The Strange Disappearance of Joe Cardona *and* The Hand

TWO CLASSIC ADVENTURES OF

THE Shadow ™

by Walter B. Gibson
writing as Maxwell Grant

and Historical Essays by Maggie Thompson,
Will Murray and Anthony Tollin

EDD CARTIER TRIBUTE EDITION

SANCTUM BOOKS

International Standard Book Number:
978-1-60877-012-0

First printing: December 2009

Series editor: Anthony Tollin
anthonytollin@shadowsanctum.com

Consulting editor: Will Murray

Copy editor: Joseph Wrzos

Cover and photo restoration: Michael Piper

The editors gratefully acknowledge the contributions of Dean Cartier and Jim Amash in the preparation of this volume.

Published by Sanctum Books
P.O. Box 761474, San Antonio, TX 78245-1474

Visit The Shadow at www.shadowsanctum.com.

THE Shadow ™
Volume 33

CONTENTS

Two Complete Novels From The Shadow's Private Annals As told to Maxwell Grant

Thrilling Tales and Features

Cover art by George Rozen
Interior illustrations by Edd Cartier

The weird purple death menace
which The Shadow battles is but a
prelude to a more amazing event—

The

Strange Disappearance
Of Joe Cardona

CHAPTER I
THE PURPLE DEATH

"LOOK at this, Cardona."

Fiercely, Police Commissioner Ralph Weston brandished a newspaper before the eyes of his ace inspector, Joe Cardona. The headline, in a big-typed streamer, read:

PURPLE DEATH STRIKES AGAIN

His swarthy face grim, Cardona received the newspaper with tight-fisted hands. He grimaced when he noted that the newspaper had foregone the usual red ink that it used for sensational head-lines. The big letters were printed in purple; the very hue that represented death itself.

Cardona watched Commissioner Weston pace

From the Private Annals of The Shadow, as told to

Maxwell Grant

the floor. Weston seemed cramped for space, in this little office that was situated in his apartment. Cardona saw the commissioner pause and stare through the darkened window, where the rattle of an early winter sleet storm was clashing against the panes.

Beyond were the lights of Manhattan, blurred by the sweeping sleet. The tops of skyscrapers were lost, enveloped by the swirl. The frown that showed on Weston's firm, square-jawed face was proof that the police commissioner was utterly befogged by the trend of recent crime.

PROFESSOR KINGSLEY MURKDEN—scientist and inventor

Cardona took another look at the newspaper. He saw a subhead in smaller type:

Detective Missing After Finding Button Clue

Cardona grunted.

"These morning sheets work quick," commented the ace. "I didn't think they'd get the news of Doolan's disappearance in time for the bulldog edition."

Weston swung about from the window.

He said wearily, "Five deaths in three nights; four of our best men missing. Lacey, Kirk, Jenkins—now Doolan. What's become of them, Cardona?"

Joe shook his head. Even his poker-faced countenance could not conceal the emotion that he felt. Murder was bad enough; the evanishment of every detective detailed to a case made the situation acute.

"Five disconnected deaths," mused Weston. "An obscure mechanic, a university instructor, a radio announcer, a Wall Street promoter, a pawnbroker. None, apparently, ever knew the others. Four competent detectives missing. Two—Lacey and Kirk—gone before they learned anything. Two others—Jenkins and Doolan—vanished after delivering clues that have not helped us.

"Jenkins found a fountain pen, significant only because it contained ordinary purple ink. Doolan found a common button from a shirt cuff; not the commonest sort of button, but one that is common enough. These clues may be valuable, should we find a suspect; but in themselves, the clues are useless."

CARDONA pondered over Weston's words, then remarked:

"Maybe the clues mean more than we think, Commissioner. They were important enough for the man who's behind these deaths to snatch the detectives who found them."

Weston shook his head.

"I don't think so," he declared. "The perpetrator of the purple death is merely flaunting his power in our faces. He wants us to know that our efforts to unearth him will prove futile."

Weston drove a heavy fist down upon his desk. This was characteristic of him.

"Five men have died," announced Weston, "from the effects of some baffling poison that turns their bodies purple. We know that the poison is similar to known ones, but it coagulates the blood of the victims to such extent that we have been unable to learn the time at which death struck them. That fact, Cardona, has masked the murderer's movements."

Cardona nodded, listening to facts that he already knew. Suddenly, however, he put a question:

"What about those new types of blood tests, Commissioner? The ones you mentioned yesterday?"

"I have talked with three experts," returned Weston. "Only one believes that results are possible. He is Professor Kinsley Murkden. He has made a special study of chemical reactions in the blood stream. In fact, he has been delivering lectures on the subject."

"Did Murkden make any tests for you?"

"Yes. Using blood from the most recent victim. The test failed because the victim had been dead too long. Murkden believes that he could ascertain the exact time of death if he could make tests within twelve hours after a victim's death."

"Perhaps he may have the chance."

Weston glared, for the moment, at Cardona's utterance. Then he sank back in his chair, nodding soberly.

"You may be right, Cardona," he declared, solemnly. "We may have to meet new murders. If they come, let us hope that we learn of them soon enough to take advantage of whatever aid Professor Murkden may give us."

A minute of silence passed, disturbed only by the sweep and rattle of the outside sleet. At last, Weston spoke methodically, passing Cardona a sheaf of report sheets.

"It is unfortunate, Cardona," he remarked, "that you were away on vacation when these deaths began. However, beginning with tonight, you will have full charge of investigation. These reports are copies of those supplied us by the missing detectives. They are quite sketchy.

"You will, at least, learn something about the purple death itself, as the descriptions of the victims are quite detailed. I may say"—Weston seemed to shudder as he spoke— "that the horror of the purple death is something that can not be described with mere words. If you had seen the victims, as I have, you would understand that fact."

Cardona received the duplicate reports. Rising, he donned a heavy overcoat.

WHILE Cardona was tightening his overcoat collar, the telephone rang. Weston answered it; Cardona heard the commissioner's end of a brief conversation.

"Hello..." Weston's brisk tone slackened. "Ah, good evening, Mrs. Tabor... Quite an agreeable surprise, to hear from you... Certainly, I shall be glad to do the favor... Yes, a message to Mr. Tabor, at his studio..."

Weston wrote an address on a pad. Cardona saw the commissioner smile, as he added:

"I understand... Yes, I shall detail a tactful man to the duty. I have such a man right here at present..."

Hanging up the receiver, Weston chuckled.

"There, Cardona," he declared, "is an example of how results can be obtained by going to the man higher up, no matter how slight a task is required. The Tabors are friends of mine; socially prominent persons who live on Long Island.

"Frederick Tabor is an architect; he has a studio here in town, where he goes when he does not wish to be disturbed. Here is the address." Weston passed the memo to Cardona, added, "It is ten o'clock. Tabor promised to arrive home before that hour. Mrs. Tabor thinks that he has forgetfully remained at the studio. Since there is no telephone there, she called me and asked me to send someone to the studio to remind him."

Cardona stared.

Weston saw Cardona's gaze and chuckled anew.

"It is making a messenger service out of the police department," admitted Weston. "However, the Tabors are important people. I assured Mrs. Tabor that I would send an experienced man who would not unduly alarm her absent-minded husband."

Weston was still chuckling when Cardona left, but Joe was muttering to himself when he arrived outside the apartment house. Hailing a cab, Cardona gruffly gave his destination. Riding along, Cardona continued to fume. The ace inspector knew that the commissioner was actually using his office to curry favor. With all his efficiency, Weston had that one fault. And it antagonized Cardona.

THE taxi stopped in front of an old building on a secluded side street. Alighting, Joe looked up at the darkened windows. He shrugged his shoulders, deciding that Tabor must have already gone home. But when Cardona turned about, his taxi was gone. The driver had received his fare, and had pulled away while Cardona was staring at the building.

There was a small lunchroom several doors away. Muffling his face against the slicing sleet, Cardona strode in that direction. Entering, he sat down at the counter, threw back his coat collar and ordered a cup of coffee.

"I'm looking for an architect's studio," Cardona told the man behind the counter. "The fellow's name is Tabor. I thought maybe I'd picked the wrong building, because I didn't see any lights there."

"You want Mr. Tabor?" returned the lunchroom man. "You'll find him there, probably. His studio's on the third floor at the back. That's why you saw no lights. Mr. Tabor must be there. He didn't bring back his coffee cup."

"His coffee cup?"

"Yes. Every time he works at night, he comes here with a big thermos bottle. I fill it up with coffee and give him a cup with it. When he leaves the studio, he stops here to leave the cup."

"He stopped for coffee here tonight?"

"Yes. At eight o'clock."

Cardona gulped his own coffee and left the lunchroom. He entered Tabor's building, went up two flights of stairs that were lighted by a small incandescent on the second floor; a glow that had not been noticeable from the street. Reaching the third floor, Cardona saw a door that had a glass pane, illuminated by a light from the other side. On the door, was the lettering:

FREDERICK TABOR ARCHITECT

Cardona rapped lightly on the door. There was no response. Cardona rapped more loudly. Still, Tabor did not answer. Cardona shrugged. Probably, Tabor was working in an inner room and could not hear the knocks.

Cardona tried the door. It opened. The inspector stepped into a little anteroom. There, he saw two chairs and a table, which supported a lamp. On the table Cardona observed the corked thermos bottle. Beside it was a cup that contained a half-inch of coffee.

There was a door beyond, marked "Private." It apparently explained why Tabor had not heard the knocks. Joe rapped against the inner door. There was no response from the studio. Deciding that he had wasted enough time, Cardona opened the inner door.

JOE'S first impression was one of complete disarray. The studio that he viewed was lighted only by a large lamp that stood in a corner, shining upon a table that supported a draftsman's board. A T-square, angles, protractors, drawing instruments and slide rule, were lying on the floor. Beyond, Cardona saw the gaping front of a metal file cabinet, from which the drawers had been yanked and left on the floor. Papers and building plans were strewn on the floor. Scanning that area, Cardona spied a rack in a far corner, saw a coat hanging there. A man's still form showed bulkily on the darkened floor below.

With a grim exclamation, Cardona sprang to the corner. Cardona knew that this hunched man who lay face downward must be the architect, Frederick Tabor. The man's dark trousers matched the coat upon the rack.

Gripping Tabor's shoulders, Cardona rolled the man toward himself. Tabor's head tilted face upward. From past Cardona's shoulder came the revealing light. With a blurt, Cardona dropped the inert shoulders, let the body sag as he dropped back to stare.

Frederick Tabor was stone dead. It was not that fact, however, that had appalled Joe Cardona. The ace inspector was accustomed to viewing death; he had guessed that Tabor was dead from the moment that he had begun to roll the body. It was sight of Tabor's face that made Cardona spring away as instinctively as if he had just escaped stepping on a rattlesnake.

Never had Joe Cardona seen a face so contorted. Whatever handsomeness Tabor might have once possessed, his dead features showed no trace of it. Cheeks were puffy, swollen. Lips were twisted and bloated. Eyes were bulging orbs that looked like imitation chunks of glass, ready to drop from the sockets that held them. Below them was a nose, with widespread nostrils like those of a primitive savage.

It was a feature that completely banished all semblance of a human countenance. Doom had left a mark that could never be erased, for it dominated every inch of Tabor's face.

The dead man's visage was dyed a deep purple; a color deeper than a stain. That lurid hue seemed to have crept from within, to reach the outer flesh and tinge it with the evil dye. Hands, crossed on the dead man's chest, were puffed and purple. The penetrating stain had even purpled the fingernails.

Cardona had learned the truth of Weston's words, the moment that he had viewed the dead face of Frederick Tabor. Embarked upon a seemingly unimportant errand, Joe Cardona had stepped squarely into the chain of crime that he had been ordered to investigate.

The ace sleuth had found Frederick Tabor, the latest victim of the purple death!

CHAPTER II
CARDONA'S CLUE

ONE hour later, Joe Cardona was standing in the center of Tabor's studio with an audience about him. In the group was a police surgeon and two grim-faced detectives; also the proprietor of the downstairs lunchroom. Most important, however, were Ralph Weston and a man whom the police commissioner had brought with him.

Weston's companion was Professor Kinsley Murkden, the blood expert who had expressed the belief that tests could solve the riddle of the purple death. Tall, stoop-shouldered and frail of build, Murkden was craning forward with one hand cupped to his ear. The professor was hard of hearing, but his keen eyes showed him to be alert.

That fact had offset Cardona's disappointment at first meeting the professor. Joe's original impression was that Murkden was a deaf old dotard. He had changed that view after watching Murkden make a sharp visual survey of the entire studio.

"I've made a thorough inspection, Commissioner," announced Cardona, to Weston. "I'm ready to reconstruct the crime."

"To begin with," continued Cardona, in a loud tone that brought a pleased nod from Murkden, "Tabor came up to this studio at eight o'clock. I arrived here soon after ten. So we know for a fact that he died between eight and ten.

"The doctor here"—Joe waved toward the police surgeon—"has been unable to fix the time of death. That was to be expected. It's the way the purple death has worked before. However, we both are agreed on how death was dealt. The murderer put poison in Tabor's coffee cup."

Striding over to the door that led to the ante-room, Cardona pointed to the thermos bottle and the cup, which still stood on the outer table. He also indicated the hallway door. In loud tone, he continued:

"Tabor came in here at eight o'clock. He set down the thermos bottle and the coffee cup. He left the door unlocked, came in here and went to work. Soon, he went out and had a cup of coffee.

He left a little coffee in the cup. He came back to work again.

"That's when the murderer moved in. Tabor didn't hear him, because Tabor was here in the studio. The murderer dropped a pill, or some other poison in the coffee cup. After a while, Tabor came out for another cup of coffee. The murderer was gone before that.

"Tabor filled his coffee cup, took a long drink of it and came back to work. That's when the poison hit him. He collapsed. The murderer came in here and rifled the place. Figuring the whole job, I would say that he could have done it in about fifteen minutes."

WESTON considered Cardona's summary; then put a sharp question:

"The motive?"

"To grab some plan that Tabor had," returned Cardona, promptly. "To cover whatever he took, he grabbed a lot of other things, too. That leaves us out of luck, Commissioner."

"There is another possibility," decided Weston. "The murderer may simply have rifled the place to make it look as though he sought some of Tabor's building plans."

"Maybe," agreed Cardona, "but in either case, he's covered whatever he was after. It looks to me, Commissioner, as though our first step is to get the time element straight."

"Did you hear that, Professor?" inquired Weston. "Do you think you can help us?"

"I can," announced Murkden. "Especially if there is actually a trace of poison in the coffee cup."

"We're sure of that," put in Cardona. "A purple color has shown up in the little coffee that we found there. But there's none in the thermos bottle That's how we know that the poison was put in the cup. The thermos bottle is less than half full. It looks clear."

Professor Murkden raised his hand; waved a bony forefinger, as he stated:

"I have already learned enough from previous cases to make tests with what we might term synthetic compounds, resembling this purple poison. A prompt analysis of the coffee will enable me to check my previous experiments.

"More important, however, is the matter of fresh blood. My previous tests have been made too late to learn the exact rate of coagulation, which may be variable. If I begin tonight, with tests of this new victim's blood, I feel sure that I shall succeed in establishing the exact time of death."

"Good," decided Weston. "The body is already on its way to our headquarters laboratory. Doctor, take Professor Murkden there. Detective Lewis will bring the coffee samples. We shall lose no time with this."

Turning to Murkden, Weston made added query:

"Tell me, Professor, when can we count upon your first report?"

Murkden considered, then replied:

"Tomorrow evening. Let us say after my usual lecture."

"At what time do you lecture?"

"From eight o'clock until nine."

"Very well, Professor. I shall call personally at nine o'clock."

MURKDEN left with the surgeon and one of the detectives, who took along the thermos bottle and carried the coffee from the cup in a bottle that the police doctor provided. Cardona dismissed the lunchroom proprietor, then turned to speak to Weston. He saw the commissioner staring at a partly opened skylight in the slanted ceiling of the studio.

"What about that skylight?" demanded Weston. "Couldn't the murderer have come in that way, Cardona?"

"No," replied Joe. "He would have had to go right through the studio while Tabor was working here. Besides, the skylight was locked when I examined it. Jammed so tight that I decided it hadn't been opened for months."

"Why did you open it?"

"I wasn't passing up anything, Commissioner. I went out to take a look at the roof. I couldn't clamp the skylight afterward. I'd bent the bar opening it."

"Mention all that in your report."

Briskly, Weston marched about the room, studying strewn papers, looking in obscure corners. Joe and the detective watched him. Neither glanced again toward the skylight.

There, motion occurred. The skylight inched upward. Solid blackness seemed to dominate the space; there was no influx of expected sleet. Gradually, the skylight lowered into place. Outside, a hidden watcher was on hand; some being whose ways were as impenetrable as those of night itself.

A few minutes later, Weston finished his inspection. He turned to Cardona and queried.

"What do you think of the time element? When would you say that Tabor died?"

"I have no clue," returned Cardona. He paused, then added, "Only a hunch."

"I though so," smiled Weston. "You always have hunches, Cardona. I used to ridicule them, but sometimes they proved good ones."

"Thanks, Commissioner," laughed Cardona. "Since you ask for it, I'd say that Tabor died at about half past eight."

"Why?"

"Because the murderer would naturally have tried to get him as soon as possible. Tabor drank one cup of coffee in the lunchroom, at eight o'clock. Let's say he took the next at eight fifteen. The murderer had to wait until then to load the poison in the coffee that Tabor left. If Tabor took his next cup at eight thirty, that was when it finished him off."

Weston mused over Cardona's statement.

"Fifteen minute intervals," remarked the Commissioner. "Not too short for a habitual coffee drinker. Perhaps you are right, Cardona."

"What's more," added Joe, "if the killer knew that Tabor was due home at ten o'clock, he'd have planned to get him quick. Tabor would have had to leave here about nine thirty to get home at ten. Maybe he'd have gone before then. Maybe at nine."

Weston nodded, impressed. Then, with a smile, he said:

"This time, Cardona, your hunch will have opportunity to prove itself. I shall remember what you said and check it with Professor Murkden's test results tomorrow night."

Cardona grimaced, knowing that his hunch would be criticized if proven incorrect. Cardona felt resentful. Ever since he had broken in as a detective, he had played his hunches. Yet Joe had never been able to convince the commissioner as to their accuracy.

Weston saw that he had touched a sore spot. He tried to mollify Cardona as they went out through the anteroom. Clapping Joe on the back, Weston gave a grave reminder:

"Don't forget what happened to the detectives on these cases, Cardona. You are too valuable a man to have disappear. I'm counting on you to smash the purple death."

WITH that, Weston was gone, followed by the remaining detective. Cardona was closing the door between the studio and the anteroom. Slow footfalls on the stairs indicated that Weston expected Joe to join him below. For the moment, however, Cardona paused. A hunch had gripped him.

"Clues," muttered Cardona, half-aloud. "That's why they've dropped out of sight. They picked up clues—"

Joe had remembered the fountain pen found by Jenkins, the shirt button uncovered by Doolan. There was a chance that Kirk and Lacey might have discovered some items also. At least, it was certain that in the last two cases of the purple death, prior to Tabor's murder, some trace to the killer had been found.

Why was there none here? Had the murderers been more careful, after reading of previous clues in the newspapers? As Cardona considered this factor, he stared across the anteroom. His gaze stopped upon a tiny object just within the door.

Popping over, Joe picked up a square-shaped newspaper clipping. Unfolding it, he saw the diagram of a chessboard, with chessmen indicated on squares. Below the diagram was the statement: "White to Mate in three moves."

Though Cardona was no chess player, he was familiar with the regular contents of most New York dailies; and there was only one newspaper—a morning one—in which he had seen daily chess problems. Noting the position at which the clipping had fallen, Cardona wondered if only the murderer could accidentally have dropped the clipping at that spot?

Cardona hurried to the outer door. In the hallway, he stopped, the clipping still between his fingers. He could hear Weston's footsteps.

With a grim smile, Cardona pocketed the clipping.

Others had made the mistake of proclaiming their clues to the police commissioner. Weston, anxious to convince the newspapers that results were being gained, had let the news reach the press.

But Cardona, for once, was decided on an independent policy. Dragged back from a vacation, thrown on to an assignment that promised danger, he felt that he was entitled to full leeway. Weston had offered him complete charge of the case; then had proceeded to crimp Cardona's favorite method of following hunches.

Joe had made one mistake; that of revealing his first hunch. He did not intend to repeat it. His present hunch was that too much talk of the chess clipping clue would mean disaster. The best way to avoid such complication was to keep his find to himself.

The clipping safely in his pocket, Joe Cardona closed the outer door of Tabor's studio and indulged in a satisfied smile as he started down the stairway to rejoin the awaiting police commissioner.

So intent had Cardona been with his discovery that he had failed to notice any sound while he was still within the anteroom. Since Joe had closed the connecting door to the inner studio, it was no wonder that his ears had failed to hear the noise.

The sound was a soft scrape from the skylight of the deserted studio. It was accompanied by an odd sight; the encroachment of solid blackness from above. The skylight had opened wider; the

darkened mass that entered slowly molded itself into a human form.

A *swish* followed as a tall shape dropped quietly to the floor. A tall stranger from the night stood in the studio where death had struck. Joe Cardona would have recognized that arrival, had he remained to witness this entrance.

The tall being was cloaked in black. His hands were encased in thin black gloves; his face was obscured by the upturned collar of his cloak, the downturned brim of his black slouch hat. Yet from the space between the collar and the brim, eyes peered so keenly that their flash was visible.

This being of blackness was The Shadow. Master crook who hunted men of crime, The Shadow, like the law, was on the trail of the purple death. With contacts everywhere, The Shadow invariably learned when crime was uncovered by the law. He had done so tonight.

ARRIVING at Tabor's studio, The Shadow had passed policemen stationed outside while the commissioner was present. He had chosen his own route to reach the scene of crime; namely, by the roof. Finding the skylight that Cardona had opened, The Shadow had looked in and listened while Cardona had summarized the circumstances of Frederick Tabor's death.

Men of the law had gone. It was The Shadow's turn to study the premises; to learn what other clues might be present. Conversant with Cardona's full report, The Shadow had gained a distinct advantage before beginning his search.

Nevertheless, The Shadow had entered too late to peer into the anteroom in order to learn of Cardona's secret clue.

A simple item, that clipped fragment of a newspaper; yet it could produce complications in the quest to learn the source of crime. Held by Cardona, that clipped chess problem promised trouble to its finder.

Far better that The Shadow should have gained it; for he alone could have used the clue to full advantage.

CHAPTER III
BATTLE BY NIGHT

THE search that The Shadow made through Tabor's studio was swift, yet detailed. The result, however, was negligible. Whoever had rifled this room had done the job swiftly, but with definite care to avoid any traces. Articles had been swept from Tabor's table. Files had been ripped from the cabinet.

The Shadow granted that the murderer had worn gloves. Cardona had looked for fingerprints, but had found none. Many of the papers from Tabor's files were gone. That was proven by The Shadow's discovery of architect's estimates that had missing pages. From this, The Shadow drew the definite conclusion that the murderer had actually wanted certain documents.

A man faking a robbery would not have had to search for the items that he wanted; hence he could have bundled batches at random and strewn the rest about. The murderer, scattering papers, had been on the lookout for certain ones. Finding them, he had taken them; then snatched up groups of strewn papers. That was why some sheets of lengthy estimates had been left behind.

This conclusion, however, was of little value. Tabor's papers were in chaos; obviously a large percentage of them were gone. There was no way to gain a lead to the particular type of documents that the murderer had purposely stolen.

STEPPING to the outer anteroom, The Shadow studied the table where the thermos bottle and the cup had been. He saw a circled mark that indicated where the thermos had once stood on spilled liquid; to leave a stained ring in the woodwork.

From the size of the circle, The Shadow decided that the thermos bottle had been a quart container. He recalled the statement that half the coffee was gone from it. Cardona had estimated that Tabor had finished two cups of coffee; one at eight fifteen, the next at eight thirty. Two cups, however, would not account for a missing pint.

Even granting that Tabor drank coffee at fifteen minute intervals, The Shadow estimated that he would not have consumed a quart within an hour. Calculating on his own, The Shadow figured that

The Shadow paused when he reached the hinged extension that formed the last six feet of the fire escape. He heard sounds that were barely audible.

the coffee clue would show that Tabor had died at about quarter past nine.

Nevertheless, The Shadow made allowance for the possibility that Tabor might have drunk two or three cups at one sitting. Like Weston, The Shadow was willing to let the time element wait until after Professor Murkden had made his blood tests. Science—not speculation—offered the best solution to the evasive time element that invariably marked the purple death.

While in the anteroom, The Shadow glanced at the spot where Cardona had found the clipped chess problem. The fact that The Shadow looked over the exact spot where the clue had been found was new proof that the murderer of Frederick Tabor had experienced real luck tonight.

His search ended, The Shadow returned to the studio. He went up through the skylight, closed it exactly as he had found it. In darkness, he began a precarious course along the roof. Sleet had hardened into ice; moving along a frozen slant, The Shadow held his position in uncanny manner. His fingers and toes seemed to dig into a surface that offered no apparent security.

The Shadow reached a projection of the roof; swung from its icy edge. This time, his fingers could not keep their clutch, but despite their slip, The Shadow gave himself an inward swing beneath the projection and landed on the platform of an old fire escape. Gripping the sleet-crusted rail, he descended toward a space at the rear of the building.

Usually, The Shadow moved with absolute silence. Tonight, that proved impossible. Steps in the fire tower were loose; The Shadow was forced to step heavily upon them, in order to gain a footing. The Shadow paused when he reached the hinged extension that formed the last six feet of the fire escape.

Listening, The Shadow was rewarded for his caution. He heard sounds that were barely audible. Whispers that only his keen ears could have detected. No patrolmen, these. There were lurkers in the darkness just below; enemies who had somehow guessed the presence of The Shadow and had moved in during the time that he had been engaged in upstairs investigation.

Those foemen had heard the slight clangs from the fire escape. Trouble might begin at any moment. The Shadow's position was a bad one; though the steps of the fire escape were iron, they were openwork and offered no bulwark.

THE SHADOW did not hesitate. Rising on the rail beside him, he reached high and gripped a step above his head. Forcibly, he clanked the step; then the next one below it. The sounds, this time, were accurate. They gave a distinct token of the exact spots where they had occurred.

The clanks, however, did not tell the most important fact; namely, that The Shadow was *beneath* the steps that clattered, not upon them. Stooping, The Shadow swung across the level rail of the lowest platform, ready for a six-foot vault to the area below.

The Shadow was not an instant too soon. As his form swung from the rail, revolvers barked upward; simultaneously, big flashlights clicked their glare. The barrage that ripped the night came from half a dozen guns.

Bullets found nothingness. Flashlights were luckier. As thugs fired uselessly, their companions with the lights gained a chance glance at blackness that was hurdling from the rim of their glowing circle. Harsh voices roared the fact that The Shadow had been spied.

A clank marked The Shadow's thud upon the cement courtyard. It came from an automatic that he had whipped from beneath his cloak. Though half sprawled, The Shadow gained his feet, just as a flashlight swept in his direction. With quick aim, The Shadow boomed a shot for the thug who held the light.

A sharp cry answered; the flashlight dropped from the thug's shattered hand. Revolvers ripped blindly. They were answered by new shots. A laugh of challenge accompanied the echoes of The Shadow's gun. Crooks were spurred to new fury. A sudden barrage opened from The Shadow's left.

Though he had successfully shifted in the darkness, The Shadow had not gained the stroke he needed. He had scoured this courtyard previously; had found it an open space that lacked cover. In the interim, the situation had changed.

Crooks had brought their own entrenchments. The clang of bullets told that the thugs had carried in steel ashcans to serve as bulwarks. With the opening of The Shadow's fire, they had ducked for cover. Failing to locate The Shadow with chance shots, they were prepared to rake the whole area wherein he stood.

Instantly, The Shadow remembered one spot that he had noted when first entering this courtyard. That was a broad basement window in the building just behind the one that housed Tabor's studio. The low window was The Shadow's one chance of refuge, yet as he dived for it, he shifted. His hands found the wall beside the window. The Shadow dropped flat in the cement.

Potshots were whistling from ashcans. With brief whines, bullets were thudding walls. Slugs pounded above The Shadow's head; yet the cloaked fighter did not move. He was listening for sounds close by. He heard them, from the very window that he wanted.

"HOLD the glim, Skeet," came a whispered tone. "Don't use no rod, neither."

"Other guys are shootin'" was the response, in a low growl. "We got as much chanct of baggin' The Shadow as they have."

"Yeah. But they're behind the ashcans. They're foxing him. Our job is to cover. Get ready to duck when you hear three quick shots."

"I know. That means the typewriters. You told me that before, Jake."

"I'm telling you again—"

Metal swished through sleety darkness to end Jake's sentence. With a short forearm stroke, The Shadow had sliced at downward angle through the opened window. His sledge blow was perfect, despite the darkness. The weight of a .45 automatic slumped Jake into temporary oblivion.

"Skeet" heard the blow; uttered a snarl and jabbed his revolver through the window. Two arms drove through like pistons. Diving in from the night, The Shadow clutched Skeet's gun wrist with one fist; dropped his automatic to grip the thug's throat with the other. As the big .45 bumped the basement floor, two figures plunged upon it.

One was Skeet, sprawling backward, to crack the stone flooring with the back of his skull. The other was The Shadow, his swift drive finished. He had plunged in from the night to gain this basement stronghold.

As Skeet succumbed, there came three shots from the courtyard; their quick succession was a signal, delivered by an entrenched leader. An instant later, machine guns clattered from two entrances to the walled area. The "typewriters" were speaking, as Jake and Skeet had prophesied.

Bullets streamed through the window, as the spraying machine guns raked every inch of the courtyard. Wisely had thugs been told to duck as soon as the triple signal was given. Otherwise, they would have been clipped in the thorough barrage that had been intended for The Shadow.

Crouched below the window, The Shadow heard the drilling cease. He knew what was to follow. He bobbed up to the window, ready for it.

LIGHTS flashed everywhere. Shouting their triumph, crooks leaped from their strongholds. They were as ready with the bull's-eye lanterns as they had been with their guns. Each wanted the first sight of The Shadow; all expected to see a cloaked figure sprawled by a courtyard wall.

Instead, they viewed blankness. As they gaped, they heard a chilling sound. A burst of mocking laughter pealed from somewhere; most of the ruffians thought the challenge was delivered in their very midst. One man spied the window where Jake and Skeet had been on guard. He shouted, aimed with a revolver. The gesture was useless.

Swinging away, The Shadow ducked low and crossed to the rear of the basement room. He blinked a tiny flashlight, saw a doorway and went through it. Ahead, he saw a flight of stairs up to the ground floor. He took that route.

Out in the courtyard, crooks were firing from cover, speeding bullets through the open window that The Shadow had left. Their leader shouted a command; thugs rose en masse to drive across the court, firing as they came. They were sure that they had forced The Shadow to drop to cover; by closing in with their barrage, they hoped to smother him in his temporary stronghold.

As the first attacker reached the center of the courtyard, a strident cry halted them. It came from above; not from below. Before the crooks could understand it, the laugh was followed by the blast of automatics, pumping downward from a high ground-floor window.

The Shadow had gained a new position. He had caught his opponents flatfooted in the center of the courtyard. Their own guns had betrayed their positions. The crooks had but one choice. They scattered.

No longer did they seek cover; they dashed for complete escape. They took to the passage that led to streets, their snarling leader running with them.

Loaded, then reloaded, those automatics had done valiant work. Thugs were scattered; there was no need to pursue. Already, shots were sounding from outer streets. Patrolmen and police cars were closing into this neighborhood. Only the luckiest of the crooks could hope to evade that gathering cordon.

Finding a side window, The Shadow dropped to a passage from the courtyard. He gained the night; took his own course, away from the shrill wail of sirens that marked the approach of the law. Driving sleet blotted the cloaked fighter's course. The Shadow was gone again, into the depths of night. Several hoodlums had been wounded.

Fierce fray had produced one important discovery. Whoever the perpetrator of the purple death might be, he feared The Shadow. The killer had guessed that the black-cloaked sleuth might be on hand tonight. That was why he had tipped off hordes of crooks to the possibility of The Shadow's arrival. The hidden killer had counted on the fury of the underworld to dispose of The Shadow.

The stroke had failed. The Shadow, his very path unknown, remained the master of darkness. Lone master who battled crime, The Shadow would continue to defy all odds in his campaign to end the scourge of the purple death.

CHAPTER IV
CROOKS GIVE CHALLENGE

AT eight o'clock the next evening, Police Commissioner Weston was seated at a late dinner in the grillroom of the exclusive Cobalt Club. He had come here to escape being hounded by reporters. Influential persons knew that Frederick Tabor had been the commissioner's friend. Couldn't he, Weston, do something about the purple deaths, they asked.

Newspapers assumed that new murders were due. Some tabloid journals had intimated that Tabor's death might have been a slap at Weston. That suggestion did not assure other friends of the commissioner. They felt that they, too, might be marked for death.

The rules of the exclusive Cobalt Club forbade loud conversation among the members. Hence, the commissioner had come here knowing that he could not be button-holed. Moreover, he had chosen an hour at which the grillroom would be nearly empty. Thus the commissioner had found the seclusion that he wanted.

While glaring at the headlines of an evening newspaper, Weston noted blackness glide across the page. He looked up to see a tall, calm-faced personage clad in tuxedo. He recognized this person as Lamont Cranston, a millionaire globe-trotter who habituated the Cobalt Club.

"Sit down, Cranston," invited Weston. "I wanted to talk to someone; and you're the only chap I know here who won't harp on the mistakes I've made. This purple death has made fanatics out of all my acquaintances."

A quiet smile showed on the lips of Lamont Cranston. Seating himself, the arrival made calm query:

"Are there any new developments, Commissioner?"

"None," replied Weston. "I expect some tonight, however. You probably read in the newspapers that we are making special blood tests to learn the exact hour of Tabor's death."

Cranston nodded.

"Professor Murkden is producing the analysis," continued Weston. "I am to see him at nine o'clock."

"At his home on East Sixty-sixth Street?"

"Yes. How do you happen to know the address, Cranston?"

"A friend told me about Murkden's lectures. I had intended to join the group that attends them. I believe that knowledge of blood conditions would be valuable to me."

"Of course. Well, then, Cranston, our meeting is fortunate. I am going to Murkden's shortly. You may accompany me and meet the professor."

WESTON paused to pour cream on a baked apple; hence he did not notice the keen glow that showed in the eyes of Lamont Cranston. That momentary burn revealed a fact that Weston did not know. Those eyes were the same ones that had shone last night, from beneath the brim of a shading slouch hat.

This personage who passed as Lamont Cranston, friend of the police commissioner, was none other than The Shadow.

Purely by coincidence, Weston happened to note a headline in the newspaper. He mentioned it.

"Last night," remarked the commissioner, "there was a gun fray outside the building where Tabor died. We rounded up several wounded crooks. None of them, however, knew anything concerning Tabor. When questioned, they stated that they had come to combat The Shadow."

"Quite interesting, Commissioner," inserted The Shadow, in the quiet tone of Cranston. "Apparently you no longer hold to the theory that The Shadow is a myth."

"I thought that once," admitted Weston. "Afterward, I gained actual evidence of The Shadow's existence and the power that he possesses. My own life was saved by his timely intervention."

"You believe, then, that The Shadow is investigating the purple death?"

"Yes. Also, that the master murderer guessed it; and tipped off certain persons in the underworld. The purple killer hoped to eliminate The Shadow; but failed. However, we have learned nothing from the episode. We believe that the hoodlums were commanded by a crook called Slook Howdrey; but we doubt that he knows the actual perpetrator of the purple death."

The Shadow's fixed smile was proof that he agreed with Weston; but the commissioner did not gain any significance from the slight curve of The Shadow's lips. Calling the waiter, the commissioner signed the check. Accompanied by The Shadow, who strolled in leisurely fashion, Weston stalked from the grillroom.

Outside, the pair entered the commissioner's car.

THE professor's residence was an old brownstone affair that squatted among decrepit buildings. Ascending the high steps, the visitors were admitted by a solemn-faced servant who ushered them into a large room. Entering quietly, Weston and The Shadow found a group of twenty persons listening while Murkden lectured from a small platform.

Peering over the tops of bifocal spectacles, the stoop-shouldered professor recognized the commissioner and nodded affably; then resumed his lecture.

A clock on the wall showed five minutes of nine when Murkden finished his lecture. The members of the group congregated to ask questions. Murkden answered them briefly. One by one, the questioners departed; in less than five minutes, all were gone. Murkden approached Weston and shook hands. The commissioner introduced the professor to The Shadow.

Murkden's eyes showed interest when he learned that Lamont Cranston was a traveler. The professor remarked that he had made many tests with the venom of poisonous reptiles, including the cobra; that he would show his visitor charts that gave the percentages of fatalities among the victims of snake bites. Then, with a wan smile, the professor remembered that he had a more important duty; that which concerned his analysis of the purple death.

Murkden unlocked a door at the back corner of the lecture room. Murkden led his visitors through a series of doors down to the basement. There, he unlocked another door and conducted them into a square room that was equipped like a laboratory.

The windows of this room were covered with crisscrossed gratings; that was evidenced by one raised window. The panes of the windows were frosted; hence other gratings could not be seen beyond the closed sashes. The Shadow eyed the barriers; saw that while they were strong enough to offset ordinary prowlers, they would not tax an expert. The same applied to the locks on Murkden's doors. However, The Shadow made no comment. As Lamont Cranston, he was not supposed to be an authority who could criticize methods of anti-burglary protection.

Furthermore, The Shadow had something more

important to command his attention. Murkden had stopped at a table in the corner; there, the professor was indicating a row of glass beakers that bore various labels. He chose a beaker marked "F."

HE said, "This beaker contains the equivalent of the poison that caused the purple death." Murkden briefly told them of his experiments.

Then, laying the last tube aside, Murkden picked up a sheaf of papers and passed them to Weston.

"These are the opinions of consulting chemists," declared the professor. "I called them in this afternoon. They checked my results; gave certified reports. You will see that all agree."

While Weston was looking at the sheets, Murkden went to another corner. There, The Shadow saw a large crate well stocked with guinea pigs. Murkden stopped at a table, opened a small box and displayed three more of the rodents. All of these guinea pigs were dead.

"I experimented with these," declared Murkden. "I gave each an injection of compound F. Each guinea pig died within five minutes. I performed the first experiment alone; I called in a physician to witness the second; and your own police surgeon was here for the last, just prior to my lecture. Here are their opinions."

Weston had come to the corner. He received the new statements that Murkden gave him.

"What are these references to microscopic slides?" queried Weston, reading the reports. "Do they concern the post mortem effects?"

"Yes," replied Murkden. "Here are the slides. They show specimens of blood taken from guinea pigs at regular intervals after death."

Producing a box of glass slides, Murkden stepped to a projector and focused it upon a screen. Extinguishing the room's brighter lights, he inserted the first slide. Its microscopic details were projected on the screen.

"The blood condition immediately after death," announced Murkden. "Note the slight coagulation that the poison instantly produced. This second slide"—he clicked another glass sheet into place—"shows greater coagulation. It has blood that was tested fifteen minutes later."

In progression, Murkden inserted new slides, stating the time element as he displayed them. He called attention to the fact that the coagulation became more rapid with each interval. When he reached the slide that marked exactly three hours, Murkden paused and inserted a darker slide.

"From the police laboratory," he announced. "A specimen of Tabor's blood, tested at precisely half past eleven last night. Its condition corresponds exactly with that of the guinea pig."

"Then Tabor was dead three hours!" exclaimed Weston. "That places the time of his death at half past eight!"

"It does," assured Murkden. "Look. Here are two more slides. Tabor's blood at twelve thirty; the guinea pig's blood at the end of four hours. They are identical."

As further proof, Murkden inserted slides that showed the fourth and fifth hours. They corresponded. The next slides, showing six hours, scarcely differed from the ones before.

"By six hours," explained Murkden, "the coagulation has lost its increasing ratio. It gradually continues, but with decreasing speed; until at twelve hours, it takes a final level. That is why fresh blood was needed to solve the riddle of the poison. Tabor's blood has enabled us to settle all facts for future reference."

"Humph," muttered Weston, to The Shadow. "Cardona was right in his hunch. He told me last night that he believed eight thirty to be the time of Tabor's death."

THE SHADOW made no comment. He, like Cardona, had made a conjecture that was partly guesswork. The Shadow's calculation had tended to show death at half past nine, an hour later than Cardona's. The blood tests, however, had shown Cardona's estimate to be correct. Because of this scientific evidence, The Shadow conceded that he had been wrong. The answer could be the long shot guess that The Shadow had not ignored; namely, that Tabor had drunk two or three cups of coffee in prompt succession.

Finished with the slides, Murkden turned on the laboratory lights. Weston commended the professor's work, in a loud enough tone for Murkden to hear. The professor smiled at the commissioner's approval. He placed the certified reports in a large envelope and tendered them to Weston.

Glancing at his watch, Weston noted that it was nearly quarter past nine. He suggested to The Shadow that they return to the Cobalt Club, as Cardona was due there shortly. Accompanied by Professor Murkden, they went upstairs and left by the front door. The commissioner's car was standing in front of the house, the chauffeur beside it. The chauffeur turned to open the door the moment that the commissioner appeared.

Entering the limousine with The Shadow, Weston waited until the chauffeur had taken the wheel; then he gave a brisk order:

"Cobalt Club, Larkin."

The big car started. Simultaneously, the door on Weston's side swung open. The commissioner reached to grab it; at that instant, a figure sprang into the moving car. Timed to the same moment, a head bobbed up from the front seat, beside the chauffeur. A passing street lamp threw its glimmer on masked faces; below them, it showed the glitter of aimed revolvers.

The man who had leaped in from the curb issued the growled order:

"Stick 'em up!"

Weston gaped as he stared into the masked man's leveled revolver. The Shadow, too, was eyeing a straight-aimed weapon. He was looking into the muzzle of the gun from the front seat.

Crooks had sprung a daring trap. With sheer boldness, they had invaded the police commissioner's car, to cover its two occupants. Thuggish outlaws had captured Police Commissioner Weston; and with him they had bagged The Shadow!

CHAPTER V
THE SHADOW'S RIDE

EVEN to The Shadow, the turn of events was sudden. The crooks had staged a clever coup. Nevertheless, their game would have failed had they tried to trap The Shadow alone.

At the very instant when the first man arrived from the dark, The Shadow had shifted to the left. His hand had gone beneath his overcoat; it was gripping the handle of an automatic. One quick sweep of the wrist and The Shadow could have blasted the thug in the front seat, then gone for the fellow at the door.

Circumstances made The Shadow halt. A life was at stake other than his own.

As Weston's hands came up, The Shadow released his gun and copied the commissioner's move. Murder could not be the intent of these invaders; they would stir up unnecessary trouble if they slew the police commissioner. And to them, The Shadow was merely a companion of the police commissioner. The guise of Lamont Cranston was serving well.

Weston was fuming as he faced the revolver just before his eyes. The Shadow merely settled back, his arms well raised, to observe what was due to follow.

"Head for the park, Hunk," rasped the leader who had entered the rear of the car. "Take your time so Jerry can tail us; and pick some places where there ain't much traffic. I want to talk to the commissioner."

For the first time, Weston realized that the chauffeur was not Larkin. Another thought struck him, also. The masked leader of this tribe must be "Slook" Howdrey, the crook who had sought The Shadow's death last night. Unwisely, Weston blurted his guess:

"You're Slook Howdrey—"

"SLOOK" HOWDREY—captures The Shadow and police commissioner.

For an instant, The Shadow saw a finger tighten on its trigger. At that grim instant there was no chance to save the commissioner's life. Weston's own blunder had placed him at the mercy of a killer.

Slook, himself, was on the point of signing his own death warrant with that of the commissioner. Had Slook tugged the trigger, he would not have lived long to enjoy his triumph. The Shadow was ready for a quick leap; a swift draw; a speedy bullet that would serve as vengeance in the event of Weston's death. Fortunately, the need of such action passed.

SLOOK'S finger relaxed. A snarl came from the crook's mask. Slook had decided to defer Weston's death; partly with the hope that it might not prove necessary.

"Sure," he growled. "I'm Slook Howdrey. I'm lamming out of town tonight, savvy? But before I lam, I want to know what the old prof spilled tonight. About those blood tests he was making."

The car had reached Central Park. The Shadow, gazing toward the mirror, could see the headlights of another car that was covering the commissioner's. Again, The Shadow counted upon Weston to use discretion. He believed that the commissioner had recognized his previous blunder and would not commit another.

"The tests," spoke Weston, slowly, "were not conclusive. I learned nothing of consequence from Professor Murkden tonight."

Weston managed to put the falsehood in a deliberate tone. For the moment, it seemed to

HUNK—henchman of Slook Howdrey

satisfy Slook. Then the killer snarled:

"Nothing important, eh? What about that envelope you were shoving in your pocket when you came out the door?"

"It contains reports of the tests—"

"Shove it over. Easy does it. Reach for a rod and I'll drill you."

Gingerly, Weston drew the big envelope from his coat pocket and extended it to Slook. A park light enabled The Shadow to see the strained look on Weston's face. The commissioner knew that if Slook examined the contents of the envelope, the bluff would be known. The Shadow, however, hoped that Slook would inspect the envelope. By so doing, Slook would relax his vigilance, thus giving The Shadow opportunity for action without danger to Weston.

"Let me explain the contents of the envelope." Weston, expecting trouble, was trying to make ready for it. "The papers that you will find there are actual reports of tests, but they represent the opinions of different persons. No one alone could vouch for all the statements."

"Maybe you could."

"Hardly." Weston was quick with his comment. "I merely glanced at the reports."

"Does the prof have duplicates?"

"No. These are the only ones."

"He can make new tests, though."

"That would be impossible. Frederick Tabor has been dead too long."

Slook grunted in pleased fashion. He spoke to the thug at the wheel:

"Pull up somewhere."

THE big car rolled along a quarter mile, then turned into the entrance of a deserted bridle path and halted. "Hunk" clicked off all the lights except the dash. Its feeble glow barely showed the masked faces of Slook and his two followers.

Half a minute later, the following car pulled up in back of Weston's. Its lights went out. Slook chuckled his satisfaction at the closeness of the cover-up crew.

"Listen, Commish," began Slook, in a cold, harsh tone. "I'm telling you some straight facts. Savvy? I had nothing to do with croaking Tabor, or any of the other lugs that were wiped out by the purple death. I got into this last night, on a tip-off that I could get The Shadow, if I was smart enough.

"That's why I showed up outside of Tabor's. The dope about The Shadow was the McCoy. He was there, right enough, but we didn't get him. Today, like yesterday, I get another telephone call. From the same guy that wised me about The Shadow—a gazebo with a funny, drawly voice. He said he was sorry I missed out on The Shadow. Told me he'd sweeten things by handing me ten grand, if I'd take on an easy job tonight.

"The job was to snatch you, outside of Prof. Murkden's. The guy in back of these purple deaths is wise that the prof knows this blood test business. I told the guy on the telephone to show me the ten grand. He said it'd be delivered to my hideout, and it was. That's why I'm on the job tonight."

Slook paused, as if expecting comment from Weston. None came. After silence that was broken only by the throb of distant traffic, Slook added:

"You wised to who I was. If you weren't the police commissioner, I'd have given you the works. But I got what I wanted—the envelope the prof handed you. Shall we call it quits?"

This time Weston responded. His voice was as cold as Slook's.

"Go on," suggested Weston. "Just what do you propose?"

"I'm leaving you here," returned Slook, "tied up along with your friend. I'm lamming with the outfit. We'll leave word somewhere, so you'll be picked up in a couple of hours; and your chauffeur can be pulled out of the alley. That's where we left him.

"But you're making a promise first—your word that you and this friend of yours will forget just one thing; that Slook Howdrey was the guy who snatched you. I wouldn't chance that with any dick, not even a guy like Cardona—they're double-crossers, all of 'em. But you and this mug with you are a couple of stuffed shirts; the kind that are dumb enough to stick to their word.

"Even if you are the police commissioner, I know you'll go through with whatever you promise. I'm giving you an out. What's your answer?"

COLD silence followed. Weston was considering Slook's statement.

Thick darkness seemed to envelop the car. Amid the gloom, The Shadow's arms moved slowly downward. His ungloved hands were doubled; they were almost out of sight in the sleeves of his overcoat.

"You are right," announced Weston, suddenly, to Slook. "My word, once given, would be kept. Nevertheless, I am not free to give such a promise. My oath to the law prevents me from declaring any truce with criminals."

Slook edged closer to the commissioner.

"Then you're figuring on a break," growled the killer. "Hoping that when we use the gats, some coppers will hear it. Hero stuff, eh? I'll show you how little it'll get you."

The Shadow's hands were on a level with his shoulders, their downward drop still unnoticed by the crook who covered him. That thug was still ready with his revolver. So was Hunk.

The driver had turned from the wheel and pulled a gun. But both were waiting for Slook's move. The Shadow's silence had given the impression that the only opposition would come from Weston. They were set to back Slook when he handled the commissioner.

"Here's how I dish it."

Growling the words, Slook shoved his face close to Weston's. The Shadow caught the side glimmer of a revolver; knew instantly what was coming. The Shadow's slow motion ceased, his hand shot to his overcoat. With a sudden side jab of his arm, he elbowed Weston squarely in the ribs, sent the commissioner sprawling against the wall of the car.

The move was timely. Slook's creeping hand had already gone into a vicious swing; the revolver was driving for the base of Weston's skull. One blow there would have finished the commissioner. The sprawl saved Weston. Instead of taking the crash at the back of his brain, he received a glancing stroke upon the top of his head.

Weston's hat broke the force; nevertheless, the whack stunned the commissioner. The Shadow had counted on it doing so. Weston, crumpling to the ample floor of the limousine, was out of the path of combat.

His elbow serving as a pivot when it struck Weston's ribs, The Shadow's forearm snapped forward, straight in the direction of the front seat thug who covered him. With the swing, The Shadow pressed the trigger. His .45 roared within the confines of the car. The bullet found its target before the crook could fire. The dashlight's glow showed a head drop from sight in the front seat.

As his arm recoiled, The Shadow rolled to the side, over Weston's slipping form. His quick move brought him under Slook's guard; for the killer had lost his balance when his gun had glanced from Weston's skull. Instantly, The Shadow and Slook were in a grapple.

Hunk's raucous shout came while The Shadow's shot still echoed. To Hunk, the grapple was confusion. He could not distinguish The Shadow from Slook. Hunk jabbed his free hand for a button at the side of the car, pressed the switch to illuminate the dome light. The glow came on. Hunk aimed.

He saw the face of The Shadow; that masklike visage that represented Lamont Cranston. It was showing above Slook's shoulder, a perfect target for close range. But Hunk, in that gloating sight, did not spot the dark automatic muzzle that tilted upward beneath Slook's arm.

As he steadied to do sure work with his trigger, Hunk was greeted by a cannonlike roar that issued from the muzzle. Again, The Shadow had dispatched a timely blast. The blinding spurt of flame was the final impression of Hunk's life. With it came a bullet that found the thug's brain.

Slook Howdrey wrenched free as Hunk fell. Hurling The Shadow half across the car, Slook jabbed his revolver for his foeman's heart. The Shadow's gun arm was wide, but his free hand hooked the handle of the door. With Slook driving down upon him, The Shadow yanked. The door swung under the double weight.

Sprawling, two figures hurtled to the dried grass beside the bridle path. Slook's trigger finger tugged, but The Shadow's body was no longer at the muzzle. Bullets dug the ground. As Slook rolled over, wildly seeking new aim, The Shadow came up on one elbow and gave his third quick shot. Slook flopped to the earth.

FIRST shots had not aroused the thugs in the other car. They had expected death in the limousine. The opening door made them think that Slook and the others were jumping out to join them. Their inkling of trouble came when The Shadow opened fire in their direction.

Fortunately for the thugs, The Shadow had struck hard. Luckily, too, for them, he had carried along but one automatic on an expedition that had promised no great chance of battle. The inside pocket of Cranston's tuxedo jacket was not as ample a stowing place as the spaces beneath The Shadow's own cloak.

The bullets that The Shadow drilled toward the thug-manned car were wide as the machine backed suddenly to the road. Jolted by his fall, The Shadow fired hazily at this longer range. As the car started away, The Shadow sprang between the trees, to avoid shots that were spurting in reply. Swinging out, he fired a last shot as the car came toward him. The driver had dropped almost prone; the bullet skimmed a half inch above his head.

The car jolted, skidded in the ditch. As it righted, a thug leaned out, saw the white of The Shadow's tuxedo shirt and aimed with a revolver. Already The Shadow's arm was on its way. His automatic came flinging from the dark to crash the would-be killer's skull.

The crook slumped. The Shadow's gun clattered beside him, a trophy to which the crooks were welcome, as it had served as well as a bullet. An instant later, the car was roaring through the darkness, its driver up at the wheel counting upon flight as the only sure policy.

Only one of those departing crooks had seen The Shadow. That thug would not remember it. He was the one who had taken the hard-flung .45, from only eight feet distant.

Central Park was well patrolled. Already, whistles were blowing; the chug of motorcycles could be heard. Mounted police were heading for the scene of gunfire. Quickly, The Shadow hurried back to Weston's limousine. He saw the one-eyed glare of motorcycle headlights rounding into the bridle path.

Diving aboard the car, The Shadow rolled beyond Weston, who was still on the floor. Finding the far door he slumped beside it; and became as silent as the other figures that occupied the limousine.

When police arrived half a minute later, they stumbled over the dead form of Slook Howdrey; then discovered the bodies of Hunk and the other thug in front. A moment later, a patrolman saw a stirring figure; and dragged the groggy police commissioner from the limousine.

Barely recovered, Weston stared dizzily into the glow of flashlights; then looked anxiously to the interior of the car. He smiled in relief as he saw policemen bringing out the slumped, but moving, figure of Lamont Cranston.

Weston was pleased because his companion had also been saved from death. Not for a moment did he suspect that it was the supposed Lamont Cranston who had waged battle as The Shadow!

CHAPTER VI
CRIME STALKS ANEW

"IT was The Shadow who rescued us, Cranston."

Commissioner Weston was firm in his announcement as he and The Shadow rode southward through Central Park. The two were seated in the rear of a large sedan that the police had commandeered in place of Weston's blood-spattered limousine.

The Shadow made no comment. He smiled in the darkness. He knew that Weston had experienced the usual mental lapse that follows a hard blow on the head. The commissioner's recollection would remain blank concerning the quick action that The Shadow had delivered at the moment of Slook's vicious swing.

As they reached Fifty-ninth Street, Weston glanced at his watch; noted that it was not quite ten o'clock. Not much more than half an hour had passed since the departure from Murkden's. That fact satisfied Weston immensely.

"By this time," he announced, "officers whom I sent to Murkden's will be there. If any attempt is intended against the professor's life, they will protect him. I feel convinced, however, that such a possibility has been completely thwarted. If the purple killer—whoever he is—planned harm for Professor Murkden, the job would probably have been delegated to Slook Howdrey.

"Moreover, the killer must have believed that he would accomplish enough results by dealing with me alone. Slook's warning was intended to make me drop the investigation of the purple death. Thanks to The Shadow, the law's work can proceed."

As he finished speaking, Weston tapped the envelope that contained the reports on the purple poison and the blood tests. That valuable packet had been reclaimed from the floor of the limousine, where Slook had dropped it.

The sedan pulled up in front of the Cobalt Club. Entering there, Weston made a prompt call to Murkden's. He chuckled as he talked across the wire; finished the call and turned to The Shadow.

"The professor is safe," stated Weston. "He was asleep when the officers arrived, but the servants aroused him, and he learned of our experience. The news quite bewildered him. I assured him that all was well; that I had instructed men to guard his house."

An attendant interrupted to announce that the commissioner was wanted on the telephone. Weston answered the call. His face showed immediate alarm. Without a word, Weston motioned to The Shadow, then started from the club. They entered a taxicab. Weston gave an address on East Fifty-eighth Street. He told the driver to hurry.

"Grave developments, Cranston" was Weston's only comment as they rode along. "That call was from Inspector Cardona."

There was a grimness to the air of secrecy that Weston had adopted. Keeping to the role of Cranston, The Shadow leisurely lighted a cigarette and gazed languidly from the cab window. The taxi reached Fifty-eighth Street; slackened speed in front of a row of pretentious houses.

JOE CARDONA was standing on the front steps of a house when the cab stopped there. He greeted the commissioner, nodded to The Shadow, whom he, like the commissioner, knew as Cranston.

"This is Rythe's house," announced Cardona, to the commissioner. "I was called here at ten o'clock."

"Trumbull Rythe," explained Weston, to The Shadow. "You've heard of him, Cranston. Rythe gained great wealth through his financial transactions. Always eccentric; but a remarkable financier."

Weston's tone was tinged with gloom that indicated he was speaking of the dead. That did not surprise The Shadow. From the very beginning of the hurried ride, he had anticipated that the conclusion of the journey would bring them to a scene of crime.

Cardona conducted the arrivals into the house, ushered them into a front parlor. There they found a long-limbed man in evening clothes, who was seated on a divan. The man's head was bowed. As the visitors entered, he looked up to reveal a sallow, pointed face. The Shadow saw the man wince at sight of Weston. He also caught the quick blink of evasive eyes.

"Courtney Grell" exclaimed the commissioner. "What are you doing here? Is this man a suspect, Cardona?"

"Please, Commissioner," began Grell. "Don't accuse me—"

"I made no accusation," interrupted Weston. "I asked a question. Let me tell you once again, Grell, your shady stock transactions cannot be tolerated. On your last visit to my office, I gave my final warning."

"I took it, Commissioner," pleaded Grell. "I told you that I was through."

"Yet I find you here—"

"Because I sought to help the law."

Grell's tone carried weight. Weston showed surprise; then looked to Cardona. The ace nodded.

"That's correct. Grell phoned me," declared Cardona. "That's why I wanted you to hear his story first, Commissioner."

Weston looked mollified. He turned to Grell, expecting the man to speak. Instead, Grell trembled; his eyes shone wildly. Cardona whacked him on the back. Grell steadied. Rising, the long-limbed man went shakily to a cabinet in the corner of the room, where he helped himself to a drink from a decanter.

"Guess it jolted him pretty bad, what he saw upstairs," confided Cardona, to Weston.

Grell had steadied by the wall. Turning to Weston, the sharp-faced man began his story, in a voice that shook with occasional tremolo.

"Trumbull Rythe understood me," declared Grell. "He knew that I sold good propositions along with bad ones. I always dealt on the level with him."

"Reserving your fake transactions for dupes," put in Weston, sourly.

Grell winced.

"I called Rythe at eight tonight," resumed Grell. "His servant, Timothy, answered; told me that I could call at ten. When I rang the doorbell, Timothy did not answer. I found the door unlocked and entered.

"No one was on the ground floor. I went upstairs. The door to Rythe's den was ajar, so I looked into the room. I saw"—Grell faltered, then fairly shrieked—"I saw Rythe!"

As he gave the utterance, Grell stared toward the floor as though visualizing some horrible sight. He flung his hands in front of his eyes, staggered to the divan and sagged there. Cardona motioned to a detective to stay with Grell. Cardona led the way upstairs.

INSTEAD of conducting Weston and The Shadow to Rythe's den, Cardona pointed to a front room. They entered to find a stocky, somber-faced man who was seated in a chair, staring moodily. The Shadow knew that this must be Timothy, the servant.

"Hello, Timothy," spoke Cardona, in an assuring tone. "Here is the commissioner. Tell him what you told me."

"There isn't much to say, sir," announced Timothy, sadly. "Mr. Rythe was upstairs in his den. I was reading in the kitchen. I chanced to remember that I had left the front door unlatched. I came to the front hall. I noted that the light was out.

"I heard a stir from the stairs; I called to Mr. Rythe; he did not answer. I started upstairs in the darkness. When I reached the top step, something clapped upon my face. It was rubbery, like a sponge. Its odor overcame me."

"Chloroform," explained Cardona. "Whoever used it stowed Timothy here in the front room. Tied him with those curtain cords; gagged him with his own handkerchief."

Cardona pointed to exhibits that lay in a corner of the room.

"At what time did this happen, Timothy?"

The question came from Weston. The servant shook his head.

"I don't know, sir," he declared. "The kitchen clock was stopped. All that I can say is that the time was somewhere between half past eight and half past nine."

"You did not recognize your assailant?"

"I had no chance, Commissioner."

Weston turned to Cardona. The inspector led the way to Rythe's den. They entered the little room to find the very sight that The Shadow expected.

On the floor lay Trumbull Rythe, a huge, portly man who had crumpled crazily with his fall. He was clad in trousers and shirt that had no collar.

All eyes were directed upon the dead man's face. It was a bloated countenance; large enough in life, hugely increased by death. Lips were pudgy; nose was swollen; eyes were goggly. Dyed deep in the dead visage was the fateful purple that told the cause of Rythe's sudden death.

The purple death had taken a new victim, as terribly as it had struck down Frederick Tabor and others before him.

CARDONA pointed to a couch.

"Rythe could have been lying there," declared Joe, "or he could have been standing over near the wall. Anyway, the murderer didn't give him a chance. I can tell you how he killed him, Commissioner."

Cardona ran his finger along paneled wood-work, showed that it glistened with some sticky substance. Looking at the wall, Weston noted stickiness throughout the corner; even on the plush of the couch, although there it barely fringed the edges.

"A spray gun!" exclaimed Weston. "The murderer administered a vaporized poison, like one would spray insects."

Cardona nodded.

"What's more, Commissioner," affirmed the ace, "I'll tell you when it happened. At half past eight!"

"How do you know that?"

"On a hunch. Timothy says that sometime between eight-thirty and nine-thirty, he came from the kitchen. Let's say that it was nine o'clock. What did Timothy do first? He called for Rythe, but there was no answer.

"That shows Rythe was dead. The murderer was on his way out. He must have killed Rythe along about eight-thirty; then torn up the place." Cardona pointed to tables and a desk, from which the drawers had been removed. As at Tabor's, there were scattered papers. "Naturally, he would have made a quick getaway, after putting Timothy out of the way."

Weston nodded his agreement; then recalled that he was endorsing one of Cardona's hunches. The commissioner chewed his lips, looked to the person nearest him, namely The Shadow.

"What do you think of Cardona's theory?" queried Weston. "Do you agree with us that Rythe must have died at half past eight?"

Weston stressed the word "us" as a sop to Cardona, but he wanted to thrust the burden of final agreement upon some other person. Weston expected The Shadow to agree.

"We may presume," remarked The Shadow, "that Rythe was asleep upon the couch when the murderer entered. With the door closed, he would not have heard Timothy's call; but the murderer would have. The fact that the murderer waited for Timothy and disposed of him could indicate that he had not started his crime."

THE SHADOW'S disagreement with Cardona's hunch pleased Weston. He liked the logic of this new theory.

"Timothy was reading in the kitchen," added The Shadow. "Time would have passed more rapidly than he supposed. We might place the time of the murderer's entry later, on that account. Let us say at about half past nine."

"Good reasoning, Cranston," approved Weston. "You have a rival, Cardona, in the matter of hunches. You say that Rythe was killed at eight-thirty; Mr. Cranston argues—quite as logically—that Rythe was slain an hour later."

"Either could be correct," remarked The Shadow. "Perhaps, Commissioner, it would be best to await the new blood tests that you will certainly have Professor Murkden make."

"Of course," nodded Weston, his face looking sour. "We shall send the body to Murkden's at once, with a surgeon in charge of it. I meant to tell you, Cardona"—Weston turned to the inspector—"that Murkden obtained results from his tests on Tabor's blood. He learned the hour of Tabor's death last night."

"What time was it?"

"At half past eight."

The Shadow smiled as he saw Cardona repress a grin.

Commissioner Weston finished up briskly. He ordered Cardona to attend to all details. That done, Weston departed with The Shadow. On the way out, they passed Courtney Grell, sitting glumly in the lower parlor. Outside, The Shadow parted from the commissioner and hailed a cab of his own.

Riding toward Times Square, The Shadow sat immobile. His eyes, staring fixedly from the window, caught the glitter of passing lights. Those keen eyes showed a burning sparkle that did not change.

In the purple death, The Shadow had encountered crime more subtle, more baffling than any of its sort that he had met before. He was planning a new campaign—one that would cover every possible detail—in his effort to solve the riddle of the purple death.

CHAPTER VII
THE SECOND CLUE

A CURIOUS clock showed the hour of five. That clock was a singular arrangement of dials, set in concentric circles; three different rings for minutes, hours and seconds. The clock was revealed beneath the glow of a blue-rayed lamp. Everywhere else was darkness.

Hands were moving across the polished surface of a table, beneath the bluish glare. They were the hands of The Shadow; long-fingered, tapered, busied with many tasks. Upon the table lay a map of Manhattan; typed report sheets; filing cards that listed names. The right hand held a fountain pen; it was making inked notations on a blank sheet.

The Shadow was in his sanctum, a hidden room of darkness, somewhere in Manhattan. Night had passed; day had followed. Still, The Shadow was at work.

The master sleuth had gleaned many details both in and out of his headquarters. As Cranston,

he had received a call from Weston, during a short stop for lunch at the Cobalt Club. The commissioner had heard the results of Professor Murkden's new tests. Specimens of Rythe's blood had been tested as thoroughly as Tabor's; they had been matched by new experiments with guinea pigs. Again, Joe Cardona had been supported in his hunch.

The tests proved conclusively that Trumbull Rythe had died at half past eight. This backed Cardona's theory that the killer had been on the way out when he encountered Timothy, the butler.

Twice, therefore, The Shadow's own theories had proven wrong. That was not disturbing; in both instances, The Shadow had conceded that circumstances might not fit his conjectures. Nevertheless, it seemed certain that some unusual element was present in the chain of purple crimes.

To trace it, The Shadow was using many measures. He had delved deeply into possible motives behind the deaths. Typed report sheets, culled from various sources, listed the various victims of the purple scourge. What could be the connection between such persons as a mechanic, a university instructor, a radio announcer, a promoter, a pawnbroker, an architect and a financier?

The last two victims—Tabor and Rythe—had added to the chaotic situation. Nothing in all The Shadow's reports showed connection between any victims. The answer, as The Shadow saw it, must be an interwoven chain. All depended on a missing link—the murderer.

Some supercrook was after great wealth. He must have gained control of something valuable. To hold it, he had murdered men who might have blocked his path. Some may have died purely because they could reveal facts later, when the killer's schemes reached the public eye. Others, The Shadow was sure, had died for different reasons, as yet unknown.

Behind the purple death lay subtle strategy; the scheming of a mighty brain.

The Shadow was sure that seizure of papers had been necessary at Tabor's, but not at Rythe's. This added to the problems that blocked The Shadow's progress.

DROPPING the question of the victims, The Shadow considered other factors. First, Slook Howdrey. The Shadow dealt but briefly with the thug whom he had eliminated the night before. Slook was nothing more than a pawn that the purple killer had moved across the board. Once, to trap The Shadow; again, to cow the police commissioner. Slook had failed to interfere with either The Shadow's investigation, or that of the law.

Second was Courtney Grell.

Last night, Grell had chanced upon a scene of crime. Had that been purely by coincidence, or had the purple killer expected Grell to arrive at Rythe's? Considering these probabilities, The Shadow saw little choice between them. He doubted that either would matter.

More important was the possibility that Grell knew who the murderer was. Grell, himself, was a shady character, the sort who would serve a master crook. That fact, however, made it seem unlikely that the murderer would employ him for so grueling a service as the discovery of a victim; unless Grell happened to be far more clever than appearances showed.

The Shadow had not forgotten Grell. He intended to consider the fellow later. For the moment, however, The Shadow was concerned with another important person; namely, Joe Cardona.

Until Cardona had taken charge of the investigation, no victim of the purple death had been found soon after murder. That had changed with Joe's entry. Moreover, no theories had been offered concerning the times at which victims had died, until Cardona put them. He had guessed eight-thirty for both Tabor and Rythe. Professor Murkden's certified blood tests had proven Cardona right. In addition, there was another element. Every detective covering the purple deaths had vanished, until Cardona had stepped on the scene. Nothing had happened to Cardona.

What was the answer?

The Shadow had one. Astonishing though it was, the answer fitted. Joe Cardona, despite his efficient work, might actually be falling in line with what the murderer wanted. If that chanced to be the case, it explained why Cardona was still at large.

Clues intrigued The Shadow. Other detectives had found them: a fountain pen and a button. There was a possibility that Cardona had uncovered clues but had kept them to himself. The Shadow intended to investigate that matter.

The Shadow's clock showed quarter past five. Long fingers lifted a sheet of paper that bore the notation:

Cardona. 5:30 p.m. Channing 5-3827.

This brief report was from Clyde Burke, one of The Shadow's agents who posed as a newspaper reporter. Visiting headquarters, Clyde had heard Cardona making an appointment for half past five. He had noted the number that Cardona dialed. It was Channing 5-3827.

The Shadow had checked on the telephone number. It belonged to a suite of offices, numbered 650, in the Landis Building, near Times Square. That suite was occupied by Courtney Grell.

The Shadow's light clicked off. A whispered laugh sounded amid total darkness. The Shadow was ready for departure; from the sanctum, he would travel to the office in question. Arrival there at five-thirty would enable him to observe two persons: Grell and Cardona. Both were individuals upon whom The Shadow must concentrate. A conference between them promised real results.

ANOTHER storm was sweeping Manhattan. Even at this early hour, the city was blanketed with night. Striving streetlamps produced illumination amid a driving swirl of mingled sleet and snow; but above, the sky was as black as the Stygian depths of The Shadow's sanctum.

Glittering windows, etched against night's velvet, indicated the lighted offices where late workers still lingered after the five-o'clock hour. One skyscraper that showed its quota of illumination was the Landis Building.

Five-thirty showed crowds in the lobby of the Landis Building; for it afforded entrance to a subway and the rush hour was still strong. Among those passers appeared a tall stroller who carried a well-packed briefcase. The Shadow had arrived at the hour of Cardona's appointment with Grell.

Seven minutes later, Cardona himself appeared from the street and went up to Grell's suite. Joe entered without knocking.

The shady speculator smiled wanly as he arose to shake hands with Cardona. Joe doffed his overcoat, thwacked a newspaper upon the table. Grell noted the folded journal; saw a conspicuous automobile advertisement showing from the uppermost page. He recognized it as a morning newspaper; wondered why Cardona was carrying it instead of an evening one. Cardona must have noted Grell's glance, for he immediately picked up the newspaper and stowed it in a pocket of his overcoat.

Seating himself across from Grell, Cardona delivered a gruff opening:

"You wanted to talk to me. All right. I'm here."

"I appreciate the visit," acknowledged Grell. "You see, although you have not arrested me, I feel that you suspect me in the matter of Rythe's death."

"What gave you that idea?"

"Ever since last night," replied Grell, "I have noted headquarters men shadowing me."

"Certainly," returned Cardona. "That was for your own protection."

"But not at my request—"

"I considered that unnecessary."

Grell smiled. He was glancing at the desktop. Cardona was watching him.

Neither saw the blackish streak that edged into the office, from the connecting door. Flat against the floor, that blotch formed a silhouette. Barely visible, it was the only indication of The Shadow's presence. Motionless, the silhouette became so inconspicuous that it could no longer have attracted attention.

"RYTHE'S death was a shock," declared Grell, changing the subject in suave fashion. "I, too, wish to see that justice is gained; and I feel that you should appreciate my attitude, Inspector.

Police Commissioner Weston seems to understand my sentiments."

"The commissioner?" snapped Joe. "When did you talk to him?"

"This afternoon," replied Grell. "When I called him on the telephone, he apologized for last night's hasty remark. In fact, he invited me to accompany him this evening to see Professor Murkden."

Neither man saw the blackish streak that edged into the office from the connecting door.

Cardona fumed inwardly. He realized that Grell, probably by flattery, had talked himself into the good graces of the police commissioner. Cardona regarded that as interference with his own activities. So he took it out on Grell.

"I suppose," growled Cardona, "that you squawked about being covered by headquarters men. Going over my head, despite the fact that I sided with you last night—"

"No," interrupted Grell, smoothly. "On the contrary, I spoke highly of you to the commissioner. I said nothing about being shadowed."

Cardona was stumped. He saw how cleverly Grell had established himself. By speaking well of Joe, Grell had impressed Weston. Established with the commissioner, he was working the game in reverse. The humor of it finally brought a smile from Cardona.

"All right," he acknowledged. "Go ahead and meet the commissioner tonight. I'll call off my men."

"Thanks," smiled Grell. "Incidentally, I might add that I said nothing to the commissioner regarding the clue you found at Rythe's last night. I suppose that you chose to keep it to yourself."

"The clue?" demanded Cardona, quickly. "What clue?"

Grell leaned across the desk.

"When I saw Rythe's body," he declared, in a confidential tone, "I was badly shaken, but I observed the slip of paper that had apparently dropped from his hand. It had writing on it, in blue pencil."

Grell eyed Cardona as he spoke. Joe sat silent.

"Large writing," added Grell. "I could read it easily. All it said was: 'Call me at noon tomorrow'; and it was signed with the letter 'L.'"

Grell paused to note the effect of his statement. Cardona's silence was proof that Grell had a hit. The sallow man settled back behind his desk; his eyes became shrewd.

"You were the next person who entered Rythe's den," reminded Grell. "Yet nothing more was said about that written memo. I fancied that perhaps you preferred to keep certain clues a secret. So I remained silent."

Cardona saw no further use in blunt silence. He snapped a question:

"Have you any idea who 'L' could be?"

Grell shook his head.

"I knew nothing of Rythe's affairs," he insisted. "Timothy might tell you."

"I quizzed Timothy on my own," admitted Cardona. "He couldn't answer it. You struck it right, Grell. I found that piece of paper. But this case is mine. I've got a right to keep quiet about the clues I find. If the commissioner is to know about them, it's my business to tell him."

Grell's eyes showed a sudden gleam; one that could be seen from the doorway where The Shadow watched. Grell had caught Cardona's reference to 'clues'; it indicated that Joe might have found something at Tabor's also. Cardona, however, was unconscious of the slip that he had made. Grell did not enlighten him.

METHODICALLY, Cardona drew a small envelope from his inside pocket. Opening its loose flap, he peered within; drew out the blue-penciled memo that Grell had mentioned. Again, Grell's eyes were sharp. Cardona's action indicated that something else was in the envelope.

"Here's the memo." Cardona showed it to Grell; then replaced it in the envelope. As he did, Cardona kept the envelope turned so that Grell could not see another item, the chess clipping that Joe had picked up at Tabor's. "All right, Grell. I'm glad we had this talk. You won't be bothered with anybody trailing you. In return, I'm counting on you to cooperate."

Grell smiled. By cooperation, he knew that Cardona expected him to make no mention of this meeting, especially to Commissioner Weston. Grell nodded his agreement, arose with Cardona and helped the inspector put on his coat.

The Shadow was gone when Cardona left by the outer office. Grell remained; but he was no longer watched by The Shadow. The reason for The Shadow's complete departure was explained when Cardona reached the lobby. There, Joe dismissed the detective whom he had told to keep tabs on Grell; then went out and took a cab. Hardly had Cardona's taxi pulled away before The Shadow appeared, carrying his briefcase, to enter another cab.

The Shadow had heard every word that passed between Cardona and Grell. He had recognized the importance of the blue-penciled memo that was signed with the letter 'L.' Whether or not Grell was positive that Cardona must have found a previous clue at Tabor's, The Shadow was certain that Joe had. Moreover, The Shadow was convinced that Cardona had gained a link between them.

Cardona's prompt agreement to Grell's requests stood as proof that Joe had some important move in mind. The briskness of Cardona's departure fitted with it. Clearly, The Shadow could see the idea that was in Cardona's mind. The ace inspector did not fully trust Courtney Grell. Moreover, Cardona would not have kept important clues too long without telling Weston, unless those clues promised some quick result.

Cardona's hurry was proof that he intended to follow a lead that he had gained; to accomplish some startling result between this hour—six o'clock—and the time when Grell met Weston. By trailing Cardona, The Shadow stood a chance to learn the link for himself. Events were fitting with The Shadow's theory that Cardona had become a vital factor in the plans of the super-crook who ruled the purple death.

Trailing Cardona, The Shadow hoped to learn all that the inspector knew; to pick up further facts if Cardona failed to find them. This was a quest that promised results. Yet The Shadow, though prepared for unusual developments, did not consider his present trail as more than a preliminary one.

The Shadow had not yet foreseen that circumstances might hold a real surprise in store, that his present mission was to bring him to the threshold of new mystery.

CHAPTER VIII
THE VANISHED SLEUTH

FROM the moment that Cardona's trip began, it proved that some new development lay ahead. Joe's cab took a roundabout direction from Times Square. Obviously, Joe wanted to throw off trailers by picking side streets where he could watch for following cars.

The Shadow, however, was equipped to match such a game. The cab in which he was riding was his own. It was an independent taxi driven by one of the cleverest hackies in New York; a driver whom The Shadow had chosen because of his skill. Instead of closing in on Cardona's taxi, The Shadow's cab kept well behind.

At Sixth Avenue, Cardona's cab had made a quick turn southward, beneath the elevated pillars. The Shadow's cab turned also; trailed at a distance of nearly two blocks.

Cross-traffic suddenly blocked the chase. It came just as The Shadow's cab was speeding to get by a cross street as all lights went red. Sleet and snow quickly blotted out Cardona's cab. Ten swiftly covered blocks failed to show new traces of the missing cab. Then, on one side street, The Shadow saw a parked cab that looked like Cardona's. The standing taxi had no lights. The Shadow ordered to keep ahead; then round the block. A few minutes later, his own cab entered the street with lights extinguished and stopped fifty feet behind Cardona's.

The Shadow alighted and started forward through the hazy sleet that blurred the infrequent streetlamps. He had gone but a few yards when he saw a figure step from a small alleyway near the cab ahead. Pausing by a doorway, The Shadow saw the outline of a gray hat and overcoat; he watched the wearer of the garments enter the taxi.

The light was insufficient to distinguish more than a general impression of the gray-clad form; but The Shadow had recognized Cardona's garb. Obviously Joe had ordered a halt at this spot; then gone through the alley on foot.

Cardona's cab shot suddenly away, as soon as its passenger had entered it. Its lights came on while it was moving. By the time The Shadow was back in his own cab, the taillight ahead was disappearing around a corner. The Shadow ordered quick pursuit.

THE new chase was a short one, performed in zigzag fashion. The first cab gained a long lead on a cross street where the avenues were wide apart. It turned right; by the time The Shadow's cab reached the avenue, there was no sign of Cardona's. The Shadow ordered a quick spurt on the avenue; a prompt turn to the right at the next street. He had gauged the situation to perfection.

As his own cab turned right, The Shadow saw Cardona's taxi parked a short way down the block. Its lights were still on. It started from the curb just as The Shadow spied it. The trick was a cute one, if intended to shake off followers; for there was no way to tell whether or not Cardona had remained in the cab. It was possible that he paid the driver while on the move; stopped long enough to drop off and tell the driver to keep going.

The Shadow, however, knew that he could depend upon Moe Shrevnitz, the driver who was handling his cab. With a quick command, The Shadow ordered Moe to slacken speed; then keep up the chase. Moe obliged. In the moment that the cab was almost halted, The Shadow opened the door and dropped off to the curb, easing the door shut as he went.

Ten seconds later, The Shadow was at the very spot where Cardona's cab had stopped.

Groping, The Shadow studied his surroundings. He soon found that he had picked the only spot where Cardona could have gone during the short time allotted him. The Shadow was in front of a little shoe repair shop. The tiny building was an old relic wedged between a loft building that had no side street entrance and a warehouse that displayed a blank wall.

The shoemaker's shop was closed for the night. It was wide enough for a door and one display window that started from two feet above the sidewalk. Avoiding the blackened glass window, The

Shadow tried the door. It was unlocked; hence it was possible that Cardona could have entered it quickly after leaving the cab.

TWO possibilities occurred to The Shadow: one, that Cardona had arranged this trick to watch for pursuers; the other, that Joe had learned something about the shoe repair shop and had come to investigate it. In either case, the darkness was sufficient for The Shadow to attempt a silent entry.

Soon after the chase had started, The Shadow had donned black garments from his briefcase. Clad in that garb, he was as invisible as night itself, when favored by the presence of a darkened doorway. His mode of entry, edging in as he opened the door, cut off all draughts and whistling sounds of wind.

One minute later, The Shadow was in the shoe shop, the door closed noiselessly behind him. The silence was so intense that The Shadow could have detected the slightest sound. Moving with absolute stealth, he assured himself that the little shop was empty.

The Shadow used a flashlight, its tiny ray masked by a fold of his cloak. Foot by foot, he scoured the place. He found a row of shoeshine chairs on one side; a shoemaker's lathe and machinery on the other.

At the front, by the window, was a small desk with a telephone. The Shadow discovered this, probing without his light. At the rear of the narrow room was a door. It was bolted from the other side.

It was possible that Cardona had gone through to the back of the building. The door could have been unlocked when Cardona found it. The Shadow's path was definitely blocked.

Half a minute passed while The Shadow listened in darkness, to learn if anyone could be listening from the other side of the door. He heard no sounds; but one suddenly came from the front of the shop. It was the ring of the telephone bell. Drawing away from the rear door, The Shadow waited a full two minutes. The bell kept up its persistent intermittent ringing all the while.

Confident that no one could have detected his entry, The Shadow took it for granted that Cardona must have gone on through the rear of the shop, using the bolted door to cut off trailers. Joe was probably calling the number, to learn if anyone had entered the shoe shop, hoping that such a person would answer. With a soft, whispered laugh, The Shadow moved forward. He lifted the receiver from the telephone hook; but did not speak. Instead, he listened.

CARDONA'S voice came across the wire, as The Shadow had expected. But it lacked its gruff, demanding tone. The words that The Shadow heard were excited ones.

"Whoever you are, listen!" came Cardona's quick tone. "This is Inspector Cardona, New York police. Get word to Commissioner Weston, at once. Tell him that I—"

A *click* ended Cardona's outburst. Simultaneously, The Shadow sensed a puff of chill that penetrated the narrow shop. Dropping the receiver, he wheeled away from the telephone, whipped out an automatic and stabbed a shot to the rear door.

Simultaneously with The Shadow's blast, revolvers barked in his direction Their shots were wide. Aiming men had picked the telephone as their target. Bullets shattered the glass show window. But The Shadow's shot told. He had picked the one spot from which an attack could come. He heard a cry; snarled oaths as crooks dragged back a companion whom The Shadow had wounded.

Three quick shots roared through the shoe shop as The Shadow bombarded the opened door. Enemies had dived for cover, but The Shadow's bombardment served its purpose. Crooks could not close the door while it was under fire. If they took to flight, their scurry would tell The Shadow of their move.

Then came the token that gave The Shadow knowledge of instant danger. As his automatic made its last recoil, he felt a barely perceptible quiver of the floor; heard a rumble from the front street. The Shadow was standing against the thin front door; to his left was the show window.

With a quick dive, The Shadow flattened himself below the show window; between it and the telephone table. He was not an instant too soon. From the front street came a terrific rattle—the outburst from a battery of machine guns.

The rumble had told The Shadow of an approaching truck. That vehicle had stopped. With downward tilted machine guns, crooks were riddling the whole front of the shoe shop.

The door was splintered by a hundred drilling bullets. The broken window was shattered into nothingness, its glass fragments bouncing over and beyond The Shadow. The whole interior of the shop was ripped and peppered, except at one spot.

That was the narrow, two-foot space where The Shadow lay prone; the only possible place where a person could have lain and lived. The Shadow was below the lowest possible angle of the machine guns. He was bulwarked behind a thick brick wall that the bullets could chip, but not demolish.

The terrific bombardment ended. The truck roared away, its occupants satisfied that they had covered every square foot of the shoe shop with their bullets. The door at the rear of the shop slammed shut, its bolt clicked. The small crew behind the wall of the rear room were satisfied that The Shadow had been riddled. They had no time to investigate and gloat. They had to carry away a wounded member of their band before the police arrived.

AS he arose, The Shadow stumbled over the telephone. The table had been riddled. The telephone had been hit, but it had fallen so quickly that its wires still remained intact. The receiver had been cracked by a bullet, but The Shadow could hear the dial tone. Calmly, he fingered the dial, found that it worked.

Sirens wailed from an avenue. The terrific clatter had aroused the neighborhood. Still, The Shadow persisted with his call. A quiet voice answered; it was that of The Shadow's contact man:

"Burbank speaking."

"Report."

"Report from Shrevnitz," responded Burbank. "He trailed Cardona's cab to the Cobalt Club. It is across the street—"

Burbank's voice faded as the receiver crackled. The split had yielded; the wiring was useless. The Shadow dropped the telephone, turned to the front door. Sirens were closer. Soon they would reach the shoe shop. The Shadow stepped out into darkness, moved rapidly along the street. He was obscured by the sleety blackness by the time the first patrol car arrived.

Elsewhere, The Shadow stepped aboard a cab that was parked near a corner, gave the driver a destination. Finishing a quick trip, The Shadow dropped a bill through the front window; stepped out and merged with darkness, leaving the driver wondering where his passenger had gone. A half block's walk brought The Shadow to a spot across the street from the Cobalt Club.

The Shadow saw two cabs. Up ahead was Cardona's. Its parking lights were on; the driver was sitting patiently at the wheel. Behind was The Shadow's cab. Approaching, The Shadow stepped up from the darkness, gave Moe the whispered order:

"Report."

"Never lost sight of it," stated Moe, referring to Cardona's cab. Moe could not see The Shadow in the darkness beside the driver's window. "It came straight here, but nobody got out of it. What the hackie's waiting for, I can't guess."

"Report received."

Moe saw ghostlike blackness move beneath the glow of a streetlamp; then fade as it reached the shelter of Cardona's cab. The Shadow had arrived there without the knowledge of Cardona's taxi driver. Noiselessly, The Shadow opened the rear door, peered into the back of the car. He could see the interior by light from the street side.

As The Shadow had expected, the cab had no passenger, but it was not entirely empty. Carefully folded upon the back seat was Cardona's gray overcoat; on it was perched the old felt hat that Cardona had worn when he left Grell's office.

Silently, The Shadow closed the door. He went back to his own cab, entered it and stowed away his black garments. Donning a hat and overcoat of his own, he spoke to Moe. The cabby started the taxi, drove around the block and pulled up in front of the Cobalt Club. There, The Shadow alighted in the guise of Lamont Cranston.

A fixed smile was registered on The Shadow's disguised lips as he left hat and cloak at the club cloakroom. Attired in faultless tuxedo, he strolled slowly toward the grillroom, where he knew he would find Commissioner Weston.

The parked cab outside the Cobalt Club, the one in which Cardona had traveled, was a token which The Shadow knew would soon be explained. It had been sent here as a contemptuous challenge to the law. Some message from a master crook would surely come to give notice of its presence.

The Shadow expected a prompt aftermath to the mysterious disappearance of Joe Cardona.

CHAPTER IX
CRIME'S SEQUEL

COMMISSIONER WESTON was in the grillroom when The Shadow arrived there. Weston had come to dinner earlier this evening, for the grillroom clock showed that the time was only ten minutes after seven. Moreover, tonight, the commissioner had guests. With him were two newspapermen, special writers who conducted columns that covered society news.

The press had found a way to gain interviews with Weston, even in the seclusion of the Cobalt Club. Ostensibly, these society writers had come merely to chat with the commissioner, disclaiming any interest in crime news. Actually, they were hoping for any wedge that might enable them to question Weston regarding the purple death. Weston knew that. He could not afford to be brusque with the society columnists. Nevertheless, he was wary. His interviewers had so far arrived nowhere.

Weston smiled when he saw The Shadow. He knew that the columnists would be impressed when they learned that the commissioner was on close terms with Lamont Cranston. The globetrotter was much sought, socially; but seldom seen at society functions. Shaking hands with much gusto, Weston invited The Shadow to join the group for dinner.

While they were waiting for The Shadow to finish his first course, Weston remarked that he had an appointment at eight o'clock. One of the newspapermen promptly questioned if the appointment happened to be Professor Murkden's lecture. Weston admitted that it was.

"Some valuable facts may be mentioned tonight," declared the commissioner, tartly. "That is why I am attending the lecture."

"And afterward?" persisted the newspaperman. "Will you discuss the blood tests that the professor has made?"

"Probably," replied Weston. "The newspapers, however, have already received full reports of the tests that the professor made today."

That closed the subject. Weston felt that he was sitting easily, until he saw a man walk hurriedly into the grillroom. The arrival was Courtney Grell. The sallow man's anxious expression told that he was looking for the commissioner. Before Weston could signal Grell to stay away, he arrived at the table. One of the newspapermen recognized him, for Grell had formerly tried to splurge in society. Weston was therefore forced to admit Grell's identity.

"What is it, Grell?" he demanded angrily. "I told you to meet me at Professor Murkden's at eight o'clock. I did not say to come here."

"But I was told to come here—"

"By whom?"

"By your secretary. He called up my hotel and—"

"My secretary has gone away on vacation."

"That is singular, Commissioner. The man who called wanted me to tell you that the taxicab was still waiting outside the Cobalt Club."

WESTON arose, fuming.

"What nonsense is this, Grell?" he fairly shouted. "Why should I keep a cab waiting? I have my official car."

"But the cab is there, Commissioner. I spoke to the driver. He said that he was waiting for word from you."

"Who told him to wait there?"

"He said that Inspector Cardona sent him here."

Weston glared, more perplexed than ever. At that moment, an attendant entered the grillroom, to announce that there was an urgent telephone call for Commissioner Weston.

As soon as Weston left the grillroom, the newspapermen arose and followed. The Shadow saw Grell watch the departure with shrewd gaze; then the sallow man followed. The Shadow had just finished his course. He arose and strolled after the throng.

Weston was in the lobby, shouting over a telephone, oblivious to all about him.

"Yes... This is Commissioner Weston!... Hello... Cardona?... What?... Where?..."

The receiver went dead in Weston's hand. Hanging up, Weston started to say something; then stopped and turned to Grell, whom he saw standing by.

"Send someone for that taxi driver," snapped Weston. "Bring him here at once."

Grell dispatched a pair of attendants. They returned, with a worried-faced cab driver. One of the attendants was bringing a gray hat and overcoat. He gave them to Weston, with the remark:

"These were in the back seat, sir."

"Cardona's hat and coat!" exclaimed Weston. "Then it *was* Cardona who just called me. Something *has* happened to him. Come, my man"—this was to the taxi driver—"give me your story."

"I don't know nothing much," blurted the hackie. "I was cruising near Times Square, along about six o'clock, when a passenger got aboard and told me to drive for Sixth Avenue."

COURTNEY GRELL—crooked stockbroker

The Shadow was watching Grell. He saw the man indulge in a tight-lipped smile, when the cabby failed to mention that Cardona had boarded his cab outside the Landis Building.

"When we got to Sixth Avenue," continued the hackie, "this fare of mine tells me to go back to downtown. I thought maybe he was kidding, until he flashes a badge; says he's Inspector Cardona. Downtown, he tells me to swing on Twenty-eighth Street and park near a sort of alley, with the lights out."

THERE was an interruption; another call for Weston. This time, the caller was not Cardona. Weston held brief conversation; announced that he had received a routine report from headquarters. He told the cabby to proceed.

"The inspector was gone a while," continued the hackie. "He showed up again, talked gruffer than he did before. Told me to turn one corner after another; then he stopped me all of a sudden in front of a joint that looked like it didn't amount to much. He shoved me five bucks, told me to chase up here and wait until I heard from the commissioner."

"What about the hat and coat?" demanded Weston. "When did Cardona leave them?"

"I don't know," admitted the hackie. "I didn't know they was laying in the cab until we just found them, a couple of minutes ago."

Weston looked quizzical. Suddenly a thought struck him.

"The second place you stopped," he inquired, "was it a shoe repair shop? Between a loft building and a warehouse?"

The cabby nodded.

"Yeah," he said. "That could have been it. On Twenty-fourth Street, I think."

Weston turned to the others. The commissioner's face was strained.

"This man has told the truth," announced Weston. "It fits with the report that I just received from headquarters. Cardona must have entered that shoe shop. Not long afterward, a truck stopped there and riddled the place with machine gun bullets. The assassins escaped."

"After killing Cardona?"

The question came from one of the newspapermen. Weston was too worried to realize who had asked it.

"No," declared Weston. "Fortunately, Cardona is still alive. I know that, because I heard his voice across the telephone, only a few minutes ago. But he has certainly been captured. He had something that he wanted to tell me; he said that this might be his last chance."

"Another investigator missing," said one newspaperman to the other. "This time, it's Joe Cardona, best inspector on the force. He tried to tackle the purple death. He's gone. The best he could do was put in a last call—"

Weston was roused to sudden ire. He began to denounce the men who had so recently been his guests. While Weston was storming, the columnists made a scramble for the cloakroom, obtained their coats and hats and headed for the street.

"They'll call their offices!" fumed Weston. "There will be special editions on the street inside an hour. What can be done about it, Cranston?"

"Notify the other newspapers," suggested The Shadow, calmly. "Give them the whole story, so that those two chaps won't have a scoop. Then come to the grillroom and finish dinner."

Weston managed a chuckle.

"That's taking it calmly, Cranston," he decided. "I shall do as you suggest. In addition, however, I shall notify headquarters that Cardona is missing. We must begin an intensive search for him."

SOON afterward, Weston joined The Shadow and Grell at the dinner table. Weston had made his calls; he had calmed considerably and announced that he intended to go to Murkden's lecture at eight.

"Professor Murkden may be our last resort," affirmed Weston, gloomily. "He is not an investigator, but his scientific tests have given the only tangible results to date."

The Shadow noted Grell, who was poker-faced. He knew that Grell was thinking about Cardona's clues. The Shadow, too, was considering that subject. He was positive that Cardona had picked up some small item at Tabor's, the night before he found the memo at Rythe's.

In addition, however, The Shadow was considering Cardona's disappearance. He had solved certain details of that riddle. The Shadow, from his own experience, knew that Cardona could not have entered the shoe repair shop. That was a trap that crooks had arranged for anyone who might be following Cardona, particularly The Shadow, himself. It proved that the purple killer had acquired another band of gunners, like the crew that Slook Howdrey had commanded.

The Shadow knew that Cardona had definitely left the cab at the first stop it made—on Twenty-eighth Street. Joe had been gone for twenty minutes before The Shadow located the parked taxi. It was during that period that the ace inspector had been seized.

Cardona had been captured not far from the cab. Another man—one of the captors—had donned Joe's coat and hat. That substitute was the man whom The Shadow had seen returning to the cab. Crooks had picked a man of Cardona's stocky build for the assignment. Viewing the fellow in darkness, The Shadow had seen only the outline of the gray coat and hat.

In the cab, the substitute had told the hackie to drive to the shoe repair shop; then continue to the Cobalt Club. The substitute had left Cardona's hat and coat. He had ducked into the shoe shop, gone through the back door and bolted it. There he had joined other waiting thugs.

Meanwhile, crooks had imprisoned Cardona. They had dialed the number of the shoe repair shop, had given Cardona a chance to get hold of an extension telephone, while thinking he was unobserved. Cardona had taken a chance on reaching the commissioner through the person at the other end.

A clever trick to surprise The Shadow if he happened to be in the shop. Crooks in the rear room had been ready to fire when they heard the ringing cease. Another had signaled the machine gun truck, from the back door of the old shop.

The call to Grell could have come from anyone claiming to be Weston's secretary. As for Cardona's call to Weston, that was simply explained. Crooks had let Cardona get to a telephone on his own; had kept watch and broken in upon him before he could tell too much.

This time, the work of henchmen showed that they were under direct orders from the purple killer. Only a master crook could have devised such a crafty sequence. Only the purple killer would have been so bold as to fling deliberate, disdainful challenges at the police commissioner.

Cardona's capture was plain to The Shadow; yet he still needed facts before he could learn where crooks held their prisoners. To gain such facts, The Shadow intended to follow his accepted course. Blind search would prove of no avail against a superplotter.

Only by uncovering the purple killer, by learning the master crook's identity and methods, without the fiend's own knowledge, could The Shadow plan the rescue of Joe Cardona and bring a final finish to the run of crime.

CHAPTER X
THE NEEDED LINK

WHEN eight o'clock neared, Weston departed for Professor Murkden's accompanied by Courtney Grell. The Shadow remained at the Cobalt Club, stating that he had an appointment. He remarked, however, that he might be able to visit Murkden's after the lecture. That pleased Weston. In this time of stress, the commissioner appreciated the presence of his friend Cranston. For some reason that Weston could not explain, he felt more confident when Cranston was about.

Soon after the commissioner had gone, The Shadow left the club. Moe's cab wheeled over, picked up the supposed Lamont Cranston. The Shadow gave a destination; the address was close to Murkden's. As the cab headed in that direction, The Shadow donned his garb of black.

To The Shadow, the disappearance of Joe Cardona marked a crisis in the sequence of purple death. Until this time, The Shadow had been forced to play a waiting game, even though other lives—those of unknown persons—might be at stake. All along, The Shadow had recognized some blockading factor; tonight, he had discovered what it was. Joe Cardona, by holding out important clues, had unwittingly restrained The Shadow.

Cardona's disappearance was doubly unfortunate; for The Shadow was convinced that Joe had gained two clues. Something that Cardona had found at Tabor's must have linked with the penciled notation at Rythe's. In some way, Cardona had managed to gain a definite lead, and had gone after it too soon.

For the present, The Shadow's policy could not be altered simply because Cardona had blundered and made himself a prisoner. If Joe should be slated for death by his captors, the chances were that he had already been put on the spot. If they intended to hold Cardona as a hostage, there would be no need to attempt a hasty rescue. The Shadow saw that it would be wiser to wait until his plans were fully formed; unless some emergency made it imperative to take great risks in Cardona's behalf.

Cardona's disappearance had, in a sense, helped The Shadow. It had given him two definite leads of his own.

The first concerned Courtney Grell.

Today, The Shadow had learned definitely that Grell was playing a cagey game. That did not necessarily implicate Grell in the crime chain of the purple death. Grell's discovery of Rythe's body could have been an accidental one, as Grell himself claimed.

Nevertheless, Grell had smartly looked out for certain interests of his own. He had played Cardona against Weston; then vice versa, in order to put himself in right with the law. That, of course, was understandable. His smartest trick had come when he mentioned the memo clue to Cardona. At that time, Grell had learned—if he had not guessed it before—that Cardona held a clue from Tabor's as well as from Rythe's.

Grell had not even suggested to Cardona that he suspected there was a first clue. As for the second one, Grell had promised not to mention it to Weston. True, he had kept that promise, but under unusual circumstances. When he heard that Cardona had vanished, Grell should have told everything to Weston, so as to aid in the search for Cardona.

Grell's silence proved that one of two situations existed. Either Grell saw how he could gain some personal advantage through Cardona's disappearance, or else he was in some way connected with the purple deaths. In either case, Grell would be due to make a move. The Shadow intended to watch Grell.

HE had postponed such a vigil partly because Grell would be with Weston until nine o'clock, when Professor Murkden's lecture ended. Grell could make no move until after he left the commissioner. For the present, therefore, The Shadow was actually using Weston to hold Grell inactive.

Also, The Shadow needed the hour between eight and nine; at least a portion of it. He wanted to follow the second lead that he had gained through Cardona's disappearance.

Joe Cardona had established the deaths of Tabor and Rythe at identical times on successive nights; namely, at eight-thirty. In making blood tests, Professor Murkden had proved Cardona's findings. Yet Cardona had not been seized because he had settled the time element, nor had any threat been made against Murkden after the results of the professor's tests had been published.

That was singular; because the greatest subtlety of the poison used in the purple murders lay in the way of baffled physicians when they tried to ascertain the hour of each death.

Therefore, The Shadow had considered the possibility that both Cardona and Murkden might be wrong in their conclusions.

Cardona had relied upon guesswork; and The Shadow had already doubted Joe's hunches. Murkden, however, had made exact tests, scientifically conducted and properly attested by competent observers. In his tests, though, Murkden had relied upon a synthetic formula that he called Compound "F." There was a chance that the chemist had erred slightly in his preparation of the compound; that it was not exactly identical with the purple poison used by some master murderer.

To settle that, The Shadow had resolved to make tests of his own. The coming hour offered the best opportunity for The Shadow to obtain the materials that he needed.

It was ten minutes after eight when The Shadow's cab stopped at a spot not far from Murkden's. Stepping into darkness, The Shadow merged with the sleety night. Snow was increasing; large flakes settled on the shoulders of The Shadow's cloak, but they vanished before they could serve as white markers to indicate the passage of a form amid the darkness.

Nearing Murkden's, The Shadow saw Weston's car out front; near it, a pair of uniformed policemen. The officers were not regular watchers. Guards had been deemed unnecessary because Murkden's house was strong and he had three competent servants. The pair of bluecoats had been stationed to protect Weston's chauffeur, in case another ruffian like Slook Howdrey tried to take over the commissioner's official limousine.

GLIDING into a side passage just short of Murkden's house, The Shadow escaped the notice of the officers. He reached the windows of Murkden's basement laboratory. There, with a small screw driver and a compact jimmy, The Shadow began the task of entry.

The job was speeded because The Shadow had previously studied the inside fastenings, when he had visited Murkden's. At the finish of five silent working minutes, The Shadow had removed the outer bars. Noiselessly, he pried the inner sash. Raising the window slightly, he slipped into the laboratory. A corner light was illuminated, but the room was empty.

After closing the window, The Shadow operated rapidly. He found a box of new test tubes; from dozens the few that he took would not be noticed. Into these, he poured samples of the various compounds that were on Murkden's shelf. New corks were plentiful in a special box. The Shadow corked the tubes, carefully packed them in a pocket beneath his cloak.

Searching among a stack of notebooks, The Shadow found one that he wanted. It contained neatly typed pages, covering the results of Murkden's blood tests. Rapidly The Shadow chose the notations that he knew would be necessary for his own experiments. He copied these, thus gaining needed formulas and complete data concerning the blood changes that had occurred both with human victims and guinea pigs.

That done, The Shadow examined some of the slides that Murkden used with the projector; noted their labels and made brief written descriptions concerning certain slides. He passed the corner where a small box of dead guinea pigs lay upon the crate that was filled with live ones. The Shadow ignored the cavies since there was no need to carry away live guinea pigs. As for the dead ones, their purpose had been served. All that was important concerning them could be found in The Shadow's notes.

It was not quite quarter of nine, The Shadow decided to look in upon the lecture before he departed. Choosing a set of thin passkeys, he unlocked the door to the stairs. He ascended and opened the next barrier as easily. At the third door, The Shadow paused; probed the lock with consummate care. This was the door to the lecture room. The Shadow handled it without noise.

Inching the door open, The Shadow viewed the lecture room through a narrow crack. He could not see the platform where Murkden stood, for that was against the wall beside The Shadow's door. He could hear the professor's dry voice, however; and he caught the thuddy sounds that came when Murkden tapped a big chart with a pointer.

Murkden's listeners were visible. They formed an attentive group of notetakers who were looking toward the platform. Near the back of the room, The Shadow saw two who were not taking notes. One was Commissioner Weston. Arms folded, face set, Weston was methodically taking in everything that Murkden said.

The other was Courtney Grell. His attitude was a contrast to Weston's.

GRELL looked bored and restless. He was slouched in a chair. His jaw was moving as he chewed gum to pass the time. Even that annoyed him. The Shadow saw Grell take out his wad of gum and throw it into a wastebasket a few feet away. Sourly, Grell reached in his pocket and produced a cigar. He chewed the end from it and brought out a pocket lighter, to ignite the stogie.

Murkden's drone now ceased. The Shadow heard the rap of the pointer upon a table.

"Attention, please!" came Murkden's sharp voice. "We can tolerate no smoking during the lecture."

Students stirred to look toward Grell, for Murkden's gaze must have been directed on the visitor. Grell quickly thrust the cigar in his breast pocket. He looked apologetic when Weston gave him a reproving gaze. Grell straightened in his chair. Murkden resumed.

Immediately, Grell slouched again. Since he could not smoke, he brought out a package of chewing gum and took a fresh stick. Again, his eyes roamed restlessly; they stopped suddenly on a table that was near the wastebasket.

The Shadow saw a shrewd look on Grell's face. Noting that Weston was not watching him, the sallow-faced visitor edged toward the table and reached for a newspaper that was lying there. Bringing the newspaper to his chair, Grell stooped and began to turn the pages.

The newspaper crinkled slightly, but none of the listeners noted it. Only Professor Murkden could have seen what Grell was doing, but this time the professor was apparently too busy with his lecture to again note the disturber. The Shadow saw Grell raise the newspaper; then turn it over.

On the side toward The Shadow was a large automobile advertisement. It was the same page that Grell had seen on the newspaper that Cardona had brought to the office. Grell had remembered that newspaper the moment that he saw its duplicate here in the room.

The Shadow recognized the large advertisement as one that he had seen; thereby, he

The Shadow ascended to the door of the lecture room.

identified the particular morning newspaper which Grell held. But The Shadow had not seen Cardona's newspaper. When he had visited Grell's offices, Joe had stowed that copy in his overcoat pocket just prior to The Shadow's entry.

Grell's interest in the newspaper, however, impressed The Shadow as important. The result proved it. Grell's eyes lighted as he found an item. A look of sudden elation swept the swindler's sallow countenance. Folding the newspaper, Grell reached over and replaced it on the table.

Looking to the left, Grell saw the door that led out to the little reception room that formed an entrance to the small lecture hall. His jaws slowed their chewing motion as he turned his gaze toward the platform; then glanced at Weston. The Shadow understood the move that Grell intended.

As soon as a convenient opportunity offered, Grell intended to leave. He wanted to get away before the lecture finished. He planned to depart without attracting Commissioner Weston's attention. Grell's reason for departure concerned something that he had noted in the morning newspaper.

THE SHADOW edged the door shut, locked it noiselessly. He made a quick descent to the laboratory, rapidly locking the other doors as he passed them. Out through the window, he closed the sash, planted the crisscrossed bar that he had removed. A single minute was all that The Shadow required to jam that outer fastening.

Gliding through darkness, The Shadow regained Moe's cab. Stowing his black garb in his briefcase, he ordered the driver to head for the corner nearest to Murkden's. As they reached the corner, The Shadow saw someone coming down the steps of the professor's house. He knew that it must be Grell.

The Shadow dropped off. The cab arrived in front of Murkden's and Grell hailed it. The Shadow saw him step aboard. The cops outside offered no objection. They were not under instructions to stop persons who came from Professor Murkden's lecture.

The Shadow had given Moe brief instructions. Watching the departing cab, he saw its stoplight give two slow blinks, as Moe pressed the footbrake. Then came four short ones. The two meant twenty; the four stood for four. That told The Shadow the number of blocks. All that he needed was the direction. The cab turned southward at the corner.

This was Sixty-sixth Street. The Shadow knew that Grell had told Moe to take him to Forty-second. Probably to Times Square, where Grell would change cabs. That did not matter; Moe would manage to trail him. Grell would not walk far, looking for another cab amid the driving sleet.

On foot, The Shadow made for the nearest subway. Reaching a local station, he had time to stop at the newsstand before the train arrived. The Shadow asked for a copy of the *Morning Sphere,* the journal that he had seen Grell consult. The dealer had a few odd copies beneath the counter.

Riding southward in a half-empty subway train, The Shadow opened the newspaper in the calm, indifferent fashion that suited his guise of Lamont Cranston. He found the page with the automobile advertisement. He scanned the page opposite it.

Chess diagrams showed near the bottom of the page. They belonged to a half column of chess problems. Below were answers to problems printed on the previous day. In addition, The Shadow saw an extra diagram. There was a notation stating that this was a problem that had appeared one week ago. It was reprinted because a reader of the column had submitted a better answer, wherein White could produce checkmate in two moves instead of three.

With the diagram was a terse letter of half a dozen lines from the reader who had presented the new solution. It was signed by a man named Louis Lenger. It gave Lenger's address, a number on Twenty-sixth Street.

THE subway train was nearing Forty-second Street. The Shadow did not rise. He intended to keep on the local until he arrived at the Twenty-eighth Street station. Thin lips showed the semblance of a smile that meant an important discovery by The Shadow.

The Shadow had guessed the nature of the clue that Cardona had found at Tabor's studio. It was a copy of the original chess problem, clipped from a week-old newspaper. In Rythe's den, The Shadow knew, Cardona had picked up a penciled memo signed with the letter "L."

Cardona had been noting the chess column in the *Morning Sphere* in hope of some lead that would help him. Today, he had seen this reprint of the problem; he had read the letter signed by Louis Lenger. Those initials looked like a sure hit. Either "L"—Louis or Lenger—would fit the initialed memo!

That was why Cardona had halted his cab on Twenty-eighth Street. It was close enough—yet not too close—to Lenger's address. Cardona had evidently intended to return to the cab; instead, he had been captured during his round trip.

The Shadow remembered a newspaper that had bulked from Cardona's overcoat pocket, when the inspector had left Grell's offices; but The Shadow had not seen the newspaper closely nor had he regarded it as important. He recalled that there was no newspaper in Cardona's overcoat when it arrived in the empty cab; but had logically supposed that Cardona had simply disposed of it.

Courtney Grell must have noted the paper in the office and observed that Cardona valued it. That was why Grell had gone after the duplicate copy among the newspapers on the table at the lecture room. Grell must also have noticed the page at which Cardona's journal had been opened.

Spying the letter signed by Louis Lenger, Grell had naturally hit upon the connection between that name and the letter "L." Grell, too, knew that Cardona had been near Twenty-sixth Street. For some reason, Grell had taken upon himself the dangerous job of visiting Louis Lenger.

The Shadow knew that he would find Grell at Lenger's. He would be present when the two men met. To The Shadow, that coming meeting would offer facts that might aid him in solving the riddle of the purple death.

CHAPTER XI
THE LAST NAME

THE address on Twenty-sixth Street was of a small apartment house; a building that looked new when compared to the old houses near it. The Shadow came along the street on the side where the apartment house was located. He passed the small entry where a light shone through a glass door.

Again, The Shadow was obscured by darkness. He had brought his briefcase with him. After leaving the subway, he had put on his blackened garments. On this secluded section of Twenty-sixth Street, lights were feeble, encrusted with freezing sleet. The terrain was well suited to The Shadow's mode of unseen motion.

The Shadow avoided the front of the apartment building; not only because there the light was stronger, but because he expected the arrival of Courtney Grell. The Shadow knew that the sallow-faced schemer could not have arrived as quickly by cab as The Shadow had by subway.

With time to spare, The Shadow crossed the street. From a darkened spot, he viewed the little apartment house. An angled outlook gave The Shadow a good idea of the building's construction.

The apartment house was nothing more than a pair of converted residences that had been joined and equipped with a false front. From straight across the street, the structure presented a good appearance; its modern style indicated that the added construction had been done within the past few years.

From an angle, however, the roofs of the old houses showed at the sides and gave an ugly contrast. The chief reason why they were visible was because they extended deep into the building block. Furthermore, there were spaces on each side of the apartment house. Those indicated routes to the back of the double building. The Shadow conjectured that there must be a regular rear entrance.

The apartment house was four stories high. There were dim lights in windows on the first three floors, but none on the fourth. The top-story apartments were either vacant, or the occupants were out.

Soon after The Shadow had completed his survey of the building, a taxicab pulled up and a man alighted. It was Courtney Grell. The Shadow watched the sallow man pay the driver. The cab went away. Grell entered the apartment house. Immediately, The Shadow crossed the street. He drew close to the doorway, stopped on the very fringe of the lighted space in front.

Grell was standing in the entry thumbing a button on the wall. He had evidently found Lenger's name card.

There was no answer to Grell's ring. The sallow man brought out a watch. He eyed the time, turning the dial toward the light that topped the entry. The Shadow saw the face of the timepiece, noted that it was quarter past nine.

Grell gave a few more futile jabs at the button, shrugged his shoulders and turned toward the door. The Shadow drew back in darkness farther than necessary to avoid Grell's observation. The reason for his extended move was a taxicab, slowing as it came along the street. Like Grell's cab, this taxi stopped in front of the apartment house.

GRELL had paused in the lighted doorway. Sharp-eyed, he was studying a man who stepped from the cab. The newcomer turned into the light. He was tall and heavy of build; his face, though rugged, seemed that of a thinker rather than a man of action. The tall man was almost shabby in attire; his heavy coat was opened, his derby hat was tilted from a jolt that it had received in the cab.

The tilted hat displayed a shock of gray hair that showed no signs of recent brushing. The tall man's face was unshaven, another indication that he cared nothing about his personal appearance. He was not bothered by the tilt of his hat. He left the derby canted. Deep in thought, he stepped toward the door of the apartment house, his ungloved fingers fumbling the change that he had received from the taxi driver.

Almost at the door, the tall arrival saw Grell and pulled up with a start. For the moment, The

Shadow saw large eyes glare and study the sallow man with suspicion. Grell smiled; then queried affably:

"Are you Mr. Louis Lenger?"

Eyes hardened; then the tall man nodded. Grell held out his hand.

"My name is Courtney Grell," he explained. "I happened to be in the neighborhood; stopped by to see if you were busy. I hoped that you would not mind the intrusion. I am a chess player like yourself."

Lenger stroked his stubbly chin. He seemed torn between two sentiments: a natural dislike of strangers, and a feeling of friendliness toward a fellow chess enthusiast. At last he motioned toward the doorway and extended the gruff invitation:

"Come up to the apartment, Mr. Grell."

Grell let Lenger go past to unlock the inner door of the entry. He was still chewing gum; his slow-moving lips formed a suave smile. Then his eyebrows arched as he saw Lenger open the door without unlocking it. Evidently anyone could gain access to this apartment house.

The reason for the unlocked inner door was apparent to The Shadow when he approached. Though he did not enter, The Shadow made a careful study of the entry that the two men had vacated. He saw that the telephone receiver, used for conversation between visitors and tenants, was one that had no wire. On that account, the front door was open. People could go up and knock at the doors that they wanted.

The uselessness of the receiver indicated that the bells, too, were out of order. On the other side of the entry, above a row of mailboxes, The Shadow observed a square-cut block that indicated a space for a new telephone installation. Evidently new equipment had been planned but not completed.

Instead of going in by the front, The Shadow moved through darkness, skirted the double building and came to the expected rear entrance. He found a locked door, but opened it with little difficulty. He entered a long, dimly-lighted hallway. There, The Shadow saw the door of an automatic elevator. Its glass panel was dark. Lenger and Grell had evidently taken the elevator upstairs.

THE SHADOW found a darkened stairway, ascended it. He stopped at the second floor and noted the frosted glass panel in the metal door of the elevator shaft. He found it dark. Keeping on to the third floor, he found another darkened panel. On the fourth floor, The Shadow saw the glow of the elevator through a door panel. He knew that Lenger's apartment must be on this floor.

The fourth floor was smaller than those below; it had only two apartments and neither bore a name card. Light showed beneath the crack of one door. The Shadow knew that it must be Lenger's. Looking for a suitable way of entry, he went along the hall. Past an arch that had been cut in an old house wall, The Shadow saw doorways on each side of a short hallway. These had no numbers. They looked like service entrances to the two apartments.

Working the door on Lenger's side of the house, The Shadow silently unlocked it. He stepped into a dusty kitchen, where pots, pans and dishes were stacked in untidy heaps. The kitchen was partly lighted by a glow that came from a hall. Thanks to that illumination, The Shadow avoided a blocking soap box that was stacked with opened tin cans.

The Shadow crossed the hallway, peered into a fair-sized living room. He saw Lenger seated in front of a small table, busy with a board and chessmen, while Grell looked on; The Shadow had expected this. He knew that Grell would have talked about the chess problem, to follow up his method of introducing himself to Lenger.

"Very good," commended Grell, as Lenger looked up from the board and pointed to his final move. "Your method of mate is far superior to the one originally published. I wish that I had more time to devote to chess problems."

As he finished speaking, Grell removed his chewing gum and looked about for a wastebasket. He finally found one; tossed the gum there. A wastebasket looked out of place in Lenger's living room, for the place was strewn with papers and other rubbish. Lenger observed Grell's survey of the room and smiled apologetically.

"The apartment is untidy," he admitted. "Unfortunately, my servant was offered a better situation and took it. I have not yet replaced him."

"I see," nodded Grell. Then, suavely: "You live entirely alone?"

"Yes. My investments bring me a small income. I cook my own breakfast and lunch, read, and do chess problems most of the day. I always dine at six; after that, I call on my friend Howard Feasley."

"A chess player?"

"Yes. Feasley is a recluse like myself. For a while, he was an invalid; but his health has improved. He still insists on retiring at nine. That is why I always go to Feasley's to play chess. Every night we play from seven until nine."

Lenger was becoming quite confidential with Grell. The ice once broken, he seemed talkative. He did not, however, state where his friend Feasley lived, although Grell's face showed that the visitor would have liked to learn that fact. Instead, Lenger went to a bookcase, rummaged among stacks of volumes and found a tin box. He brought it to the table, where Grell was starting to chew another stick of gum.

"I have worked on all these problems," remarked Lenger, opening the box to show a pile of clippings. "Whenever I work out a better solution than one in the newspaper, I write a letter to the chess editor."

AS Lenger tilted the box to rearrange the clippings, something clicked and rolled to the table. The Shadow saw Lenger pick up a blue pencil and replace it with the clippings. So did Grell. The sallow man pursed his lips, glanced at his watch.

"Nine-thirty," he remarked. "I must be going, Mr. Lenger. By the way, do you retire early, like your friend Feasley?"

"Seldom," replied Lenger. "Why?"

"I thought that I might drop by some evening," returned Grell, "and play a few games, after you have returned from Feasley's."

"Fine!" agreed Lenger. "We could play from nine until midnight."

"How would tomorrow evening be?"

"Excellent. Can you come at nine, Mr. Grell?"

"I am not certain. But jot down your telephone number"—Grell motioned toward a pad that lay on the table—"I can keep it as a sure reminder to call you—"

"I have no telephone here."

Grell's eyes narrowed. The Shadow knew why. Grell had failed in his effort to gain a specimen of Lenger's handwriting. He dropped that endeavor rather than arouse Lenger's suspicion.

"I shall drop by again," promised Grell. "If I cannot stop off, I shall leave a note in your mailbox. Good night, Mr. Lenger."

Grell picked up his hat and coat. Lenger reached for his own frayed overcoat and derby.

"I'll accompany you downstairs," suggested Lenger. "I forgot to make some purchases at a drugstore. We can chat about chess as we go along."

The two left by the main door of the apartment. The Shadow listened until he heard the dull rumble of the descending elevator. Then he entered the living room; there, he went to the bookcase and examined the tin box that Lenger had replaced. Thumbing quickly through the stack of chess clippings, The Shadow found that many of them were duplicates. There was one copy of the original problem that Lenger had answered in today's newspaper; but no duplicate.

Newspapers were stacked everywhere on the floor. They showed gaps where Lenger had clipped chess problems. Many of the journals were from out of town. Whether or not Lenger had other interests—murder, perhaps, included—it was certain that he was a true devotee of chess.

Most of the books on the narrow shelves were volumes that referred to chess. The bottom shelves were stacked with dusty magazines; beneath them were boxes of various sizes. As a result, the old magazines formed a wavelike line. Carefully, The Shadow withdrew some of the boxes, so that he could examine them without disturbing the arrangement.

Some of the boxes contained chessmen; others held articles clipped from magazines, referring to chess. A few were filled with miscellaneous items. It was in one of these that The Shadow made an important find. He saw a page that had been cut from a college catalog. It bore names of faculty members. Around one was a circle, marked in blue pencil.

THE name was that of James Ardess, the university instructor who had been one of the earlier victims of the purple death.

Beneath the torn page was a pawnbroker's ticket. It carried the name of William Gringew. He was the pawnbroker who had been another of the mysterious victims.

Farther down, The Shadow found a business card, of neatly engraved pattern. It was old and dusty; the card bore the name of Frederick Tabor, with the title: "Architect."

Next, The Shadow discovered a small-typed page, roughly torn from a copy of "Who's Who." Names on that page began with "R." Among them, circled in blue pencil, was a brief biography of Trumbull Rythe, the financier who, like Tabor, had been a victim of the purple death.

At the very bottom of the box, The Shadow unearthed a folded sheet of paper. It bore a list of typewritten names, in capital letters, badly off line. This list carried the names of the victims of the purple death, in the order of their doom. Ardess and Gringew were early in the list. Later came Frederick Tabor; then Trumbull Rythe.

There was an old typewriter near the bookcase; probably the list had been typed on that machine. The Shadow did not wait to check that matter. Something more important concerned him. The name of Trumbull Rythe was not the last one on the list. There was another below it.

The final name was Horace Selbart. A name that had been in the news today. Horace Selbart, big time gambler; controller of gaming interests throughout the United States, had arrived in New York this afternoon, aboard a liner from Europe. He had been photographed by cameramen, on the roof of his penthouse near Park Avenue.

Thus The Shadow knew who Selbart was, and where the man could be located. Both facts were vital. Selbart's unsavory past could be disregarded. All that mattered was that Horace Selbart had been slated as a victim of the purple death. Apparently, doom's chain had been timed to fit Selbart's return to America.

Quickly, The Shadow replaced the box beneath the magazines. He left by the front door of the apartment. The elevator was on the ground floor; The Shadow did not waste time in pressing the control button and waiting for the slow car to ascend. Instead, he took the stairs. Reaching the ground floor, he hurried out through the rear door.

The lack of a telephone in Lenger's apartment made The Shadow's spurt imperative. An instant warning must be dispatched to Horace Selbart. Yet with all his speed, The Shadow knew that his present cause would probably be useless.

It was almost ten o'clock, the approximate time at which the last two victims of the purple death— Tabor and Rythe—had been discovered dead. Unless some unusual factor had delayed the purple murderer, The Shadow would be too late to save Horace Selbart from his scheduled doom.

CHAPTER XII
DOOM'S LONE CLUE

FIVE minutes distant from Lenger's apartment house, The Shadow reached a telephone, located in the gloom of a side entrance to an antiquated office building that stayed open for the benefit of late tenants.

The Shadow made a quick call to Burbank, for he knew that Selbart's number would be unlisted. Burbank, however, had an excellent collection of unlisted numbers, always in readiness. The Shadow knew that Selbart's would be among them.

Burbank's response was prompt. To the contact man The Shadow delegated the duty of calling Selbart and delivering a warning. Burbank was excellent at that sort of job. His even, methodical tones carried an impressive touch across a telephone wire.

The call finished, The Shadow returned to the street. He saw a chance cab parked near the corner; its fidgety driver was ready to pull away as soon as a traffic light turned green. Evidently the hackie figured that he would make out better cruising on this stormy night than by standing still.

The hackie was wrong. As he shoved the car in gear, he heard a quiet voice speak from the back seat. Turning about, he stared into darkened depths. The voice gave a destination near Park Avenue, told the hackie to hurry. The fellow gawked no longer. He had the passenger he wanted. The fact that his fare had seemingly come from nowhere was a secondary matter.

As he drove along, however, the cab driver was determined to keep tabs on his passenger. He did not want to let that unseen rider slip away as weirdly as he had arrived. Nonetheless, the hackie's vigilance failed him.

One block from the given destination, the cab slowed to make a final right turn. Something fluttered from the driver's shoulder; when it reached his lap, the man saw that the object was a five-dollar bill. Jamming the brakes, the hackie looked into the back seat. He turned on the dome light. The mysterious passenger was gone.

The Shadow had seen another cab coming from a side street. It was the one manned by Moe. Burbank had evidently contacted The Shadow's speedy cab driver after calling Selbart's penthouse. The Shadow boarded his own cab as it slackened on the crossing. Once inside, he whispered the word:

"Report."

MOE gave the news. Burbank had called Selbart but there had been no answer from the gambler's penthouse. Burbank had dispatched Moe to be in readiness, should The Shadow need him.

The cab neared the apartment house where Selbart lived. Dropping off, The Shadow noted the front entrance of the building. It was an old structure, only ten stories high; but its nearness to Park Avenue had kept it fashionable. The Shadow saw a uniformed doorman pacing the lobby. Ordinarily, the attendant belonged outside; but he had gone indoors because of the miserable weather.

Looking upward, The Shadow barely discerned the outline of the penthouse against the sullen illumination of the city's lights, a glow that persisted despite the driving storm. The Shadow noticed that the penthouse was situated at the front corner of the building on the side toward Park Avenue.

Passing that corner of the building, The Shadow observed a small side entrance to the apartment building. He guessed its purpose. The door must be a private entrance to a special elevator that took visitors to Selbart's penthouse.

Entering the doorway, The Shadow found a small entry; he saw the double door of an elevator shaft, beyond it a small, keyless door that looked like the entrance to a closet. The elevator doors were a half-inch apart, a glow showed between them. The elevator was here on the ground floor.

The Shadow wedged the doors far enough to grip the inner lever. He opened the doors, saw that the small elevator was empty. Quickly, The Shadow stepped to the closet door and whipped it open. On the darkened floor, he saw a slumped figure in uniform, trussed and gagged.

The man was the elevator operator. He had been treated like Timothy had been handled at Rythe's. The closet reeked of chloroform. There was no time to wait longer. The Shadow left the door open so that the bound man could get more air. He stepped aboard the elevator and closed the doors.

There was only one control button, marked: "Penthouse." The Shadow pressed it; the elevator, one of a modern type, made the ascent swiftly. Reaching the top, The Shadow silently opened the doors, stepped quickly from the elevator, a drawn automatic in his fist.

Lights were on in the penthouse; their glow was indirect and mellow. The soft light was like a pall. That effect was increased by the unearthly silence that seemed to dwell within these spaces.

There was no need for The Shadow to tread softly as he crossed the floors of huge, hushed rooms. Thick-tufted Persian rugs drowned every footfall.

Every doorway was heavily curtained; those draperies looked like lurking spots for hidden watchers. The Shadow recognized the possibility of spying eyes. He adopted a course that allowed for them. As he entered each room, The Shadow edged along the wall, his motion barely visible against dark oak panels. At each curtain, he performed a quick sweep with his gun; a move of the drapery, the muzzle jabbed behind it.

Any hidden watcher would have been caught completely off guard, but The Shadow found no lurker. He came to the last of several doorways; frisked the curtains and stepped across the threshold. The Shadow had reached a square-lighted room that served as Selbart's library.

There, The Shadow stopped.

ON the floor lay a portly body, sprawled face downward. The figure was attired in a dressing gown that had pressed upward, high above the sprawled man's neck. It did not, however, cover the bald pate that showed above a fringe of thin, dark hair.

Light glistened from the smooth bald head. The reflected glow was purple. The dye of death had tinged the skin that covered the sprawled man's skull.

Stopping, The Shadow rolled the body sidewards. He recognized the pudgy small-eyed face that he saw. It was the fat, piggish countenance of Horace Selbart; but it had retained only a mere semblance to the photograph that The Shadow had seen in today's newspaper.

Selbart's face was completely purple. Its puffy features had gained in size. His small, deep-set eyes were still tiny in proportion to the rest of his face, but they had definitely enlarged. They looked like purple agates that had been poked into the fatty sockets that held them.

While The Shadow stooped, his hand upon the dead man's shoulder, a clock whirred in another room; then chimed the quarter hour. The Shadow had uncovered this case of the purple death at exactly half past ten.

Letting the body sag face downward on the floor, The Shadow made a brief survey of the room. Little had been disturbed, but The Shadow noticed one spot where books had been removed from a shelf and clumsily replaced. Taking out the books, he saw an opened panel in the wall beyond. Someone had slid back the woodwork to reveal an open space that served as a small, shallow wall safe.

There were papers visible; The Shadow examined them. Some were promissory notes, made out to Selbart. Several were signed by gamblers; but two bore the names of prominent New York artists; another was signed by a man who had recently acquired a large theater near Times Square.

Others were letters. One was from a man who wanted money to open an abandoned gold mine; two were from inventors, one mentioning a new automotive device; another described the merits of a special process for taking motion pictures in natural colors, which would cut production costs below those of existing methods.

The Shadow replaced the papers. He put the books back as he had found them. He looked at Selbart's body. The Shadow's lips phrased a whispered laugh, solemn and mirthless.

THE SHADOW had long known that Horace Selbart had other interests than the precarious game of running gambling establishments. Being a multimillionaire, Selbart had always had plenty of money to invest. It was not surprising that he had figured in various types of transactions, for Selbart had always preferred to keep himself technically within the law.

That, in a sense, had been his most pernicious practice. Selbart had backed many shady deals; his process was always to deal with a lone individual. Often, when gambling establishments had been raided in various cities, the proprietors had squealed that Selbart was the actual owner. None had ever proven that claim. Invariably, they had taken the rap themselves, because they could furnish neither witnesses nor written evidence.

Selbart's own gaming establishments were always located in cities where the laws were lenient.

The Shadow had suspected Selbart's past game; but had not interfered with it, for the big time gambler had been dealing with rats of his own ilk. He had also suspected Selbart's simple method.

Selbart had simply advanced the gambling proprietors all the money that they needed; and in return, received promissory notes far in excess of the amount he gave them. If the men made out well, they were quite willing to pay their silent partner from the profits, even though he doubled or tripled his investments. If the game went sour with any of the gamblers, Selbart never produced the notes. Arrested gamblers went to the penitentiary, but did not have to pay their debts.

What The Shadow had not suspected was that Selbart had used this method in dealing with persons who offered him legitimate opportunities to make money. Artists, theater men, inventors; all had pawned their future in the hope of getting a start. Selbart, cannier than the men with whom he dealt, had only advanced cash to those who he felt positive would gain success.

The Shadow stepped back to Selbart's body, rolled it face upward. He studied the body closely, observed a small but deep gash on the heel of Selbart's hand. Closely, The Shadow pictured how the gambler had died.

Some visitor had come to discuss the matter of an invention, probably bringing a model that Selbart had seen before he went to Europe. When Selbart had taken the object, a hidden spring had snapped, to jab a knifelike point into the gambler's pudgy hand. That cutting device had been loaded with the poison that delivered the purple death.

The opening behind the bookcase indicated that Selbart had himself removed the documents that pertained to the invention—letters and promissory notes—to discuss them with his visitor. The killer had taken those documents away with him, but had not lingered to search the library for papers that pertained to other persons. Probably the murderer had not guessed that Selbart kept such documents at the penthouse. Having the papers that he required for himself, the killer had preferred rapid departure.

CALMLY, The Shadow turned Selbart's weighty body face downward, so that it took its original position. As the form settled on the floor, The Shadow spied a tiny bluish object that pushed from beneath the dead man's shoulder. With gloved hand, The Shadow picked up the object. It was a stubby, blue pencil.

The pencil was a round one; it was thicker than most. It was topped with a metal ring, but was not equipped with an eraser. The lead, like the painted surface of the pencil, was blue. Under usual circumstances, the pencil could have been classed as ordinary, although it differed from most standard makes of blue pencils.

This pencil, however, was doubly important. Not only did it appear to be an object Selbart's murderer had dropped; the pencil was the exact mate of one that The Shadow had seen before, less than an hour ago. It was identical with the blue pencil in Lenger's box of chess clippings.

Carefully, The Shadow replaced the pencil beneath Selbart's shoulder. Rising, he stood motionless while he viewed the dead man's body. Again, The Shadow delivered a whispered laugh. He had found a repetition of a former circumstance.

There had been odd clues at the scenes of earlier murders: a fountain pen, a shirt button. Better clues had come with later deaths: a chess clipping and a blue-penciled memo with the letter "L." Despite the cleverness with which the purple deaths had been delivered, some odd clue had been left behind on every occasion.

The Shadow knew that Joe Cardona had stolen the clipping and the memo. But Cardona, strangely vanished, would not be here to find the final clue. This time, The Shadow had discovered a clue before the law had opportunity; but he wanted to witness the reaction that would come when the clue reached the law.

There was one way to accomplish that; namely, to summon the law to the scene of death. The higher up The Shadow went, the better the result would be. There was one man who would come here hot on the trail, if properly summoned.

That man was Commissioner Ralph Weston. The Shadow's next move would be to reach him. With that decision, the cloaked investigator turned and strode silently from the room of purple doom.

CHAPTER XIII
THE LIPS THAT FAILED

WHEN he had descended by Selbart's private elevator, The Shadow took another look at the gagged elevator operator. Fresh air had partially revived the prisoner; but the man's brain was still too clouded to sense happenings about him. The Shadow was satisfied, however, that no injury had been sustained; the man's stupor was due entirely to the effect of chloroform. Enough clear air had filled the closet; so The Shadow again closed the door with the prisoner inside.

Reaching his cab, The Shadow ordered Moe to drive him to Professor Murkden's. On the way, The Shadow gave instructions regarding a call to Burbank. Arrived at Murkden's, The Shadow observed that Weston's limousine was gone; however, some lights still showed from the gloomy windows of the chemist's residence. The Shadow alighted. Moe pulled away.

A servant answered The Shadow's ring at the front door; but he was not met by a cloaked visitor. The Shadow had resumed the guise of Cranston; he was wearing gray overcoat and hat. The servant recognized him as Lamont Cranston and ushered him into the reception room. The menial went to summon Professor Murkden.

The stoop-shouldered chemist arrived from the laboratory. He greeted his visitor, then cupped one hand to his ear when The Shadow inquired regarding Weston's whereabouts. Catching his visitor's query, Murkden explained that Weston had gone to the Cobalt Club.

"The commissioner expected you at nine o'clock," stated Murkden. "When you did not arrive, he became impatient. He went to the club almost immediately."

"I thought that he would remain here quite a while," returned The Shadow. "Didn't he come to talk over blood tests with you?"

"He had already received my report on the blood tests."

"That's right. You established Rythe's death as occurring at eight-thirty, the same as Tabor's."

The professor nodded, then added:

"Commissioner Weston was disturbed because Inspector Cardona is missing. He was also quite incensed at a man who came with him here tonight."

"You mean Courtney Grell?"

"Yes. He left before my lecture was finished and did not return. I am to notify the commissioner if Grell comes back here. I believe that he intends to order Grell's arrest."

THE SHADOW made his departure. Outside the house, he strolled for the corner, pausing every now and then to look for a cab. Moe's taxi showed up suddenly. The Shadow boarded it. He told the driver to take him to the Cobalt Club; then to call Burbank again.

As The Shadow had arranged it, Burbank was to call Murkden's if The Shadow did not come out of the professor's house. Moe, cruising by, was to inform Burbank if The Shadow remained at Murkden's. Since The Shadow had come out of Murkden's, Burbank would still be waiting for the final order. This time, Moe would relay the order to call the Cobalt Club instead of Murkden's.

At the club, The Shadow found Weston in a fumy mood. Searchers had been unable to locate Cardona; but that was only one reason for the commissioner's indignation. Weston was particularly aroused because of Grell. His mental state fitted with what Murkden had said.

"Grell is gone, Cranston!" shouted Weston, to The Shadow. "The rogue walked out on me, in the midst of Professor Murkden's lecture. His actions have aroused my suspicions."

"Of what do you suspect Grell?" queried The Shadow. "Of murdering Tabor and Rythe? Or of abducting Cardona?"

"Either. Or both. Yet the fellow puzzles me. He had won my favor; it would have been good policy for him to retain it. Instead, he did the worst thing possible. He had no excuse for leaving Murkden's without my permission. However, he will answer for his indiscretion. I have just telephoned headquarters, telling them to send two plainclothes men to Grell's hotel and bring him here."

The Shadow repressed a smile. Again, Weston was showing bad logic. If Grell returned to his hotel at all; it would be evidence of the man's innocence of murder and abduction. However, The Shadow expected Weston to forget Grell for the present. He saw an attendant coming to summon the commissioner to the telephone.

Weston went to answer the telephone call, remarking that it might be news about Grell. When he returned, he was excited. As he had done the night before, he motioned his friend Cranston to come with him. They hurried outside and boarded Weston's limousine. The Shadow anticipated the direction that they took.

The Shadow knew that the telephone call had come from Burbank; that the contact man had anonymously tipped off the commissioner to the fact that matters were not right at Horace Selbart's.

Weston gained full evidence of that when he and The Shadow reached the gambler's apartment house. A patrol car was there ahead of them; the officers had found the elevator man in the closet and were arousing him. Weston had no time to wait until the prisoner's stupor ended. He ordered an immediate trip upstairs. The Shadow accompanied the commissioner in the little elevator, which was crowded to capacity. With them were two bluecoats, a pair of headquarters men, a police surgeon and the manager of the apartment house.

THEY found Selbart's body as The Shadow had left it. One look at the gambler's dyed bald head told Weston that Selbart was another victim of the purple death. Weston took immediate charge of the investigation. He ordered blood specimens to be taken at once to Professor Murkden's. Then he began to go over the ground that The Shadow had already covered.

Weston found the blue lead pencil as soon as the body was moved at his direction. The clue intrigued him. The commissioner expressed the belief that it might lead somewhere. He found nothing else, however, until The Shadow casually pointed out the disturbed books on the shelf. It was then that Weston uncovered Selbart's papers.

After a deliberate inspection of the documents, Weston formed the conclusion that The Shadow had already drawn. Enthusiastically, he developed his version of the theory.

"Someone came here to see Selbart!" exclaimed Weston. "Someone to whom he had loaned money. A person who felt himself swindled; unfairly treated. Selbart produced papers—one most certainly was a promissory note—and the visitor saw a chance to seize them."

"Quite likely, Commissioner," agreed The Shadow. "Of course, the killer came here with the deliberate intent of murdering Selbart."

"Not necessarily," objected Weston, who usually disagreed with anyone who made prompt editions to his theories. "The murderer might have performed his crime through sheer desperation."

"Odd then, that he should have come equipped with some device that delivered the purple death."

Weston chewed his lips.

"That is true, Cranston," he admitted finally. "Yes. The murder must have been premeditated. But the motive is plain. The man had been swindled by Selbart."

"I suppose then," remarked The Shadow, "that he was swindled by many other persons. Seven to be exact."

"What seven?"

"The previous victims of the purple death."

Weston considered. His face showed perplexity.

"You're right again, Cranston," he decided. "It doesn't fit, does it? The other purple murders looked like thrusts against innocent parties. This one is quite the reverse. It baffles me. However"—Weston's eyes showed one hopeful gleam—"we can at least establish the time at which Selbart died. He only arrived in New York this afternoon; his blood will be fresh enough for another analysis by Professor Murkden."

A patrolman arrived to announce that the elevator operator had recuperated, but that he was too sick to bring upstairs immediately. Weston decided to go down to the ground floor. The Shadow accompanied him.

When they stepped from the elevator, they saw the operator propped on a chair near the outside door. The released prisoner looked very white; the aftereffects of the chloroform had sickened him. He was wrapped in a big overcoat, with a blanket around his legs so that he could benefit from fresh air whenever the door was opened and at the same time could avoid a chill.

"IT was at eight o'clock they got me," informed the man. "A couple of huskies wearing masks. They rang for me and I came down. They piled on me so quick I didn't have a chance."

"Eight o'clock," mused Weston. "Then this could have been another eight-thirty murder like the others. This time, the murderer had to send some toughs to clear the way for him. He must have another rowdy working for him like Slook Howdrey. Yes, that fits. It could be the same group that captured Cardona earlier."

The commissioner eyed the operator; then demanded:

"Why were you up at the penthouse with the elevator?"

"I had just delivered a note," explained the operator. "A messenger brought it for Mr. Selbart."

"You saw Selbart alive, at eight?"

"Yes, sir. There were others, too, that must have seen him just before then. His niece and three friends. I brought them down just a little while before the message came. They were going to the opera."

Weston consulted his watch. It was just eleven o'clock; not yet time for the party to return.

"We'll investigate that message," decided Weston. "It could have come from the murderer; perhaps to tell Selbart to expect him later. The murderer probably took the message away from him. I wonder"—Weston paused, reflectively—"I wonder if Grell could be in on this. He could have sent the message. It might explain why he hurried away from Murkden's—"

Weston stopped short. The door was swinging open. In from the snowy night came two headquarters men, dragging a prisoner between them. Each had locked his own wrist to one of the prisoner's. The man was helpless as they hauled him. Face to face with Weston, the fellow glared as the commissioner ejaculated his identity:

"Courtney Grell!"

Grell grimaced sourly. His sallow face showed indignation; but with it, there was an air of triumph.

"Hello, Commissioner," greeted the sallow man. "So they brought me to you after all. I thought it was a stall, when they grabbed me at my hotel and said you wanted to see me. That's why I put up an argument."

"You'll put up an explanation," snorted Weston. "You'll tell me why you left Professor Murkden's lecture without my permission."

Grell's eyes opened. His lips phrased a laugh.

"SO that's it!" he exclaimed. "Say—I didn't think you'd get so huffy over a little thing like that. You can't arrest me for just leaving Murkden's—"

"I can arrest you for murder."

"Whose murder?"

"The murder of Horace Selbart, which occurred this evening. Also for the murder of Trumbull Rythe, last night. The fact that you found Rythe's body did not prove that you first visited his home at ten o'clock. Similarly, unless you have an alibi for this evening, you will be in a bad way, Grell."

The sallow man winced.

The Shadow knew the reason. Grell's only alibi for nearly an hour after leaving Murkden's would be Louis Lenger. Knowledge of that fact made Grell shaky. He sank back. The plainclothesmen jerked him forward with the handcuffs.

"So we've found the murderer," accused Weston, as he noted Grell's expression. "Take him to headquarters. We'll grill him there—"

"No, no, Commissioner!" Grell's tone was excited, pleading. "I'll—I'll talk. I'll tell you what you want to know—who the murderer really is. But I never met the man before tonight. But take the handcuffs off me—"

"Take him away," roared Weston. Then, suddenly: "No, wait! Has he a gun on him?"

The plainclothes men shook their heads.

"Remove the handcuffs," ordered Weston. "Grell, I'll give you five minutes to come clean. You claim that you know who the murderer is. Tell us all that you know about him."

Grell grinned wisely as the handcuffs came off. He rubbed his chafed wrists; then thrust a hand into his overcoat pocket. One of the headquarters men grabbed for his arm. Grell's hand came out bearing a fresh package of chewing gum. The headquarters man looked sheepish while Grell chuckled and opened the pack of gum.

"Come, Grell," insisted Weston. "Your five minutes have begun."

"I can tell you everything in three minutes," promised Grell. "So I'll wait two, Commissioner, just to put you in the right mood. When I've told you my story, you'll be ready to hand me a medal. I'll have all the time I want. You'll be willing to listen to anything I tell you."

Deliberately, Grell began to chew his stick of gum. Shoving the wad to the side of his mouth, he eyed Weston and spoke methodically.

"Inspector Cardona held out a couple of clues," announced Grell. "The first was a clipping from a newspaper, that showed a chess problem. He found that at Tabor's; at least I think he did. I'm guessing at that part of it.

"The second clue, I'm sure about. It was a memo signed by the letter 'L.' Cardona found it at Rythe's, where I'd seen it ahead of him. Cardona came to see me this afternoon. We talked about that memo then. Cardona knew a lot; too much for his own good, because he wasn't smart.

"Tonight, I picked up where Cardona left off. I found out about the first clue; knowing the second. I hooked the two and they led me straight to the murderer. I went to see him, like Cardona did; but I was smarter. I came on my own; not as a representative of the law."

"If you know who the murderer is," bellowed Weston, "tell us! I give you one minute, Grell!"

Headquarters men gripped Grell's arm, ready to clamp the bracelets again if Weston gave the order. Anger showed on Grell's face; then his lips formed a smirk.

"The murderer's name?" remarked Grell. "Certainly, I shall tell it to you, Commissioner. Of course, it begins with an 'L'—"

A SUDDEN choke broke Grell's voice. He gulped, slumped in the arms of the headquarters men. They yanked him upright. Like Weston, they thought it was another bluff. Only The Shadow realized the real cause. Springing forward, he gripped Grell's neck and chin; tilted the man's head forward with a snap. Grell's jaws spread, his wad of gum plopped from his mouth and struck the stone floor of the entry.

Yet with all his speed, The Shadow was too late. As he released Grell's head, the sallow man's chin sagged downward. His body sank to a dead weight, dragging forward the men who gripped him. A death gasp hissed as Grell's jaws clamped.

Weston gave a startled shout. The headquarters men saw why, for they were looking at Grell's face. A rush of blood had come to that sallow countenance; as it spread, its crimson hue darkened. Grell's features enlarged, his eyes bulged. Over all came an indelible dye.

Grell's staring face, his limp hands, were turning purple. The transformation was a swift one that could not be revoked. The men who gripped him lost their nerve; they released their burden. Grell toppled hard upon the floor, rolled over face upward, as men shrank back, avoiding him like they would a victim of the plague.

Only The Shadow did not recoil. He was

stooped beside the body, Grell's head raised in his hands. His face retained the calm composure of Lamont Cranston, but his eyes—which none could see—held a burning glint as they studied the death-frozen countenance beneath them.

The Shadow was viewing a new victim of a powerful murderer; a victim whose name was not on the list, but who had been added through necessity. The name of Louis Lenger would never be spoken by Courtney Grell. Sallow lips had failed at the last moment.

Again, the purple death had claimed a victim, this time in the very presence of The Shadow!

CHAPTER XIV
THE SHADOW'S TESTS

POLICEMEN carried Grell's body up to Selbart's penthouse. They handled the corpse gingerly. Sight of the purple death in actual progress had unnerved these witnesses. Only The Shadow's bold handling of the body had stiffened the men to whom Weston gave the order. The commissioner, however, decided to come up on a second trip, claiming that the elevator was too crowded.

That second trip included The Shadow and the officers who had brought Grell from the hotel. Weston questioned his men during the ride; they mentioned that they had merely frisked Grell for weapons and had not inspected other contents of his pockets. The incident of the chewing gum made Weston decide that there might be important finds on Grell's body.

Reaching the penthouse, detectives began a search of Grell's clothing. For a while it looked as though Weston's guess was wrong; then came a discovery. Deep in an inside pocket of Grell's overcoat, a detective found a sealed manila envelope. On it were penciled notations, the names of Talbot and Rythe, with the dates when their bodies had been found.

"Cardona's writing!" exclaimed Weston. "Let's see what's in here!"

He ripped open the envelope. Inside, he found two items. One was the chess clipping that Cardona had picked up at Tabor's. The other was the memo that Joe had found at Rythe's. Weston read the notation with the signature that consisted solely of the letter "L."

"Grell told us the truth about these," decided Weston, solemnly. "But he said that they were Cardona's clues, not his own. How did Grell happen to get them?"

Weston put the question to The Shadow; but before he received a reply, the commissioner had another inspiration.

"Look!" he exclaimed, "The memo is in blue pencil. Here are two clues to begin with—and we have a third! The blue pencil that we found here with Selbart's body!"

The Shadow made no comment. He had recognized the blue pencil link from the time of his first visit to the penthouse. Seated in a corner of the room, The Shadow merely watched Weston's expression.

It was plain that the commissioner was piecing facts together. His square face looked grim; then his lips formed a convinced smile. Looking about, Weston saw headquarters men standing expectantly, as if waiting for him to solve the mystery. He noted The Shadow sitting silent. Weston's smile tightened.

"Tell me, Cranston," he suggested, "what do you make of these facts? I want your whole opinion. I would value it highly."

The Shadow saw that Weston was asking for an opinion merely as a build up to his own. Therefore, when he answered, he confined his remarks to a simple statement.

"GRELL was right," asserted The Shadow. "Cardona found the two clues: one at Tabor's; the other at Rythe's. Crooks seized Cardona because he pushed those clues too rapidly. Grell had an inkling of the situation. He looked for a man whose name began with 'L'—"

"We heard all that," interrupted Weston, impatiently. "What I want to know, Cranston, is if you think Grell actually met the murderer tonight."

"Grell must have met the murderer," returned The Shadow. "Otherwise, the two clues would not have been in Grell's pocket."

"You think the murderer gave the clues to Grell?"

"Not necessarily. He could have placed them in Grell's pocket at a time when Grell had taken off his overcoat. That is when he also placed the chewing gum in Grell's pocket, substituting it for a pack that Grell already carried."

There were nods from the listeners. They remembered how The Shadow had been the first to recognize that Grell was chewing poisoned gum. Weston saw the nods. His smile increased.

"Your theory is good, Cranston," declared the commissioner, "but it has one weakness. Since the murderer abducted Cardona because he had the clues, why should he have returned those same clues through Grell?"

"You would like the answer?"

Weston smiled and shook his head.

"There is no answer, Cranston," he declared. "Grell's story was a lie. We do not need to search for a man who plays chess and whose initial is

'L.' We have already found the purple killer—and there he is."

Dramatically, Weston pointed to Grell's body. While The Shadow smiled, others stared astounded at the commissioner's new theory.

"Grell committed the murders," asserted Weston. "When he realized that he was leaving clues behind him, like a fountain pen and a button, he became worried. The chess clipping that he accidentally dropped was actually a mistake. It worried Grell more than ever.

"So he purposely left the memo with Rythe's body. It was a note that he had probably picked up somewhere. Cardona, however, was smart enough to trace both the clipping and the memo to Grell. That was why Grell abducted Cardona; and took the clues from him."

Weston paused. He was coming to the crux of his theory.

"Though he failed to bluff Cardona," declared the commissioner, "Grell believed that he could trick me. He tried it tonight; thought that he had won my confidence and could leave Murkden's without arousing my suspicion. Nevertheless, Grell was prepared for a last resort.

"His weapon of death was the purple poison. He knew that in an emergency, he could escape the electric chair by suicide. Downstairs a short while go, Grell knew that his game was through. He made a last bluff, saw that it was failing. He did not even produce the clues, with some cock-and-bull yarn to explain how he acquired them. He took that stick of chewing gum and ended his life in our presence."

Listeners had new nods. These were in support of Weston's theory. The Shadow arose; spoke quietly to the commissioner.

"I SUPPOSE, however," said The Shadow, "that you would like to know the identity of the man who signed himself 'L.'"

"Why?" demanded Weston. "The case is closed. I shall tell the press that Grell was the murderer. Grell was a crook at heart. Let us hope that his underlings will weaken; that Cardona and the missing detectives may still be alive. The fact that we have trapped the master murderer may lead others to release them."

"Yet 'L,' if you found him, might tell you facts concerning Grell."

"Bother 'L.' He is simply the herring that Grell drew across our path. Of course, we shall try to trace the clipping, the memo, the blue pencil; as a matter of routine. But I can assure you, Cranston, that this supposed man 'L' is either imaginary or unimportant."

The Shadow shook hands with Weston as though congratulating the commissioner on his theory. He departed; a detective took him downstairs in the elevator, remarking on the way that the commissioner "sure knew his stuff when he got started." Outside, The Shadow rode away.

Later, he arrived at the sanctum. There, The Shadow's hands busied themselves beneath the bluish light making notations in an ink that faded after each thought had been inscribed.

Tonight, The Shadow had been willing to give Commissioner Weston some facts regarding Courtney Grell. Since Weston had refused to accept them, The Shadow intended to pursue those facts on his own. He did this with the knowledge that emergency existed.

Though he would have prevented the deaths of Horace Selbart and Courtney Grell, The Shadow had few regrets concerning them. Both men were crooks; that stood proven. Selbart's death marked the last that the purple killer had listed. Grell's death—together with his actions—had sufficient explanation.

Many of Grell's past activities had approached blackmail. Tonight, Grell had seen a chance to deal in that gentle art. Picking Louis Lenger as the purple murderer, Grell had made friends with the chess expert. Keeping in right with the law, Grell had hoped to press that acquaintance, to wind it up with a demand of cash for keeping silence.

That was why Grell had not intended to turn his findings over to the law. The fact was obvious to The Shadow; he believed that others could have seen it, even though Commissioner Weston had not. One, however, who was capable of spotting Grell's game was the purple murderer.

Therefore, the murderer had planted the clues that had been taken from Cardona. He had also placed the chewing gum in Grell's pocket. He had figured that Grell would chew the gum before finding the envelope that was so deeply tucked away. Once Grell died, the clues and the chewing gum would both be found.

The purple murderer had disposed of Grell because the sallow man was a troublemaker. It had worked out as the murderer wanted; circumstances, however, had chanced to make the finish a close call. Grell had not taken a stick of chewing gum as soon as the murderer expected he would. Thus Weston's men had found their chance to grab him.

When had the goods been planted on Grell?

Not at Lenger's. Grell had removed his overcoat there, but The Shadow had been on watch. The planting had come later, after Grell went out with Lenger. Therefore, the answer lay in learning partly how long Grell had been with Lenger, and just where Grell had gone.

Why had the murderer sent back the clues by Grell?

The answer was that he wanted the police to have them, that he considered those clues insufficient, in themselves, to incriminate him. The murderer believed that the clues would mislead the law. The only break had come when Cardona and Grell had noticed Lenger's letter to the chess column; but the newspaper that printed that letter was now one day old. Weston would not search the back files; particularly since he believed Grell a suicide. The murderer had made a good guess as to Weston's actual reaction toward Grell's death.

THE bluish light went out. Soon afterward, a light appeared in a room that was walled with shiny black. The room was a laboratory; all its equipment was of that same ebony hue. Here, The Shadow returned to the task that he had originally scheduled.

From his cloak he brought the slides that showed the blood clots. He produced the test tubes that contained samples of Professor Murkden's lettered compounds. He begin an analysis of the liquids. After an hour, The Shadow came to the conclusion that the chemist had done an exacting task. Compound "F," when compared with the attested formula, had the expected elements of the purple poison.

There was one way to make a final proof. The Shadow had gained important evidence when he had seen Grell die. He had witnessed the actual effect of the purple death; no longer did he need to rely solely on post mortem data.

From a chest in the corner, The Shadow brought a guinea pig. He gave it an injection of Compound "F." The result was instantaneous. A tinge appeared upon the whiteness of the guinea pig; became a purple. As the dye increased, the cavy fell dead.

Immediately, The Shadow began a series of blood tests, at timed intervals. One hour later, he injected the compound into another guinea pig, thus starting a new sequence of blood tests. At regular intervals, The Shadow continued the tests and made microscopic examinations.

It was not long before The Shadow discovered an important factor. The tests were conforming to the findings of Professor Murkden, but with one exception. The professor's tests—according to the data available—showed a slower rate of coagulation than did The Shadow's experiments.

This meant that The Shadow's test made *one* hour after the guinea pig's death corresponded to the professor's test at the end of *two* hours. From then on, the tests corresponded, but always, The Shadow's slides retained that one hour advantage.

This was singular as The Shadow was using the chemist's own compound.

Professor Murkden's tests had shown that victims of the purple death had died at half past eight, in accordance with the time that Joe Cardona had set them. The Shadow's tests proved The Shadow's own theory that the victims had died at half past nine.

TO account for this discrepancy, The Shadow decided to make another test. He had more guinea pigs available; but he had used up his supply of Compound "F." The Shadow decided upon departure. He extinguished the lights of the laboratory.

Half an hour later, The Shadow arrived at Professor Murkden's old house. The building was completely dark. Silently, The Shadow effected entry into the professor's basement laboratory.

Shading the windows, The Shadow turned on a single light. He took the large bottle of Compound "F" from its shelf; began a careful analysis of a small quantity. It tallied exactly through The Shadow's own test of the compound. The Shadow was ready to make a new blood test. He went to the corner and obtained one of the professor's guinea pigs. The Shadow injected the compound into the guinea pig. He watched the result. The guinea pig seemed loath to release its hold on life, but the effects of the deadly compound could not be resisted. Gradually the chemical mixture overpowered it. The Shadow began to study the blood coagulation. After the first two tests, he discovered that they fitted Murkden's analyses and not his own. Although the compound was identical, the coagulation proved slower. Taken as an example, this test bore out the professor's tabulations.

The Shadow ceased his work at the end of the second hour. He put the guinea pig with the other dead ones that had perished in the interests of science. He extinguished the lights in Murkden's laboratory and made his exit by the window.

The storm had ceased. Dull dawn was knifing through the clouds that still clustered above Manhattan. The Shadow saw lights in the third floor of Murkden's house. The servants were rising early. Today Murkden had more work to do, he must test the blood of new victims—human ones— who had died last night by the purple death.

No streaks of dawn revealed The Shadow. He was enshrouded in the darkness that still clung in the thoroughfares where traffic had not commenced.

The Shadow's task had been completed. He could sleep during the coming day, leaving the laboratory work to Professor Murkden.

Night, perhaps, might bring a new thrust of the purple death; but it would be hours yet before the purple killer moved abroad.

Before that time arrived The Shadow would be ready to delve more deeply into matters that concerned Louis Lenger. Once those were settled The Shadow could thwart the purple killer.

More than that, in his coming quest, The Shadow saw opportunity to remove the pall of mystery that enshrouded the unsolved disappearance of Joe Cardona.

CHAPTER XV
LINKS TO CRIME

IT was seven-thirty the next evening. Commissioner Weston was at the club, beaming enthusiastically over a newspaper as he spoke to his friend Lamont Cranston.

"The press has accepted my views," announced Weston. "Grell is recognized as the purple murderer. The chain of death is ended. Our next task is to find Cardona and the missing detectives."

"It is time that they were located," observed The Shadow. "But just how do you intend to find them, Commissioner?"

"Through a complete checkup of Grell's affairs. We have searched his suite of offices and his hotel room. I believe that we shall unearth some important clues."

"Even though you have found none so far."

Weston was irked by the quiet remark. Though the commissioner firmly believed that Courtney Grell was the purple murderer, he knew that he was short on evidence. Search had as yet produced no expected results. Grell's effects had lacked any documents that pertained to murdered men; and the police had found neither weapons nor supplies of the purple poison that could have been in Grell's possession.

"We learned much from Professor Murkden's tests," declared Weston, suddenly, hoping to drop the subject of the futile search at Grell's. "He estimated eight-thirty death in the case of Tabor and Rythe. Today, he made blood tests to learn when Horace Selbart died, and he found—"

"Eight-thirty again."

Weston stared at The Shadow's interruption; then laughed.

"Good guesswork, Cranston," he remarked. "Since Tabor and Rythe both died at eight-thirty, you figured that must be the usual time of action. Yes, you are right. Professor Murkden proved conclusively that Selbart was slain in his penthouse at exactly half past eight last night."

Weston was about to leave the club. He extended an invitation before departure.

"I am going to Professor Murkden's usual lecture," stated the commissioner. "Would you care to accompany me, Cranston?"

"I have another appointment," replied The Shadow, "but since you are going to Murkden's, I would recommend that you have him perform another test."

"Another test?"

"Yes. To find out when Courtney Grell died."

"But we saw Grell die! It was after eleven o'clock, when my men brought him to Selbart's. What use would there be to make a blood test in Grell's case?"

The Shadow smiled; then gave the reason.

"Since you know when Grell died," he stated, slowly, "tests of his blood would serve as a basis for exact computation of the time element. From Grell's case, you can learn if Murkden was right in his calculations of the previous cases."

"I never thought of that, Cranston," admitted Weston. "Nor did Professor Murkden. I shall speak to him about the matter tonight. Of course, the tests are actually unnecessary, for Murkden's Compound "F" closely resembles the purple poison; hence his calculations cannot be in error. Nevertheless, a test of Grell's blood would silence any doubtful persons. Your suggestion is a good one, Cranston."

As soon as Weston had gone, The Shadow left the club. Riding southward in a taxi, he indulged in speculations regarding the purple death.

THE SHADOW'S own tests had shown an hour's variation from Murkden's. They indicated that Tabor and Rythe had died at nine-thirty; therefore, Selbart's death could also have occurred at half past nine, since it tallied with the others. Still, there was another element to be considered: that was the last test that The Shadow had performed, in Murkden's laboratory instead of his own.

Using the same formula and the identical methods, The Shadow had found that his last test tallied with the professor's. If that test stood, eight-thirty would have to be considered the time of death. Nevertheless, The Shadow was satisfied despite the odd discrepancy. Whatever his reason, it was known to him alone.

At present, The Shadow had another matter to consider.

It was plain that the chain of murders involved some important invention that had been backed by Horace Selbart. Someone had acquired the invention by murdering the inventor; then killing other persons who knew about it or who could have blocked its commercial success. Among the dead, perhaps, were persons whose connection with the matter had been peculiarly remote.

Selbart had been left to the last. The murderer had decided that the gambler would hear little of the purple death while en route home from Europe; that whatever he did hear, he would keep to himself because of his own hidden connection.

Reaching Selbart had been an easy task. The murderer had probably posed as a person whom Selbart would not fear; it was also likely that he had promised to divulge valuable facts that Selbart would want to hear alone. Since an investigation of the victims would prove too long a task, The Shadow had decided to concentrate upon living persons.

Louis Lenger was important. Clues, properly linked, pointed directly to him. Should the law link those clues as The Shadow had, Lenger would be promptly arrested. Yet the law, if it found Lenger, would be blocked by what it had already learned from Professor Murkden's tests.

Those tests showed that the murderer had delivered purple death at half past eight, on every tested occasion. To pin the murders on Lenger, the law would have to prove that he had been at large at half past eight on at least one of three successive nights. The Shadow, had overheard Lenger tell Grell that he played chess every night from seven o'clock until nine, with a friend named Howard Feasley.

Lenger, if arrested, would depend upon Feasley for an alibi. If that alibi could prove as acceptable to the law as Murkden's blood tests had been, Lenger would never be convicted. Hence The Shadow's first step on this important evening was to look in on Howard Feasley.

NEARING the outskirts of Greenwich Village, The Shadow left the cab. He soon found the address which was listed with Feasley's name in the telephone book. At the front door, The Shadow noted name cards that indicated that the house was divided into improvised apartments. Feasley's bore the number "3"; it was evidently the top floor of the residence.

Skirting the block, The Shadow came to the rear of the building. Looking up from the darkness, he saw that the top floor had a porchlike projection at the rear. The house next to Feasley's was empty. It also had a top rear porch.

Cloaked in black, The Shadow worked at a rear door of the empty house. He found no difficulty with the simple lock. His entry effected, The Shadow used a tiny flashlight, found a stairway and went up through the empty house. Soon he stepped out on the rooflike porch at the back of the third floor.

There was a separating wall between this porch and Feasley's; but The Shadow swung around it. The shift was a nervy one, for he swung outward above thirty feet of space, but the move was not difficult. It proved that it would be quite an easy matter for anyone to visit Feasley's apartment by this unseen route.

There was a door that led into Feasley's apartment; it was unlocked. The Shadow stepped into a darkened room. He reached a door at the front, opened it slightly and peered into a lighted room. There he saw two men seated at a chessboard.

One was Louis Lenger. The heavy man was bowed close to the chess board, stroking his chin, which was as stubbly as it had been the night before. Facing Lenger was a man who fitted the description of Howard Feasley.

Frail of build, wan of countenance, Feasley was propped in an armchair. He was wearing a dressing gown and was well swathed with blankets even though the room was not chilly. Feasley's appearance indicated that he had gone through a long illness; but the man's smile, his keen interest in the chess game, were proofs that he was well recovered.

Both Lenger and Feasley were too intent upon their game to suspect The Shadow's presence. Looking about the room, The Shadow noted that it was in good order. Probably Feasley had someone come to arrange it every day. One oddity, however, commanded The Shadow's notice.

On a far wall of the room was a blackish square, covering a space that had once held a wall bracket. Evidently some electrical installment had been started and not completed. The important point, however, was that the black plate matched the square block that The Shadow had seen in the entry of Lenger's Twenty-sixth Street apartment house.

A clock showed a few minutes after eight. A brief view of the chessboard told The Shadow that the players had just begun their game; that they were proceeding with slow, methodical tactics. It would be quite a while before they finished their game; perhaps it would have to be called at Feasley's nine o'clock bed hour.

The Shadow waited no longer. He left by the route through the back of the building. He descended through the empty house, found a cab on a side street. Boarding the taxi from darkness, The Shadow quietly ordered the driver to take him to an address on Twenty-sixth Street.

THE SHADOW had looked into the matter of Lenger's alibi; he had found that it existed. Lenger's presence at Feasley's fitted his statement that he played chess with the invalid between the hours of seven and nine. It did not, of course, prove that Lenger had been there the last three evenings. Only Feasley could have settled that fact.

However, since Lenger was at Feasley's, he could not be at his own apartment. Therefore, The Shadow had opportunity to visit Lenger's. Such a trip had become important from the moment that The Shadow had observed the black plate in the wall. Such devices were not common. To see one in Lenger's entry; another on Feasley's wall meant a definite connection.

When he reached the apartment house on Twenty-sixth Street, The Shadow avoided the entry until later. Instead, he went in by the rear door; took the stairway up to Lenger's. Once inside the untidy apartment, he began a rapid inspection.

All the bits of evidence that The Shadow had noticed the previous night were undisturbed. Looking through a bureau drawer, The Shadow uncovered two other items. One was an old box that had once contained a fountain pen; another was an old, frayed shirt that had one button missing.

The absent fountain pen could be the one that a detective had found on a murder scene. The buttons of the frayed shirt were identical with a photograph that The Shadow had seen of the celebrated "button clue" that had been picked up by another missing dick.

It was among some papers in another drawer that The Shadow found an item which he regarded as more important than all the rest. This was a certificate of title made out to Louis Lenger. It named Lenger as the owner of this apartment house in which he lived.

This discovery fitted with the picture that Lenger gave the world concerning himself. Lenger was ostensibly a man with moderate income, living on the interest of investments. One of his assets was the modest apartment house. Unable to rent the fourth floor apartments, Lenger had moved into one. Nothing could have been more logical.

It fitted also with a definite theory that The Shadow had formed. When Joe Cardona had started on his trip to Lenger's, The Shadow had followed him. The Shadow had seen no other trailer. Therefore, The Shadow had divined that Cardona must have run into trouble close to Lenger's. He had considered it a likelihood that Joe had been captured in the apartment house itself, but The Shadow had avoided a detailed search while matters were requiring solution.

There was one odd feature that would have perplexed an ordinary sleuth. That was why Grell had not been grabbed like Cardona. To The Shadow, that could be easily answered. His whispered laugh told that he knew why Grell had come and gone, to be handled elsewhere. That token from The Shadow's lips brooked trouble for the purple murderer.

LEAVING the apartment, The Shadow descended to the ground floor. He found the elevator there, opened the door and peered into the car. It was his first view of the elevator's interior; it must have suited some theory that The Shadow had in mind.

Closing the elevator, The Shadow found a stairway to the basement. He looked about, discovered that the cellar was a comparatively small one; that it showed a large expanse of heavy concrete wall that had evidently been installed to form a new foundation. Ascending to the first floor, The Shadow left by the rear door. He went to the front of the building, peered into the entry but did not pass the lighted threshold.

Again, The Shadow viewed the black plate on the entry wall.

Moving back, The Shadow edged into the darkness close to the building line. He had gained facts that he wanted; to them, he had added other possibilities. His thoughts were concentrated upon one matter that he had never forgotten—the disappearance of Joe Cardona.

The Shadow knew that Cardona must have been quickly and efficiently captured; yet Joe had recovered promptly from whatever attack he had met. Although a prisoner, Cardona had managed to make two telephone calls soon after his capture.

Those facts told The Shadow what would probably be encountered by anyone who sought to follow Cardona's actual trail. It offered The Shadow the very challenge that he wanted; for he had guessed the route that Cardona had taken.

The Shadow's plans were made. A quick trip to the sanctum, a prompt return, that would bring him here before nine o'clock, the time when Lenger usually left Feasley's.

In the short interval that would remain, The Shadow would attempt to solve the riddle of Cardona's disappearance. That done, he would have another task ahead.

For The Shadow foresaw that the purple death had not reached its limit. He had divined that a new murder would be necessary to the schemes of a master crook. Through quick thrusts, The Shadow planned to balk the vital move of the purple killer.

CHAPTER XVI
THE LAW LEARNS

WHILE The Shadow was on the move, completing speedy plans, Commissioner Weston was complacently seated in Professor Murkden's lecture room. Though he had found Murkden's previous lecture an interesting one, Weston was bored upon this occasion. Murkden had passed the subject of blood coagulation; his remarks concerned chemical conditions that had but little bearing on the purple death.

Had Weston felt in his present mood the night before, he would not have been piqued by Courtney Grell's departure from the lecture room. Last night, Weston had been tense; everything seemed important while he still sought facts regarding the purple murder. Tonight, satisfied that the riddle was solved with Grell's supposed suicide, Weston felt that matters were monotonous.

The commissioner wanted to talk with Murkden; to settle any minor details. He was anxious for the lecture to end. The professor must have noticed it. Instead of prolonging his lecture until nine o'clock, Murkden cut it short ten minutes before the hour.

Disposing of the lecture group, Murkden greeted Weston. He conducted the commissioner to the laboratory. As Murkden was preparing a set of slides, one of his servants appeared accompanied by a police surgeon who had come at Weston's order. Murkden looked up from his projector and smiled.

"Excellent, Commissioner," observed the chemist. "I am pleased that you summoned a physician here. I am going to compare the slides that show the blood changes in all three victims. This demonstration marks the completion of my experiment. Therefore, I am glad that a qualified observer is on hand to attest my findings."

The projector glimmered. On the screen, Weston and the physician saw four enlarged representations of blood specimens. They were labeled; the names showed on the screen: Tabor, Rythe, Selbart; below them, a slide that bore the title: "Certified Test."

"The three upper slides," stated Murkden, "show blood specimens tested at precisely half past eleven on three successive nights. The certified test shows the blood condition of a guinea pig exactly three hours after death. It is identical with every other test performed with guinea pigs.

"This proves conclusively that every victim of the purple death died at half past eight. Let me show you another set of slides. These show the blood condition a half hour later. Again, you will observe that they match."

Murkden projected a new set. The later blood conditions were identical. The professor was about to introduce another set of slides when Weston stopped him.

"Those are sufficient," declared Weston. "There is another matter that I should like to discuss with you, Professor." Weston turned to the police surgeon. "Have you brought the specimens, Doctor?"

THE surgeon nodded. He brought a cardboard cylinder from his pocket, produced a corked bottle from it.

"A specimen of Grell's blood," remarked Weston, reading the label, "taken at eight o'clock tonight. We should like you to test it, Professor."

Murkden looked puzzled, then remarked:

"This seems superfluous, Commissioner. You already know the time at which Grell died. A test is not necessary."

"That was my original opinion," admitted Weston, "but it occurred to me this evening that a test of Grell's blood would serve as a final key to the others. Better than your tests with guinea pigs."

Weston expected Murkden to raise an objection. He would not have been surprised to see the professor flare in indignation. Instead, Murkden shook his head sadly.

"You should have thought of this before, Commissioner," declared the chemist. "Or, perhaps, the blame can be placed upon me. Late last night, I was on the point of calling you, to ask for specimens of Grell's blood."

"Why didn't you call me?"

"Because I was satisfied with my formula. I was sure that Compound "F" contained every needed element of the purple poison. You agreed with that opinion. If I had called you, Commissioner, you might have misunderstood my request for specimens of Grell's blood. You would logically have believed that I doubted my own tests."

"True, Professor. Yet a test of Grell's blood would have finally proven the correctness of your experiments."

Murkden smiled.

"My tests were already established," reminded the professor. "They were accepted and attested. Since you had expressed your full approval—"

"I understand," interjected Weston. "The fault was mine, Professor. However, there is still time to make a test with Grell's blood. He died after eleven o'clock last night. It is now nine o'clock— less than twenty-four hours since his death."

"Too long an interval," returned Murkden. "I originally set twenty-four hours as the maximum limit for tests. Since my actual experiments with the blood of fresh victims, I have learned that the chemical changes reach their final state in twelve hours. Here are the attested experiments, Commissioner."

Murkden produced a sheet of typewritten notes. Studying them, the commissioner saw that Murkden's statement was correct. Weston shrugged his shoulders. After all, the idea was Cranston's, not his own. The commissioner decided that his friend should have thought of it sooner.

PROFESSOR MURKDEN, meanwhile, was removing a slide from the projector. Weston saw no need for further demonstration. He motioned for the surgeon to leave; then turned to speak to Murkden. A ring of the telephone interrupted.

Murkden put away the slide that he held. Methodically, the professor answered the telephone. The call was one that had been received upstairs and relayed to Murkden's laboratory telephone. Weston stood by impatiently while Murkden talked. The professor was having his usual difficulty hearing over the telephone.

"Louder, please!" insisted Murkden. "Yes. The connection must be bad... Yes... I hear you... Wait. I shall write it down..."

Murkden made notations upon a pad. Apparently, all was clear until he came to write a final name.

"What's that?" he queried. "No. I can't catch the name... Wait a moment, please... You can speak to the commissioner... What's that? No, no. I am not the commissioner... You said you wanted to talk to him? I thought you simply asked if he happened to be here... Certainly. It would be better if you spoke to him... Hold the line, please..."

Murkden turned around and nodded to Weston, who had strolled away impatiently. The commissioner paced over to the table; snatched the telephone as Murkden gave it to him. Weston's wrist tangled in the receiver wire. Angrily, he wrenched it free.

"Hello... Hello..."

A click came with Weston's words. The call was ended. Weston joggled the receiver hook. Finding the line dead, he hung up and glowered.

"It must have been your man upstairs," snapped Weston. "He thought that when you finished talking the call was ended. Anyway, I was cut off. Perhaps the person will call again."

"He gave me the message," reminded Murkden, passing over the paper with its notations. "I understood everything, except the last words. These notes, though, are meaningless to me."

Weston read the notations:

One dozen blue pencils.
Azure Specials, Number 3.
Purchased by Louis Lenger.
Deedham Apts., Twenty-sixth Street.
Other purchases, chess books.
Company, Retail Stationers.

"This is plain!" exclaimed Weston, in high enthusiasm. "We sent out a flier to all stationery stores, asking them to check on blue pencils that they had sold. Azure Special, Number 3, is the type of pencil that we found last night at Selbart's. The brand is obsolete. We thought that the purchaser might have bought some leftovers.

"So a man named Louis Lenger bought those pencils! Wait! That memo at Rythe's was signed with the letter 'L.' That fits. Look at this, Professor: Lenger bought chess books also! That covers the chess clipping that Cardona found at Tabor's."

WESTON paused; pointed to the final notation on the list.

"That was the name I couldn't understand," explained Professor Murkden. "The man on the telephone was trying to tell me who he represented. It was someone and company, retail stationers; but I couldn't catch the actual name of the concern."

"Which doesn't matter," put in Weston. "Our flier went to thousands of such stores. I don't care which one called up. Lenger's name is the one that counts; that and his address."

"You think that Lenger is involved in the purple deaths?"

"I intend to find out. I was satisfied that Grell was the murderer, but that was because there were no links between the clues. This news changes everything, Professor. I must call headquarters at once."

Five minutes later, Commissioner Weston's limousine pulled away from the front of Murkden's house, followed by two officers in a patrol car. A whining siren cleared traffic for Weston's speedy trip; but the commissioner did not plan to ride with such hubbub as far as Twenty-sixth Street.

Over the telephone, Weston had ordered headquarters men to form a silent cordon all about the block where Lenger's apartment house was located. When Weston reached the scene, that cordon would close in, performing the move with stealth.

For Commissioner Weston had admitted to himself that he might be wrong about the identity of the purple murderer. For the present, he had put aside the name of Courtney Grell. His whole purpose was to surprise Louis Lenger; to capture the man without a struggle.

Unwittingly, the police commissioner had found a scene of action already chosen by The Shadow. Surprises would be due when the law reached its goal.

CHAPTER XVII
BATTLE BELOW

AT the very moment of Weston's start upon his new and active mission, two men were standing in a square-walled windowless room. Stone walls told that this chamber was located underground. The only breaks in the square walls were two doorways, each in a different wall. Both doors were closed.

The room was furnished only with chairs and tables, but upon one table stood a large, square-shaped box that looked like a radio receiving set. The front of the blocky object formed a black screen. Upon the wall above was a blackish plate like the one in the entry of Lenger's apartment house.

One of the two men was tall and long-faced, his features showed a shrewd grin that revealed yellowed, ugly-shaped teeth. The grin identified him. He was a product of Manhattan's underworld, a one-time racketeer named Bert Thayler. Bert was a crook whose past resembled that of Slook Howdrey; but he was smoother, craftier than the rowdy who had lost the battle in Central Park.

The man with Thayler was a thuggish rogue of squatty build. His greasy face carried a brutal leer; his wolfish eyes watched Thayler expectantly. This ruffian was Bert's lieutenant; he was also a character well known in the underworld. He was "Rink" Leed, notorious as an organizer of strong-arm squads. Like Bert, Rink had disappeared from the underworld months ago.

"We're all set, Rink," announced Bert, in a purring tone.

"All we got to do is pack the telesighter"—he indicated the cabinet on the table—"and yank the special set off the wall." He pointed to the black square above the telesighter. "You hop upstairs and get the finder that's in the entry."

"And lam from there?" queried Rink. "Or do you want me back here, Bert?"

"Come back here. We'll go out by the route the chief uses. The crew can travel with us."

"What about the finder that's at Feasley's?"

"The chief will get that."

Rink turned toward a doorway. As he did, there was a sharp click from the wall. Both Bert and Rink stared in that direction. A sudden change had come to the black square that was set in the wall.

The plate was illuminated. It was grayish instead of black, for the light came through it. On the plate was a picture, projected as upon a screen. The picture showed the little entry of Lenger's apartment house. Bert and Rink watched the screen intently.

"NOBODY there," growled Bert. "That's about the tenth time it fooled us, Rink. It's set too sensitive, that's what. Anything going past the front door—like somebody's shadow—is likely to click it. Look—there it goes off again!"

The light disappeared as Bert spoke. Again, the black plate showed dully from the wall. Bert turned to Rink.

"Better let it stay a couple of minutes," he decided. "Help me pack the telesighter. Then go up and yank the finder."

"What about the crew? Want me to call them?"

"I'll take care of them, Rink, while you're upstairs."

"What're we going to do with the dumb dicks?"

"We'll leave them where they are. They don't know what it's all about. There's only one bird in the lot that's got any brains. But he made a dumb duck of himself, too."

Rink grinned. He knew the person to whom Bert referred.

"Wait until I show you the route we're taking out of here," chuckled Bert. "Then we can pack the telesighter. Look, Rink—this is the way the chief uses."

Bert stepped to a blank wall, jammed a thin key deep into a corner crack. There was a muffled click; another crack widened. Rink gaped as a portion of the wall swung away, to reveal a narrow underground passage. Bert pointed along the blackened corridor, looking toward it as he spoke.

"It goes clear into the next block," he stated. "Comes up into the old garage where we've got those cars parked. We can make a clean getaway in five minutes, Rink."

While Rink was speaking, a motion occurred at one of the doors. Slowly, the barrier came open. Rink heard a squeak of a hinge, turned quickly toward the door. As he did, a stocky figure came lunging headlong. Rink tried to pull a gun. He was too late. The attacker was upon him.

Bert wheeled about, startled by the sudden fray. He saw a hand grab for the revolver that Rink had pulled halfway from his pocket. The attacker almost gained the weapon, for he had shoved Rink to the wall beside the telesighter and had the rowdy helpless. Rink managed to defeat the grab by the only move that was still open to him. He jolted his shoulders sideways; let go of the gun. It sped from his hand, took a long bounce on the floor and skidded straight for Bert Thayler.

The stocky attacker threw Rink aside and started a dive for the lost gun. Bert coolly took command. He clamped his left foot on Rink's revolver; at the same moment, whipped out a .38 of his own, to cover the man who had made the wild attack. The stocky invader stopped short, raised his head and eyed Bert with a scowl.

For the first time, the light showed the man's face plainly. The frustrated attacker was Inspector Joe Cardona.

"THOUGHT you'd stage a fast one, eh?" sneered Bert. "Well, you didn't get away with it, Cardona. Back up against the wall and keep your dukes high."

Cardona obeyed. Bert kicked Rink's gun toward its owner.

"Grab your heater, Rink," ordered Bert. "Keep Cardona covered. I want to talk to him."

As Rink regained the revolver, Bert concentrated upon Cardona. Bert's tone was vicious.

"We figured you for a lug," he told Cardona. "You acted like it, too, right after we grabbed you. We let you get out of that cell we had you in, so you could make a couple of phone calls. We wanted you to make them.

"Guess you figured they could be traced back here. They couldn't. Those calls went over a tapped wire; and afterward, we unhooked it. Nobody could trace them after that."

Pausing, Bert watched Cardona eye the tele-sighter and the black block on the wall. He also saw Cardona note the exit to the underground passage.

"Take a good gander," jeered Bert. "It's all you can count on, Cardona. We were going to leave you in that cell of yours, like we're doing with those dicks we grabbed before you came along. But since you managed to bust loose from it, we'll give you the works instead. You've got a chance to look at some things you weren't supposed to see."

Rink looked expectantly toward Bert. Rink's finger was itching on the trigger of his reclaimed gun.

"How about it, Bert?" queried Rink. "Ready for me to drill him? Nobody's going to hear me give it. These walls won't let no noise go through them."

Bert shook his head.

"I've got a better way, Rink," he declared. "One I was holding in case this happened." Bert looked toward Cardona. "Remember how we handled you when we came here?"

Cardona gave no reply.

"I'll remind you," chuckled Bert. "We gave you a shot of tear gas, when you were in a place where you couldn't get away from it. So we're putting you back in the same place. But this time the gas tank is filled with the same kind of purple stuff that finished Trumbull Rythe."

BERT stepped forward, nudged Cardona with his gun. Joe had only one course; to take the route that Bert indicated. It led to the door that was still closed. With Rink covering Joe, Bert opened the door. The pair moved Cardona into a small room that looked like an entry. In front of them was the door of an elevator shaft.

"Call the crew." Bert snapped the order to Rink. "They can stay with me, keeping Cardona covered, while you go up to the front door and

yank the finder. As soon as you're back with the elevator, we'll put Cardona aboard. It's going to be swell, having them find this mug all purple."

"Not so swell for you, though," said Cardona, suddenly ending his silence. "You want to bump me because I finally found out who you were. But remember—anything you do to me will pin the goods on Louis Lenger. You'll be traced through him."

"Lenger can take care of himself," chuckled Bert. "Don't worry about him spilling anything that will make trouble for us. Even you couldn't make Lenger give the lowdown on the purple death. But you won't be around to try."

While Bert spoke, Rink stepped over to a side wall to press a button that would summon the hidden crew. His hand stopped short as a peculiar buzz sounded from above the door of the elevator shaft. A light glimmered from a panel. It showed the figure "1."

"Wait a minute, Rink!" snapped Bert. "Somebody's gone on board that elevator. But whoever it is didn't come in through the front door."

"He may have," remarked Rink. "We weren't watching the detector panel."

"I was listening for it," returned Rink. "I'd have heard it click on and off. Whoever is on that elevator sneaked in through the back door."

The number "1" went out. A second later, a new number showed on the panel. It was the figure "4." Bert gave a prompt grunt.

"Somebody's going up to the fourth floor," he commented. "It isn't Lenger. He always comes through the front door. Nobody else would be going up there except—"

"The Shadow!"

Bert nodded as he heard Rink's exclamation. He reached into a niche beside the elevator shaft. He pulled a switch that Cardona saw there. Immediately, the number "4" light went out. Instead, a bulb glimmered showing the letter "B."

"That will bring him down," grinned Bert. "Like it did you, Cardona. It's a lucky break for you. We'll have to give you bullets, after all. We'd been hoping that The Shadow would show up for the purple gas treatment."

CARDONA tightened. He edged toward Bert; all the while, he could hear the rumble of the elevator. It was coming downward. Soon it would strike the basement level. Well did Cardona know the hopelessness of The Shadow's position. Joe had ridden in that same elevator.

Bert's pull of the switch had locked the inner door of the car. Solid-walled, with heavy roof, the elevator was a prison from which no occupant could escape in the short time that the descent required. Cardona was ready to make a last thrust, in the hope that he could avert the doom that threatened The Shadow, even if it cost his own life.

Bert's gun was aimed toward Joe, but Bert was watching the elevator shaft. The rumble was louder, the car was almost at the bottom. Cardona started his forward spring. It ended instantly. Powerful hands caught his arms from behind, yanked him backward, pinning him helpless.

Joe had forgotten Rink. The lieutenant had seen the coming move. He had shoved away his gun to make the grab. Catching Cardona helpless, Rink gave a sideways heave. Joe crashed the wall, jolted the back of his head. He sagged to the floor, half groggy. Rink produced his gun and again covered Cardona.

The elevator's rumble ended. Staring hazily, Cardona saw Bert Thayler reach to the top of the little niche and grasp a metal ring. Bert gave a tug; a chain came into view. There was a muffled hiss beyond the elevator door; the surge of the poison gas through tiny holes that lined the walls of the car.

Cardona came to hands and knees. His head swirled dizzily. He sagged back, rested limp as he tried to regain his scattered senses. He saw Bert calmly studying the dial of a watch. He heard Bert's remark:

"The gas settles inside a minute, Rink. We'll give it two, though—"

The two minutes passed like a few hazy seconds to Joe Cardona. He steadied slightly as he saw Bert step to the door of the shaft. The metal barrier clanged open with Bert's pull. Cardona saw the lighted interior of the car.

There, on the floor of the elevator, lay the sight that Joe Cardona had hoped he would never view. A black-cloaked figure was sprawled crazily, in a crumpled posture that indicated instant death.

One long arm was extended toward the door of the elevator. Its gloved hand was limp; from the unclenched fist had fallen a huge automatic. Beside the shoulder of that same arm was a downward tilted head, its face obscured by folds of a cloak collar. The head itself was hidden, for a black slouch hat had tipped backward, to rest loosely upon head and neck.

The interior of the elevator glistened as the walls had shone at Rythe's. Drying drops of condensed vapor caused that shine. They told that the gas had completely filled the elevator.

Crooks had gained the chance they wanted. They had loosed the full force of the purple death upon The Shadow.

CHAPTER XVIII
THE UNDERGROUND WAY

BERT THAYLER stepped forward gingerly. He reached the threshold of the elevator, gave a cautious sniff to make sure that the gas had cleared. Satisfied, he stooped and reached downward to pluck the slouch hat from The Shadow's head.

Bert paused as he heard Rink approach. He looked over his shoulder, glared angrily at his lieutenant. Bert snapped an order:

"Watch Cardona!"

"He's groggy, Bert," insisted Rink. "He can't make no trouble."

Bert looked toward Cardona, saw that the stocky sleuth was again trying to come to his hands and knees.

"Call the crew, then," ordered Bert. "As soon as they get here, tell them to plug Cardona. I'll haul The Shadow out of here. The outfit can take a gander at this mug while you're on your trip upstairs. Make it snappy, Rink. Time's short."

Rink swung toward the wall, to press the button. Cardona made a wild effort to rise and stop him; then sagged back. On hands and knees Cardona came, face toward the elevator. His chance position enabled him to see what happened there.

As Bert swung to reach for The Shadow's hat, his arm went past the extended, black-gloved hand. Momentarily out of Bert's sight, that hand came to life. It dropped; its fingers tightened on the automatic that lay on the floor.

Bert yanked away the slouch hat, gave The Shadow's body a roll, so that he could stare at the cloaked fighter's face. What Bert saw must have startled him. Cardona saw a reflected glimmer as Bert suddenly jabbed his revolver straight for the figure on the floor. Cardona also heard the ugly snarl that came from Bert.

Simultaneously, Joe saw The Shadow's gloved hand snap upward. Time seemed disjointed to Cardona. He heard a roar from the interior of the elevator. It was the echoing blast of a gun. Almost like a separate occurrence, Cardona saw a flash of flame.

To Joe's dazed mind came one distinct impression. That tongue of fire had thrust upward. Therefore it was from The Shadow's gun. The cloaked fighter had beaten Bert Thayler to the shot.

Rink Leed heard the blast just as he pressed the button on the wall. Rink swung about with a leer, thinking that Bert had decided to drive a bullet to The Shadow's heart, just for the evil satisfaction that the deed would bring. Rink stopped rigid.

Rink ... saw no trace whatever of The Shadow's actual visage. The Shadow, restored to life, looked like some monstrous being.

He saw Bert's body crumpling, spilling across The Shadow's form. He saw black shoulders rising, he saw a face above them. In that instant, Rink expected to view a purpled countenance. Instead, he saw no trace whatever of The Shadow's actual visage.

THE SHADOW, restored to life, looked like some monstrous being. His face was covered with a darkish cloth; from it extended a metallic hose that ran downward to the folds of The Shadow's cloak. Rink saw the glare of eyes that burned through thick, protecting goggles.

The object that covered The Shadow's face was a gas mask. The Shadow had recognized the method by which crooks captured unwanted visitors who came to Lenger's. He had seen the elevator as a trap. He had known that only tear gas could have accounted for the capture of Joe Cardona, since it had been followed by the recuperation that Joe had shown through his telephone calls.

The Shadow had foreseen that if he entered the trap, he, too, would experience a gas attack. Whether it would be tear gas or a deadlier vapor had not mattered. He had come equipped for either, wearing a gas mask brought from the sanctum.

Rink's gun wrist, thrust the crook's hand upward. Though his head was swimming, Joe fought instinctively. He jammed Rink backward; gained a momentary advantage. But with that attack, Cardona came between The Shadow and Rink.

Only by a quick halt of his finger did The Shadow hold back his shot. His restraint was timely; the bullet, had it been dispatched, would have clipped Cardona instead of Rink. For a moment, The Shadow eyed the strugglers. Seeing that Cardona had the edge, he changed his tactics. The Shadow made a quick leap to the door on the other side of the elevator passage.

The Shadow had heard the pound of footsteps. He knew that Rink's crew was coming, spurred to greater speed because they had heard the boom of The Shadow's gun. Reaching the door The Shadow sprang into the main room just as four hoodlums surged from the other doorway.

The crooks saw The Shadow the moment that they arrived. All were swinging ready revolvers; they leveled their weapons toward the gas-masked figure of The Shadow. Hasty aim did not serve them. The Shadow was a move ahead.

Not only had he met his foemen on the way; he was ready with two automatics instead of one. He was past his door before the thugs could pick it as their point of aim. He was sidestepping across the large square room, toward the wall where the telesighter rested.

THE SHADOW'S automatics stabbed together. Like knife thrusts, their tongued flames cut toward the entering crooks. The foremost arrivals took the opening bullets. They staggered as the others shoved them aside. The second pair fired, swinging their guns in The Shadow's direction.

One bullet was high. It thudded the wall above The Shadow's head. The other was wide. The crook who fired it was too hasty in his aim. He fired for a spot from which The Shadow had sidestepped. The slug whizzed past The Shadow's shoulder.

Instantly, The Shadow returned the fire. His aim was as accurate as before. One ruffian floundered; the other jounced back against the wall beside his doorway. He snarled as he tried to aim. His arm was unsteady; his gun hand wavered.

Another fighter might have stayed to fire more shots at this sagging crook, but The Shadow did not remain. Split seconds still counted. He had business elsewhere. Speedily, The Shadow sprang back to the doorway that led to the elevator. He was just in time to see Cardona lose his grip on Rink Leed's gun.

There were shots from the big room, fired by the crooks who sagged there. They were futile; as The Shadow had expected. They did not even find

His sprawl upon the floor had been a ruse. He had wanted crooks to think him dead, so as to catch them off guard.

Rink's rigidity ended. Hastily, the lieutenant aimed for The Shadow. He was late. Already The Shadow had him covered. One instant more would have spelled death for Rink Leed. Only a misguided intervention saved him.

Joe Cardona saw Rink aim. With a heroic effort, Joe sprang for the crook. He grabbed the doorway through which The Shadow had passed. Concerned only with Cardona, The Shadow aimed for Rink, just as the lieutenant twisted and drove his gun hand downward.

Rink had unwittingly come into the path of The Shadow's aim. A single shot was all that The Shadow needed. It found Rink's left side. The bullet jolted the crook toward the wall; but it did not stop his gunstroke. The revolver, though it slipped, delivered a glancing blow to Cardona's bobbing head.

Both strugglers rolled to the floor. Rink kicked the cement; then quivered and lay motionless. Cardona fell heavily, tried to clamber to hands and knees, but slipped. Again, he made the effort. He clamped his hand upon Rink's dropped revolver, managed to grip it. But he was too dizzy to rise.

The Shadow reached the elevator, whipped up his hat that lay beside the body of Bert Thayler. Stepping out, he clanged the door of the elevator, then those of the shaft. He turned to see Cardona trying to rise beside the wall. Joe's fingers slipped as they clawed the stony surface. He was still hanging grimly to the gun that he had claimed from Rink. One-handed in his effort to rise, Cardona slumped.

The Shadow aided Cardona to his feet. Groggily, Joe recognized his cloaked rescuer. He let The Shadow guide him to the big room. There, Cardona tried to gasp out words as he pointed to the telesighter and the opening in the wall, that led underground to the distant garage.

FROM the side door of the room came a clamor. Imprisoned detectives were hammering the bars of their cells, hoping that they would soon be rescued. For a moment, The Shadow was ready to move to their release. A click from the wall made him stop.

Supporting Cardona beside him. The Shadow watched the black panel that showed pictures of all that happened in the entry of Lenger's apartment house. The light appeared; The Shadow viewed the lobby. A man had entered. The Shadow recognized the face of Police Commissioner Weston.

Other faces appeared. With Weston were headquarters men. The Shadow saw that one of them was a detective sergeant named Markham, who frequently worked with Joe Cardona. A whispered laugh came from The Shadow's lips.

The arrival of these representatives of the law saved him the delay of opening the cells that held the prisoners. Soon, Weston and the others would find this underground lair. They could come here in safety. No longer would the elevator be a trap.

The way was clear for The Shadow to travel elsewhere.

A quick start was imperative. The Shadow still had work to do. He wanted to reach his next destination without delay. He had the route that offered rapid departure; that tunnel through which Bert, Rink and the others had intended to depart.

The Shadow looked at Joe Cardona. He saw that the ace sleuth was steadier. Cardona had shown his nerve tonight; he had risked everything to aid The Shadow. Cardona was entitled to a reward, and there was a way whereby The Shadow could deliver one.

With a whispered order to Cardona, The Shadow pushed Joe through the opening in the wall. As Cardona steadied in the darkness of the passage, The Shadow used a flashlight, found a switch and pressed it. The wall swung shut, closing so perfectly that the opening could not be detected.

The underground vault was empty of living beings. The Shadow was gone, through the passage beyond, taking Joe Cardona with him. The only evidence of The Shadow's visit were the silent bodies that lay upon the floor.

The last sagging thug had toppled with his final hopeless shots. The Shadow had gained full triumph over Bert Thayler, Rink Leed and the four henchmen who served them. Underlings of the purple death were vanquished.

The Shadow's next meeting would be with the master murderer himself.

CHAPTER XIX
THE LAW SEES

COMMISSIONER WESTON, standing in the entry of the apartment house, was completely ignorant of the fact that his presence had been observed from a lair below. Like everyone else who had visited this entry—with the exception of The Shadow—the black finder plate on the wall was meaningless.

Weston's sole purpose was to invade these premises and trap Louis Lenger in his fourth-floor apartment. With that plan in mind, he tried the inner door and found it unlocked. Leading the way through the first floor hall, Weston found the elevator shaft.

Instead of sending men up on the elevator, Weston ordered them to use the stairway, so that they could inspect the intervening floors. As soon as a small squad had started, he ordered Markham to remain with him and keep watch on the front door. Weston had already posted men in front of the apartment house and in back.

The commissioner was standing by the elevator

shaft when he saw someone come into the entry. Thanks to a glass panel in the inner doorway, Weston observed a pair of shoulders; above them a rugged face topped by shaggy hair and derby hat. Suspecting that the arrival might be Lenger, Weston stepped out of sight beyond the elevator. Markham promptly joined him.

A few moments later, the man came in from the entry. He approached the elevator; turned to open the door. Looking past him, Weston saw a face at the entry door. He caught a signal of an upraised hand. It was one of the outside detectives. He had seen the rugged-faced man open a mailbox in the entry. The dick had thus learned that the arrival was Louis Lenger. The signal transmitted the news to Weston.

The commissioner stepped into view; Markham was beside him with ready revolver. Lenger turned as they approached; his eyes glared with suspicion. His fists tightened as he saw Markham's revolver; then relaxed as he saw the detective sergeant display a badge.

"What is the trouble?" inquired Lenger. "I was rather startled, gentlemen, before I realized that you were police."

"I am the police commissioner," informed Weston. "I have come here to interview you, Mr. Lenger."

Surprise showed on Lenger's face. Weston bluntly added the statement:

"I have some questions to ask you regarding Courtney Grell."

"Courtney Grell?" questioned Lenger. Then, in a reminiscent tone: "Ah, yes. I remember him. He was here last night; a chess enthusiast like myself."

"How late was Grell here?"

"I disremember. We went out together; stopped in a little restaurant to chat while we had a cup of coffee. Tell me, Commissioner, is Grell wanted by the law?"

Weston stared; then demanded:

"Don't you read the newspapers, Mr. Lenger?"

"Only the chess columns. Why?"

"Then I am to suppose that you are ignorant of the fact that Grell died last night?"

LENGER looked dumfounded.

"Grell died a victim of the purple death," stated Weston, eyeing Lenger closely as he spoke. "Suppose we go up to your apartment, Mr. Lenger. No, not by the elevator"—he stopped Lenger as the heavy man reached to press the button. "The stairway would be better."

Weston chose the stairway knowing that Markham would be joined by detectives during the ascent. Moreover, the commissioner kept up a running fire of remarks as they went up the stairs.

"We thought that Grell was a suicide," he told Lenger, "but we need more facts to be sure. It was odd, Grell dying from the purple death. Of course, you have read about the purple death?"

"Yes, I did," returned Lenger. "But I am not interested in such matters."

"You live here alone?"

"Yes. I am the owner of this building."

They reached the fourth floor, to find two detectives in Lenger's apartment. The dicks had already begun a search, losing no time when they found that Lenger was absent. One detective gave the immediate announcement:

"We've found plenty, Commissioner."

Weston motioned Lenger to a chair; told Markham to watch the suspect. He began to examine the evidence that the detectives had uncovered. Their finds popped thick and fast.

The detectives produced the box that had contained a fountain pen of the type found on the scene of one murder. They showed Weston the frayed shirt with the missing button. Weston, himself, spied the bottle of purple ink. A detective produced the box of chess clippings; his teammate displayed blank memo pads. Among the chess clippings, Weston discovered the blue pencil.

Then came the items that concerned dead victims. First, the blue-marked page from the university catalog, containing the name of Ardess, the murdered instructor. Next, the pawn ticket from Gringew's shop. After that, Tabor's business card; the page from "Who's Who" that displayed Rythe's biography.

The final touch came when Weston opened the folded list; read the typed names of victims, ending with Horace Selbart. One of the detectives shoved a sheet of paper into Lenger's old type-writer; typed a few lines and compared them with the list. It was obvious that the names had been typed on Lenger's machine.

Weston turned coldly to Lenger; handed the man a blue pencil and a sheet of paper, with the request that he write a few words and sign them with the letter "L." Lenger looked puzzled; then nodded and complied. The commissioner examined the writing. It corresponded with the memo found at Rythe's.

"I was wrong about Grell," declared Weston, in a harsh tone. "He was not the murderer who perpetrated the purple deaths."

LENGER stroked his stubbly chin.

"I thought that chess was a game for a keen mind, Commissioner," he asserted. "I learn, at last, that it is no more than a childish pursuit. You come here; you pick out odds and ends from among my papers. From them, you form the remarkable conclusion that Courtney Grell, whom I met but once, is not a murderer. I would not be astonished if, from this same evidence, you discovered who actually is the murderer."

"I have done that," retorted Weston. "Your bluff is finished, Lenger. You are under arrest for the perpetration of those crimes."

"I?" exclaimed Lenger. He stared; then gave a short laugh. "This is preposterous, Commissioner. I do not even know who was murdered."

"Perhaps," returned Weston, "you will try to tell me that you never saw these before."

He handed Lenger the catalog page that bore the name of Ardess; then the pawnbroker's ticket; the card that bore Tabor's name; finally, the page from "Who's Who" that referred to Rythe. Lenger studied the exhibits. He passed back all of them except Tabor's business card.

"I never saw any of those," he insisted. "How they came here is a mystery to me. The business card, though, was among my own papers; but I never met Frederick Tabor personally."

"Then how do you happen to have his card?"

"I told you that I owned this apartment house," explained Lenger, calmly. "Tabor was the architect who drew up the plans for its reconstruction. All the details, however, were handled by the contractor."

Weston studied Lenger intently. The commissioner realized that he needed stronger tactics to jolt Lenger's calmness. Weston produced an envelope from his pocket.

"Three nights ago," he told Lenger, "Frederick Tabor was found dead in his studio. This chess clipping"—Weston exhibited the item—"was found on the premises."

Lenger eyed the clipping and nodded.

"An interesting problem, that one," he remarked. "But the answer given is not the best one. I remember that Grell and I discussed that very problem—"

"Two nights ago," broke in Weston, "Trumbull Rythe was murdered in his home. This blue-penciled memo, signed with the letter 'L,' was found there."

"That is curious!" exclaimed Lenger. "That looks like a memo that I left in my mailbox one day when I expected a visitor. Someone must have taken it—"

"Last night," interrupted Weston, curtly, "Horace Selbart was murdered in his penthouse. This blue pencil was found with his body."

"It looks like one of my pencils," admitted Lenger. "I have a lot of them here in the apartment. I mislay them often. Do you suppose that someone has—"

"I suppose that you are the murderer who slew those three men. Let me add another statement, Lenger. Tabor, Rythe and Selbart were murdered at half past eight, on three successive nights. Where were you at that particular hour, on each of the last three nights?"

Lenger arose from his chair.

"That is easily answered, Commissioner," he stated in a pleased tone. "Every night at eight-thirty, I am with my friend Howard Feasley. We play chess until nine. Feasley lives on the outskirts of Greenwich Village. I can give you his address; you can go there and see him."

"HE'LL come to headquarters," retorted Weston. "That's where I am taking you, Lenger."

Grabbing the suspect's arm, Weston shoved Lenger out into the hallway and headed him toward the elevator. On the way, Lenger began a protest.

"You cannot call Feasley to headquarters," he insisted. "The man is still an invalid. He cannot be taken outdoors in this chill weather."

Weston pressed the button for the elevator.

"I shall attend to Feasley," he said, coldly. "We shall check whatever alibi he gives you, Lenger."

The accused man smiled. Apparently, Lenger was willing to bank entirely upon Feasley's statements. Silence followed, except for the ascending rumble of the elevator. Lights appeared beyond the frosted glass of the shaft door. Weston opened the door; he stepped back with a startled exclamation. Lenger gulped an odd cry.

On the floor of the elevator lay the body of Bert Thayler. Markham stepped aboard; lifted the dead crook's head and turned to the commissioner.

"Bert Thayler," informed Markham. "A bad egg. As bad as Slook Howdrey. He's probably the guy who took over Slook's job, Commissioner."

"Working for the purple murderer!" exclaimed Weston. "But where could the body have come from, Markham?"

"From the basement, maybe," suggested Markham, unable to think of a better answer. "If we went down there, Commissioner—"

"Remove the body. We are going to the basement."

Soon, the elevator descended minus Bert's corpse. The passengers were Weston and Lenger, accompanied by Markham and a pair of detectives. They reached the basement. The moment that Markham opened the door, they saw Rink Leed's body. Markham identified Thayler's lieutenant.

Weston heard shouts as he stepped to the door of the big room. Bringing Lenger with them, the investigators found the bodies of the dead thugs. They saw the door to the side passage; took it and discovered a row of small cells. Behind the bars were the missing detectives.

Weston snapped queries while Markham and others were pounding the locks with revolver butts. Every prisoner had the same story. Each had received a telephone call, telling him to call on a man named Lenger. Each had come to the same apartment house, had been gassed in the elevator.

Weston inquired for Cardona. The prisoners told him that Joe had broken free tonight; that there had been gunfire, but Cardona had not returned. Weston had just finished this inquiry when the final lock was smashed. The prisoners crowded out into the corridor.

With eight men at his heels, Weston marched Lenger out into the big room. The suspect was handcuffed and helpless; he seemed totally bewildered by the new discoveries. Weston decided on another quiz.

"THE facts are plain, Lenger," snapped the commissioner. "You arranged this lair. These crooks served you, just as Slook Howdrey and his ruffians did. You can gain nothing by useless bluff. You are the only man who could have engineered the purple deaths."

Weston waited for Lenger to reply. Tense silence was broken by a sudden click from the wall. Weston looked in that direction. The black panel had lighted. It showed the entry. In the picture, Weston saw the faces of two outside detectives.

"A television device!" exclaimed Weston. "It must be controlled by a photoelectric cell. The moment anyone enters the building, the scene is registered down here. That is how the crooks knew when to use the elevator as a trap!"

The panel darkened. The detectives had stepped from the entry. Weston eyed the big cabinet that Bert had termed the "telesighter." Approaching it, Weston noted that the device had a special regulator that was set at a number. He saw a switch. He pressed it.

Immediately there was a buzz from the cabinet. The front became a grayish screen; its scene was indistinct at first. In low tone, Weston spoke.

"A television device," declared the commissioner. "Let us hope that it is tuned in to some given place. Perhaps from this we can gain new clues."

The screen was clearing; a scene began to appear. With it were sounds. The watchers could hear a wheezy cough just as the picture made itself plain.

They were looking into a room where a man sat at a chessboard. Frail and wan-faced, the man was coughing. He recovered from his spell and reached for one of the chess pieces. The background of the room was plain. At one side was a closed door; at the far end of the room, the viewers saw heavy curtains.

Louis Lenger gave an exclamation that betokened recognition. He knew the identity of that frail man who was garbed in dressing gown. Lenger craned closer to the telesighter screen.

"Howard Feasley!" he exclaimed. "The man I told you about, Commissioner. He is working on a chess problem that we discussed after our game tonight. He must have forgotten that it is after nine o'clock. Otherwise he would be in bed."

Weston motioned for silence. Lenger quieted, stood as tense as the detectives who surrounded him. Weston had spotted a change in the scene. The door at the side of Feasley's room was opening. Those who watched could hear the groan of a hinge; but Feasley, actually in that pictured room, did not apparently notice it. He was too deeply engrossed in his chess problem.

Something about the scene presaged a coming menace. The men who watched the television screen were helpless to intervene. They could do no more than gaze in rigid horror at the changing picture that revealed those distant events.

Commissioner Weston somehow sensed the significance of the slowly opening door. From his lips came an involuntary statement:

"The purple murderer!"

CHAPTER XX
THE LAST DEATH

HOWARD FEASLEY shifted back in his chair. His wan face showed a satisfied smile. He had completed the problem upon which he worked. Casually, the invalid glanced toward a mantel. He saw a clock and noted that it was after half past nine. He started to rise from his chair, his eyes still on the clock. He stopped; his lips twitched.

In the mirror behind the clock, Feasley saw the reflection of the opening door. From his position, he could see a face beyond it; one that was not visible across the television apparatus, because the door intervened.

Feasley spun about; clutched the arms of his chair. A man stepped into the room and closed the door behind him. Calmly, the intruder stepped toward the quaking invalid.

Though Feasley had never seen his visitor before, he knew that the man had come with evil intent. The intruder's expression showed it. The face that Feasley saw was a gloating one; the approach that the intruder used was an insidious creep.

There were others who saw that face and recognized it, despite the fact that its usually friendly expression had changed to a vicious gloat. The man who had entered Feasley's isolated abode was Professor Kinsley Murkden.

Feasley sank into his chair as the professor neared him. Murkden reached the side of the chessboard and eyed Feasley as a snake studies a hapless bird. Stupefied, the chess player blinked. He recognized that Murkden intended ill; but he could not understand why.

From a coat pocket, Murkden produced an object that glistened. Feasley saw it, recognized that it was a hypodermic needle. The invalid quivered, tried to twist away from his chair. Murkden shot his free hand forward, thrust Feasley downward and held him helpless.

"Death will be prompt," declared Murkden, in a dry, insidious tone. "Unfortunately, Feasley, I am forced to end your life."

Feasley found words.

"Why—why kill me?" he blurted. "Whoever you are—I have never harmed you."

"Quite true," agreed Murkden, his voice carrying an ugly sneer. "I owe you an apology for my action. Therefore, I shall give one. Perhaps you have heard of the purple deaths—"

Murkden paused as Feasley's face showed white with terror. He saw his victim make an effort to nod.

"I devised the purple death," announced Murkden, proudly. "I reserved it for some important use. Not long ago, I learned of a remarkable invention; a television apparatus that can be added to an ordinary set. It is an invention, I might state, that is worth millions. Its transmission and reception are of such high quality that messages, when sent, can be heard only in a limited area.

"With this device, it will be possible to revolutionize the entire broadcasting systems of the world; to control, through international patents, companies that will produce greater wealth than any enterprise in modern history. I have tested the device from this very room." Murkden chuckled as he paused to motion toward the wall. "That black plate that covers your unused wall bracket is both a finder and a transmitter that picks up all that occurs here."

FEASLEY was staring; his eyes had temporarily lost their horror and were displaying interest. Murkden's sudden switch from the subject of death had given the invalid hope that the professor might be humored.

"An obscure mechanic invented the device," explained Murkden. "It was improved by a college instructor. A radio announcer was called in secretly to aid in its tests. A promoter learned of it, offered to sell the idea. He tried to raise money from a pawnbroker, but failed."

Feasley, who read the newspapers, realized that Murkden had explained the reason for the first five purple deaths. They had eliminated all men concerned with the development of the television device.

"They finally went to a man named Horace Selbart," continued Murkden. "He financed the invention, upon terms that gave him control of its future. At about that time, I learned of it. I proceeded to use the purple death to eliminate all those whom I have named.

"I needed a dupe; one upon whom the murders could be pinned. I chose Louis Lenger, a friend of yours, because it was an easy matter to turn the evidence against him. Chiefly because Lenger had a set policy of being absent from his apartment every night between the hours of seven and nine."

"When he came here," blurted Feasley. "That is why you chose Louis Lenger—"

"Yes. It was a simple matter to visit his apartment soon after seven o'clock. There I acquired bits of evidence to incriminate him. I also planted items that would serve against him. Lenger's place was in such disarray that I knew he would never find the objects that I had placed."

Murkden paused. Feasley's breath came tensely. Murkden heard its sighing tone and his eyes gleamed wickedly. The scheming professor had not only proven that his usual mild manner was a pose; he had also demonstrated that his supposed deafness was a pretense.

"I planned this long ago," chuckled the murderer. "I had picked Lenger for my future dupe. I intercepted rough plans that Lenger had made for the reconstruction of two old houses into an apartment building. I added instructions of my own. As a result, the architect added a stronghold in the basement. That architect was Frederick Tabor. I killed him, took the old plans from his files. That murder, too, will be pinned on Louis Lenger.

"Looking to the future, I could see but one man who might block my great plans for international control of television. That man was Trumbull Rythe, the financier. Among his many holdings were options on certain forms of radio equipment that are at present regarded as unimportant; but which will be vital to the production of the television apparatus that I required. By eliminating Rythe, I removed the one obstacle that night have blocked my path to commercial supremacy."

With that statement, Murkden changed his manner. He had lessened his evil glare. Viciously, he resumed it. His left hand settled clawlike upon Feasley's shoulder. His right hand approached with the deadly hypodermic. Feasley was too paralyzed to writhe.

"My apology is ended," sneered Murkden. "It is time that you should die."

"BUT why?" gasped Feasley. "I have not tried to block your schemes."

"You are Lenger's alibi," croaked Murkden. "The law is ready to class him as a homicidal maniac. When you are found a victim of the purple death, Lenger's last hope will be gone. Particularly"— Murkden's tone was gloating—"because the law believes that every victim died at half past eight.

"Tonight, my henchmen watched—as they have always watched—to see when Lenger left here. Tonight, they saw him leave. They sent a tip-off to the police. I answered the call myself, in Commissioner Weston's presence. By this time,

my men have left their stronghold. Lenger is in the hands of the law. The police will come here; that plate on the wall will be gone. But they will find you dead and purple—"

Murkden halted. Feasley's wild, hopeless eyes had gained a sudden light. They were looking past the hand that held the hypodermic; beyond Murkden's shoulder to the curtains at the rear of the room. Sharpness came to Murkden's gaze. Instantly, the murderous professor spun about.

Straight before him, Murkden saw The Shadow. Curtains had parted to admit the black-clad avenger. With leveled automatic, The Shadow

The murderous professor swung about. Curtains had parted to admit the black-clad avenger.

approached. Murkden backed away from Feasley. Though his livid lips still showed viciousness, Murkden knew that he was trapped.

With long stride, The Shadow stepped between Murkden and the door. Burning eyes fixed themselves upon the half-crouched murderer. Murkden glared back. His fists were clenched; the right one still held the hypodermic. For a moment, Murkden seemed ready for a spring; then he recognized the futility of such a move. The looming muzzle of The Shadow's .45 was too powerful a threat.

"You forgot the mention of one victim." The Shadow's tone came in sinister syllables. "I refer, Murkden, to the man that you were forced to kill. That man was Courtney Grell."

Murkden scowled, but made no response.

"You wanted clues to reach the law," continued The Shadow, "so that Lenger could be incriminated. But your methods required that those clues be held back until you had completed your chain of murder. That was why you trapped the law's investigators.

"Grell investigated also; but he was not trapped, even though he visited Lenger. That was proof that Lenger was not the purple murderer. I looked for an answer to the riddle of Grell's death. I found it. Grell was the only man who visited Lenger and found him at home. Grell entered the elevator trap; but Lenger was with him. Since Lenger was to remain at large, an unsuspecting dupe, your henchmen could not spring the trap on Grell.

"Instead, they let him go, knowing that he would return to your residence, either to inform the commissioner of what he had learned or to continue with a bluff that would suit his own plans. Commissioner Weston was gone when Grell arrived, but you talked with Grell and lulled him into thinking that Weston was not angry. Meanwhile, you had prepared the poisoned chewing gum. One of your servants planted it in Grell's overcoat pocket, while Grell was with you."

A SNARL formed on Murkden's lips, plain proof that The Shadow had been right in his reconstruction of events. Realizing that his expression was a betrayal, Murkden stiffened. Forgetting that he was trapped in an attempted murder, the professor suddenly reverted to the past.

"You have no proof," he grated. "No one will believe your statements. My tests—certified by experts—proved that the purple death was delivered each night at half past eight. I can bring dozens of witnesses to prove that I was always in my lecture room at that precise time."

"Your proof will be useless," asserted The Shadow. "Your scheme was clever. It began when you hired Slook Howdrey to intimidate Commissioner Weston, with the demand that no tests be made. You hired Slook without revealing your identity. Facts seemed to show that some hidden killer regarded your blood tests as a menace to his career of crime.

"Established as the one man who could solve the riddle of the purple death, you prepared your Compound 'F' and made it almost identical with the poison. The tests that you made were genuine. They were thoroughly checked by experts and accepted. But no one thought to examine the guinea pigs that you used.

"I performed the tests with other specimens. I learned that the purple death had struck at half past nine, a time when you were free to deliver it in person. The guinea pigs that I used were ordinary ones. Your guinea pigs were inoculated; you tinged their blood beforehand with a small dose of the purple poison. When you killed them with a full injection, their first blood changes were slow, and did not reach the correct ratio for a full hour. Thus your tests with guinea pigs gave false proof that the human victims had died at half past eight instead of half past nine."

Murkden's glare was gone. The Shadow had revealed the facts behind the murderer's cunning game. For a few moments, Murkden cringed. His expression showed no vestige of its former confidence. Then came a sharp glint from evil eyes; simultaneously, a warning gulp from Feasley, who had been an awed and silent spectator during The Shadow's denouncement.

The Shadow needed neither warning. A groan of a door hinge told him that Murkden and Feasley had seen something occur behind him. The Shadow was spinning about as the door swung violently inward. Gun ready, he sprang straight for the doorway to meet a massed surge of three attackers.

The men were Murkden's servants. The professor had brought them along to stay on watch outside. They—like Murkden—had arrived after The Shadow had already entered to take his post behind Feasley's curtains.

The blast of The Shadow's automatic dropped the first attacker. The second, springing past the cloaked fighter, turned to aim. The Shadow sledged him unconscious with a hard swing of the automatic. With his stroke, The Shadow made a complete spin, came upon the third henchman before the startled man could fire. Wildly, the last of the trio grabbed for The Shadow's gun arm.

The Shadow's hand twisted free, poised for a downward stroke that would end the conflict. His back was toward Murkden. The murderer saw the opportunity he wanted. Murkden had forgotten Feasley and with good reason. All that the invalid could do was shriek a warning as Murkden bounded toward The Shadow.

Down came The Shadow's gun arm. Murkden's

last servant fell. Simultaneously, Murkden swung his hand above The Shadow's back. The hypodermic glistened from the claw that clutched it. One second more, Murkden could have driven the needle home, to change The Shadow's triumph into doom. The gloating murderer was sure that he could claim The Shadow as the final victim of the purple death.

As Murkden's poised hand moved, the report of a revolver echoed through the room. The shot came from the curtains that had been The Shadow's hiding place. A steady gun had aimed for Murkden. The bullet found the murderer's body. As Murkden wavered, smoke curled from the curtains; then the draperies parted. A stocky marksman sprang into view. The sharpshooter was Joe Cardona.

The Shadow had brought the missing inspector with him. From the moment that The Shadow had confronted Murkden, Cardona had been holding a bead upon the murderous professor. Joe had hoped to capture the killer alive. The chance arrival of Murkden's reserves had made it imperative for Cardona to fire.

One bullet, though well aimed, was not enough to finish Murkden. The professor wavered; then recuperated. His lips snarled as his right hand tightened. The Shadow wheeled about to see Cardona stopping for new aim. Before the ace inspector could fire, Murkden jabbed his hypodermic for The Shadow's turning shoulder.

A gloved fist, quick as a trip hammer, came up to clutch Murkden's driving wrist. The thrust stopped short, the needle point pricking the folds of The Shadow's cloak. With a powerful twist, The Shadow turned back Murkden's hand, pointing the needle in the opposite direction.

For a moment, Murkden was rigid. Suddenly his strength faded. He toppled forward, a dead weight, succumbing to the mortal wound caused by Cardona's bullet. The full pressure of the killer's chest struck squarely on the back-turned needle. The long point pierced straight to Murkden's heart.

The Shadow released the crumpling body. Murkden folded on the floor, face upward. Cardona, staring downward, saw a weird change come upon the murderer's frozen countenance. A crimson flush covered Murkden's features. The tinge darkened; grew to a terrible purple that brought a gruesome swelling to the dead man's face, a purplish bulge to evil eyes that were staring fixed in death.

DISTANT observers saw the sight. Weston, Lenger and those with them were staring at the telesighter screen. They had heard every word that had passed at Feasley's. They had learned the full truth of Kinsley Murkden's crimes. They viewed the aftermath.

Murkden prone and lifeless, his purple face showing dark upon the screen. They saw Cardona gazing at the dead murderer; Feasley, half up from his chair, gasping in relief at sight of the doom that he had missed.

Beyond that tableau was The Shadow. The cloaked victor turned, stepped slowly to the far curtains and paused there for a final view. Gloved hands spread the curtains; The Shadow took a backward step between. The curtains dropped. The Shadow was gone. There was a pause as the curtains ceased their rustle.

Then, from that hidden spot, came a final token; a sound that quivered through the room where Cardona and Feasley stood and carried its chilling echoes through the ether to those who watched and listened at the telesighter.

That sound was a laugh that rose to weird crescendo, then faded into nothingness, yet seemed to echo in the brains of those who heard it. That peal of solemn mirth betokened The Shadow's triumph. It marked the black-clad victor's departure.

There were ears that that weird tone could not reach; ears that had gained a deafness more permanent than they had once pretended. Those were the ears of Professor Kinsley Murkden. That master murderer would never again move to crime.

Purple death had ended his reign forever. The Shadow's hand had turned its final thrust. The last dose of the purple poison had found its proper lodgement in the death-stilled form of the murderer who had created it.

But The Shadow's hand would be thrust forward again, in the future, grimly clutching for the lead that would bring together *The Seven Drops of Blood*. Priceless rubies from the storehouse of an Oriental potentate, then the prize piece of a wealthy gem collector—The Shadow battles the master thief who separates the seven glittering stones, and traces them one by one in a relentless struggle against the pick of the underworld.

THE END

Coming soon in **THE SHADOW Volume 34:**
The Blackmail Ring *and* **Murder for Sale**

INTERLUDE by Will Murray

The Strange Disappearance of Joe Cardona was written in May 1936 and published in the November 15, 1936 issue of *The Shadow Magazine.* Editor John L. Nanovic added the descriptor "Strange" to Gibson's working title, and no doubt he was tempted to retitle it "The Purple Death." The lavender background of George Rozen's striking cover illustration seems to suggest this possibility. One of the fascinating things about Walter Gibson's Shadow stories is how they transport you back to the Manhattan of the Great Depression. Some of this fascination lies is the then-contemporary world he depicted— which now no longer exists. Much of its charm lies in Gibson's Dickensian-style touches of matter-of-fact reality, whether it be the old elevated trains or the simple details of places that may or may not still exist in 21st century New York City. His editor, John L. Nanovic, was well aware of this gift, even back in the glory days of The Shadow. In 1941, he wrote:

> Walter Gibson, who has been doing a ... *Shadow* novelette twice a month for the past ten years, and getting fatter and fatter on the job right along, has a technique that is as amazing as the feat he has accomplished in making *The Shadow* such a tremendous success. One block from the office is an automobile accessory store. Usually, they have a pile of secondhand tires near the entrance. Gibson, always keeping his eyes open for something new for The Shadow, was the first one of dozens of writers who passed there often to realize it would make an excellent hiding place for The Shadow. Slipping inside the piled-up tires, he could simply lift any one of them slightly and peer through, observing without being seen. If, by good fortune, we have some steel rims on these tires, they can prove a veritable fortress against gunfire, while The Shadow's automatic, sticking out between the tires, blasts crooks to pieces! This made an excellent scene in one of The Shadow novels.
>
> Another time, sitting on the roof of Gibson's hotel, he remarked about the taller buildings which surrounded it. Looking around, he noticed the ornamental corners on some of these buildings— and immediately figured out that The Shadow, if he wanted to make a quick trip from the point where we were sitting to one of the other buildings, could simply throw a boomerang around one of these ornamental corners, thereafter trail a heavier rope around it, and thus construct a "pulley" device in a matter of seconds, rather than go downstairs in one building, cross the street, and up the elevator in the other to get to the same spot. This, too, made a great incident in another Shadow novel. A quicker, more dramatic means of getting to a place which it seemed he would not be able to reach in time otherwise.

Now, Gibson's great appeal is the fact that he can make you feel every one of his stories can happen to you. The tricks and devices he uses are clever adaptations of things you see and know in everyday life, but never think of in that light until The Shadow, or one of his agents, makes such use of them. It makes the reader realize how clever the hero is to take such advantage of common things; it makes him feel that he is part of story because the things which are a part of his life play so important a role in the yarns. Gibson does not need to try any peculiar style, either in construction or plotting. The straightforward, simple, direct style is the best for such everyday devices.

Gibson himself often talked about this writing technique. "Not only were they realistic stories," he once remarked, "they stand out as reflections of what life was like in those days. For instance, I had some scenes where the crooks bang into another car with their running boards. This is realistic to readers." He recalled walking down a New York street with artist Jack Binder, who was then drawing his scripts for *Shadow Comics.* Noticing a fence with side-slanted iron rails, Gibson recounted to the interested Binder how The Shadow could put them to good use in a gun battle, simply by concealing himself behind them and firing through the slating rails, which would deflect any incoming fire. No doubt they collaborated to introduce that very scene into a Shadow strip before long.

The quaint shoemaker's shop into which Joe Cardona disappears no doubt existed back then, as did the apartment house which hosts the climactic gun battle of this novel's shattering climax. Gibson describes them in such careful detail that they could hardly be imaginary. In fact, the Deedham Apartments is probably Gibson's name for the Gilford, the 15-story neo-Georgian apartment building where he resided between 1934-36. It was located at 140 East 46th Street, and was built in 1923 on the former site of the old Gilford Mansion.

Modern readers might be surprised to read that television—which did not become part of the American cultural fabric until after World War II—plays a role in this 1937 story. But prototype television receivers date back to the late 1920s, and experimental TV broadcasts were a reality in Depression America.

The first U.S. pioneer was no less than Hugo Gernsback, publisher of magazines such as *Electrical Experimenter, Science and Invention, Radio News, Amazing Stories* (the first science fiction pulp) and *Modern Magic* (with features by Walter Gibson). On August 13, 1928, Gernsback's radio station, WRNY, inaugurated the first scheduled daily television programming in the nation. Primitive by today's standards, it consisted of a

Television pioneer Hugo Gernsback

still image transmitted after each of WRNY's programs, usually depicting the featured performer of that program. Receiving sets were all home-built kits, from plans Gernsback published in his own magazines! The experiment was short-lived.

The first metropolitan TV broadcast antenna was mounted atop the Empire State Building on December 22, 1931. NBC was the new tenant of what had originally been the building's impractical dirigible mooring mast. Experimental telecasts to area homes began over station W2FX on June 29, 1936, around the time Walter Gibson wrote this story. Receiving sets were rare. Only about 100 existed—most in the hands of RCA officials.

All through the 1930s, the Depression suppressed the development of commercial TV. Not until the opening of the 1939 New York World's Fair were the first sets offered to the general public. President Franklin D. Roosevelt's opening-day speech was telecast as the kickoff. Regular programming began simultaneously. The first commercial telecast took place on July 1, 1941 over WNBT's Channel 1. However, just when TV was poised to take off, World War II intervened, delaying the medium's progress until the late 40s. WNBT is now WNBC Channel 4.

Switching from supercrime to organized crime, we begin a celebrated series of stories pitting The Shadow against The Hand. Although he battled everything from masked supercriminals to shadowy spies, the Master of Darkness first came into existence to combat big city crime.

"When The Shadow stories began in 1931," explained Walter Gibson, "mob crimes were rampant. New Number One [Public] Enemies were popping up as fast as the newly activated FBI could shoot them down. Prosperity was giving way to the Depression and the New Deal was still unknown. So it was only logical that the Shadow should be doing his part to bring order out of chaos."

One outfit The Shadow never tackled was The Mafia. Partly that was because Street & Smith understood that they would receive complaints from Italian-Americans if they did. Perhaps they did, early in the Dark Avenger's career.

Gibson recalls his editor telling him early on, "Make the crooks good, solid Americans, so you don't offend anybody."

In any event, mobsters with Italianate names were seldom seen in the pages of *The Shadow Magazine* after the Master of Mystery tangled with an Al Capone clone named Nick Savoli in 1931's *Gangdom's Doom*. But The Shadow continued battling ethnically neutral crime lords and racketeers of various types. Perhaps only the names were changed to protect the guilty.

In one 1938 novel, *The Rackets King*, the Master Avenger crushed Manhattan's existing web of rackets. This set the stage for an unusual experiment, a sub-series pitting The Shadow against a criminal organization known as The Hand, which had moved in to fill the vacuum. Earlier in the 20th century a pre-Mafia Sicilian extortion group known as the Black Hand Society was operating with impunity in New York, Philadelphia, Chicago and other major U.S. cities. Therein lies the likely root inspiration for the premise.

If so, the execution was pure pulp. For the Hand consists of five master racketeers, all nick-named after a different digit of the human hand, all affiliated but working independently of one another in different municipalities, specializing in individual rackets, such as blackmail, kidnapping, murder for hire, and the like.

The kickoff novel, *The Hand*, was written at the end of 1937. *Murder for Sale* followed in January. *Chicago Crime* came along in February. Then mysteriously, Gibson stopped the series. His plan seemed to be to write a Hand story every month, alternating with an unconnected adventure.

Strangely, given that The Shadow was barreling along at a two story a month clip, Gibson stopped writing Shadows altogether after turning in *Shadow Over Alcatraz* at the end of February 1938. Not until May did he pick up the pen of Maxwell Grant again, concluding the final hand tales in June and July.

There is much more to the story behind The Hand. But it can wait. Over the next four Shadow volumes, we'll present in sequence the remaining episodes of The Shadow's campaign against the ferocious Fingers of The Hand—each story laid in a different city. This is not a serial. In each adventure, a separate member of that far-flung criminal organization will be dealt with. While the stories do not have to be read in publication order to be enjoyed, this is the best way to experience them.

And now, Maxwell Grant begins the saga in Manhattan as The Shadow launches his epic campaign to dismember The Hand in this riveting tale ripped from the pages of the May 15, 1938 issue of *The Shadow*. •

From out of darkness comes

THE HAND

to confront The Shadow—and only he could read completely the terrible message it held!

A Complete Booklength Novel from the Private Annals of The Shadow.

As told to

Maxwell Grant

CHAPTER I
CRIME FORETOLD

THE man on the corner looked like a Bowery bum. He was bent-shouldered, droopy-faced, with a bleary gaze that seemed to have two purposes. The first was to find prosperous-looking passers-by who could be touched for a drink; the other, to avoid any patrolman who might come along.

The panhandler had chosen a place frequented by those of his ilk. He was beneath the high-built elevated structure at Chatham Square, near the outskirts of New York's Chinatown. Many visitors who scorned the Chinatown busses came to the Oriental quarter by the elevated. It was easy to halt them and make the old plea for a cup of coffee.

The one trouble was that too many other bums had the same idea. There was a horde of them about—furtive, vulture-eyed, all hoping to gain their quota of small change.

A squatty hard-faced man came down the steps from the elevated. He gave a contemptuous glance that took in the array of panhandlers. Most of them shifted away. This guy wasn't the sort who would fall for the old flimflam. But the bent-shouldered man thought differently.

He shambled toward the squatty arrival. Plucking a cigarette stump from the pocket of his ragged coat, he raised it toward his pasty lips, while he whined the query:

"Got a match, bud?"

"On your way, bum," growled the squatty man. "Here comes a harness bull. Want me to turn you over?"

"All I asked for was a match!"

"Yeah! The old buildup! That stall don't work around here. I got you labeled; you're one of them mission stiffs that tries to find a few dimes before crawling in to beg for an overnight bunk!"

The squatty man turned away, only to twist angrily when he felt the panhandler's fingers pluck his sleeve. Again, the whine: "Honest, bud —all I'm lookin' for is some guy to give me a hand."

There was a hard look in the squatty man's eyes. He saw a slow grin on the pasty lips of that face above bent shoulders. In a lower tone, the panhandler reminded:

"And all I asked for was a match."

From his vest pocket, the squatty man drew a pack of paper matches, thrust them into the bum's fist.

"There's some matches," he guffawed. "You wanted 'em, so keep 'em!"

He strode away, while watching bums grinned at the sour look displayed by the stoopy panhandler. Evidently, that episode was enough to settle the unsuccessful fellow.

HUNCHING his bent shoulders, the droopy-faced man shambled toward Doyers Street, taking the route to the old Bowery Mission, where bunks awaited those of his breed.

Out of sight along the curving street, the shambling bum didn't stop at that logical destination. Instead, he shuffled onward, through Chinatown and out again, to the gloom of a street where many cars were parked. Some of those automobiles were pretentious, for they were owned by persons visiting Chinatown.

The bum picked the best car in the line—a huge, imported limousine, in which a uniformed chauffeur sat drowsing at the wheel. Opening the rear door softly, the stogy bum shifted inside. As soon as he had closed the door, he lifted a speaking tube. His voice awoke the chauffeur.

"Very well, Stanley." An even tone had replaced the whine. "Drive uptown."

The big car started. Crouched in the rear seat, the ex-bum flicked a tiny flashlight. Its gleam showed the match pack that the squatty man had given him. That pack was open; on the inside flap, keen eyes saw markings made with a rubber stamp.

One token was a clock dial, with an indicator pointing to the hour of nine. Beneath it was another stamped design that served as signature. It was crudely shaped, badly stamped, but easily recognized.

That emblem represented a human hand; fingers and thumb were close together, but extended.

A whispered laugh filled the confines of the soundproof limousine. That mirth, too, was a token.

It was the laugh of The Shadow!

MASTER investigator who battled men of crime, The Shadow had gotten information that he wanted. One hour's pose as a Bowery bum had proven highly profitable. His next step was to link his findings with those of workers who served The Shadow and his agents. Earphones came from a hidden space in front of the limousine's folding seats. A buzzing announced shortwave contact. The Shadow heard a voice from the ether:

"Burbank speaking."

"Report!"

The Shadow's whisper was all that Burbank needed. The contact man gave news from The Shadow's agents. When the reports were finished, The Shadow spoke instructions.

Replacing the earphones, The Shadow gave Stanley a new destination, using the quiet, even tone that suited Lamont Cranston, the wealthy owner of this limousine and the man whose identity, at times, The Shadow adopted. As the big car wheeled into a side street, The Shadow drew a hidden drawer from beneath the rear seat.

In the next few minutes, the guise of the bum was obliterated. The Shadow didn't bother to alter his facial makeup; he merely smothered it. A black cloak slid over his shoulders, its upturned collar hiding The Shadow's disguised lips. Long hands clamped a slouch hat on the head above; the hat brim obscured The Shadow's upper features.

When the limousine halted beside a darkened curb, a shrouded figure glided from the door. Patiently, Stanley sat at the wheel, supposing that his master was still within the car.

The Shadow had chosen a hidden pathway through the night.

SOON, a bluish light flooded the corner of a black-walled room. The Shadow was in his sanctum—a secret abode in the heart of New York City. Long-fingered hands moved above the surface of a polished table. Into view came newspaper clippings, mostly from tabloid journals. All told the same story.

After months of comparative quiet, following the smashing of Manhattan's racket rings, crime had again reared itself. It was crime with a sensational touch, although it hadn't brought big monetary results. The main feature was the chief criminal involved. He, at least, was picturesque; although his ways were foolhardy.

The newspapers called him the "Masked Playboy."

Heading a small band of marauders, their faces covered like his own, the Masked Playboy entered nightclubs and small hotels. In every case, he had forced someone to open the safe and hand over its contents.

Staring through a slitted bandanna handkerchief, holding a .38 revolver in his fist, the Masked Playboy had meant business. When he dropped his Harvard accent to suggest that victims "fork over," they invariably forked.

The Playboy's constant mistake had been his picking of the wrong places. True, he had chosen spots where the police were not around; but real money had been as absent as the law. In four of these surprise raids, the Masked Playboy had netted a total that scarcely exceeded a thousand dollars.

That made it seem a sure conclusion that he and his crew would soon be on the move again. The law wanted to know when and where. So did The Shadow. He, himself, had found out "when"—from the message that he had picked up in Chatham Square.

Through reports from agents, The Shadow hoped to find out where the Masked Playboy intended to appear.

WEEDING through the typewritten information, The Shadow added further data, obtained verbally from Burbank. His whispered laugh toned the darkness beyond the sphere of the shaded lamp. This present run of crime had become the talk of the underworld. As a result, many tips had leaked out.

By the weeding process, The Shadow found the tip that looked best. The clock on his table showed twenty-two minutes past eight. There was time, plenty of it, for The Shadow to be on hand at the place where he expected the Masked Playboy to arrive at nine o'clock.

The bluish light went out. From then, The Shadow's paths were covered until eighteen minutes before nine o'clock, when a tiny flashlight flickered along a low roof that wedged between two squatty, old-fashioned office buildings near Twenty-third Street.

The Shadow reached the window of a darkened office. He forced it, silently; crept through the office to a corner door. Opening that barrier, he stepped into another office, where he gleamed the flashlight on the front of an old safe.

The strongbox bore the lettering, in faded gilt: "NU-WAY LOAN COMPANY."

The safe was as antiquated as the office. Five minutes was all that The Shadow required to handle the tumblers, taking his time in the process. When he opened the safe door, The Shadow whispered another laugh.

There was nothing of value in the safe. All that it contained were stacks of old papers: bundles of closed accounts that had been stowed here in case of fire. That explained why the offices of the Nu-Way Loan Company lacked protection in the way of burglar alarms.

The Shadow closed the safe door, gave the dial a twist. He retired to the adjoining office, but went no farther. He was waiting on the hunch that he had found the right place: that the Masked Playboy, always a poor picker, would be running true to form.

There was another reason why The Shadow lingered. Behind this chain of profitless crime, he could discern a hidden purpose. So far, The Shadow had no clue to the underlying reason, but in assuming that one existed, he was far ahead of the law.

Tonight, The Shadow intended to learn the real motive that concerned the Masked Playboy. This would be the ideal spot to gain the required facts. The Shadow would be looking over crime from the inside.

Such measures, with The Shadow, usually brought complete success, unless an unexpected element entered.

This night was to provide the unexpected.

CHAPTER II
TOOL OF CRIME

NINE o'clock proved that The Shadow's surmise was correct. Promptly with that hour came sounds from the outer corridor that fronted the office of the Nu-Way Loan Company.

Crooks were arriving by the route that The Shadow expected them to use, the straight road to their goal. Since they were coming in through the front door, The Shadow's post in the adjoining office seemed well-chosen.

There was no reason for criminals to suspect trouble on these premises. Once they cracked the ancient safe, they would logically depart by the route which they had used to enter.

Logic, however, was due for a severe blow.

Scraping sounds ended at the front door. Flashlights gleamed as the door came open. Those rays were flicked along the floor; but against the outlines of the windows, The Shadow could see a cluster of entering invaders.

More than that, he noted the appearance of the man who entered first, with two others at his elbows. The leader's face was masked with a bandanna handkerchief; below his chin was the whiteness of a shirt front, with a black splotch that indicated a bow tie.

He was the Masked Playboy, attired in tuxedo.

The Playboy reached the safe, still accompanied by his two pals. Those three weren't all that composed the band; there were others, in the background, making about six in all. But evidently, the Masked Playboy depended chiefly upon the two who were at his elbows, for they stayed with him, engaging in whispers.

Audible words reached The Shadow.

"Go ahead—open it!" The whispered tone was rough; it didn't suit the description of the Playboy's accent. "You got gloves on, ain't you? Two to the right, four to the left—that's it."

The two men moved away, leaving the Masked Playboy alone. Against the window, The Shadow saw the glimmer of a revolver; but it wasn't in the Playboy's fist. One of the other men gripped the gun, keeping it as a threat.

Instantly, The Shadow saw the setup of the game.

The Masked Playboy wasn't the real leader of the outfit. The man who handled matters was the fellow with the gun. He was forcing the Playboy to go through with the job of opening the safe!

JUST why had the tuxedoed dupe become a tool of crime?

The Shadow answered his own question almost as soon as he had mentally asked it. He was watching the Playboy's laborious work with the dial. Although he had been told the combination, the dupe was finding the job difficult.

His unsteadiness proved that he was either drunk or doped; probably the latter.

The man with the gun had ceased to bother about the Playboy. He was at the telephone, dialing a number. This time, The Shadow heard no more than snatches of his words.

"Yeah, he's at it..." The tone became a mutter. "Sure. We're counting on the stoolies... It don't look like the grapevine worked too soon..."

The rest was lost. The phone conversation ended. Intruders waited until the Masked Playboy had finished with the combination. He was wavery clinging to the dial with one hand. That was when one crook shifted to a spot between The Shadow and the safe.

The shifter was carrying a squarish object. The Shadow learned its purpose when a gruff voice told the Playboy to look to the right. He swung slowly in obedience; there was a sudden flash of light that filled the whole room like a lightning streak.

In that moment, The Shadow saw the squarish object. It was a camera, trained on the masked features of the Playboy. The light was the illumination from a photographer's flashlight bulb.

There was nothing in that quick glimpse by which to identify the Masked Playboy, except his tuxedo. The bandanna covered his face; crouched as he was, his height was difficult to estimate. The crooks themselves recognized those facts. Their next move showed it.

Swinging the Masked Playboy about, they faced him toward the windows at the left. The man with the camera stepped between them. Rough hands snatched the Playboy's mask, tugged it down to the dupe's neck. Again, a flash bulb puffed.

This time, they caught a more than candid shot of the Masked Playboy, in his same attire, in front of the very safe shown in the first photo.

But this time, the Playboy was unmasked!

Chance had worked against The Shadow. The thugs had turned their tool away from his direction, to take that all-important picture of the fellow's face. They had begun to work in a hurry, for the camera job was finished. Again, the Masked Playboy had the bandanna across his face, for crooks had lifted it there.

The real leader of the crew had yanked the safe open. Inside went a box; The Shadow heard the sizzle of a fuse. The safe door clanged shut.

BEFORE The Shadow could ease forward to surprise the crooks with sudden challenge, a different sound intervened. It was the shrill of a police whistle from somewhere beyond the windows.

A crook pressed the light switch; others shoved the Masked Playboy to the nearest window.

In London, in Berlin, in Madrid—in all corners of the world—crooks lower their voices when they discuss The Shadow. In Paris, skulking creatures of the underworld still mumble tales of The Shadow's prowess—of that eerie night when an unknown being clad in black had battled, single-handed, against a horde of Apaches. In Moscow, there are men who talk about the time when The Shadow had fought himself free from the midst of a regiment of troops.

When crime becomes rampant, then does The Shadow strike! A living being of the darkness, he comes and goes unseen. Always, his objective is the stamping out of super crime.

Dying gangsters expire with the name of The Shadow upon their blood-flecked lips. Hordes of mobsmen have felt The Shadow's wrath.

A man garbed in black, his face unseen beneath the turned-down brim of a slouch hat—that is the spectral form that all evil men fear; that is The Shadow, whose exploits are recounted exclusively in the exciting pages of this magazine. Hundreds of thousands of readers find his experiences thrilling, encouraging, and instructive, and hold him as the leader of law-abiding citizens in the battle against crime.

A shout from below. Police had seen the masked face, the tuxedo shirt below it. Hands yanked the Playboy from the danger spot, just as police revolvers began to crackle. A mobster doused the light.

The whole frameup had been perfectly timed, even to the arrival of the police. That was what the man at the telephone had talked about, when he mentioned stoolies. The Shadow had learned facts on his own, through leaks in the underworld; but afterward, the crooks themselves had let the same word be broadcast.

They wanted the law to know that the Masked Playboy had been concerned in this crime, so that the photographs would prove a recognized episode. But in their cleverness, the crooks had taken on a problem.

They had to be out of the loan company's office in a hurry, not only before the safe was blown, but before the police reached the place.

There was only one route that offered them security. That path was through the adjoining office from which The Shadow watched.

Promptly, The Shadow stepped back into darkness. Bold, sudden attack was unneeded. Not that he preferred to supply lurking tactics; on the contrary, he would rather have driven in upon the crooks.

Worried by the thought of their own time fuse; trapped between The Shadow and the law, they would have shown themselves as frantic rats, quite as helpless as others that The Shadow had adeptly handled in the past.

The Shadow's reason for sudden retirement concerned the Masked Playboy.

The Shadow knew that he could not depend upon the dupe's cooperation; not even to the point where the groggy man would scramble for safety. He couldn't risk the chance of that victim's death. It was obvious that the crooks wanted to keep the Playboy alive, and get him out of danger. The Shadow decided to let them accomplish that much.

Close beside the window that led to the low roof, The Shadow heard the clatter of the connecting door. Mobsters were coming through, dragging the Masked Playboy with them. They didn't need their flashlights; they could make out the shape of the window. Thanks to the darkness of the office, they couldn't see The Shadow.

As The Shadow expected, three of the thugs went though the window first. The others started to shove the groggy playboy to the men outside. Some seemed jittery, but the growl of their leader steadied them. He was telling them that there was another minute for the fuse; that the blast couldn't reach this room, anyway.

As for the cops, they were still trying to break into the building, as muffled crashes proved.

THE Masked Playboy lay half across the sill when The Shadow acted. His move was a swoop from blackness, as powerful as it was unexpected. His hand thrust in unseen, to arrest the shoves that the crooks gave. His fingers clamped the dark cloth of the Playboy's attire.

The Shadow's other hand held an automatic. He didn't release the gun. He simply hooked his arm beneath the Playboy's body. Coming up from his crouch, The Shadow voiced a taunting shivery laugh squarely in the ears of the men that flanked him.

With that burst of startling mirth, he whipped the Playboy from the rigid hands of the mobbies. With a hard back-fling, he launched his burden toward the corner behind him. That shove was the sort that could have damaged the human who took it, if it hadn't been for the retarding grip of The Shadow's free hand.

Crooks didn't see that part of it. One man— their leader—jabbed a flashlight. It showed only The Shadow, one hand behind him, the other fist thrusting forward. That leading hand was gloved, and it gripped a big-muzzled gun.

Thugs surged. A blast mouthed from the .45, dropping the first attacker to reach The Shadow. From the recoil, The Shadow made a cross-slash that thwacked the flashlight from the fist of the man who held it.

In darkness, he was among his foemen, slugging for their heads, while the crooks outside the window huddled helpless, unable to pick The Shadow in the darkness.

With enemies sprawled about him, The Shadow swung for the window, his mocking laugh telling the outer trio that their turn was next. Shakily, they arose to flee; then, as one, they took a head-long sprawl.

The blast that produced that result was not from The Shadow's gun. It came from the next office—a titanic burst when the safe blew open. That charge was more powerful than intended. It shattered windows; shook the building.

Amid the rattle of loosened brick and spattered chunks of walls and ceilings, all fighters were flattened, The Shadow among them!

CHAPTER III
TRIPLE BATTLE

THE outside mobbies were the first to recuperate from the explosion's shock. Regaining their footing, they stared at the window, where a ghostlike wraith was creeping forth.

The shape wasn't The Shadow. It was white. As the crooks eyed the phenomenon, they saw that it was smoke trailing from a cloud of fumes that had poured through from the next office.

Partly startled by the sight, the thugs remembered The Shadow's weird laugh. They decided upon a parley before they invaded the battleground. That delay was fortunate. If crooks had attacked at that moment, it would have gone badly with The Shadow.

The cloaked fighter was rising from the floor, too jolted to recognize fully his surroundings. A portion of the window frame had broken; in its fall, the chunk of wood had found The Shadow's head. He was as groggy as the thugs that he had slugged.

Right then, he couldn't have combated invaders; but despite the smoke, he was gaining some return of his ability. The half minute that the crooks allowed him was enough. When they suddenly poked guns and flashlights in from the window, The Shadow sensed the menace.

He still had his gun, but didn't wait to raise it. He wheeled for a corner, using the smoke as cover. Instinctively, he reversed his course amid the fumes. Guns stabbed wide when his foemen sought to follow his course with bullets.

Through The Shadow's returning senses thrummed thoughts of the Masked Playboy.

He remembered that he had flung the dupe to safety, but couldn't recall the direction, except that it was toward a corner. He wanted to get to that spot and make sure that the man was safe, then spring a surprise thrust on the crooks.

Ordinarily, that would have been easy for The Shadow. In his present condition, the task went awry.

The corner that The Shadow reached was the one leading into the wrecked office. Perhaps it was the thickness of the smoke that invited him in that direction; for he was depending chiefly upon the instinct to take cover.

Whatever the cause, the result came when The Shadow reached the wall and took a roundabout swing to brace himself there.

He fired as he went backward; the gun's recoil sent him off balance. There wasn't a wall to stop him. He went sprawling through the blasted doorway, to land amid the wreckage near the ruined safe.

THE SHADOW'S one wide shot proved that he wasn't in form. It not only missed the crooks at the window; the spurt also betrayed where The Shadow was.

Again, guns began to tongue through the smoke. First shots were high; but later ones scored the floor at the doorway.

The Shadow wasn't present to receive the final barrage. He was crawling clear of the doorway, blindly seeking new cover along the wall within the loan office. Tortured by the smoke, he was forced to rest with his face muffled in the folds of his cloak sleeve.

Two figures arose in the thinner smoke of the next office. One was the leader of the invading crooks. He had received a hard blow from The Shadow's gun; so had the thug who arose with him. The two stooped above a third: the hoodlum who had taken The Shadow's bullet.

That pal wasn't worth carrying away.

Mobsters at the window reached through to help the rising pair. The leader snarled, gave a look about. He saw a figure crawling toward him on hands and knees. Shaking free from his helpers, he pounced upon the Masked Playboy.

Again, crime's tool was in the hands of his persecutors; and with their prisoner, crooks were carrying away the battered camera that contained their precious photographs.

Sounds of the scramble through the window roused The Shadow. Though in the next office, he was aware what had occurred. He still had time to overtake the mobsters and their dupe. On his feet, he started for the connecting door.

Three men swept in from the hallway. They roared for surrender as they fell upon The Shadow. In the smoky darkness, they thought they had bagged the Masked Playboy. These new invaders were the first members of the police headquarters squad that had come here on advice from stool pigeons.

In the next dozen seconds, The Shadow added to the false reputation that the Masked Playboy had acquired.

Three against one, the detectives were overconfident, each anxious to claim credit for the capture of a badly wanted criminal. Their lack of concerted action gave The Shadow a split-second opportunity to handle them.

He flung the first attacker aside; tripping over the unhinged safe door, the dick took a long tumble. The second man made a grapple and The Shadow closed with him, for it enabled him to sidestep the third.

A moment later, two bodies were lunging, bowling the third man ahead of them. When the pair spilled, they floored the free detective beneath them, letting him take the full weight of the fall. The Shadow broke the hold of his grappling opponent, landed a hard punch that sent him rolling.

Neither of the other two detectives were on their feet when The Shadow dashed away to take the route across the roof.

THOUGH he hadn't much time to spare, The

Shadow detoured when he reached the roof. He sprang to the back edge, where he hissed a quick call to the alleyway below. Men heard it; they were agents of The Shadow. In a trice, they understood.

Dashing to the rear of the next building, they were there when mobsters came out bringing The Masked Playboy. Though The Shadow's agents didn't know the innocent part that the Playboy had acted, they recognized that he was the man The Shadow wanted.

Falling upon the startled crooks, they wrested the tuxedoed man from them and lurched him toward a waiting cab.

It was timely work, aided by the fact that the crooks were still disorganized. Before guns could bark, the taxi was starting for the corner, while The Shadow's agents dived for cover, from which to wage combat.

Wild shots didn't halt the cab. It was gone, with its passenger slumped upon the floor where he had been none too gently placed.

Maddened crooks hoped to massacre The Shadow's two agents. Guns were speaking from doorways and alleys, with the odds much in favor of the criminal crew. But The Shadow's agents held their ground, knowing that aid was due.

It came. The Shadow had come down through the building. His big guns began to boom; crooks recognized the marksman. They scattered, their flight spurred by the tone of a gibing laugh that seemed to echo from every wall about them.

The Shadow headed for the corner, to see how the cab had made out. There was a chance that the police might have blocked its flight.

Such was actually the case. Around another corner, the cab was halted, while its driver argued with a pair of officers. He had just about convinced them that the cab was empty, when a stir occurred within the taxi itself.

A cop yanked open the door, to see the Masked Playboy rising from the floor. His bandanna handkerchief was still across his eyes; sensing that he was wanted, he was keeping it there. But numbed wits hadn't calculated further. Blindly, he was shoving himself into the hands of the law.

The taxi driver was one of The Shadow's agents. He recognized his passenger's plight; knew that he could handle the groggy fellow later. He decided to make a spurt, but by the time he pressed the accelerator the Playboy was rolling to the sidewalk, wrestling with the policemen.

THE cab was away without its passenger. Shots suddenly began to whistle about the driver's head. Where they came from, he couldn't guess; but it was his cue to keep on going and come back around the block.

The officers heard the shots, and saw their origin. Guns were spurting from a passage between two old houses; with the cab in flight, the crooks aimed for the police.

Forgetting their prisoner, the officers dived for cover of their own. By the time they had reached it, crooks were piling the Masked Playboy into an old sedan.

As luck had it, the taxi episode had taken place within fifty feet of the spot where mobsters had left their car parked for the getaway.

This time, the officers supplied the shots that followed a fleeing vehicle; but they opened fire from cover, and their aim was bad. From back at the next corner came the only intervention that could have halted the sedan's escape. The Shadow had arrived there; he was beginning long-range fire for the sedan's gas tank.

The officers saw the new marksman vaguely. Deciding that he was an enemy, they returned his fire. This time, the cops were close. The Shadow was forced to wheel for cover, his chance to halt the sedan ended.

The end of The Shadow's fire brought an exultant shout from the policemen. They dashed toward the corner, expecting to find a sprawled victim. As they came, they saw the same taxi that had eluded them a short while before.

Blackness detached itself from a wall. A living shape, it reached the slowing cab, to spring aboard. Stopping their run, the officers fired; but their bullets peppered nothing but the corner of the building. The taxi was away again, this time with a different passenger.

Riding from the scene, The Shadow delivered a grim mirthless laugh. In triple battle, the issue could only have been decided by luck; and the breaks had gone against him. Crooks had won the point they wanted: escape, with the Masked Playboy still in their clutches.

The dupe was safe, however, for he was useful to their game. It was the game itself that concerned The Shadow, more than the helpless man who had participated in it.

Some hand of crime lay hidden behind tonight's events. That schemer was the master foe whose plans The Shadow intended to learn, and, later, frustrate!

CHAPTER IV
CROOKS TALK TERMS

THE next morning, two men entered a huge office building near Wall Street. They rode to the fifty-fifth floor, which was entirely occupied by the offices of Eastern Refineries, Incorporated. When they stopped at the anteroom desk, one of the men inquired for Mr. Martin Meriden.

The girl at the desk looked doubtful.

As treasurer of Eastern Refineries, Martin Meriden seldom had visitors that the girl had never seen. Eastern Refinery, it happened, was one of several subsidiary concerns all controlled by World Oil interests.

These men certainly weren't from World Oil. Nor did their appearance assure the girl that Mr. Meriden would want to see them.

One man was short and barely the average weight for his height. He looked wiry, though, and pugnacious. His face was sallow, his lower lip, had a thrust that the girl didn't like. His eyes, too, were ugly; they had a way of fixing themselves, then opening wider, in a glare.

The other man was tall, almost lanky; his long face had a wise, close-mouthed expression. His eyes didn't glare; they just set themselves half shut and stayed that way, as though hiding what lay behind them.

It was the short man who asked for Meriden; to the query the girl inquired if he had a card. He gave her one which seemed important enough to take in to Mr. Meriden. The card read:

J. B. CORSTON
Manager
Interstate Service Stations

When the girl had left the desk, the short man's lower lip formed a grin, while his upper lip raised, displaying stained, misshapen teeth. He turned to the tall man beside him.

"I'm J. B. Corston," he undertoned. "Got it? Just forget that I'm Pinkey Findlen. And forget that you're Slick Thurley."

"Easy enough, J. B.," replied Thurley, "I'm Bill Quaine, from headquarters. I've sprung that gag often enough."

Martin Meriden didn't like the looks of his visitors any more than the girl had. From behind his desk, the portly, baldish treasurer of Eastern Refineries was prompt to express his opinions regarding the visit of J. B. Corston.

"This is our first interview, Mr. Corston," spoke Meriden, testily. "You can take it for granted that it will be our last."

"That's sure enough," returned Pinkey, in a raspy tone. "After you've bought the Interstate Service Stations, I won't have to see you anymore."

"But I don't intend to buy!" Meriden pounded the desk with his pudgy fist. "I told you that in my letter. Your chain of service stations exists only on paper. It is worth nothing to us!"

Pinkey leaned back in his chair; he tucked his thumbs in the armholes of his vest, as he turned his head toward Slick, with the comment.

"You talk to him, Quaine."

SLICK produced an envelope from his pocket. He drew out some clippings, slid them across to Meriden. They were old newspaper accounts relating the exploits of Detective William Quaine, ace of the racket investigation squad.

Quaine's photograph was printed also; and—as Slick had often privately expressed it—the picture might as well have been Slick's own. Though he and Quaine might have been distinguished if together, separately, either could pass for the other.

It happened, too, that they had never made the test of meeting face to face. If there was one man that Slick dodged consistently, that fellow was Bill Quaine.

Meriden took it for granted that Slick was Quaine; but he couldn't see any connection between that fact and the proposed purchase of the Interstate Service Stations.

The treasurer of Eastern Refineries was soon to be enlightened. Pinkey Findlen observed that Meriden had fallen for the first step in the game. Pinkey spoke to Slick Thurley:

"Show Mr. Meriden those other clippings, Quaine."

"Certainly, J. B.," returned Slick, in a brisk tone that suited his false part. "Look these over, Meriden. They tell about a crook called the Masked Playboy."

Meriden was nodding as he eyed the recent clippings. Still, he couldn't understand the link, until Pinkey opened a large envelope and shoved two photographs across the desk.

They were the pictures snapped the night before, during the phony crime at the office of the Nu-Way Loan Company. The first that Meriden saw was the picture wherein the Playboy was masked. He laid that photo aside; looked at the one below it. He saw a pale strained face with worried eyes. He recognized those features.

Martin Meriden sank deep in his chair. His lips took on a fishlike gape.

"Reggie!" gasped Meriden. "My—my own son Reggie! And I—I thought he had—"

"You thought he'd been behaving himself," sneered Pinkey. "But he hadn't! You gave him cash for a trip to Europe, but you didn't know he blew it and had to make it up, somehow."

"But Reggie is sailing—at noon—today—"

"You mean he *will* be sailing, if you come through with the deal on those service stations."

A new expression showed in Meridian's eyes. His tone was indignant when he uttered:

"This is blackmail!"

"That's what they call it," agreed Pinkey. "Or a shakedown. It's all the same in this case. You come through, Meriden, or the kid does a stretch in Sing Sing!"

MERIDEN'S hands were fidgeting on the desk. Pinky liked the sign. He'd seen others act that way before. Pinkey's rasp became less noticeable. He was trying smooth encouragements.

"You're not the first guy," he said to Meriden. "Others were up against the same proposition. They came through. Quaine, here, will tell you it's the easiest way."

Meriden looked toward Slick; he saw the fake detective reach for the incriminating photographs. From now on, apparently, the pretended Bill Quaine was to keep the evidence.

"So you've turned crook," accused Meriden. "That means you're not to be trusted, Quaine, any more than this man"—Meriden thumbed toward Pinkey—"who appears to be your boss."

Slick's only reply was a sarcastic smile.

"How do I know that you won't blackmail me further?" demanded Meriden, hoarsely. "This could go on and on—"

"Only it won't," interposed Slick. "You and I are in the same boat, Meriden. You've got to cover up on this deal that you make with J. B. here. I've got to cover up that I was in on it. One shakedown to one guy is all we can chance."

Slick looked to Pinkey for corroboration. The big shot gave a nod.

"That's the way it stands," assured Pinkey. "But if you don't come through, Meriden, Quaine will turn in these pictures to headquarters and make himself a hero again.

"He'll be the guy who outsmarted the Masked Playboy, by figuring where he was due and placing a camera there. Quaine will identify your son Reggie, and he'll also deny that he tried this shakedown."

Meriden saw the logic. He knew that the false Quaine could explain this visit by saying that he came to ask questions regarding Reggie's identity. As for Pinkey, he would back anything that the false Quaine said. Believing Slick to be a real detective and Pinkey to be a bona fide business-man named J. B. Corston, Meriden could find no loophole. He looked dazed; but he managed to gather his wits and ask one important question.

"What about my son?" queried Meriden. "Where is he?"

"On the boat," returned Pinkey. "Getting some sleep after a bad night. The bulls nearly nabbed him, after that job. Why don't you call him, Meriden? They've got a telephone service to that ship. Make sure that he's all right."

MERIDEN made the call. He controlled his tone while he talked to his sleepy-voiced son, and made no remarks that Reggie could have interpreted as knowledge of last night's episode. From that conversation Meriden convinced himself that Reggie was not in the clutch of crooks.

"Satisfied?" queried Pinkey, when the call was ended. "You ought to be. Why should we be worried? We don't have to keep our mitts on the kid. That packet doesn't sail till noon. Bill Quaine, here, has still got two hours to show up with a squad and yank Reggie off the boat."

Meriden nodded. His lips were firmly pressed. Pinkey produced an agreement of sale, laid it on the desk.

"The price for Interstate Service Stations," he announced, "is two hundred and fifty grand."

"You mean"—Meriden was amazed—"a quarter million?"

"Why not?" returned Pinkey. "Your company has got plenty of dough. You can make this look like a swell buy! Use the phony reports that I sent you."

Meriden winced; mechanically, he reached for his pen. He applied his signature to the agreement. Pinky reminded him that a check would be in order. Meriden wrote one for fifty thousand dollars, stating that he would have to make the payments in installments.

"Write out the rest of them," ordered Pinkey. "Date them ahead, a month apart. We know you won't welsh on them. We've got the goods on you, now, Meriden, along with your son Reggie."

Meriden made out the remaining checks; he passed them weakly across the desk. Pinkey arose, beckoned to Slick. Together, the crooks went out toward the elevators. At the information desk, Pinkey spoke to the girl.

"Better look in on the boss, sister," remarked Pinkey. "He wasn't feeling so good when we left him. Maybe he's feeling sort of sick!"

Slick was waiting at the opened door of an elevator. Pinkey stepped in with him. As the door clanged shut, the girl at the desk heard the finish of two ugly chuckles that came from the lips of Meriden's visitors.

Two crooks were mutually agreed on the proposition that crime, when properly framed, could pay in plenty.

CHAPTER V
LINKS TO CRIME

IN all the reports of the Masked Playboy's final crime, there was no inkling of the real purpose. The public, like the law, assumed that the tuxedoed criminal had merely led his crew in another profit-less expedition—this time with such bad results that the Playboy might well be tired of his crooked business.

One badly wounded thug had tried to slow the police, and had received more bullets. That thug was dead; hence, he couldn't talk. It seemed plain, though, that something had gone wrong before the police arrived. That made the law decide that rival crooks had tried to muscle into the Playboy's ill-timed game.

There were reports of flashes that had been seen from the windows of the loan office prior to the blasting of the safe. Those were attributed to tests with fuses, before the charge was set.

No investigators guessed that flashbulbs had been used for photographs; that the whole episode of the Masked Playboy was a frameup. That knowledge belonged in one lone personage, who had been an eyewitness; namely The Shadow.

From his personal observation, The Shadow knew that blackmail was the motive behind the game. To prove that case was a more difficult proposition.

The identity of the Masked Playboy was a riddle. The Shadow correctly sized him as a dupe; probably a young man of good social status, fallen in with bad companions. That helped little. There were probably a few thousand such young men in New York. Any one of them might be eligible for the part of the Playboy.

Similarly, it was a hazy problem to identify the crook who had actually led the invading crew.

The Shadow classed him as a small-time mobleader; and the underworld was full of such ugly characters. Recently, New York had undergone a cleanup, wherein a special prosecutor had smashed a widespread racket ring. Lots of little fish had slipped through the mesh, but they were big enough to be leaders of hoodlum crews.

Last came the mobbies themselves. There, again, The Shadow drew a blank.

The actual thugs had been recruited from here and there, through an endless chain wherein each knew only a few others and none was acquainted with the persons higher up.

The Shadow had personal knowledge of that situation, for he had posed as one who was "in the know." That was how he had managed to receive the hand-stamped message down at Chatham Square.

The man who had passed the match pack to The Shadow was merely a messenger, slipping partial information to anyone who gave him the password. By mentioning a "hand," The Shadow had become one of the recipients.

From that incident, however, The Shadow gained a link with the past. He knew the meaning of the crudely stamped hand symbol. It went back to conditions that had existed many months ago, during the clean-up of the so-called "racket ring."

There hadn't been a single racket ring; there had been several. All had learned the advantages of cooperation, shaking money from prosperous businesses. New York had been a land of plenty for the racketeers. Expecting trouble from the law, they had avoided strife among themselves.

In fact, their organizations had reached an interlocking stage, even to the point where they had "fixers" and other peacemakers, who had kept everybody satisfied and happy. Eventually perhaps, gang wars would have come; but the law hadn't let it get that far.

Rackets had been shattered right and left, with The Shadow and his agents playing an active but hidden part in the cleanup.

Prominent racketeers had been brought to trial; to be rapidly convicted and sentenced. The public thought that those men had been the brains of the racket ring. That was true; but only in part.

For every big shot who had found the interior of a prison cell, there had been three or four who had fled from New York before crime's citadel crumbled.

The Shadow had not forgotten those who had vanished.

SEATED in the corner of his sanctum, The Shadow was at work beneath the bluish light. From a stack of files he drew one that was stamped with an appropriate symbol: human hand, with extended thumb and fingers.

This was a casebook dealing with one group of racketeers who had teamed together, with double result. Not only had they made their profit while rackets were going strong; every member of the group had cleared New York before the cleanup.

Where they were, what each was doing, were matters that concerned The Shadow. That was why he laid a stack of recent reports close at hand, where he could refer to data as required.

Upon a sheet of paper, The Shadow inscribed five names:

"Thumb" Gaudrey
"Pointer" Trame
"Long Steve" Bydle
"Ring" Brescott
"Pinkey" Findlen

One by one, The Shadow checked the list. Gaudrey was in Bermuda posing as a retired business magnate seeking a rest cure. Trame had headed for Havana to gamble some of his ill-gotten gains at the casino. Bydle had actually gone into business, in Chicago.

Brescott had made a trip to California, probably to test some racketeering enterprise; but without result. Latest reports stated that he would soon be coming East.

One man alone was unaccounted for. He was Pinkey Findlen, the last crook on the list.

The Shadow laid the sheet aside. He began to visualize recent crime in terms of Pinkey Findlen. It was plain that the pack had become lone wolves; that each was dangerous in his own right. Of the five, Pinkey was the first to start an individual enterprise. Therefore, The Shadow had to deal with him alone.

Pinkey knew rackets, thoroughly. Therefore, he certainly recognized that the usual sort of racket would be hopeless in New York, at present. Rackets depended upon numerous small collections from many harassed businessmen. They required too many collectors, all weak links in the chain.

So Pinkey had simply reversed the procedure. Instead of building up many small profits, he was working to gain a few large sums. That meant contacts that Pinkey could handle personally, with enough precautions to prevent leaks.

He needed his strongarm men; but he wasn't using them as collectors. Their job was to frame dupes like the Masked Playboy, thus giving Pinkey opportunity for big-time blackmail on a high pressure basis.

UPON the table came clippings: past reports of the Masked Playboy. The Shadow's laugh was audible beyond the bluish light. He was studying the past crimes attributed to the Playboy. They had simply been buildups to the final one.

Whether the Playboy had been shoved into those crimes, or whether someone had impersonated him, did not matter to The Shadow. He was interested in the crimes themselves; and among the list of pitiful raids, he saw one that stood out strongly.

That robbery had been committed at a place called the Bubble Club. The Masked Playboy had marched in upon Claude Ondrey, owner of the nightclub trapping him in his own office. Ondrey had passed over some cash; he provided the police with an elaborate report of the episode.

From The Shadow's viewpoint, Ondrey had talked too much. That happened to be a habit with Claude Ondrey.

When the police had cracked the nightclub racket, during the big cleanup, Ondrey had been one of the most talkative informants. As a victim of the racket, he had paid many visits to the special prosecutor's office.

The Shadow had records of Ondrey's testimony. Oddly, with all his talk, Ondrey had provided nothing new. He simply corroborated statements that other victims had given before him. That marked Ondrey for what he was.

The Shadow had him labeled as a man leagued with crooks. For everything that Ondrey told the prosecutor, he brought back valuable facts for the big shots who ruled him.

Claude Ondrey could be blamed for the fact that five big men of crime had left New York before the prosecutor was ready to order their arrests. The law had missed that fact, but The Shadow hadn't.

From the past, The Shadow had his key to the present. Pinkey Findlen, back in New York, was employing the human tools that he had used before. Claude Ondrey was one of them; and his Bubble Club was also valuable. It was one place that Pinkey Findlen could use as a headquarters, when he wanted.

But Pinkey hadn't been there the night when the Masked Playboy had visited the Bubble Club. That was just the old game over again. It had strengthened Ondrey's position with the law, enabling him to retain his pose as a victim of crime, instead of a man leagued with crooks.

THE SHADOW clicked off the sanctum light. His whispered laugh brought shuddering echoes from walls that were invisible in the pitch-darkness. Those echoes faded. The Shadow had left the sanctum. But he still chose paths of blackness.

Evening had come to Manhattan. In the darkness of narrow side streets, The Shadow was no more than a gliding shape as he chose a route to his waiting limousine, a few blocks away. Stepping into the big car, The Shadow dropped his hat and cloak.

A streetlamp showed his face at the window. No longer was The Shadow disguised as a droopy-faced panhandler. His features were hawklike; impassive and distinguished. He was immaculately attired in evening clothes.

The order that The Shadow gave the chauffeur was spoken in a calm but lazy tone—that of a man who seemed bored with life and was looking for some diversion:

"Bubble Club, Stanley!"

CHAPTER VI
AT THE BUBBLE CLUB

THE Bubble Club was located on a side street not far from Times Square. It rated high among nightclubs, and many well-known persons chose it as their favorite bright spot. Drinks and meals were reasonably priced, and no other nitery provided a better-balanced floor show.

In fact, every evening was a triumph for Claude Ondrey, who was always on hand to greet his patrons. Ondrey was portly and genial, with a bald head that kept bowing as he walked from table to table. His handshake, though, was flabby, and his smile a sham. Ondrey didn't make his real money from the customers who thronged the Bubble Club.

That was apparent on this present evening, when Ondrey finished his rounds and returned to his fancy office at a back corner of the club.

Three men were seated in the office. One was Pinkey Findlen, who wore a hard grin on his lippy, sallow face. The second was Slick Thurley, maintaining his usual wise pose, in constant imitation of Detective Bill Quaine.

The third arrival was a chunky block-faced man, who looked presentable despite the squinty way he shifted his eyes and the side-mouthed manner in which he grinned. He was "Bugs" Hopton, leader of Pinkey's strongarm crew.

Ondrey was pleased to see his visitors. From his coat pocket, the nightclub owner brought a notebook that he handed to Pinkey. While the big-shot studied red-ink figures, Ondrey spoke an explanation.

"The place is packed," he said, "but it can't make money. Not at the prices we give them. If I could put on a cover charge, we'd break even."

"Forget it!" snapped Pinkey. He pulled a roll of bills from his pocket and counted off the required amount. "This clears you, Ondrey. Keep running things the way you have. I don't want you to run no clip joint. That brings squawks."

"But some of the best places have cover charges—"

"So what? That makes this joint better than them, don't it? Better than the best; that's the way I want it. I'm willing to pay for a front that every-body falls for. When you spend dough that way, it ain't wasted."

Pinkey gestured Ondrey to a chair. Then:

"We're sitting pretty, Ondrey," declared the big-shot. "So pretty that we're going to tell you all about it. We've finished three jobs out of four; and when that one goes across, we'll have a million bucks in the bag!"

Settling back in his chair, Pinkey began to recount the victories to date.

"FIRST was Howard Milay," Pinkey declared. "General manager of Sphere Shipping. He was a cinch, because he had a past that he was trying to forget. We dug up the dirt; he had to come through.

"So he let one of his boats go to the bottom, when we fixed it for him. Only an old tub that ought to have sunk anyway. It was loaded with a cargo of junk metal, and that helped the dive. That cargo"—Pinkey chuckled—"was on the books as supplies worth three hundred grand. Milay collected the insurance dough and passed it to us."

Ondrey knew of the case, but hadn't heard all the details. His shammy smile took on a genuine appearance.

"Next was John Thorry," continued Pinky. "He was the president of a company called Western Oil Fields. He won't forget that trip he made to New York. We framed him a couple of ways, and let him crawl out by buying some punk oil wells. He'd been lucky at picking good ones, so he can laugh off some lemons. Anyway, that brought the total up to half a million."

"And after that"—the interruption came from Bugs Hopton, who spoke with raspy tone—"the going got tough!"

Pinkey swung about angrily in his chair. "Whatta you mean by 'tough'?"

"I mean last night," retorted Bugs. "You said it would be soft, framing young Meriden. But it wasn't—not with The Shadow barging in on us."

"Forget The Shadow!" scoffed Pinkey. "He got left behind, didn't he? And today, Slick and me put the deal through with the kid's old man. That's one thing The Shadow ain't wise to."

Bugs didn't continue the argument. He helped himself to an expensive cigar from a box on Ondrey's desk. Scratching a match on the mahogany, he lighted the cigar and puffed it in silence.

"The next job is soft," assured Pinkey. "We've already put through a lot of forged checks and notes with World Oil interests. There's only one guy who can spot that phony stuff. He's Lewis Bron, the auditor. He'll smell a rat as soon as he goes over the books.

"What we're going to do is get to Bron before he sees the books. When we've done that, he'll see things the same way we do. Once the books have his O.K., there'll be no more worry."

No one asked Pinkey how he intended to handle Bron. The big-shot's word was good enough for the listeners. Even Bugs had no objection. He knew that Pinkey always changed his game when occasion required. There wouldn't be another tangle like the Masked Playboy proposition.

IT was Ondrey who voiced the main thought that all the others held.

"Over a million bucks," said the nightclub owner, in an eager tone. "You get half of it, Pinkey, and we three divvy the rest. Fair enough."

"That's only half the story," inserted Pinkey. "This ain't just a million dollar proposition. I'm going to double it, before I've finished."

Eyes popped, including those of Bugs Hopton. That was unusual; it took plenty to surprise the chunky mobleader.

"Here's the lay," confided Pinkey. "All these companies we've nicked are owned by one outfit, and that's the World Oil interests. They call those companies subsidiaries; but that's just a business term. Big business is just a racket anyway, from my way of looking at it.

"Western Oil Fields pumps the oil. Sphere Shipping runs the boats that bring it here. Eastern Refineries peddles the gasoline to the public. The gravy all goes to World Oil, because it owns the rest of them.

"The biggest guy in the whole game is Giles Jondran, because he's the president of World Oil. It's the head of what they call a fifty-million-dollar corporation; and he's worth about ten million on his own. So when we've finished with the rest of them, we'll work on old Jondran himself.

"We'll tell him that we've snagged a million, and how we got it. We'll say to him: 'All right, old buzzard, you're going to double the ante!' And if he don't, we'll spill the whole works. It won't be us that'll take the rap. It will be guys like Milay, Thorry, and Meriden, along with this auditor Bron—"

A buzzer interrupted. It meant a house call for Ondrey. Pinkey waited while the nightclub owner spoke over the telephone. Ondrey was brief; when he hung up the receiver, he turned promptly to Pinkey.

"There is a gentleman who wants to see me," explained Ondrey. "He wants to arrange a banquet; and he's the sort of customer that I ought to bring in here. His name is Lamont Cranston."

"You mean the guy that pals around with the police commissioner?" queried Pinkey. "Say—

that's neat! You're right, Ondrey: he's one guy that oughtn't to be kept waiting. Come on you lugs"—Pinkey turned to his other companions—"we're moving out—"

SLICK was nearest to the wall behind Ondrey's desk. He pressed the edge of a panel; the woodwork slid apart to reveal a tiny elevator. The three men entered it; Slick was about to close the secret door when Pinkey stopped him.

"Listen, Ondrey," remarked Pinkey, "we're going back to the hideout. I got a phone there, but there's some calls I'd rather make from here—"

"You mean to Maude Revelle?"

"Yeah. So you call her for me. Tell her I'll meet her at the usual place an hour from now. That'll give you time to talk to this Cranston guy, first."

Ondrey nodded. Mention of Cranston reminded him that he didn't want to keep the visitor waiting. He reached for the telephone, gave the order to usher Mr. Cranston into the office. While Ondrey was doing that, Slick closed the elevator door.

Ondrey prided himself on that secret elevator. It was slow in operation, because it was designed for silence. There wasn't the slightest rumble from the hidden shaft; nor even the vibration of a cable as the elevator made its ascent.

Ondrey stepped to the office door. He opened it to see Cranston coming through the passage from the nightclub.

A few moments later, Ondrey was bowing a hawk-faced visitor to a seat in front of the desk. Reaching into a drawer, the nightclub owner brought out a box of very special cigars, finer even than the brand that Bugs liked to smoke.

It was while Ondrey was bent above the desk drawer that Cranston's ears caught a distant sound, so slight that Ondrey did not notice it. That noise was the muffled *clang* of an elevator door, closing, somewhere, a few floors above.

With the sound, Cranston's eyes went instinctively to the paneled wall behind Ondrey. There, his keen eyes picked a vertical line in the ornament woodwork. Gauging sight with sound, Cranston had the answer. He knew that Ondrey had talked with at least one visitor tonight.

More than that, Lamont Cranston could name the man who had departed. He was sure that Ondrey's principal visitor had been the lone-wolf racketeer, Pinkey Findlen.

For behind the masklike countenance of the supposed Lamont Cranston lay the brain of The Shadow!

CHAPTER VII
THE MEETING PLACE

IT required only ten minutes for Lamont

Cranston to make arrangements for a banquet to be held at the Bubble Club. He named the date as ten days in the future; and Claude Ondrey was more than pleased to learn that Cranston intended to invite the police commissioner to the affair.

That was the sort of news that Ondrey knew would go over well with Pinkey Findlen.

However, Ondrey's beaming smile began to fade, when Cranston continued the discussion further. For some reason he wanted to settle many matters, including such details as the banquet menu. Thus he prolonged his interview with Ondrey until nearly half an hour had passed.

During the first ten minutes, The Shadow sensed that Ondrey had something on his mind. He foresaw that subtle stalling tactics might reveal more; and the system worked.

Toward the end of the half hour, Ondrey's fingers were itching to get at the telephone; and his constant glances in that direction flashed the fact that he had an important call to make.

Ondrey was at last relieved to see Cranston arise, ready for a leisurely departure. Ondrey bowed the visitor out to the nightclub; then, after a quick handshake, the portly man hurried back to the office.

Ondrey would have been startled had he taken time to look over his own shoulder.

Idly, Cranston turned about, as if he had forgotten something in the office. His easy action attracted no attention from the waiters. But once he was within the little passage leading to the office, Cranston disappeared.

In fact, as he stopped within a darkened corner of the passage, he seemed to draw blackness all about him.

That phenomenon was explained by the fact that The Shadow had planted his cloak and hat in that particular corner. He had entered the nightclub by a side door, carrying the garments over his arm. Starting first for Ondrey's office, he had left his garb in that convenient spot; then had stepped into the nightclub to find someone who would announce his arrival to Ondrey.

CLOAKED in black, The Shadow made quick strides to the office. The door was unlocked, as he expected, for Ondrey hadn't wasted time in getting to the telephone. The nightclub owner had just managed to get his number, when The Shadow peered in upon him.

Through the crack of the door, The Shadow could see Ondrey at the desk; and every word that the man uttered was plain.

"Hello... That you, Maude?" Ondrey was smiling when he recognized the voice. "Yes, this is Ondrey... Yes, Pinkey was here; but he didn't have time to call you... Yes. He'll meet you. At the usual place..."

There must have been a flow of talk across the wire, for Ondrey fidgeted for the next two minutes. At moments, he opened his mouth as if to say something; but he couldn't manage to insert a word. When his chance finally came, Ondrey spoke pleadingly.

"Don't be angry, Maude," he insisted. "It was actually my fault that you weren't called sooner... I know you don't like The Hayrick, but it's one of the few places where Pinkey can go...

"Here? Certainly he comes here; but he always stays in the office... No, he never goes into the nightclub... No, it wouldn't be safe. At least, that's what he says. Pinkey's supposed to be on the lam...

"You'll meet him? That's good! But you'd better hurry... Yes, he'll be at The Hayrick within the next half hour..."

The call finished, Ondrey mopped his forehead, shaking his head as if in testimony that the ways of women baffled him. He came out to the nightclub proper. Ondrey saw no sign of The Shadow in the passage.

The cloaked intruder had stepped to that blackened corner where he had formerly placed his cloak and hat.

Moving into Ondrey's office, The Shadow, began a rapid search of the desk. He found nothing in the way of evidence that linked Ondrey with Pinkey Findlen.

In fact, The Shadow wasn't at all certain that Ondrey knew the details of Pinkey's present racket. The only way to settle that point would be to accost Ondrey and question him. But with the chances to the contrary, it was preferable to leave Ondrey alone, particularly because he might prove useful later.

Moreover, The Shadow saw an excellent chance to meet Pinkey himself, when the racketeer reached The Hayrick. Mention of the place by name was all that The Shadow had needed. The Hayrick was well-known as a nightclub in Greenwich Village.

FINISHING his short search of Ondrey's desk, The Shadow tried the paneled wall. He found the hidden catch, opened the panel and looked into the elevator shaft. There he saw a switch and pressed it to bring the car downward.

The elevator hadn't quite reached the bottom, when The Shadow heard muffled footsteps beyond the door of Ondrey's office. He waited coolly, calculating that the car might arrive before Ondrey entered. It did.

The Shadow was aboard and closing the panel when Ondrey opened the office door. He caught a glimpse of the portly man speaking to someone in the hall. The panel went shut while Ondrey was turning about. The fellow did not notice its motion.

This time the silence of Ondrey's private elevator worked against its owner. The Shadow made the slow trip to the top of the shaft. He found himself in the deserted fourth floor of a building that had once been a private residence.

There was a door that led into an adjoining house; it was probably the route used by Pinkey and other secret visitors. There was another exit, however, that pleased The Shadow better.

It was a fire escape outside the window at the end of the hall. It had a metal ladder leading to the roof, and The Shadow raised his head above the edge, to learn facts for future reference.

One thing that he saw was a trapdoor that evidently topped the hidden elevator shaft. That was something that could prove useful later. His inspection finished, The Shadow descended by the fire escape.

TWENTY minutes later, The Shadow was in Greenwich Village; near an alleyway that afforded entrance of the side door of The Hayrick. Looking along the street, he saw a man loafing near the corner; another, shambling along in aimless fashion.

These were agents of The Shadow. He had summoned them through a shortwave radio call to Burbank. With his agents on the watch, The Shadow could later receive reports on any outside developments.

Entering the side door, The Shadow stopped for a view of The Hayrick.

The place formed one big barnlike raftered room, with the stacks of hay around the sides. There were about forty tables, half of them occupied by customers. In the center was a dance floor; an orchestra dressed as farmhands occupied the far end of the room.

To his right, The Shadow saw a little stairway that led up to a gloomy balcony. Beyond the rail were the doors of small private dining rooms, which explained why Pinkey had chosen to meet Maude here. By using the side door, Pinkey could reach one of those little rooms unnoticed by the patrons on the main floor.

The Shadow took the stairway to the balcony. He entered the first empty room and closed the door behind him. Using a tiny flashlight, he decided that this room was probably unused, for its table and chair were stacked in a corner.

There was a connecting door next to the little room. It was locked, but The Shadow opened it with a skeleton key. Again he found a little-used room; so he took another door into the third room in the row. There, the gleam of his flashlight showed a table set for two.

Positive that this was where Pinkey intended to dine with Maude, The Shadow approached the table, his flashlight cleaving a path before him. He hadn't taken five steps, before there was a *click* from beside the partly closed door that led to the balcony passage.

The room was filled with light. Just inside the doorway stood a striking blonde, whose large blue eyes were fixed upon the center of the room. The girl was Maude Revelle.

She wasn't the type that The Shadow expected her to be. She was attractively attired in a black velvet evening gown that sparkled with a line of small rhinestones from neck to hem. That decoration was tasteful; quite different from the cheap finery worn by the usual racketeer's moll.

There wasn't any question, though, regarding Maude's identity. She recognized The Shadow when she saw him, and the sudden narrowing of her eyes told that she knew him to be the arch-foe of crooks like Pinkey Findlen.

Whatever else happened, Maude intended to make sure that Pinkey didn't walk into a surprise meeting with The Shadow in this room.

Nervily, the girl ignored the gun that The Shadow whipped from his cloak. Yanking the door fully open, she made a dive to the balcony, at an angle which took her from The Shadow's range. As she went, Maude delivered a long warning scream.

The Shadow reached the same doorway, hoping that his arrival would cause the girl to end her tactics. His move proved a bad one. Hardly had he leaped out to the balcony, when someone turned on another string of lights.

Those bulbs glimmered along the balcony, revealing The Shadow where he stood. Tough faces bobbed suddenly among the patrons of The Hayrick, while quick fists went for guns. As The Shadow wheeled to find cover, he faced along the balcony toward the stairs. There, he saw another menace. On the steps stood Pinkey Findlen, revolver gleaming from his lifting fist.

Luck had reversed the trap. Pinkey had attained an advantage over The Shadow!

CHAPTER VIII
MAUDE FINDS A FRIEND

THE next two seconds provided The Shadow

1 Acting on information that he had garnered from overhearing a telephone conversation, The Shadow hastens to a nightclub known as the "Hayrick." He wants to be present at a meeting between a mobster and his moll. Entering the night club through a side door giving onto an alley . . .

2 The Shadow heads up a small stairway to a balcony off which open small private dining rooms. Searching the rooms, he is discovered by the mobster's moll, who screams out a warning . . .

3 Finding himself in a trap, The Shadow glides down the balcony seeking escape, and is confronted by the mobster himself on the staircase. Flinging himself at the gunman, The Shadow and his underworld opponent roll down the steps, locked in battle. Other mobsters, planted in the nightclub, rise to attack The Shadow in a surprise move . . .

with one of the tightest pinches in his long career. By all the laws of ordinary chance, that interval should have produced his doom. This predicament, however, was the sort that urged The Shadow to extraordinary measures. In the emergency, he took a long-shot method.

Not Pinkey, but the rising gun muzzle, was The Shadow's focal point. At the last instant, he gave a twist that preceded the blast of Pinkey's gun. The bullet scorched through The Shadow's cloak, so close to his body that Pinkey thought he had scored a hit.

Pinkey's triumphant shout made others believe the same. So did The Shadow's own course. He didn't slacken as he reached the steps. Shoulder-first, he took a plunge straight downward. To the enemy, that topple indicated that Pinkey's shot had reached The Shadow.

Even Pinky didn't realize that The Shadow's fall would be broken. It was Pinkey, himself, who became the buffer when the black-clad fighter hit his shoulder first. The two went rolling down the steps together; and with the finish of Pinkey's raucous shout came the sudden burst of The Shadow's mocking laugh.

A gun blow settled Pinkey for a while to come. That stroke was swung for the racketeer's skull; through sheer luck, Pinkey partly warded it, with upraised arm. He flattened, groggy at the bottom of the steps, and The Shadow promptly forgot him, to wage battle with others.

They were coming across the floor—half a dozen mobbies planted here by "Bugs" Hopton, Pinkey's strongarm crew leader. They expected victory through that rush; instead they put themselves in trouble. By deserting the tables, they came clear of innocent patrons. That give The Shadow full opportunity to fire.

Two automatics in his fists, the black-cloaked battler sent shots through the stairway rail. Crooks

The Shadow didn't halt to beat Pinkey in a gun duel. That would have been suicidal, with other revolvers coming up to aim. Nor did he wheel away to make himself a more difficult target. That would have worked with the more distant crooks, but not with Pinkey.

The Shadow took the one direction that offered sure surprise. He drove straight for the spot where Pinkey awaited him. By the very swiftness of his lunge, he accomplished the unexpected. He arrived by the time that Pinkey's gun was leveled at him.

began to spill; their fire was belated when they tried to return flying lead.

Two of them reached the balcony, jumped up, and hauled themselves over its high rail. Maude was in their path, trying to stop the conflict; they hurled the girl aside and started for The Shadow.

He was up the steps to meet them. Instead of wasting bullets that might be needed, he came like a living avalanche, before the pair could aim. The foremost thug took a hard stroke on the head; his companion made a desperate grapple with The Shadow.

Bold patrons who peeked from beneath tables saw a mass of blackness heave upward, hoisting a struggling thug above. The crook took a long, sprawly dive over the balcony rail; the jolt that the floor gave him left him senseless.

BY this time, new fighters had arrived. Bugs Hopton and a trio of picked gorillas had dashed in

The blonde recognized The Shadow when she saw him....
Nervily, the girl ignored the gun that he whipped from his cloak.

through the side entrance. They aimed for The Shadow as they snatched up Pinkey, to haul the big-shot out of danger. Guns spoke anew, The Shadow's quick shots hurrying the crooks in their aim.

Amid that preliminary barrage, a new attack came from the side door. The Shadow's agents had closed in, to surprise Bugs and his crew with a rear attack.

Mobsters turned, hoping to reach the door. Into the melee came a batch of waiters, thinking that they could drive out the troublemakers.

The Shadow waited, watching the struggle. He couldn't risk shots at the moment; he was depending upon his agents to handle themselves in their usual competent style. Probably they would have done so, if the waiters hadn't mixed in it. As it was, the fight became a free-for-all.

Bugs and two pals dragged Pinkey out through the side door, the brawling figures shielding them against The Shadow's aim. That getaway made the waiters realize that the real trouble-makers were in flight.

They took up the chase, out through the alleyway, leaving The Shadow's agents in control, with one man of Bugs Hopton's crew lying limp and helpless.

The Shadow saw that further pursuit would be useless. Bugs had managed an escape, and had taken Pinkey with him. Probably they had a waiting car in readiness.

It was time for The Shadow to make his own departure, taking his agents with him; and the best route would be through a window of one of the little dining rooms. That was why The Shadow's sibilant tone gave quick command for his agents to join him on the balcony.

As they arrived, The Shadow observed a forgotten figure. Maude Revelle lay dazed upon the floor. The Shadow told the agents to take her with them, and added brief instructions. They hurried through a little room, just as a squad of police arrived at the front entrance to The Hayrick.

The officers saw The Shadow fading into a doorway. They shouted for him to halt, and followed the order with a rapid volley. Those shots were wide of their mark. With their echoes came the trailing tone of The Shadow's parting laugh.

OUTSIDE The Hayrick, Pinkey and his carriers had vanished. Police whistles were sounding everywhere. The Shadow's agents found themselves confronted with a difficult task, for they had to make their own departure and carry Maude with them.

They were aided, though, by shots that took the police in the wrong direction. The Shadow had provided those shots, knowing that they would draw the officers away. By the time the police reached the spot where the shots had been fired, The Shadow was gone.

Two blocks away, a pair of The Shadow's agents crept through the darkness, taking Maude with them. The girl had recovered her wits; she supposed that these men were two of Pinkey's followers. They reached the street, to hear the sound of a police siren. Maude shrank back.

One of the men nudged the girl, pointing to a limousine parked near the curb. Maude nodded, then made a dash for it. She reached the limousine and climbed hurriedly aboard. The chauffeur didn't notice her; he was looking across the street toward a little cigar store.

A tall man strode from the store and entered the limousine. He spoke quietly through the speaking tube; the big car started forward. Then, lighting a cigarette, the owner of the limousine turned to look beside him. For the first time, apparently, he noticed Maude.

The girl became breathless. She felt she could trust this calm-faced stranger whose well-tailored evening clothes gave him the mark of a gentleman. Maude gripped the man's arm.

"You've got to trust me," she pleaded. "Honest—I'm on the level! My name is Maude Revelle. I was in The Hayrick, when a lot of shooting started."

"I am quite pleased to know you, Miss Revelle," returned the owner of the limousine. "Let me introduce myself. My name is Lamont Cranston. You are quite welcome to share my limousine"—he broke off, suddenly, to utter through the speaking tube, "Come, Stanley!... What is the delay?"

The big car had jolted to a stop. Stanley didn't have to explain why. A heavy-jowled patrolman was opening the door, to poke a flashlight inside.

"What is the trouble, officer?"

Cranston's quiet query brought the flashlight in his own direction. The cop mumbled that there had been a riot; that they were looking for a girl who had helped start it. He turned the flashlight toward Maude; eyed her suspiciously as she shrank away.

"Don't be frightened, Maude," soothed Cranston. He tendered a card to the patrolman. "My name is Lamont Cranston. I am a friend of Police Commissioner Weston."

"And this lady?"

"She is Miss Maude Revelle. Please do not

delay us, officer. You see these tickets?" Cranston held them in the light. "I am taking Miss Revelle to the opera, and we are anxious to reach there before curtain time."

A MINUTE later, the limousine was rolling clear of the police cordon. Maude's big eyes were full of admiration, as they turned toward Cranston.

"Gee, you're swell!" exclaimed the girl. "Helping me out of a jam, the way you did! Maybe I'd be a lot better off if I'd met up with real guys like you, instead of some of the mugs I've known."

Cranston's gaze showed a sympathetic interest that caused Maude to say more.

"I tried to help a fellow out tonight"—Maude's tone was bitter; she was thinking of Pinkey—"and he left me to scramble for myself. Maybe he's a right guy, but he's in the wrong racket, whatever it is. Only, I'm not the sort that blabs."

The car stopped at a traffic light. Maude reached for the door, intending to alight. Cranston's hand restrained her; his voice was persuasive.

"I told the officers that I was taking you to the opera. I might have to prove that story."

Maude settled back in the cushions her eyes were eager.

"You mean that?" she exclaimed. "You'll take me to the opera with all the other swells?"

The Shadow nodded. The limousine rolled ahead; Maude felt herself riding in air. She didn't realize that keen eyes were watching her, grasping the thoughts that she betrayed by her facial expressions.

Maude was getting something that she really wanted: a chance to appear among fashionable people, as one of them. She wasn't a selfish sort; but the joy of that triumph made her so, for the present. She wanted to feel that Cranston had invited her to the opera because he liked her.

Maude made that plain, as they stepped from the limousine in front of the opera.

"If I go with you," she remarked, "I won't be cutting out someone else, will I?"

From her tone, The Shadow knew that Maude hoped she was doing just that. He gave the slight smile that was typical of Cranston.

"I was to meet a lady here," he said, "but she can go with other friends, who asked her to join their party. I would prefer your company, Miss Revelle."

"Do you see this lady you're telling me about?"

"Yes. Over there."

The girl that The Shadow pointed out was the most attractive young woman in sight; and that was quite a distinction, for the lobby thronged with beautiful femininity. She was waiting for someone, and it could very well have been Cranston. Maude certainly thought that it was Cranston.

Penning a note, The Shadow showed it to Maude. She was pleased when she read: *"Sorry, Eleanor. I am escorting another lady this evening: Lamont."*

Folding the note, The Shadow gave it to an attendant. Adding a dollar bill as tip, he pointed out the lady to whom the note was to be delivered. Maude saw all that; what she didn't observe was the note itself.

The Shadow held it loosely, so that air reached the drying ink. The message faded before he gave it a final fold. The Shadow had used the special ink that he employed when sending orders to his agents.

The girl across the lobby looked puzzled when she opened the message. For a moment, her gaze became as blank as the paper itself. Then, supposing that someone had played a practical joke, she crumpled the paper and threw it away, staring about angrily as she did so.

By that time The Shadow was escorting Maude into the opera house. Maude had seen the other girl's piqued expression, and it had pleased her. Maude was smiling triumphantly when she and her escort reached the Golden Horseshoe.

When the opera house lights went down, The Shadow indulged in a smile of his own. Unlike Pinkey Findlen, The Shadow knew the ways of women. He would use his acquaintance with Maude Revelle in the future.

Tonight, though Maude did not guess it, she had become an ally of The Shadow in his campaign against crime.

CHAPTER IX
MOVES THROUGH THE DARK

THE next evening, Maude Revelle dined with Lamont Cranston in a little restaurant off Fifth Avenue. The place was both quiet and exclusive; the type of café where Maude had often wanted Pinkey to take her, only to have him claim that "ritzy joints" were the bunk.

Being with Cranston improved Maude's style. She liked his perfect manner, his excellent usage of the English language. She did her best to copy it, with very good results.

There were times, though, when she lapsed. Those came when she referred to the boy "friend" who had deserted her the night before.

Maude knew plenty about Pinkey; but there was much that she wouldn't tell. She would have been amazed, though, had she realized how much Cranston learned from the remarks that she dropped. Among that well-gleaned information, The Shadow obtained two important points.

One was that Maude did *not* know what Pinkey's present racket was. The other was that she had no idea as to the location of Pinkey's present hideout.

"He's supposed to be on the lam, if you know what I mean," confided Maude. "In other words, he's had to put himself where

A mass of blackness heaved upward, hoisting a struggling thug above. The crook took a long, sprawly dive over the balcony.

the police won't find him. But it wasn't on account of what he did. I guess he covered that pretty good.

"It's what he's up to, that makes him stay out of sight. He doesn't want to be seen around town, for fear they'll ask him down to headquarters. If he spends his time answering a lot of questions, they might wise up to what he's doing now."

Cranston smiled, as though amused by the adventures of Maude's boyfriend. His gaze, however, made Maude feel that he did not approve of Pinkey.

"I'm dropping the guy," declared Maude. "But I can't do it in a hurry. His kind wouldn't understand it. Give him time. He'll get an interest in some other dame. Then I can step out of the picture without an argument."

WHEN the conversation again turned to Pinkey, Maude remembered that she was supposed to telephone him. There was a booth in the hallway outside, the little room where she and Cranston were dining privately. Maude decided to make the call.

Hardly had she stepped from the room, before The Shadow reached beneath the table and drew out a single earphone. Placing it to his ear, he heard the plunk of Maude's nickel when she placed it in the pay box. This wire was connected with the telephone booth.

From Maude's first words, The Shadow learned that she had called the Bubble Club and was talking to Claude Ondrey.

Pinkey wasn't there; but he was expected by ten o'clock.

"Ten o'clock is when I'll call him," announced Maude. "Yes. Tell him I'll be at the apartment, if you hear from him before then... Yes, and listen, Ondrey. You can tell him that he's going to find out where he gets off..."

"Sure, I'm sore... Yes, Pinkey knows why... You want to know where I am right now? Out with a swell guy, who took me to the opera last night..."

There was a pause, while Ondrey spoke a piece; then came Maude's sharp laugh.

"I'm not telling you who the guy is," she said. "I don't spill Pinkey's name to anybody, do I?... All right, it works two ways. I'm keeping this fellow's name to myself... Sure, tell Pinkey if you like..."

The earphone was parked from sight when Maude returned to the little dining room. They had dined late; Maude was suddenly surprised to notice that her wristwatch said half past nine. She didn't realize that she looked at the watch, because Cranston's gaze had been idly resting in the direction of her hands and arms.

"I've got to go back to the apartment," decided Maude. "Don't worry about taking me there, Mr. Cranston. I can go alone."

Cranston wouldn't allow that; but he finally agreed to ride by subway, instead of taking the limousine. It was when they came up from the subway, a block from Maude's apartment, that the girl expressed real alarm.

"You mustn't come farther," she insisted. "It—well, it mightn't be safe!"

"Not safe?" interposed Cranston. "If this neighborhood is as dangerous as all that, I certainly cannot allow you to go the rest of the way alone."

Maude tightened her attractive lips. Her hand gripped Cranston's arm, with the sincere clutch, that her fingers had displayed the night before.

"The boyfriend's jealous," she declared. "He knows I've met you; that is, somebody may have told him. But I didn't say who you were. That's why I didn't want you to bring your car.

"And the same goes for you, Mr. Cranston. Maybe Pink—I mean, maybe this guy that thinks he's got a corner on me will be tough enough to have a couple of gorillas around here. By 'gorillas,' I don't mean monkeys from the zoo. I mean sluggers!"

CRANSTON chuckled. Then he took Maude's arm and started her in the direction of the apartment house, ignoring the girl's continued protests.

Maude's argument persisted. She became watchful, particularly when they passed the side door of the apartment house. It was dark along that portion of the street, especially in the service alley. Maude feared that there were lurkers present.

She was right. Two figures were crouched in waiting. When Maude and Cranston had passed, the pair exchanged growls. They decided they'd get Cranston on the way back.

"That's what Bugs told us," argued one. "He says to let the dame get upstairs, so she won't know what happened. Then we can handle this stuffed shirt."

"Suppose he don't come back right away?" queried the other. "Whatta we do? Wait here, maybe all night?"

"Don't worry. He'll be back. We gotta keep an eye peeled, though, to see he don't hop no cab."

The apartment house was an old one, with a large, but deserted, foyer. As he conducted Maude toward the elevator, The Shadow spoke in a lower tone than usual, but in Cranston's style.

"Go to the side door," he told her. "Wait there, and watch what happens in the street."

Maude's eyes were wide, startled. But when Cranston turned and strode out through the front, she could do nothing but obey his instructions.

What Maude witnessed a few minutes later was something that left her even more astounded.

She saw Cranston come along the side street, pausing to look over his shoulder for a cab. He spotted one coming from a few blocks away; but instead of halting, he did the one thing that Maude feared. He stepped deliberately toward the darkness of the service entrance.

Husky shapes launched from the gloom. Maude gave a scream; tried to yank open the heavy side door. She wouldn't have reached Cranston in time to warn him; but it wasn't necessary.

A sweatered arm swung toward Cranston's head; the fist at the end of it tried to sap him with a blackjack. That arm stopped short as Cranston's hand clamped it. Whipping back into the light, he flayed the thug with a terrific forward heave; then snapped the rowdy all about.

Lashed like a human whip, the husky took a long dive toward the curb. The Shadow had chosen the right direction for the fling, for he had pointed the fellow for a suitable target: a large fireplug.

The thug rammed that metal object with his skull. The quick reverse of The Shadow's swing served an additional purpose. It took him from the path of a second attacker, who was wielding a chunk of lead pipe. The fellow took a swing at Cranston, only to miss him by a foot and a half. He didn't have a chance to try another wallop.

Spinning in, The Shadow took a square punch at the footpad's chin. The jolt lifted the slugger off his feet; his head went back with a terrific snap. He didn't have far to travel, for he was almost against the wall.

Maude yanked the door wide just in time to hear the impact of the second rowdy's skull against the side of the apartment house.

IT had all happened with such suddenness that Maude hadn't judged the rapidity of Cranston's action. She saw him smoothing his clothes in leisurely fashion, as if he had scarcely exerted himself. Stepping to the curb, he waved to the approaching cab.

By the time the taxi stopped, Maude saw Cranston lifting the two limp thugs, a hand clamped tight to the sweatered neck of each. He bundled the pair into the cab. Opening a wallet, he extracted a five-dollar bill from it.

"Drop them somewhere in Central Park," he told the driver, "and keep the change. They'll be more comfortable sleeping it off in the open, than they would be in the alley."

"A couple of drunks, huh?" grunted the driver. "Well, suit yourself. You've said it with five bucks, mister, and that clinches it." As the cab wheeled away, The Shadow joined Maude in the apartment house. Her admiration for Cranston had received another boost. He rode up with her in the elevator, while she expressed her enthusiasm.

Outside Maude's apartment, Cranston spoke a quiet good-bye; then paused long enough to smoke a cigarette, while Maude continued to relate her recollections of the fight.

"Say!" she exclaimed. "The way that bird hit the fireplug! You'd have thought that was what it had been put there for! And when you handled the other guy, I thought the wall wouldn't stand the strain. I'm going to take a look at the bricks tomorrow, just to see—"

A telephone bell began to ring. It was in Maude's apartment. Cranston said good-night again, and turned toward the elevator. He heard the apartment door go shut and stepped back quickly to listen in on Maude's conversation.

Through the thin door, every word was plain.

"Oh, hello, Pinkey." Maude's tone was scornful. "So you called the Bubble Club. Couldn't wait, could you, to find out if anything happened here?... Listen, if my new friend is a cream puff, they mixed in TNT when they made him."

"Those gorillas of yours looked like baboons when he was through with them! He used jujitsu stuff, and *how* it worked!... Get this, Pinkey. If you want to keep in good with me, don't try any more rough stuff on my friends..."

"You won't see me tonight? That doesn't bother me. Go on over to the Bubble Club, since you have to. Maybe you'll get some sympathy from old Baldy Ondrey."

When Maude hung up, she looked out into the hall, hoping that Cranston had not yet gone. The hall was empty. Maude was disappointed. Since she didn't expect to see Pinkey, she would have liked to go out with Cranston. It didn't occur to Maude that since Pinkey had business at the Bubble Club, Cranston would have reason to be there also.

The Shadow had learned that a conference of crooks was due. When Pinkey and his pals discussed their next plans, they would be favored with the presence of an unseen listener.

He would be The Shadow.

CHAPTER X
CRIME'S CONFERENCE

When The Shadow reached the old residence that housed the Bubble Club, he went directly to the roof above the secret elevator. The trapdoor was tightly fixed; but it didn't take The Shadow long to jimmy it.

His method of persuasion was both efficient and noiseless; and the latter factor was important. While The Shadow was at work, he heard faint sounds of the elevator making a descent.

That meant that Pinkey Findlen had arrived to hold conference, in Ondrey's office.

The elevator was at the bottom of the shaft when the trapdoor came free. The taut cable offered a means of rapid descent. Hand under hand, The Shadow went downward, until he found a resting place upon the solid top of the elevator itself.

On his previous visit to Ondrey's office, The Shadow had observed that the wall panel was slightly higher than the elevator. Reaching from the top of the car, he probed in front of it, until he found a catch. The panel was released; but The Shadow did not spread its sections.

Instead, he was content with a mere quarter inch of space, that enabled him to peer into the office and overhear what passed there.

The Shadow was correct in his assumption that Pinkey had arrived. The big-shot occupied the center of the office and two others were present with him. One was Claude Ondrey; the other, Slick Thurley.

It happened that Bugs Hopton was absent; and from the conversation, it came apparent that the leader of the strongarm crew was not expected.

"Tonight, we frame Bron." Pinkey made that statement in positive tone. "The way we'll handle it, the job will be the neatest one we've staged. There won't be a chance of The Shadow mooching in to queer it."

Slick Thurley added a nod; he knew the general plan, but Claude Ondrey hadn't yet heard the details. His fat face showed worry; he was mopping sweaty spots from his baldish forehead.

"Don't get jittery," rasped Pinkey. "We ain't yanking you into it, Ondrey! Bugs Hopton is the guy that's going to start things."

"Which means a mob," reminded Ondrey, "and that may bring cops—and The Shadow."

"Not tonight," assured Pinkey. "Bugs is working alone. Just so you'll be posted, I'll give you the setup."

Pinkey began his explanation.

"First of all," he declared, "Bron is going to be in his office until midnight. He's cleaning up an auditing job, so he can go over the World Oil interests books tomorrow. What's more, we know that Bron will be alone in his office. That's where Bugs will walk in on him."

ONDREY'S nervousness returned. Pinkey gave a harsh laugh.

"Bugs won't begin by pulling a gat," declared the big-shot. "He's going to hand Bron a letter of recommendation given to him by a sap named Roy Parrington. Bron will think that Bugs has come to ask for a job."

"Parrington?" questioned Ondrey, suddenly. "I seem to know that name."

"Maybe you do," returned Pinkey. "Parrington goes around to a lot of bright spots; he's probably been here. He's an advertising promoter; at least, that's what he calls himself. But he spends most of his time playing the races. That's how Bugs got acquainted with him—by giving him tips on the ponies."

"And Parrington knows Bron?"

"Of course. That's why Bron won't be suspicious when he sees the letter. But he won't have a job for Bugs. That'll make Bugs mad."

For the first time, Ondrey showed a smile. Evidently, he had begun to picture certain fine points of this game.

"You know what Bugs is like when he pretends he's goofy," reminded Pinkey. "They call him 'Bugs' because of the way he can stage the nut act. From then on, its a cinch!

"Bron will get scared and try to heave him out. Bugs will yank a gat and Bron will make a grab for it. There'll be a blank shot and—blooey!—Bugs will be flopped like he was dead with Bron holding the rod."

It was Slick who put in the next approval.

"Bugs can fake that dead stuff as good as I can," declared Slick. "We've both seen so many boobs get croaked that we know the way it looks."

Pinkey strode across the floor, pointing here and there, picturing the future scene.

"Suppose this is Bron's office," he declared. "There's Bugs on the floor; Bron standing over here, with the heater in his mitt. The door opens; I step in, like some guy who heard the shot from another office.

"While I'm listening to Bron, like I was friendly and believe his story, in comes Slick. He flashes that badge of his, says he's Bill Quaine, the dick. Only he won't believe Bron's story. He'll talk about pinning a murder rap on the guy."

"That's when I'll have the way to fix it. I'll tell Bron what I want done, and that if he'll play ball he won't have to worry about nothing. Tomorrow, he'll put his O.K. on those books over at World Oil."

Pinkey's story was finished, and from Ondrey's

delighted look, the big-shot was sure that the scheme would work. Ondrey was not the only listener who nourished that opinion.

From his hiding place, The Shadow had heard all the details and could foresee the result, once the game reached completion.

Obviously, Lewis Bron would realize that he was framed by the time Pinkey came to the climax; but that wouldn't help the auditor out of his dilemma. If Bron believed that he had actually shot Bugs and that Slick was really Bill Quaine, the game would work.

Knowing the skill with which Pinkey and his pals worked, The Shadow was sure that they would sell Bron on the proposition, provided nothing intervened to disturb their scheme. It happened, though, that crooks would be due for a surprise; because The Shadow saw a way to provide one.

The Shadow, too, could be witness to all that occurred. When the game came to its high point, he could step in with a brace of guns and corner both Pinkey and Slick. Bugs on the floor, would never dare a move.

A call to police headquarters would bring Joe Cardona, Manhattan's ace police inspector. Fuming crooks would be trapped, with their whole game exposed.

WHILE The Shadow was speculating on that pleasant prospect, Pinkey stepped toward the elevator. The Shadow pressed the panel tight; rolled to the top of the car.

Pinkey slid the panel wide; The Shadow could hear him entering the elevator alone. Pinkey's words were also plain.

"I'm going over to watch Bron's office," he told the others. "You can come along later, Slick—say in about forty minutes, because Bugs won't be due until eleven o'clock.

"You look too much like Bill Quaine to be seen around Bron's place until you're needed. You might bump into some harness bull who knows that Quaine is away on vacation."

The panel went shut. The elevator moved smoothly upward carrying its two passengers. It was a curious situation—Pinkey Findlen starting off on a criminal venture, taking The Shadow right along with him. Pinky hadn't the remotest idea that such a case existed.

Nor did The Shadow disillusion him. When the car reached the top of the shaft, he waited while Pinkey went out though the door. After that, The Shadow stretched upward and opened the trap above his head, to emerge upon the roof.

Pinkey was gone by the time The Shadow reached the street below. There wasn't any reason to trail him, for the big-shot was going to the very spot where The Shadow wanted him to be. Shifting through the darkness, The Shadow reached a waiting cab. Entering it, he whispered to the agent who was at the wheel.

That aide was Moe Shrevnitz, the speediest hackie in Manhattan, but Moe didn't hurry on this occasion. He drove at an easy pace; while The Shadow contacted Burbank by radio. Over the shortwave set, The Shadow learned Bron's office address. It was in a small office building on Thirtieth Street.

The Shadow instructed Burbank to send an agent, Harry Vincent, to the Bubble Club, in case of chance developments there. That done, he put away the earphones and gave Moe the Thirtieth Street address.

But the cabby didn't stop when they reached the destination. Instead, he merely slackened speed near the less lighted portion of the curb.

Dropping from the cab, The Shadow merged close to the darkness of a building wall. Blended

ACTING INSPECTOR JOE CARDONA

with blackness, he looked across the street to the small old-fashioned building where Bron's office was located.

The Shadow saw a lighted office at the front of the third floor. Its curtains were drawn; but he knew that the office must be Bron's.

While he watched, The Shadow spotted another light that suddenly appeared at the window of a side office on the same floor. That window was also shaded; but The Shadow could picture the scene within as plainly as if he possessed X-ray vision.

The side office was the waiting place chosen by Pinkey Findlen. That fact brought a whispered laugh from The Shadow. Fake murder was shaping itself as crooks intended; and with its climax would come The Shadow's triumph.

That soft laugh would have faded, had The Shadow foreseen the change that chance was to produce. Already, events were leading to a different climax. Such matters, it happened, were unknown to Pinkey Findlen as well as The Shadow.

Real murder—not false—was in the cards tonight, and through it would come success to present schemes of crime!

CHAPTER XI
BUGS SWINGS A DEAL

VERY shortly after The Shadow's departure from the Bubble Club, two unexpected customers arrived there. One was Bugs Hopton, attired in ill-fitting tuxedo; the other was a stoopish, sly-faced man, similarly attired. The two took a table; when Claude Ondrey stopped nearby, Bugs beckoned.

Worried, Ondrey approached the table. Bugs clapped him on the back, then introduced his companion.

"Meet Mr. Parrington," announced Bugs. "Roy Parrington—one swell guy! And you, Roy—shake hands with Claude Ondrey. He's regular!"

Handshakes were exchanged; all the while, Ondrey was looking anxiously toward Bugs, wondering what twist of circumstances had brought him to the Bubble Club.

There was a burst of music from the orchestra; a trim dancer whirled to the center of the floor, amid the applause of the patrons. Bugs nudged Parrington.

"Get an eyeful, Roy," advised Bugs. "That kid is some looker—and can she dance! Here—shove your chair around for a better look."

Parrington obliged. When his back was turned, Bugs shifted in the opposite direction, grabbed Ondrey's sleeve and whispered in the manager's ear:

"Is Slick in the office?"

Ondrey nodded; then began: "But—but what—"

"Don't ask questions," undertoned Bugs. "See this hatcheck? It's Parrington's. Listen—get a gat from Slick and plant it in the guy's coat pocket. Leave the rest to me."

Ondrey hurried away, still wondering what it was all about. He reached the office, to find Slick lounging there. He told Slick what Bugs wanted. Slick was mystified; but obligingly provided Ondrey with a revolver, in accordance with the request.

Hurrying from the office, the nightclub owner reached the cloakroom near the street door. He spotted the garments that bore the ticket number. Getting rid of the check girl on a pretext, Ondrey fumblingly slid the revolver into Parrington's overcoat pocket.

The task wasn't exactly easy, for Ondrey encountered a fat bundle in one pocket and had to slide the gun to another. Since Bugs hadn't mentioned the package in the overcoat, Ondrey left it where it was.

Sidling from the cloakroom, Ondrey neared the table where Bugs sat with Parrington. Bugs thumbed the manager toward his office; then leaned forward to watch the floor show.

"How do you like it, Roy?" he queried. While he spoke, Bugs was watching an approaching waiter. "Ain't this a classy joint, with plenty for de money? I come here a lot."

The waiter had arrived. Bugs shifted suddenly in his chair, jolted the fellow and caused him to spill the contents of a tray. Mixed drinks poured over Bugs and Parrington. Both came to their feet.

In the argument that followed, Bugs blamed the waiter; so Parrington did the same. Bugs staged a portion of his "crazy act" in very competent fashion. The result was that Parrington agreed when Bugs gave loud decision:

"Come, Roy. Let's get out of this lousy dump!"

They were still arguing with a headwaiter when they put on their hats and coats. It was then that Bugs became more reasonable.

"We ought to talk to Ondrey," he decided. "After all, he's a good guy. Come on, Roy, we'll go to his office."

PARRINGTON agreed that the protest would be in order. They reached the office, found Slick with Ondrey. Bugs shook hands with Slick; introduced him to Parrington as Bill Quaine.

"A good guy," voiced Bugs, "even if he is a dick." Then, to Ondrey: "Say—wait'll you see the way one of your cluck waiters messed us up."

Bugs took off his coat to show his soaked tuxedo jacket. Parrington did the same; Bugs planked both overcoats upon the table. There was a clank when Parrington's pocket hit the woodwork.

Turning at the sound, the fake dick took the cue.

"What's that?" snapped Slick. "That your coat, Parrington? Let's see what you got in the pockets."

Uneasily, Parrington lifted the coat, pulled out the bundle and laid it with his hat. That done, he fished out gloves and cigarettes. Finally, his fingers found the revolver. Parrington didn't realize that it was a gun, until he brought it into the light.

Slick snatched the weapon from Parrington's fingers. While the man was gasping, Slick demanded:

"What's the idea of carrying the gun? Where's your permit?"

Parrington tried to protest. He failed.

He said he didn't know the gun was in the pocket; that was all, and it sounded pitifully weak. Even Bugs looked reproachful, especially when Slick cracked the revolver and found it loaded.

"Better see what's in the bundle," suggested Bugs. "Maybe it will give us one on the guy."

The bundle was filled with currency; bills totaled five thousand dollars. Slick wanted to know where the money had come from.

"I'm a promoter," panted Parrington. "This was for—well, I'd arranged an advertising campaign, and was—"

"And you flimflammed somebody out of the dough?"

"No, no!—well, this was a commission—I—"

"In cash? Sounds phony to me, Parrington." Slick shoved the money to the far side of the desk, along with the gun. "Tell us some more about the dough."

Parrington confessed that the cash was tainted. It was a cut that he had received for swinging a national advertiser to a wildcat agency. Becoming bolder, he suddenly declared:

"But you can't prove anything because of that!"

"We can prove plenty with this gun," interposed Slick. "Enough to put you in the cooler for a long stretch. Come along! We're going down to headquarters."

Parrington wilted. His head in his hands, he was moaning incoherently when Bugs motioned to Slick, signaling that the bluff had gone far enough.

Slick was mightily relieved when Bugs took over the burden; for even yet, the fake detective hadn't decided what Bugs was going to do next.

"Why don't you give the guy a break?" demanded Bugs. "His overcoat was out in the cloakroom; maybe somebody planted the rod in his pocket. Go on out there, Quaine, and ask the cloakroom doll about it."

Slick agreed that he would do so. He started to pick up the planted gun, remarking that it was evidence.

"Leave it here," suggested Bugs. "Let Ondrey lock it in that desk drawer. We'll look out for Parrington while you're gone."

THE REVOLVER was put away. Slick left the office but he didn't go to the cloakroom, because that would be of no use. Slick knew well enough how the gun had come into Parrington's pocket.

What Slick didn't know was what he escaped by staying away from the cloakroom. At that very moment, a young man was checking hat and coat there. He was Harry Vincent, one of the keenest of The Shadow's agents.

If Harry had seen Slick come to the cloakroom, he would have promptly sensed that something was up. But Slick didn't even leave the passage outside of Ondrey's office.

Meanwhile, in the office itself, Claude Ondrey was sweating more than ever.

Of all the screwy games he'd ever met with, this one was the worst. What did Bugs mean by passing the buck right back to him? Of course, Slick wouldn't come back with evidence that Ondrey had planted the gun; but Ondrey was beginning to believe that Bugs might be crazy enough to shout that out, himself.

Maybe Bugs was really as goofy as he sometimes looked.

In the midst of Ondrey's quandary, Bugs suddenly provided the reason behind his stunt.

"Listen, Parrington," spoke Bugs quickly. "I'm for you—see? I got a way to snatch you out of this mess. Ondrey, here, is a good guy. He'll help."

Parrington looked up, weakly hopeful.

"Unlock the desk drawer," Bugs told Ondrey. "Make it fast, before Quaine gets back here."

Ondrey obeyed. He was in a mood for anything that would end this crazy setup. As soon as the drawer was open, Bugs grabbed the revolver that lay within. Pocketing it, he picked up Parrington's five thousand dollars and planked the money in the drawer.

"Quaine won't find the gun when he looks for it," stated Bugs, with a grin. "He'll find the dough, instead. I'll look dumb, and so will Ondrey, here. How about it, Ondrey?"

Ondrey nodded. He didn't like the looks of things, but he couldn't find his voice.

"So Quaine will forget the gun," added Bugs, "and take the mazuma instead. That's fair enough, ain't it? You can make up that five grand easy, Roy, but you can't laugh off a stretch in the big house."

Parrington's eyes narrowed. He was becoming suspicious; but he was still worried enough so to be handled. Bugs nudged to the wall panel.

HARRY VINCENT

"Bring down the elevator," he ordered Ondrey. "Get Roy out of here before Quaine comes back."

ONDREY obeyed reluctantly. Bugs told Parrington how to make his exit through the house next door. Sight of the open elevator made Parrington suddenly eager for flight. Half a minute later, he was on his way.

Bugs gave a raucous chuckle after the panel had closed; but Ondrey didn't join with him.

The harsh mirth was heard by Slick, in the passage. Slick came back into the office, looked about, perplexed, when he failed to see Parrington. Bugs yanked open the desk drawer, told Slick to take a look.

"How's that for a neat shakedown, Slick?" he asked. "Say—you should have seen the sap fall for the finish of it!" Then, to Ondrey, Bugs added:

"Stick that five grand in the safe, along with the dough you're keeping for Pinkey. It's five thousand more in the pot."

There was an incredulous snarl from Slick.

"So *that* was your racket!" uttered Slick. "You're not smart, Bugs; you're dumb!"

"Me dumb?" rejoined Bugs. "When I picked up five grand that easy?"

"I said you're dumb," repeated Slick. "You've wasted time here, when you're supposed to head for Bron's office. What about that letter you were to get from Parrington?"

With a grin, Bugs pulled the letter from his pocket.

"Right here," he said. "I'm starting for Bron's now. Give me fifteen minutes start, Slick, and you'll get there just when you'll be needed."

Bugs pulled the switch to bring down the elevator. His grinning face was the last thing the others saw when the panel went shut.

Ondrey flopped behind the desk, mopping his bald head.

"Bugs had me nuts!" he panted. "I'm glad that's over."

Slick Thurley didn't reply. His eyes had a hard gaze; his lips were set. He was thinking that Bugs Hopton had tossed a boomerang by trying that shakedown on Roy Parrington.

Slick's hunch was right. Matters were to take a trend that crooks wouldn't like. But there was one element that Slick didn't include in his calculation; that was the part that chance was to play.

Lady Luck was already riding along with crime.

CHAPTER XII
CHANGED TRAILS

THE SHADOW'S first inkling that something had gone wrong came when the lights went blank in Bron's office. That was curious, since Bron was supposed to be there until midnight. It couldn't mean that plotters were on the move, because there was only one entrance to the office building and Bugs Hopton hadn't arrived to use it.

Furthermore, another incident furnished The Shadow with proof that crime's plans had been balked. Half a minute after Bron's lights were out, the side office went dark. Pinkey Findlen had evidently learned that Bron had gone out of the building.

Very soon, a man came from the front of the building. He was tall; his long legs made awkward strides toward the corner. The Shadow caught a glimpse of a tight-skinned face beneath a derby hat. Those features answered the slight description that The Shadow had gained concerning Lewis Bron.

Wherever Bron was going, he was in a hurry, for The Shadow saw him hail a cab. Blinking a flashlight toward the next corner, The Shadow waited until his own cab came along. Boarding it, he took up Bron's trail.

Turning the corner, The Shadow looked back. He saw Pinkey come out of the office building. There wasn't another cab in sight. That left the big-shot stranded. The fact pleased The Shadow; but it was to prove another of the grim jests that fate was supplying tonight.

Unsuspecting that The Shadow was on Bron's trail, Pinkey strode away in the opposite direction, and reached a subway station. Huddled in the corner of a half-filled car, he rode a few stations northward, muttering all the while. It didn't take him long to arrive at the house adjoining the Bubble Club.

The elevator was on the top floor when Pinkey reached there. He stepped into the car; before he had time to push the button, someone pulled the switch at the bottom of the shaft. When the car reached the ground floor, Pinkey came face to face with Slick Thurley.

For once, amazement showed on the features of the fake Bill Quaine. Slick couldn't figure what had brought the big-shot here, until Pinkey broke the news that Lewis Bron had made an unexpected exit from his office.

"We should have met earlier," rasped Pinky. "I didn't have a chance to tail the guy. Where he's gone, I can't even guess. But it looks like the deal is off for tonight; and that"—Pinkey's lower lip thrust forward—"may ruin the works tomorrow."

Claude Ondrey, seated behind his desk, put in a sudden theory regarding Bron.

"Maybe Parrington called him!" exclaimed Ondrey. "And if Parrington squawked—"

Ondrey caught himself. He didn't know just how to break the news to Pinkey.

"Squawked about what?" demanded the big-shot. "Say, you mugs"—he swung from Ondrey to Slick—"what's been going on here?"

GRUFFLY, Slick gave the details, stating the facts in brief. When Slick had finished, Pinkey raged.

"And you helped him with that screwy idea!" ranted the big-shot. "Pulled a small-change shake-down, didn't you, on a guy that was supposed to know nothing?"

"How could I know what was up?" demanded Slick. "I thought maybe Parrington had got wise to Bugs, and wouldn't give him a letter to Bron. I figured that was why he wanted to put the heat on the guy."

Pinkey saw merit in Slick's alibi. He swung toward Ondrey, to blast the portly man.

"You saw what Bugs was pulling, didn't you?" roared Pinkey. "Why didn't you do something about it?"

"Bugs made me jittery," replied Ondrey. "Before I'd catch up with him on one thing, he was off on another, until finally—"

"Until finally he stuck Parrington on the elevator! That was swell, wasn't it? If Parrington wasn't wise by that time, he got his chance to really think

it over. The guy knows all three of you were working together, so he tipped off Bron."

Silence followed. If Slick or Ondrey had any ideas, they didn't express them. They were letting Pinkey do their thinking for them; and it was the smartest system that they had yet used. Pinkey formed some rapid conclusions.

"Parrington must have called Bron right away," he decided, "from a phone down at the next corner. The question is, what did he tell Bron? There's only one answer."

"He told Bron that his friend Hopton was a phony, and he advised Bron to get out of the office before Bugs showed up there. He may have told him a lot more, but I don't think so. If Parrington is going to make a big squawk, it won't be to Bron."

"Maybe Parrington will figure that the bulls ought to know about one of their own bunch." Pinkey swung toward Slick. "For instance, about a smart dick named Bill Quaine. That would put a bad crimp in your style, Slick."

This time, Pinkey was met with a steady stare, the sort that Slick used when he meant business.

"Parrington fell for the bluff tonight," reminded Slick. "He'll fall for it again, if I drop in on him."

The suggestion awoke a response from Ondrey.

"Of course he will!" exclaimed the nightclub owner. "After all, Parrington didn't see you take the money. I've got it in the safe, Slick. You can take it with you—"

Pinkey interrupted Ondrey by shoving the portly man back in his chair.

"That dough stays where it is!" hoarsed the big-shot. "If things go sour, we'll make Bugs eat it. You're going after Parrington, but I'm the guy that's going with you. Between us"—Pinkey produced a revolver—"we'll fix Parrington so he'll never blab to nobody!"

THE next question was where Parrington lived. That was something that Bugs could have answered, for he was the only one who had traveled around with Parrington.

Bugs wasn't needed, however, for the telephone directory provided the information. There was only one Roy Parrington in the book; he lived at an address in the Sixties, which Pinkey decided must be a small apartment house.

Slick remarked that he didn't have a gun, for he had planted his revolver on Parrington and Bugs had kept it, afterward. Ondrey dug up a .32

that Slick decided would do. Shoving the gun in his pocket, Slick swung to Pinky with the words:

"Let's go."

Pinkey told him to wait a minute. He wrote out a phone number on a slip of paper; handed it to Ondrey. "Give a call there," he told Ondrey. "One of the mob will answer. Tell 'em you're calling for Bugs. They'll believe you, because they're dumber than he is. Have 'em cover up at Parrington's because they may be needed."

Ondrey asked what he was to do in case he heard from Bugs.

"Send him up there, too," ordered Pinkey, "and tell him to take charge of this outfit. Bugs ought to be calling here pretty quick, because, by this time, he's probably found out that Bron has left his office."

Pinkey glanced at his watch while he and Slick were riding up in the elevator. The big-shot was pleased to find that he hadn't lost much time by his trip to the Bubble Club. It was directly on the route to Parrington's address.

"I saved time coming by the subway," Pinky told Slick, "because the show-break had started at Times Square, and being drizzly tonight, there was a lot of traffic there."

Slick didn't reply. Pinky gave him a poke, asking raspingly what Slick was thinking about.

"I'm thinking about Bron," declared Slick. "I've got a hunch that maybe he went up to see Roy Parrington."

"Yeah?" Pinkey was enthusiastic. "Say, that would be nifty, wouldn't it?"

"Maybe. Its going to be hard to put the heat on Bron, though, if we walk right in and croak Parrington."

That comment brought a string of oaths from Pinkey; most of his remarks concerned Bugs Hopton, for the way in which the mobleader had queered tonight's setup. By the time they had reached the street, however, Pinkey's fuming had ended.

"With all that traffic jam," Pinkey decided, "Bron has just about had time to get to Parrington's. If we hop to Sixth Avenue and get a cab there, we'll be out of the tie-up. The two of them won't have time to gab much, before we show up.

"What we'll do when we get there, we can decide right then. It would be hoping too much, to croak Parrington and frame Bron, the way we wanted to. Anyway, whatever we pull, there won't be nobody around to get wise."

Slick, the hunch producer, agreed with every word that Pinkey uttered; and, thereby, both were totally wrong. Matters were to take a twist that neither believed possible. They were to find that everything could turn out as they wanted it,

more effectively than they could have planned.

They were mistaken also, on their second conjecture; namely; that whatever they did would remain unwitnessed. There was one being whose ability was unwisely discounted by both Pinkey and Slick.

That personage was The Shadow.

CHAPTER XIII
MISTAKEN MURDER

LEWIS BRON had actually started for Parrington's apartment. That had been the burden of Parrington's phone call—that he had to talk with Bron right away, regarding a matter of vital importance to both of them.

But Bron had been a long while getting to his destination; precisely as Pinky had calculated. That fact was worrying Roy Parrington, as he paced the living room of his little apartment. It didn't occur to the promoter that traffic might have delayed Bron.

Parrington's face was haggard; his lips had an increasing twitch. The gradual strain became too much for him. When his nerves finally broke, he showed it by pouncing for the telephone.

Within a few minutes, the haggard man was talking to police headquarters. Across the wire, he heard a gruff voice that announced the speaker to be Inspector Joe Cardona.

It took Parrington a few gulps, before he could talk. When he found control of his vocal cords, he was loath to explain matters fully. At last, he decided to take the line of least resistance: to blame the one man whose name would make Cardona eager to listen.

"Listen, Inspector," gulped Parrington, "I want to tell you, something about a man I met tonight—a fellow who says he's a detective. His name is Bill Quaine."

"What's that?" Cardona's query was sharp. "You saw Bill Quaine tonight? You couldn't have. He's away on a vacation. Say—who is this calling, anyway?"

Parrington gave his own name and address. He insisted that he had seen Quaine, and began to describe the detective. Parrington's memory was good; his description graphic. The sketch that he gave of Slick Thurley was a thorough one.

Cardona, totally ignorant of the fact that Quaine had a crooked double, was soon convinced that Parrington had actually met the vacationing dick. "Funny thing, Quaine being here in town," gruffed the inspector. "Just what did he have to say to you?"

"He threatened to arrest me," returned Parrington, "for something that I didn't do! If you come up here, Inspector, I'll give you all the details."

"You bet I'll be up there!"

Parrington hung up the receiver, highly pleased with himself. He resumed his pacing of the living room, to be interrupted by a hard rap at the door. Thinking that it was Bron, Parrington went to the door. As he turned the knob, he asked, hoarsely:

"Is that you, Mr. Bron?"

For reply, the door itself came banging inward, so hard that it staggered Parrington across the room. By the time the haggard man had stopped against a chair, a hard-faced arrival was upon him.

A revolver jabbed Parrington's ribs; he stared into the face of Bugs Hopton! The gun that the mobleader held was the one that had been recently planted on Parrington. With it, Bugs started Parrington toward the door. Reaching it, Bugs halted, simply closing the door with one hand, until it was almost latched.

"So you called Bron, huh?" Bugs plodded harder with the gun. "Well, I got an idea maybe you would, so I came up here instead of going down to his office. The boys seemed to have got

an idea that I ain't smart. They'll think differently after this!"

Leaving the door as it was, Bugs backed Parrington toward the center of the living room. Frightened, Parrington began to plead. He swore that he had told Bron nothing, and Bugs began to believe him.

It was mere coincidence that changed Parrington's tune. His hand brushed a table; his knuckles slid past the base of a heavy lamp. Eye to eye with Bugs, Parrington suddenly had the thought that his tormentor hadn't noticed the lamp, which stood unlighted.

A frantic scream came from Parrington's lips as he grabbed the lamp and swung it toward the other man's head. He tried to twist away from the gun muzzle at the same moment, but Bugs shoved his hand forward to prevent the victim's escape.

The dodge that Bugs gave saved him from the swing made by Parrington. Simultaneously, Bugs pulled the revolver trigger. Parrington was spinning as the lamp crashed the floor. Clamping his hands to his side, the haggard man slumped to a chair.

Ready to intervene from the doorway, The Shadow suddenly whipped back into the hall as a gun muzzle came pushing over the fallen man's shoulder.

Bugs pounced toward him, flourishing the revolver under Parrington's nose.

"Want another dose of it?" he taunted. "You're going to get it, whether you want it or not! I came here to croak you, Parrington—"

Bugs was interrupted by the victim's sudden move. Shooting his hands forward, Parrington made a frenzied clutch for the gun. He was mortally wounded, but he didn't know it, and the pain drove him to a show of strength that took Bugs totally of guard.

Bugs tried to twist away. His move merely hauled Parrington from the chair. They reeled across the floor together, and by the time they jounced the wall, the gun was in Parrington's possession.

During the next stagger, it would have been doom for Bugs, if they hadn't encountered a chair just as Parrington was shoving the revolver against the mobleader's temple. The two took a long spill; it caused Parrington to lose the gun. But Bugs didn't wait to snatch up the weapon.

The door to an inner room was open. Bugs dived through, slammed the door behind him. Parrington found the gun; came to his feet unsteadily.

He had heard the slam, but couldn't locate the door. The room was going black. All that Parrington could think of was the hallway, the natural exit that Bugs would have chosen. Parrington reeled toward the outer door.

SOMEONE was knocking when he arrived there, but Parrington didn't hear it. The knocks sent the loose door inward; staggering sideways, Parrington almost fell into the arms of a man who had arrived outside.

He didn't recognize Lewis Bron. Parrington was thinking in terms of one man alone: Bugs Hopton.

With a strength that would have suited a death grip. Parrington pointed the gun toward Bron. All Bron could do was shove the weapon upward, while he threw his weight against the attacker. He didn't realize that Parrington was badly wounded. Bron was wrestling for his own life.

The pair rolled into the living room. From the hall stairway came a figure in black. Though he hadn't kept to close to Bron's trail, The Shadow was near enough to witness the struggle at the doorway and his expert eye had noted something of Parrington's plight.

Ready to intervene from the doorway, The Shadow suddenly whipped back into the hall as a gun muzzle came pushing over Bron's shoulder.

With a final burst of strength, Parrington pulled the trigger. The bullet whistled through the space where The Shadow had been.

There was a thump; a groan; the dull *clank* of a gun against the carpet. Peering into the apartment, The Shadow saw Lewis Bron rising slowly from beside the body of Roy Parrington.

It took Bron a few minutes to recuperate from his daze. Once his wits w e r e gathered, he was horrorstruck.

He saw a broad bloodstain upon Parrington's shirtfront. The fellow was dead; and Bron thought himself responsible, supposing that the gunshot had occurred while the muzzle was pressed toward Parrington.

The Shadow waited for Bron to recover his nerve; meanwhile he looked for signs of the man who actually shot Parrington.

The Shadow saw the door to the inner bedroom. It had evidently been slammed, for a key was out of the lock and lying near the middle of the living room floor. However, the murderer, if actually in the other room, seemed to have no intention of showing himself.

That was why The Shadow continued his policy of letting Bron recuperate. Given a few minutes more, he would be in a mood to remember accurately what had actually happened. Those needed minutes were to be denied, however.

The Shadow became conscious of a sound that Bron did not hear. Creaky footsteps were coming up the stairs.

The hall was dark just past the apartment doorway. Suspecting the nature of the visitors, The Shadow stepped into that front darkness to let the arrivals pass. Once in the apartment, they would be in the light, where he could easily cover them. It would mean no danger for Bron, under such circumstances.

Two men arrived; they made a quick movement for the open doorway. The light from the apartment showed their faces: Pinkey Findlen and Slick Thurley.

That cleared The Shadow's last doubts regarding the identity of Parrington's murderer. With Pinkey and Slick accounted for, Bugs Hopton was obviously the killer.

BRON heard the two men enter the apartment. He gave a hoarse cry when he faced them; made a move as if to pick up the revolver.

Slick, snapping into his accustomed style, was prompt to wrench Bron's arm behind him, holding the man helpless, while Pinkey stooped and reclaimed the dropped revolver.

Bron slumped to a chair when Slick released him. He was burying his face, gasping that he hadn't tried to kill Parrington.

Again at the doorway, The Shadow saw the glances exchanged by Pinkey and Slick. They had been puzzled, first, when they saw Parrington's body; but their expressions were becoming triumphant.

This was better than the frameup that the crooks had planned. It wasn't necessary to display a scene of faked death to make Bron worry.

Instead, they had trapped Lewis Bron with the evidence of real crime against him!

CHAPTER XIV
CROOKS GET THE GOODS

IF ever an innocent man believed himself a murderer, the case fitted Lewis Bron. Pinkey observed that; and he saw something else. The bedroom door had cautiously opened; Bugs poked his head into sight. Pinkey nudged Slick, who also took a look.

"Do your stuff," whispered Pinkey. "Flash that badge and sell this guy Bron on the idea you're Quaine."

Slick flashed the badge. Bron eyed it fearfully; when Slick announced that he was Bill Quaine, from headquarters, Bron took it for granted. He stammered an argument of self defense, but it sounded feeble and Bron knew it.

"Suppose you write out a confession," suggested Slick. "It'll go easier with you, if you do. Better get it down."

Bron took the pen and paper that were handed him. With Parrington's body still in sight he was shaky; ready to do whatever he was told. Slick began to dictate; and Bron copied. The way the smart crook handled it would have been a lesson for the real Quaine, had he been present as a witness.

Meanwhile, The Shadow made no move.

This wasn't the sort of situation that could be cleared, like the one intended in Bron's office. There, death was to have been a sham; here, it was real. Bron had become so eager to swear that he had killed Parrington that it would be difficult to make him realize the truth.

The Shadow decided to let plotters go further with their game, before he terminated it. Apparently, they had plenty of time; but that didn't last. Crooks were due for an interruption, as sudden as the one that The Shadow had experienced.

From somewhere came the faint wail of a police car. Bugs caught that sound, gave a warning gesture that his pals saw.

"Come along!" snapped Slick, to Bron. "You've written enough. We're going to take you somewhere else to finish it."

He started Bron out through the door, with Pinkey and Bugs following. Bron had scarcely noticed Pinkey; he didn't even see Bugs.

When the group reached the stairs, The Shadow followed. He wanted to see the finish of this game; and he wasn't worried about Bron's safety. He knew that the auditor was too valuable for thugs to harm him.

At the bottom of the stairs, the crooks could hear the police car stopping in front of the old apartment house. Pinkey drew Bugs aside.

"We're going out the back," Pinkey told him. "The mob's here—you take care of the bulls; while Slick and I haul Bron to the hideout. Come around there, afterward."

IN less than half a minute, Pinkey and Slick were gone with Bron, while skulking thugs were joining Bugs in the darkness of the rear hallway. Brought in from the back alley, those lurkers were eagerly watching the men who entered from the front.

A smarter crook than Bugs would not have pitched into Joe Cardona and the detective sergeant who came with the ace inspector. In fact, Pinkey had meant that Bugs was simply to cover the departure with Bron. But Bugs, with one kill to his discredit, was anxious for more. Pinkey had said to "take care" of the bulls; and with Bugs; that meant to drill them.

Moreover, Joe Cardona was the one member of the force who had lived far too long, according to the mode of calculation used by Bugs Hopton.

Cardona was a man of hunches. He wasn't halfway to the stairs, before he scented danger. His swarthy face went suddenly grim; he shoved his stocky body in front of the accompanying detective sergeant.

"Look out, Markham!" With the words, Cardona reached for a gun. "Dive for cover!"

Foemen were leveling revolvers when Cardona shouted; but those crooks weren't the first to fire. Intervention came from the stairway. There, a strident laugh offered challenge that no crook could ignore. Thugs snarled their recognition of The Shadow's sardonic laugh; changed their aim to his direction.

The Shadow was speaking with bullets, as well as mirth.

His two guns produced a sudden staccato, as they coughed their leaden message. Crooks went diving for cover of their own, and all of them didn't make it. Their own shots might have been blanks, for their aim was halted on its way.

Those who tried to get in accurate shots were dropped where they stood. The ones who dived weren't able to keep their muzzles on the blackness where they knew The Shadow lurked.

Joe Cardona recognized The Shadow's laugh. From its tone, he knew that the cloaked fighter had a route of retreat, if he needed it. That was why Cardona made for the street, taking Markham with him.

Out front were two patrolmen; Cardona wanted them with him, when he made another sally.

From among the scattered crooks, Bugs Hopton made a sudden lunge; then turned in the direction of the alley. He wasn't anxious to face The Shadow's fire; nor were the gorillas who went with him. Nevertheless, they were due to experience more battle. They could hear The Shadow's laugh, as he pursued them.

IN the alley, mobsters spread. The Shadow kept to the doorway, stabbing shots that were aimed for the spurts of his foemen's revolvers. Occasional yells told when crooks were clipped by The Shadow's withering fire. Finally, a shout was proof that Bugs and his crew had lingered too long.

The shout came from Cardona. He and his small squad had rounded the block to reach the alleyway.

Thugs took to their heels; and sweeping close behind them came The Shadow. Bugs saw him; tried to dive away from an aiming automatic muzzle. The Shadow's arm swung; his fist sledged the mobleader's head.

It wasn't that Bugs was just lucky. The Shadow was easy with him, for a reason that was to become apparent later. That was why Bugs received The Shadow's weighted fist instead of the metal barrel of a gun. As it was, the jolt left Bugs half groggy.

Bugs didn't even wonder where The Shadow had gone. Hazily, he tried to find a car with mobbies in it. He didn't realize that his crew was hopelessly scattered.

As he thought of it afterward, Bugs was in luck when someone grabbed him by the shoulder and shoved him behind the wheel of a coupé.

"Get goin' Bugs," came a gruff voice. "You gotta drive, while I watch for the bulls."

Avenue lights were dancing ahead of him, but Bugs managed to maneuver the car, while the man beside him occasionally yanked the wheel to keep the coupé off the curb. As Bugs steadied, he kept his eyes straight ahead, while he sidemouthed the inquiry:

"That you, Joey?"

"Yeah" was the reply. "Don't waste no time, though. There's a car tailin' us. Wait! I guess it's O.K. Just, some more of the mob."

Taking a roundabout course, Bugs finally reached a darkened parking space alongside an old garage. He told Joey to wait, while he talked to the others. When Bugs returned, he ordered Joey to come up with him.

They entered a doorway; reached the second floor of an old house that looked deserted. There, Bugs left Joey in a darkened hall, while he went in to find Pinkey and Slick.

Bugs didn't have a chance to tell what had happened. Pinkey motioned for silence. Slick was still working on Bron. The confession was nearing its completion. Bugs watched Bron scrawl the last line, then apply his signature.

"Thanks for bringing me here," said Bron, plaintively. "It's quiet. I could think. I'm ready to go with you to headquarters."

It was Pinkey who snorted a rebuke to Bron's suggestion. Pinkey had snatched the confession, and was reading it.

"You won't have to take a rap for this," he told Bron. "There's an easier way out. Listen, while I tell you."

BRON listened. He was amazed when he learned what Thurley wanted done on the morrow. Even in his present plight, he foresaw bad consequences.

"If I accept those books," he exclaimed, "I can go to jail for it!"

"It would be easier than a murder rap, wouldn't it?" demanded Pinkey. "Anyway, you won't be found out. And neither will this be."

Thurley waved the confession under Bron's eyes. He made it plain that Detective Quaine was a regular guy; to which Slick added his own declaration. Bron finally capitulated.

"I'll go through with it," he gasped. "But if you blackmail me once, you may try it again—"

"Not me," interrupted Pinkey. "This is the only deal you can handle for me, Bron. So why should I bother you?"

It became evident that Bron was suspicious of the supposed Bill Quaine. He felt that he could trust an ordinary crook; but not a detective who had double-crossed the law. Pinkey listened seriously to that argument.

He nudged Bugs, who caught the idea. Pinkey wanted the gun that had the blank cartridges. Bugs slipped it to him. Shoving his face toward Bron's, Pinkey rasped:

In the alley, mobsters spread. The Shadow kept to the doorway, stabbing shots that were aimed for the spurts of his foemen's revolver.

"You've got guts, Bron. That's why I'm listening to what you tell me. You think Quaine's a double-crosser; so do I. We don't need him, neither of us!"

Pinkey jabbed the gun muzzle against Slick's ribs, so suddenly that the fake dick was startled. There was a tug of the trigger; a muffled shot. For the moment, Slick thought that Pinkey had actually handed him a bullet. Staggering back, hand against his side, Slick suddenly understood.

The fall that he made won the approval even of Bugs Hopton. Afterward, Bugs was willing to concede that he couldn't have faked a death scene any better. Slick was writhing when he reached the wall; his collapse came with the same suddenness that Bron had noted in Parrington's death.

Bron stared—partly awed, partly fearful.

"You—you've killed him!" he told Pinkey. "Like I killed Parrington!"

"Yeah," agreed Pinkey, "only there's a difference. They've found Parrington's body; but they won't find Quaine's. I know where to bury my dead. Anyway, I've done you a favor. There won't be no double-cross while I'm around. That goes for you, Bron, like it did for Quaine!"

Turning Bron over to Bugs, Pinkey told the mobleader to have one of his men take Bron

home. Bugs said he'd use Joey, because the latter was in the hall. He took Bron outside; then returned to find Slick alive again, receiving Pinkey's congratulations.

RIDING in the coupé with Joey, Bron didn't have a word to say. The hoodlum driver dropped him near his home; watched Bron walk away like a person waking from a dream. When the coupé pulled away from the curb, a whispered laugh came from Joey's lips.

That tone proved that Bugs had made a bad mistake. It wasn't one of his own thugs who had rescued him; it was The Shadow. From beneath his sweater, The Shadow was producing black hat and cloak, placing them on the seat beside him.

Once he had taken this coupé back where it belonged, he could vanish, letting Bugs think that Joey had simply gone with the rest of the crowd. But it wasn't his clever ruse, alone, that caused The Shadow's laugh.

A silent witness to the scene at the hideout, The Shadow had linked a few more facts. He was willing to let Bron go through with the matter of the oil company's books. For The Shadow knew that Pinkey Findlen wasn't through with crime.

There was a payoff coming, larger than any before. That was when The Shadow would find his greatest opportunity to expose the present reign of New York's biggest racketeer.

CHAPTER XV
CARDONA TAKES ADVICE

THE next morning, crooks had more cause to congratulate themselves. According to the newspapers, the death of Roy Parrington was something of a mystery. The gun battle that had occurred downstairs in the apartment house had merely served further to confuse the facts.

A few thugs had been captured; but they couldn't have told much, even if they had been willing to squeal. Those hoodlums who formed the core of Bugs Hopton's outfit had all managed to get away in the second car. The rest were recruits who didn't even know who commanded them.

Why had Roy Parrington died?

Even that was a mystery; for the man had no underworld connections, nor was he wealthy. There were persons, of course, who had engineered shady deals through Parrington, but they were keeping strict silence.

All that news unquestionably had its effect upon Lewis Bron. When the auditor visited the offices of the World Oil interests, he certified the books just as they stood.

That pleased Giles Jondran, the gray-haired president of the oil company, when Bron stopped in to see him. Jondran always prided himself on the efficiency of his own staff; and he felt that the auditor's unqualified approval was a tribute to the entire organization.

Despite the comfortable quiet of Jondran's office, Bron felt ill at ease, and was glad to get away. Not only was he conscience-stricken when he received Jondran's commendation; but there was a visitor present whose eyes worried Bron.

Jondran introduced that hawkfaced stranger as Lamont Cranston, one of the stockholders of World Oil. Bron had heard of Cranston; knew that he was reputedly a millionaire.

Therefore, it bothered Bron badly, when his mind went skipping back to his homeward ride from Pinkey's hideout.

Why he kept thinking of Joey, the thug who had driven the car, Bron couldn't guess. He certainly did not link Joey with Cranston.

Afterward, Bron was inclined to believe that his own imagination had been responsible for his nervousness. But he was confident that he had covered all traces of the jitters.

Bron received a telephone call, after he reached his office. When he reported that everything had gone as ordered, he heard a gloating chuckle from the receiver.

That piece of news was all that Pinkey Findlen wanted to know.

The big-shot was confident that The Shadow knew nothing of last night's factors. Pinkey assumed that The Shadow, hard up for a trail, had merely tagged along with Joe Cardona. As for Joey's arrival at the apartment house, that was easily explained.

CLYDE BURKE

Someone in another apartment must have heard the shot that Bugs fired, and put in a call to headquarters. Probably that caller had been uncertain about the affair; hence, Cardona had decided to make it a matter of personal investigation.

Pinkey hadn't the remotest idea that Parrington had made the call. In Pinkey's opinion, the fellow would have been too scared to do so. Slick had certainly put the heat on him, with that old stunt of passing himself as Quaine.

PERHAPS it was The Shadow's own lack of information regarding Parrington that caused him to suppose that the man had actually called Cardona.

The Shadow had encountered no clues to the five thousand dollar shakedown that had been staged in Ondrey's office. All he had to work on was the fact that Bron had gone to Parrington's apartment.

That indicated that Roy Parrington had suspected coming crime. Therefore, The Shadow regarded a call to Cardona as the one logical explanation for the ace inspector's arrival. Calculating further, The Shadow saw that Cardona might have facts that he had not revealed to the newspapers.

That was why, at noon, a reporter named Clyde Burke made an unexpected visit to Cardona's office. Clyde, though he worked for a tabloid newspaper called the *Classic,* was also an agent of The Shadow.

Clyde's arrival was highly opportune.

The reporter found Cardona going over a batch of papers that the inspector shoved aside the moment he saw Clyde. Hunching back in his chair, Cardona became poker-faced. Clyde only grinned.

"I thought you'd have something, Joe," he said, wisely. "What is it; new dope on the Parrington murder?"

"No. Talk to the homicide squad about that." Cardona spoke bluntly at first; then suddenly changed tone: "Say, Burke, you get around a lot. Tell me—do you think any rackets are starting up again?"

Clyde shook his head. He hadn't heard of any.

"I'm supposed to look into it," remarked Cardona as if annoyed by a new assignment. "What I need is some good men. Here's one fellow who helped a lot in the cleanup"—Joe lifted the papers from the desk—"so I've been going over his record. You've heard of him: Bill Quaine."

Clyde agreed that Quaine had a real reputation as a racket smasher. Secretly, the reporter was elated. Facts pieced perfectly. Cardona had certainly received a call from Parrington: what was more, the man had mentioned Quaine by name.

Though Cardona didn't know it, he was getting close to unsuspected facts. With more to go on, he might learn the details of the clever impersonation staged by Slick Thurley.

Working under orders from The Shadow, Clyde was prepared for such a situation. That was why he suggested:

"Why don't you talk to Quaine, Joe?"

"Quaine is out of town," returned Cardona. "On a long vacation. Anyway, he'd say he was good. I want somebody else's opinion."

Clyde jotted down several names, passed them across the desk to Cardona with the comment:

"Why don't you talk to these fellows?"

The list contained the names of managers of various nightclubs. The Bubble Club was not included. That was one place where The Shadow didn't want Cardona to drop in.

"They all knew Quaine," insisted Clyde. "Maybe they can tell you how much he really did toward smashing the nightclub racket. When you make the rounds, Joe, stick to the bunch that I have listed. They're the sort who won't stall."

IT was nearly five o'clock when Cardona completed his tour, for he had to sit around in several night clubs waiting for the managers to arrive. The whole job, however, was worth the trouble. Cardona was in a state of mental torment, when he arrived back in his office.

Detective Sergeant Markham was there; and Cardona could not help bursting loose with what he had learned.

"I've found out plenty about Bill Quaine!" exclaimed the inspector. "He's been running a racket of his own! All during that nightclub mess, he was walking in on places, getting what he called 'evidence'; but that wasn't what he was after!

"He was making trouble for those nightclubs. Every manager that confided too much in Quaine, began to find the clamps coming down on him from the racket ring; Quaine always had an alibi for it, so no one man thought he was phony.

"But when you get the same hints from a dozen of them, you know what lies behind it. If those fellows had talked together, they'd have seen through the racket themselves; but nightclub managers don't get too chummy with each other. It took an outsider, like myself, to get the real lowdown."

Cardona yanked open a desk drawer; brought out the file that he found there. He studied it with angry eyes, then flung the papers on the desk.

"Who took that stuff about Bill Quaine?" he demanded. "This isn't the data I had before. Who's been in here, Markham?"

Markham hadn't seen anyone; but he admitted that he had not been in the office all along. Cardona went to the office door; in the hallway he saw a stoopish droopy-faced janitor, busy with mop and brush.

"Come in here, Fritz!" gruffed Cardona. "I want to talk to you."

The janitor shambled into the office. Cardona took the papers on the desk.

"Did you see anybody in this office?" he roared. "Anybody who went out with a batch of papers like these?"

Fritz shook his head. His eyes were listless, dull.

"You've been around here all along, Fritz?"

"Yah," Fritz nodded. "Not all along. Only a little while."

Cardona slapped the papers on the desk. Fritz wasn't of any use; he knew as little as Markham. In fact, Joe wasn't even annoyed when Fritz began to paw the papers, looking at them curiously.

"I know him," grunted Fritz, suddenly. "Yah. Bill Quaine."

Cardona swung about. Fritz was pointing to a photograph that had come loose from the papers. It was Quaine's picture, all right, but what it was doing in this batch of records, Cardona didn't know until he looked more closely.

He started to snatch the photo from Fritz's hands; the janitor dropped it. The picture fell face downward on the desk.

Fritz was shambling away, back to his mop and bucket, while Cardona was staring at the name on back of the photo. That name wasn't Bill Quaine; it was Slick Thurley.

CARDONA scanned the papers. Amazement took control of his poker face. Here were records of a sort the police didn't have, although they were backed with certain official data that had never yet been properly linked.

"Slick Thurley!" exclaimed Cardona to Markham. "Say—he's a dead ringer for Bill Quaine, but we never knew it! I've heard of Slick Thurley; he's been in some jams, too, but he always managed to get out of them.

"That's because we never guessed his real racket. He's been doubling for Quaine! With this mug of his, he could get away with it, by talking like Bill and acting like him. But, that's something we can check up on in a lineup.

"Bill Quaine is O.K.; the guy we've got to find is Slick Thurley. When we get him, we'll know who murdered Parrington; and I've got a hunch, Markham, that we'll learn a lot besides!"

The telephone bell jangled. Cardona answered. When he heard a whispered voice across the wire, he didn't have to be told who had put the new papers in his desk drawer. Joe Cardona was listening to The Shadow.

All during that call, Cardona nodded. When he hung up, he pulled a telegraph blank from the desk drawer and began to write a wire.

"Forget all that's happened," Cardona told Markham. "We're keeping this business to ourselves. I've found out the best way to handle it."

Downstairs, Fritz, the janitor, was hanging up the receiver of a pay telephone. Hoisting his mop and bucket, he went to an obscure locker. Putting down the implements, he opened the locker and drew out a black cloak and slouch hat.

As those garments settled over the head and shoulders of the pretended Fritz, a whispered laugh came from obscured lips. Though only an echo, that mirth identified its owner.

It was the laugh of The Shadow!

CHAPTER XVI
THE GO-BETWEEN

THAT night, Maude Revelle had a date with Pinkey Findlen. Maude expected it to be for dinner only; when Cranston had called her on the telephone, she had told her new friend that she might be able to see him later.

It was thought of Cranston that made Maude give Pinkey a suggestion, when they met at the side door of her apartment house.

"Let's go to a decent place, for a change," insisted Maude. "You know what happened at the Hayrick, the time you ran out on me."

"I didn't take no powder," argued Pinkey. "The Shadow slugged me. My pals had to carry me out."

"They didn't think of me, though, did they?" retorted Maude. "Which means that maybe you didn't, either."

Pinkey was muttering when he hailed a taxi. Once in the cab, he decided to humor Maude.

"All right," he growled. "You name the place—provided it ain't somewhere that people are going to lamp me."

"It won't be," assured Maude.

The place where she took Pinkey was the one where she had dined with Cranston. Pinkey gave the surroundings a disgruntled stare, but was forced to admit that it was secluded. The little room was certainly a good spot where two people could be alone.

The dinner, too, pleased Pinkey reasonably well, after Maude had translated the French terms that appeared on the bill-of-fare.

"You've got class, kid," approved Pinkey. "I've always said you had, ain't I? That's why I never introduced you to the mugs I pal around with."

"I've met Claude Ondrey," reminded Maude.

"Yeah, but he ain't no mug," rejoined Pinkey. "I mean guys like—well, never mind who they are. They ain't in your class."

"And maybe you aren't, either."

Maude's remark brought an ugly stare from Pinkey. That glare didn't make the girl flinch.

"Figure it for yourself," insisted Maude. "You've always tried to bluff me, Pinkey. Why deny it?"

"I didn't drag you into the racket, did I?"

"You've come close to it. You haven't fooled me, Pinkey. I know you've framed things so I'd look as crooked as you are, in case you wanted to put me in wrong with the police."

Pinkey gave a short laugh. He liked Maude's direct manner, especially because it was leading up to a plan that he had in mind.

"I suppose you want to ditch me," he remarked, "because you've fallen for this silk-hat guy. Say—what's the name of this bird who's too good with his dukes?"

"That's my business," returned Maude, coolly. "I haven't mentioned your name to him; so I'm not telling you who he is."

PINKEY'S eyes showed a mingling of expressions. Through his mind were passing the thoughts that Maude wasn't the sort who would talk; also, that she was getting too ritzy in her ideas, to suit him.

After all, Pinkey decided, blondes were plentiful; and what Pinkey liked about most of the ones that he had met was the fact that he had found them dumb. He'd made a bad guess with Maude. She was smart.

That had seemed good, at first. If she'd turned crooked, and acted dumb, she could have helped in Pinkey's business. But Maude had never listened to reason along those lines.

What Pinkey wanted, most of all, was to outsmart her. He knew that if he did, Maude would be through with him forever; but that seemed likely, anyway. Right now, Pinkey saw how she could be useful; and the time was right for his proposition.

"You've taken a shine to the silk-hat guy, ain't you, kid?" he questioned. "All right—suppose we do call it quits. How would you like that?"

"I'd like it a lot," admitted Maude, frankly. "But get this straight, Pinkey: I'm not trying to make this fellow fall for me. He's just a friend, that's all."

"I'd figured that," nodded Pinkey. "What you're hoping is that he'll introduce you to a lot of other stuffed shirts, so you can go ritzy."

"That's partly so," admired Maude. "Of course—"

"Never mind the rest. If this guy is the real McCoy, and really knows people, you're welcome to him."

Maude's eyes widened. For a moment, she thought that Pinkey was getting big-hearted; then she began to look for the catch. It came.

"Tomorrow," undertoned Pinkey, "there's a swell cocktail party being thrown on Long Island, at the home of a dame named Mrs. Rothmorton. This guy you talk about ought to be able to crash the gate, and take you with him."

Maude agreed that such might be the case.

"There, you'll meet a doll named Beth Jondran," continued Pinkey. "All you've got to do is find out when she's coming into town, and how. Nobody's going to know it, if you spill me that news."

"And in return?" asked Maude.

"It's quits for you and me," returned Pinkey. "Everything forgotten. We've never heard of each other."

Maude wanted to hold back acceptance, but she couldn't. The words fairly sprang to her lips; before she knew it, she was thanking Pinkey, and giving full agreement.

"O.K., kid," declared Pinkey. "But remember"— his eyes went ugly—"you go through with it, or else—"

"I'll go through with it," interposed Maude, "provided nothing is going to happen to this Jondran girl."

"She won't be hurt. That's understood."

WHEN Pinkey and Maude went from the little café, a figure emerged from the hallway phone booth. The Shadow had been there all the while; he had overheard the entire conversation. The wiring that ran from the dinner table to the telephone booth was equipped with a two-way hookup.

Maude wasn't at her apartment very long before she received a phone call from Cranston. One hour later, they were sixty-odd stories above Manhattan's streets, watching the floor show in an exclusive nightclub. Maude found her chance to mention tomorrow's party at the Rothmorton residence.

Cranston, she learned, was a welcome guest there and would be glad to attend the party, if Maude went with him. The girl was enthusiastic with her thanks, and she was genuinely pleased at the prospect of meeting persons who were socially prominent.

But with it, Maude showed a certain restrained bitterness that few persons other than The Shadow would have noticed. He knew what was on Maude's mind. She didn't like the task that she had to perform for Pinkey Findlen.

To Maude's credit, the girl would probably have turned down the offer that Pinkey made her, if it hadn't given her a chance for absolute freedom, along with another factor.

The other item was that Maude knew how tough Pinkey would become, if he wanted his way. If she hadn't taken his promise, he would have changed it to a threat. There were probably ways where Pinkey could have forced her to go through with the plot against Beth Jondran.

There had been times, Maude had heard, when Pinkey planted phony servants in swell households. He could manage to do that with her, if he wanted; and supply a triggerman to watch her.

During the rest of the evening, Maude was impelled by a huge desire to confess everything to Cranston. At moments, she hated herself because she didn't tell her story. At other times, she calmed enough to reason that if she spoke the truth, Cranston would also be placed in danger.

All the while, Maude was confident that she had kept those thoughts from the man who had befriended her. Actually, The Shadow recognized everything that passed in Maude's mind. That wasn't difficult, since he already knew her story.

Maude reached her apartment soon after midnight. She hadn't long to wait, before Pinkey called. From his cautious tone, Maude decided that he had broken his usual rule and was calling her from his hideout.

As she heard Pinkey's voice, she wished with all her might that she knew where the hideout was, for she was in a mood to finish Pinkey's entire game.

The big-shot didn't state that information. He merely wanted to know if Maude had arranged matters for tomorrow. Listlessly, Maude told him that everything was set.

IN the hideout, Pinkey gave a gruff chuckle when he hung up the telephone. Slick and Bugs were present to hear the big-shot's glee.

"Its going to be a cinch!" announced Pinkey. "We'll snatch this Jondran doll, and hold her while we make her old man listen to the million dollar proposition. After that, we'll let her go."

"That means Maude won't make a holler. She'll be glad because I'm through with her. Only I won't be"—Pinkey's eyes went glinty; his underlip gave a shove—"because were going to rub out that blonde, after we've finished everything else.

"No dame can pull ritzy stuff on me and get away with it! I talked nice to her tonight and, for a while, I really meant it. Only I changed my mind, afterward."

None of the crooks was watching the door, as it closed a fraction of an inch. A figure glided down the stairs and out through the alleyway, where some of the mobbies were keeping guard. The watchers were on the lookout for anyone who started trouble; but they hadn't expected a shrouded prowler who could creep in and out like night itself.

Later, a voice spoke within the darkness of a soundproof limousine. Its tone was The Shadow's whisper, forwarding instructions by shortwave radio; orders that would reach his agents and have them ready on the morrow.

Burbank acknowledged those instructions; and, in his listening post, the last tone that the contact man received was one that promised full success.

That tone was The Shadow's laugh.

CHAPTER XVII
CRIME'S ZERO HOUR

MAUDE REVELLE was at her best, the next afternoon. She had expected that the guests at the cocktail party might regard her as an outsider; instead, they received her like an old friend.

That was partly because she came with Lamont Cranston; but Maude's own conduct was an added factor.

Most of Maude's society notions had been gained from watching movies; but she had profited a lot from the process. Moreover, she had an aptitude for imitating other persons, without having them realize it.

That was one reason why Pinkey had liked her. She had seemed "classy," as he put it; but she talked his own language. He had never realized that her conversation was unnatural. Nor did the guests at the Rothmorton party suspect that Maude was not of their own ilk.

There were times when Maude used slangy terms; and once in a while, she didn't grasp what others talked about. But they accepted her slang expressions as quips; and Maude was wise enough to preserve silence, when she found herself beyond her depth.

There was one girl at the party that Maude liked the moment she saw her. The girl was a slender brunette whose smile was as friendly as her eyes. She admired the tasteful way in which Maude was dressed; and that pleased Maude more than ever.

The two were not introduced at first, because most of the persons at the party were already acquainted. When Maude finally met the brunette, she was pleased until she heard the latter's name.

The girl that Maude liked so well was Beth Jondran.

As the party progressed, Maude learned that Beth's father was a very important man in the oil business. She also found out that Beth was driving into the city alone, in her roadster. The car happened to be parked just outside the window; it was the only roadster in the driveway.

Maude had no trouble learning the license number. Gloomily, she scribbled it on a bit of paper, tucked it into her cigarette case. With it, she marked the time at which Beth intended to leave; namely, a quarter past six. Beth wanted to meet some friends at seven; but they wouldn't wait for her if she was late.

That fact also bothered Maude; for it fixed everything nicely, in accordance with Pinkey's plans. Maude was hoping desperately that something might happen to prevent Beth's capture.

For her own part, she saw no other way to manage it; whether right or wrong, she had to go through with Pinkey's orders.

IT was nearly six o'clock, when Beth suddenly approached Maude and handed her an envelope. The deed was timely, for Maude had reached the point where she knew she would have to call Ondrey and give him news for Pinkey.

"I've been carrying this for the last ten minutes," laughed Beth. "Mr. Cranston gave it to me, for you. He found that he had to leave unexpectedly. I'm terribly forgetful at times. So much so, that I can never remember where I place the car keys. That's why I always leave them in the car, whenever I know that it is safe."

Maude was opening the envelope. Dusk had gathered; it was gloomy in the corner where the two girls were. Beth turned on a floor lamp. She was starting away, when Maude halted her.

With the envelope only partly opened, Maude forgot about it to express something to Beth.

"You know, Miss Jondran," she said, "there's one thing I wouldn't ever do, that's double-cross anyone."

Beth smiled sympathetically. She didn't quite understand; but she saw that Maude was badly troubled.

"I mean, anyone like Mr. Cranston," continued Maude. "Or anyone as swell as you are, Miss Jondran. But sometimes—well, there are things you can't tell a person."

Beth looked at the note, then asked: "You mean something you cannot tell Mr. Cranston?"

"That's it," returned Maude. "That is, in a way. What I mean is, if a fellow doesn't know something he ought to know, but if you've promised someone else that you won't tell him—" Her voice broke; Maude was choking when she added:

"What I mean is, a real guy like Mr. Cranston

ought to be treated right. And so should you, Miss Jondran."

"I don't quite understand," soothed Beth. "But Maude—I know you won't mind my calling you Maude—I feel that real persons can trust each other. That often solves life's problems. But I feel, too, that each person must be allowed to do what he or she thinks is best."

"You do?" blurted Maude. "Would you trust me to do that, Beth? After only meeting me once?"

"Certainly! One meeting is enough."

"Gee, you're swell!"

"Why not open the envelope?" asked Beth. "It seems to have brought up your problem. Perhaps it will solve it."

Maude didn't think it would, but she did not say so. She decided to do as Beth suggested. Maude needed a few minutes to get the choke out of her voice. Beth left her; a few moments later, Maude was reading Cranston's message.

Maude's eyes were a bit tear-dimmed. She couldn't believe the words that blurred in front of her. When she had wiped her eyes, she read them again. They were amazing; but real. They were so utterly incredible that Maude stood motionless.

SLOWLY, Maude came to life, a grim smile showing on her face. She crumpled the message, not observing that its words were fading from view. Hurrying out to a little hallway, she reached the telephone.

She called the Bubble Club. Ondrey answered, his voice impatient, worried. He'd had three calls from Pinkey; the big-shot was still awaiting news from Maude.

"Tell him to keep his shirt on!" snapped Maude. "Here's the dope he wants. The dame is leaving here in about ten minutes. She's driving a roadster, and she's going to be alone. Here—take down the license number."

Ondrey recorded the number as Maude gave it.

"When she gets into town," added Maude, "she'll leave the car in a parking lot on Sixtieth Street, right next to the old Zenith Apartments. From there, she always takes a cab. So it ought to be easy to grab her.

"But remember: Tell Pinkey there's to be no rough stuff. He's not going to know where I am, tonight, and if I hear that this dame gets hurt, it's going to go bad with Pinkey! He and I made a deal; tell him to remember it."

A few minutes later, Maude was on her way to the front door, wearing her hat and coat. Beth met her, asked if she intended to go into New York.

"You can come with me, Maude," suggested Beth. "I'm leaving in just a few minutes."

"Thanks, Beth," returned Maude. "But I can't wait. Not even one minute."

Maude's smile told much to Beth, even though it didn't give the details. Beth's tone was sweet when she asked softly:

"The message solved everything?"

Maude nodded, happily. She gave Beth's hand a squeeze, then hurried out into the darkness.

MEANWHILE, Maude's message had reached its destination. In the hideout, Pinkey repeated the details to Slick and Bugs, chiefly for the latter's benefit.

"It's your job, Bugs," said Pinkey. "Get up there to the parking lot and grab that doll in a hurry. And remember: no rough stuff. We ain't taking chances on Maude making trouble.

"Take the dame down to Ondrey's. Let him look out for her. The office is a good place for him to keep her; and Ondrey has enough sense to make her know we won't hurt her.

"Tell him to give her a feed, if she's hungry; and if he hears from Maude, to let her know that everything's being done in style. Dames are soft to handle, if you kid 'em right."

Bugs left the hideout. There was a thug in the hall; he growled for the fellow to come along. Pinkey and Slick heard the hoodlum follow him. A few minutes later, Pinkey and Slick stole out of the lair.

On their way through the alley, Pinkey undertoned remarks regarding their next step.

"We'll handle it together," he declared. "Only, this time, I'll spill my real moniker; but you're still Bill Quaine. The more we tell old Jondran, the better, provided we keep that part of the story straight."

They had neared a parked car. Slick gave a sudden shift; a quick exclamation.

"What's up?" snapped Pinkey.

Slick turned a flashlight toward a wall beside the alley. The glow showed nothing more than bricks.

"It was like some guy nudged me!"

"There's nobody here," rasped Pinkey. "Better take a look around, though. There's one guy we don't want to meet. That's The Shadow!"

Pinkey was stepping toward the car when Slick flashed the light back into the alleyway. He saw something; made a pounce. Pinkey scrambled from the car in time to hear the thud of a slugging gun; the clatter of a person in the alley.

Pinkey's oval flashlight beamed; his gun was leveled, but he lowered it a moment later when he saw the face of Slick Thurley. Stepping out to meet the big-shot, Slick beckoned.

"Douse your glim, Pinkey," suggested Slick. "We won't need it. I fixed the snooper!"

Slick led the way back, turning his flashlight on a huddled man whose hat was bashed over his eyes. The fellow lay face downward, his shoulders so hunched that Slick found it difficult to turn the flashlight on his features.

Even then, he managed only a partial view of the man's profile; and Pinkey saw no more than the fellow's chin.

"He ain't The Shadow," assured Slick. "Maybe he's some snooper The Shadow sent here; but even that ain't likely. I'd say he was just a guy that showed up where he wasn't wanted."

"Yeah," agreed Pinkey. "He probably saw Bugs and the crew sneaking out of here, and thought he'd find out where they came from. Leave him lay, Slick. We're in a hurry. What's more, we're never coming back to this hideout.

A FEW minutes after Pinkey and his companion had driven away, there was a stir from the inner reaches of the alley. A flashlight glimmered; the tiny torch was The Shadow's. The beam reached the slugged man who lay in the alley—a relic of the brief fight staged by Slick Thurley.

The huddled form was senseless. Who the man was; how he had come here, were questions that did not seem to trouble The Shadow. He simply extinguished his flashlight, lifted the victim from the cobblestones and carried the man across his shoulder.

Soft mockery came from The Shadow's lips, as he lugged the senseless burden from the alleyway. That tone was edged with prophecy—one that crooks would not have liked, if they had heard it.

Both Pinkey Findlen and Slick Thurley were later to regret this brief episode in which they had figured.

The Shadow knew!

CHAPTER XVIII
CRIME'S CAPTIVE

THE first stop on Pinkey's route was the Bubble Club; and for a very important reason. Ondrey was in the office; he looked pleased when he saw Pinkey and Slick step from the elevator. Ondrey started at once to open the safe, while Pinkey made a suggestion:

"Take a gander outside, Slick. See if there's any phonies in the nightclub. Don't show yourself much. We don't want any guys saying they saw Bill Quaine here."

Ondrey's safe bulged with swag from previous crimes, for this was where crooks stored their profits. Whenever Ondrey opened it in Pinkey's presence, he always let the big-shot see him handle the combination.

That was one reason why Pinkey had sent Slick out to look around. But there were eyes, tonight, that saw Ondrey manipulate the dial; other eyes than those of Pinkey Findlen. The Shadow was atop the elevator, watching through the panel.

Ondrey produced two envelopes; both were opened. Pinkey was going over the contents, when he saw Slick return. He showed the envelopes to the man who looked like Bill Quaine.

"This is the one we keep," said Pinkey. "The other, with the mark on it, goes to Jondran."

Slick nodded. Then: "You're going to let me handle them?"

"Sure thing," returned Pinkey. "You're supposed to be the copper, ain't you? All right, let's go."

They were starting for the elevator when Ondrey said something about Bugs Hopton. Pinkey stroked his chin.

"We'll wait a couple of minutes," decided Pinkey, "just in case we hear from Bugs."

Slick stood half in the elevator, so close, that The Shadow could have reached down to touch him. Pinkey remained chatting with Ondrey. A few minutes passed; impatient, Pinkey decided to get started, when the phone bell tingled.

It was Bugs. Ondrey turned the telephone over to Pinkey.

"It was a pipe!" Pinkey heard Bugs declare, eagerly. "The moll didn't even know what it was about! The guy in the parking lot had gone across the street to get a sandwich; so we just grabbed the skirt and shoved her into our own bus."

"Where's the car now?" demanded Pinkey.

"Our bus?" questioned Bugs. "A couple of blocks away, outside the store where I'm phoning from. We left the moll's fancy boat up in the parking lot."

"That part wasn't smart. Never mind, though. We can cover it later. Get her down here in a hurry."

Pinkey told the others how Bugs had made out; but he added that he and Slick weren't going to wait for Beth's arrival. Pinkey summed it with the comment:

"You can handle the soft soap, Ondrey. Me and Slick are the guys that will use the heat. Only, we're working on the old man."

WHEN the pair had gone, Ondrey went out for a look around the nightclub. He wasn't trusting

Slick's report, that all had been well there. But Ondrey came back, smiling broadly.

Though there were a good many strangers present, all looked to be the sort who were out for a good time. None of them appeared to be headquarters men; or the sort of snoopers that Ondrey fancied would serve The Shadow.

Fifteen minutes later, the elevator panel slid open. Ondrey turned to see Bugs Hopton and two thugs bringing in a muffled burden. The prisoner hadn't put up a battle, but the rough mob had not handled her too gently.

Her head was muffled in a piece of cloth that looked like a sack. The crooks had ripped away a portion of her dress, to bind her hands and feet. When they rolled her on a couch in the corner, Ondrey raised an objection.

"That isn't the way you were to handle her," he told Bugs. "I thought you said she didn't put up a fight."

"That's right," agreed Bugs. "But we wanted to see to it that she didn't change her mind. Dolls are that way, you know."

"This girl is limp!" declared Ondrey worried. "Cut her loose, and do it easy. Get that bag off her head. What was the idea of it, anyway?"

"So she wouldn't see where we were taking her," informed Bugs. "We gagged her first, though."

Ondrey spread his arms in anxiety. He was relieved when he saw the prisoner stir while Bugs was freeing her. The hood came away; but still Ondrey didn't see the girl's face, for Bugs was busy removing the handkerchief that gagged her. A moment later, the girl had sagged back upon the couch.

Ondrey pressed forward; he was speaking in his most ingratiating tone:

"I am terribly sorry about this, Miss Jondran. These men were ordered to treat you gently—"

"Cut the stall, Ondrey!" The girl's tone gave harsh interruption, as she swung up from the couch. "Get over there by the desk and raise your mitts! The same goes for the rest of you!"

With the start of that order, the captive tossed her head. Beneath a mass of tousled blond hair, Ondrey saw a face he recognized. This prisoner wasn't Beth Jondran; she was Maude Revelle!

MAUDE'S defiant face meant business. In her hand she held a gun, that she had whipped from within her dress. She had caught Bugs and his mobbies totally off guard, along with Ondrey. Not one of the three thugs had a gun where he could reach it.

"Pinkey thinks he's a wise guy." Maude's tone was loud; Ondrey was afraid it would penetrate to the hall outside the office. "That's why he never introduced me to any of his pals, except you, Ondrey.

"He said he was going to treat the dame right; so to make sure about it, I grabbed her car myself. Well, look at the way I am. Were these gorillas gentle? I'll say they weren't! They were dumb, though; too dumb to frisk me.

"That's why they didn't find this gat that I picked up in the car. And guess who told me to run off with that roadster. The same guy that left the gun for me! The one real guy I've ever met. The Shadow!"

The name brought a hoarse cry from Ondrey. His alarm spread to Bugs and the thugs. It was Bugs who decided to rely on force of numbers. He urged his two pals with the hoarse shout:

"Grab the dame! She won't shoot!"

Mobsters never made that surge. The door of the office flung inward. Across the threshold came three men: Harry Vincent, followed by two other agents of The Shadow. Their guns had the crooks covered.

Settling behind his desk, Ondrey recognized the faces of the invaders. All of them had been seated at a table near the passage to the office. Maude had known that they would be ready. That was why she had given her shrill denunciation of the crooks.

The Shadow's agents bound the prisoners, all except Ondrey. Maude kept the nightclub owner covered with a gun.

"I was going to bawl you out for crossing the dope," she told him, "but that wasn't needed. I didn't have to argue that there had been a mistake. I saw my chance to cover the lot of you, and I took it."

There was a ring from the telephone. Maude ordered Ondrey to answer, and talk sweet. He did his best; then gulped that he didn't know the voice on the wire. It was a quiet voice, he said; but no name had been announced.

Harry Vincent took the telephone abruptly, to speak with Burbank. He made notations during that brief conversation. Hanging up, he strode across the office and dialed the combination of Ondrey's safe.

Ondrey sat riveted with amazement. Maude's voice came to his ears.

"The Shadow knows everything, don't he?" queried the girl. "So this is where Pinkey kept his swag! Well, its going back to the people it belongs to. But not for a while, yet.

"We're staying right here, Ondrey, in case Pinkey calls. If he does, you tell him that you've got Beth Jondran as a prisoner. We wouldn't want to queer the rest of Pinkey's game, would we?"

NUMBLY, Claude Ondrey slumped deep in his chair. The sarcasm in Maude's voice had told him further details of The Shadow's scheme. Pinkey was going through with his present game; but it wasn't going to work out the way the big-shot expected. The whole setup had been turned in The Shadow's favor.

But there was one point that even Ondrey didn't realize. That was the method whereby The Shadow had arranged to turn the tables on Pinkey Findlen, in the midst of the big-shot's coming action.

If The Shadow's plan went well, Pinkey would actually feel the thrill of victory, only to have it wrenched from his grasp. For The Shadow was counting upon more than mere triumph in a final battle. The Shadow's purpose was to clear the names of helpless dupes; to gain vengeance for past crimes, as well as present; to forever squelch the man who had become Manhattan's biggest racketeer: Pinkey Findlen.

That task seemed huge, even for The Shadow. But that was because men of crime had not guessed the hidden fact upon which The Shadow depended.

CHAPTER XIX
THE FINAL TERMS

GILES Jondran lived in a pretentious mansion secluded behind a high wall that cut it off from the hubbub of Manhattan. It wasn't easy for visitors to gain entry there; but Pinkey Findlen had a way. He depended upon Slick Thurley.

"You tell 'em, Slick," ordered Pinkey. Then, with a derisive snort, "I mean, you tell 'em, *Bill.*"

Pinkey's companion told him. He informed Jondran's servant that he was Detective Quaine, arrived on an important duty from headquarters. The servant was convinced; but the two visitors didn't see Jondran right away.

Instead, they cooled their heels in a huge reception room that looked as high as it was wide.

"Who'd want to live in a joint like this?" grumbled Pinkey. "Say—that thing"—he referred to a massive crystal chandelier—"looks like it would come down and crack you on the konk. But, getting back to the point: why ain't Jondran seeing us, Slick?"

Slick didn't reply. Pinkey saw him peering out into the hallway, listening for the approach of servants. Finally, he must have heard someone, for Pinkey saw him step back wearing one of the knowing grins that suited the part of Bill Quaine.

A flunky arrived to conduct the visitors to Jondran's study. They followed a long hall; came to a massive doorway. Entering a little anteroom, Pinkey saw a heavy metal grille barring a doorway on the left.

Beyond the grille was a room; it was dimly lighted, and Pinkey spied the door of a huge vault. There was another door on the right; it was of oak. The servant rapped at that door.

There was a call to come in; the visitors were introduced to a large study, where Giles Jondran sat behind a massive desk. The only lights were near the desk itself, leaving the depths of the room vague, except at one wall, where flames were crackling merrily in a wide fireplace.

Jondran's face was kindly, but marked with lines that gave him a keen expression. His eyes had a steady sparkle, beneath the grayish brows that matched his hair. His tone was businesslike, when he asked:

"Which one of you is Detective Quaine?"

Pinkey nudged toward the man beside him. Jondran inquired regarding Quaine's business here. It developed that Quaine had come for the sole purpose of introducing Mr. Findlen, which he did.

"Just call me Pinkey," announced the big-shot, seating himself at the end of Jondran's desk. "I'd call you by your first name, too, if I knew how to pronounce it. Anyhow, we're acquainted. So let's talk turkey. Hand me those envelopes, Bill."

RECEIVING the envelopes, Pinkey opened the one that was unmarked.

"Take a gander at these," he told Jondran. "First, here's some dope on a guy named Howard Milay. You ought to know him. He runs one of your companies; an outfit called Sphere Shipping."

Giles Jondran nodded, but his expression was perplexed.

"Here's the proof of how Milay swindled a big insurance company," continued Pinkey. "Letters, showing that he knew one of the ships was loaded with junk metal and was due to hit the bottom of the ocean. Only, Milay collected on a cargo of supplies."

Stupefaction came over Jondran's features.

"Next comes John Thorry," announced Pinkey. "Here's the dope on how he bought a lot of punk oil wells and charged them off to another of your companies—Western Oil Fields. He knew those wells were phony. We've got a letter from him, admitting it."

Pinkey didn't even bother to watch Jondran wilt. He brought out the evidence incriminating Martin Meriden.

"Meriden pulled the same sort of deal," declared Pinkey. "He bought up a bunch of service stations that were only on paper. That did another of your nice little companies out of a quarter-million. Meriden gypped Eastern Refineries, just like it shows here."

Jondran started an interruption. Pinkey stopped it with a wave of his hand. He planked Bron's confession on the table along with photographs of Meriden's son, Reggie.

"You think there's an explanation," declared Pinkey. "Sure there is! Meriden wanted to keep his kid out of jail; Lewis Bron is scared he'll go there himself. That's why Bron put an O.K. on your books, Jondran.

"Get it? Your own company was doped out of the fourth quarter-million. Yes, sir—World Oil has plenty to cover up for itself. Here, Bill"—Pinkey shoved the papers and the envelope across to his companion—"put these away."

Pinkey watched Slick sort the papers. Jondran did the same. His eyes showed contempt for Pinkey; but he thought that persuasion might work with the big-shot's companion.

"I can't believe this, Mr. Quaine!" exclaimed Jondran. "You represent the law, yet you ally yourself with a blackmailer!"

Bill Quaine himself could not have registered a blunter look. Jondran heard his gruff voice:

"Yeah, I'm in on the racket. So what?"

Jondran couldn't answer but Pinkey did.

"We've got a million," snapped the big-shot. "Now we're all set to smear the front pages with this stuff about your companies. How would you like that, Jondran?"

"It would mean ruin!" gasped Jondran. "Stock of World Oil would drop, with that of all its subsidiaries!"

"Yeah. Your fifty-million-dollar company would be lucky if it was worth ten million. And half of your own money would go in the smash. But there's a way out of it, Jondran."

"There is?"

"That's right. An easy way out. Just pay us dollar for dollar. Double the ante. With another million bucks, we'll be satisfied!"

JONDRAN'S hands seemed feeble as they drummed the desktop. He, too, was thinking in terms of two million dollars; for he knew that he would have to restore the funds that crooks had already rifled. But Jondran apparently could see no other way out of the dilemma.

"Very well," he decided. "You shall have your million—but with one proviso. I must have a positive guarantee that it is all you intend to ask."

Pinkey opened the second envelope. From it tumbled a different sort of evidence. Here were facts that refuted the incriminating statements in the first envelope.

"Here's the whole way we worked the racket," affirmed Pinkey. "Copies of letters that we swiped. Forged papers pinning things where they didn't belong. Signed statements by some of the boobs that worked for us—particularly a guy named Bugs Hopton.

"For instance, Meriden's son wasn't a safe-cracker. Bron didn't shoot that guy Parrington. All this stuff will square the guys we framed, up to a certain point. Its good enough, ain't it, for you to keep as a receipt?"

He pushed the papers across the desk, with the order:

"Put 'em in the envelope, Quaine."

"Suppose I made that evidence public?" queried Jondran. "What could you do then?"

"You won't spill it," rasped Pinkey, "because you'd have to tell everything that happened. What you'll do is keep it, so that you can explain what we've got, if we use it. All right, Jondran. Let's get back to the million."

Pinkey nudged for Slick to hand Jondran the second envelope. It came over, and Pinkey noted the mark on it. Jondran fumbled the envelope between his hands.

"About the million dollars"—his tone was pathetic—"if you can wait a few days—"

"I thought you'd stall!" snarled Pinkey. "All right, we'll wait, but there'll be somebody else waiting, too!"

He reached for the telephone; dialed Ondrey's number. When Ondrey answered, Pinkey asked if Beth was all right. Mention of the name brought a startled look from Jondran. Pinkey was grinning at Ondrey's assurance that the girl was a prisoner.

"Put her on," suggested Pinkey. "Her old man wants to talk to her."

It was Maude who actually talked across the wire to Jondran; but she had Beth's tone to perfection. Jondran let the receiver chatter. Pinkey politely replaced it on the hook.

"When we get the million," he told Jondran, "you get your daughter. No strings to it; we just want to make sure that we get the dough without no trouble."

FUMBLING in his vest pocket, Jondran produced a key; he passed it weakly to Pinkey. He said that it was the key to the strong room that his visitors had seen when they entered. With a pencil, Jondran scrawled the combination of the vault.

"You've got a million bucks in there?" demanded Pinkey. "You keep all that money in the house?"

"Much of it is in securities," returned Jondran. "There are jewels, also—priceless jewels; but they mean nothing, compared to my daughter's safety! Take all of it, and be gone. If you will promise only to release my daughter—to return her—"

"We'll do that," assured Pinkey. "Come on, Bill."

"Wait a moment." Jondran arose, holding the envelope that had been given to him. "I want to show you how much I trust you, because I know my daughter's life depends upon a show of good faith. I am placing everything in your hands."

He tossed the envelope into the fire, where the flames licked it into oblivion. With a sweep of his arms, Jondran sat down in the chair at the desk, with the gesture of a man who had done all that was humanly possible.

"How was that, Slick?" chuckled Pinkey, as he and his sidekick crossed the anteroom. "The way it's worked out, we can shakedown the old geezer again, if we want to. Hang on to that envelope. Here—let me have it."

Slick made no objection. Pinkey pocketed the envelope; indulged in a short laugh, in which his companion joined.

"This is one job that's as good as done," voiced Pinkey, "and nobody can queer it. Nobody!"

By the emphasis that Pinkey put on the word "nobody," it was plain that he included The Shadow.

CHAPTER XX
THE FINAL MEETING

PINKEY FINDLEN never mistrusted his own ability when he embarked on crime. He was doubtful only of the tasks he left to others; and tonight, for once, he had no qualms regarding events elsewhere. That telephone call to the Bubble Club had convinced Pinkey that all went well there.

All had gone well—but not for Pinkey. The Shadow, through his agents, had taken over that part of the game. He was the one who had real reason to be confident.

Wherever The Shadow might be, he knew that his preliminary plans had worked. It happened, however, that circumstances were to undergo a sudden reversal.

Trouble came to the Bubble Club immediately after Pinkey's phone call, trouble in the persons of arrivals who were capable of producing it.

Maude Revelle had replaced the telephone on the desk, after her well-disguised chat with Giles Jondran. Looking toward Claude Ondrey, she saw puzzlement upon the pudgy man's face. Ondrey couldn't figure why Maude had pretended to be Beth Jondran.

"Didn't get it, did you?" queried Maude. "Well, that was to fox Pinkey. So he wouldn't start any rough stuff over at Jondran's house. See the point?"

Ondrey saw it; but Bugs Hopton apparently didn't. He stared at Ondrey, as if hoping to read the answer in the latter's expression. What Bugs actually saw was something that awoke his entire interest.

The wall panel was sliding open!

Whatever Bugs lacked in careful calculation, he was at least an opportunist. He had proven that on various occasions. Bugs could take long chances in a pinch. He proved it once again.

Bugs was the only person who saw the panel start to open. Before the noiseless wall section was fully open, Bugs guessed that the newcomers were members of his own gun crew.

"Look out!" Bugs shouted. "We're covered by guys that are working for The Shadow!"

Two men sprang from the elevator. Bugs was right; they were members of his outfit. They had come here, wondering what was keeping Bugs. Finding out, they did their best to change the situation.

Like Bugs, they didn't reckon with the ability of The Shadow's agents. Having been told about the elevator panel, the agents swung to meet the invaders.

Guns spoke. Harry Vincent beat one mobster to the shot. So did Cliff Marsland, another agent, stationed just inside the doorway.

Cliff was reputedly a tough guy, known as a killer in the underworld, which he patrolled for

CLIFF MARSLAND

the real purpose of supplying information to The Shadow.

Cliff had stayed in the background to avoid recognition. His range was more difficult; but it didn't matter. Cliff was even quicker with a trigger than Harry.

In dispatching those shots, however, both gave opportunity to others. The two thugs who had been trapped with Bugs, made maddened dives. One reached Harry; the other grabbed Cliff. Though unarmed, they put up a hard struggle.

Even Claude Ondrey came to action. He made a grab for Clyde Burke, third of The Shadow's squad. Wrestling with the reporter, Ondrey had temporary advantage, thanks to his weight. Everyone in the room was in a struggle, except Bugs and Maude.

Bugs didn't rush for the girl. He'd seen too much of Maude's nerve when she had taken things over on her own. Instead, Bugs dived for the elevator, reaching it behind a barricade of strugglers. The men who had launched forth were sprawled on the floor. Bugs cleared them with a bound.

By the time Maude was able to train her gun on Bugs, the panel went shut. The shots that she fired merely ruined the decorative woodwork that concealed the slit in the secret door.

Maude couldn't even reach the wall. She was jounced about by the brawlers. Forgetting Bugs, she turned to aid The Shadow's agents. By that time, they had matters in hand.

Harry and Cliff had beaten down the thugs; Ondrey was backing to his chair, with Clyde's automatic poking his fat stomach.

When Maude gave the details of Bugs Hopton's flight, it was too late to pursue the squinty mobleader.

OUTSIDE the Bubble Club, Bugs found the remnants of his gun crew. He decided that he wouldn't risk a counterattack on Ondrey's office. It would be too risky; furthermore, Bugs knew of someone who might need important aid.

"Listen, guys," he told his outfit. "The big-shot in this racket is Pinkey Findlen. With him is a fellow named Slick Thurley, who looks like a dick named Bill Quaine. So don't let that fool you, when we meet up with them.

"They're calling on a guy named Jondran; and that's where we're going. I'll slide in there first, and you lugs be ready when I call for you."

It wasn't far to Jondran's mansion. The street was silent; Bugs opened the gate and sneaked his five-man crew in among the shrubbery that lined the inner side of the big wall.

Approaching the front door, Bugs rang boldly. He had his gun pocketed by the time a servant appeared.

"I'm here to see a guy named Findlen," began Bugs. "He's in talking to Mr. Jondran."

The servant looked blank.

"There's a dick with him," added Bugs. "A headquarters guy named Bill Quaine. I'm a friend of his."

"You're a detective?"

"Sure! See this badge?" Bugs whipped his coat back, flapped it quickly. "That fixes it. Let me through."

The servant hadn't seen a badge; but he attributed that fact to the darkness. Obligingly, he let Bugs through, pointing out the way to Jondran's study.

Bugs reached the anteroom. He saw the grilled gate; it was wide open. Beyond, he observed the two men he had come to see: Pinkey and Slick. They had opened the main door of the vault, and were just finishing the combination of an inner barrier.

They didn't even hear Bugs enter. The inner door came wide; the room lights showed an empty space backed by a brick wall. Bugs heard Pinkey voice an oath.

"Jondran's stalled us!" rasped the big-shot. "This vault is empty! It ain't even a vault. It hasn't been finished. Wait'll we talk to Jondran. He won't get nowhere with this stuff!"

Pinkey turned about, growling for Slick to do the same. They saw Bugs; Pinkey came up with his gun. Recognizing his own man, Pinkey lowered the weapon. Angrily, he demanded:

"What're you doing here?"

Hurriedly, Bugs explained how matters had gone bad at the Bubble Club. That was all Pinkey needed to know.

"Jondran must have got wind of it!" he grated. "A wise guy, huh? Thinking he's safe because we haven't got the dame. We'll show him how safe he is! Come along!"

Pinkey strode to the door of Jondran's study; thrusting it open, he faced the big desk. Jondran was behind it; hearing the clatter, he raised his head. Pinkey expected to see a terrified face. He was disappointed.

Jondran's pose of fear had been a mask. He had dropped it, after bluffing Pinkey.

HIS face stern, Jondran eyed the invaders with a sharp, defiant gaze. Pinkey strode three paces forward, started to lift his gun.

It was a murderous gesture; but Pinkey didn't intend to rub out Jondran just yet. Maybe Jondran knew it, for he smiled.

"You're coming through with that dough, Jondran"—Pinkey's rasp meant business—"and you're coming through quick! Next time you stage a bluff, make sure you've got something to back it!"

Jondran did not budge. Nor did Pinkey's gun rise farther. The big-shot saw the full reason for Jondran's calm. The gray-haired man was not alone. Pinkey hadn't noticed that at first; nor had his companions.

For the form near Jondran's desk was immobile: a statue that might have been carved from solid ebony. That figure was cloaked; upon its head rested a slouch hat. Against the blackish background, Jondran's protector would have passed unnoticed, except for a sound that issued from his lips.

That tone was a taunting laugh: a quiver that brought shuddering echoes from every wall; a mirth that rose amid the crackle of the flames in the fireplace. The flickery glow showed other features of that living shape in black.

Pinkey faced the burn of brilliant eyes that peered from beneath the hat brim. Below those brilliant orbs, he saw the twin muzzles of two automatics trained straight toward the doorway where he stood.

Pinkey found his voice. He spat the name: "The Shadow!" But the racketeer's words were weak.

They were drowned by the strident challenge that came from The Shadow's own lips!

CHAPTER XXI
FORGOTTEN CRIME

THOUGHTS were drumming through Pinkey's brain—thoughts that he didn't like. He realized that The Shadow had been here all along; that he had talked to Jondran while Pinkey and Slick were waiting in the reception room.

That was all part of the buildup for the payoff that The Shadow wanted. Jondran had cooperated, by telling The Shadow about the unfinished vault.

A neat game. One that ought to have forced Pinkey to quit. Perhaps it would have, if Pinkey hadn't caught a sudden brainwave. He realized that he still held a threat.

That threat was the envelope in Pinkey's own pocket: the one with the evidence incriminating four men who were important in Jondran's big business enterprises.

And Jondran had overplayed the bluff. He had chucked the other envelope in the fire!

With that deed, Jondran had destroyed the only evidence that could save his huge corporation. He had evidently made the gesture to strengthen his bluff. No wonder; he had The Shadow with him. But he'd given Pinkey an opportunity.

If Pinkey could only get out of this tight spot, he would still be able to bring Jondran to terms.

Slowly, Pinkey backed away from The Shadow's guns. He tried to make his retreat seem a fear-inspired action; but all the while, Pinkey was remembering that he had two men with him. He could depend on Slick and Bugs; and he knew that Bugs had a gun crew in readiness.

But that wasn't the only way in which Bugs counted. Bugs was dumb enough to be what Pinkey termed a "fall guy"; which meant that Bugs would bear the brunt when The Shadow attacked.

Almost at the door, Pinkey made a sudden sidestep. He grabbed Bugs, who was on his left. Making a gesture with his own gun, Pinkey shouted:

"Get The Shadow!"

Bugs lunged forward. He was aiming as he came; but his shot never reached The Shadow. A big automatic spoke; Bugs went sprawling, his own gun toppling at an angle toward the floor. He served one purpose, though, in that mad endeavor.

Pinkey was out through the doorway before Bugs fell. Wisely, the big-shot had ducked behind Bugs.

As he scrambled across the anteroom, Pinkey found a man beside him. He gave hurried approval:

"Good work, Slick! You made it, too! Come on—give a yell for the crew, and we'll go back after The Shadow!"

The mob was coming without call. They had heard the sound of gunfire. They were piling in through the front door, all five of them. Pinkey pointed them toward Jondran's study, giving the only shout that was needed:

"The Shadow!"

Thugs saw The Shadow at the doorway. His guns began to boom. They were joined by other shots that came from the front of the house.

Crooks sprawled, their guns unfired. The few who turned, writhing from the floor, saw Inspector Joe Cardona heading a squad of detectives!

The Shadow had turned this house into a trap, letting the law decide the final issue!

THAT wasn't going to save The Shadow. Not if Pinkey knew it! He had reached a corner, hauling Slick with him. In the mix-up, Pinkey saw his chance. He aimed straight for The Shadow, pulled the trigger of his gun.

The bullet missed.

Pinkey was toppling when he fired, twisted by the impact of a bullet. Who had fired that shot, Pinkey could not guess. It hadn't been The Shadow; he was busy with the last of the thugs.

Somehow, though, The Shadow had known

that Pinkey would be handled; for he had not bothered with the racketeer.

While his wild shot echoed, Pinkey rolled on the floor. He dropped his gun; clamped his hands against his side. He heard The Shadow's triumphant laugh; then stared up to see eyes that were glowering down at him.

It wasn't The Shadow who stood above Pinkey; it was Joe Cardona.

Pinkey's eyes were glazing; but they took in more. He saw Slick Thurley with detectives grouped about him. Pinkey snarled his contempt for Slick's surrender:

"So you're yellow, Slick—"

Another face came into view. It was that of Giles Jondran. The gray-haired man took no delight in the fact that Pinkey was mortally wounded; but the big-shot didn't want Jondran's sympathy.

Pinkey hadn't managed to finish The Shadow; but he could fix Giles Jondran.

"You thought you pulled a fast one, Jondran," coughed Pinkey. "But you didn't. These bulls have got me; but I'll live long enough to make you squirm!"

Propped on one elbow, Pinkey pulled the big envelope from his pocket, thrust it into the hands of Joe Cardona.

"That's evidence!" gulped the racketeer. "I'm telling you that in front of witnesses. When you get evidence, you've got to use it! Screwy, ain't it? But that's the way the law works."

Cardona gruffed a stolid query: "Want me to open this, Pinkey?"

"Yeah"—Pinkey's voice came with a spasm— "open it—look it over. I want to see Jondran, when you do—"

Cardona pulled the papers from the envelope. He spreads them in front of Pinkey's eyes. Those eyes went wide, not from the approach of death, but from sheer amazement that made Pinkey forget the finish that soon awaited him.

This was not the evidence that Pinkey wanted Cardona to have! These were the other papers: the negative evidence: the batch that Pinkey thought Jondran had tossed into the fire!

It wasn't imagination. Jondran had actually destroyed an envelope. But the one that he had burned was the one that Pinkey intended to keep. Only one man could be responsible; Pinkey's gaze rolled in his direction. Blood flecked Pinkey's lips, as he coughed:

"You—you have double—crossed-me, Slick!"

There was a negative headshake from the man that Pinkey had mistaken for Slick Thurley. For the first time, Pinkey noticed that his sidekick was not a prisoner. Enlightenment dawned, when Pinkey heard the statement:

"You weren't double-crossed. I'm not Slick Thurley; I'm Bill Quaine!"

FLAT on the floor, Pinkey stared upward with bulging-eyed gaze. Recollections were throbbing through his numbed brain. He remembered how Slick had spotted someone in the alley outside the hideout. For the first time, Pinkey knew what had really happened.

Slick had encountered The Shadow there, in the dark. After the one swift blow, it was Slick who had sprawled on the cobbles. But there had been another man there also, waiting with The Shadow. That man had been Bill Quaine.

The Shadow had turned crime's own game full about.

Bill Quaine had rejoined Pinkey, to play the part of Slick Thurley! Together, they had looked at a stunned snooper, and Quaine had been smart enough to keep Pinkey from seeing that the flattened man was Slick!

Pinkey remembered how Quaine had loitered in the elevator at the Bubble Club; how he had strolled into the hallway outside Jondran's reception room. Those had been chances for Quaine to contact The Shadow; to learn what was needed.

In Jondran's study, Quaine had coolly replaced the batches of papers in the wrong envelopes. Pinkey hadn't been watching him when he did it, for the big-shot had never guessed that Quaine was not Slick Thurley.

Clutched by the final agony of his death wound, Pinkey knew who had delivered it. The Shadow had left that task to Quaine, in case of emergency. The pinch had come; Quaine had delivered.

Standing men eyed a silent figure on the floor. The motionless form was all that remained of Pinkey Findlen. The racketeer had died in the throes of those final thoughts.

A sound stirred the stillness; it was like a knell, that mirthless laugh that betokened The Shadow's departure.

The rest was easy for the law. Crooks at the Bubble Club were taken into custody, Claude Ondrey among them. Slick Thurley was found, bound and gagged in a place where The Shadow had left him.

Funds from Ondrey's safe were identified by Jondran; they were placed in Jondran's unfinished vault, with detectives on guard. All those details were completed by midnight—the hour when Beth Jondran came home with some friends.

Beth found her father in the study; with him was Maude Revelle. The story that Beth heard did not entirely surprise her. She had already recognized that Maude was a girl whose friend-ship had no limit.

And Maude knew, in turn, that she had found a lifelong friend in Beth Jondran. Maude could have wanted no better reward from The Shadow.

AT that same hour, The Shadow was alone in his sanctum. Beneath the bluish light rested the list that he had made early in his campaign against recent crime. Five names composed that list:

> "Thumb" Gaudrey
> "Pointer" Trame
> "Long Steve" Bydle
> "Ring" Brescott
> "Pinkey" Findlen

That list, however, had changed. Through the name of Pinkey Findlen, The Shadow had stroked a long line, that marked the obliteration of the racketeer, himself.

A whispered laugh stirred the black-walled sanctum, as The Shadow replaced the list within the folder that bore the stamped symbol of a hand.

One finger of that hand had been obliterated. It was the end of one phase of the work. Not even The Shadow knew how very soon he was to meet another of The Hand; how soon he would again have to meet the challenge of these racketeers.

The Hand would reach across The Shadow's path once more; and then another time, and still another, before that symbol would be wiped off The Shadow's record!

THE END

THE FOUR-COLOR HAND

Early comic book creators including Jerry Siegel and Joe Shuster, Bill Finger and Bob Kane, Stan Lee, Jack Kirby, Will Eisner and Mort Meskin were heavily influenced by hero pulps like *The Shadow* and *Doc Savage*. After all, there were no comic book superheroes during their childhoods, so these comic-book pioneers patterned their four-color creations after their favorite pulp mystery men.

Meanwhile, a number of talented wordsmiths were relocating from pulps to the burgeoning comic book industry, including Otto Binder, Alfred Bester, Edmond Hamilton and Henry Kuttner, along with Walter Gibson and Theodore Sturgeon, both of whom pounded out scripts for Street & Smith's *Shadow Comics.* Many of the pulp writers lured to the comics field were recruited by DC editor Mort Weisinger, a pulp veteran who in 1941 unveiled his own comic book version of The Hand, a crime cabal obviously inspired by Walter Gibson's 1938 *Shadow* series.

An early member of science fiction fandom, Mort co-published the first SF fanzine and was one of the first fans to break into the ranks of pulp professionals with a 1933 sale to *Amazing Stories.*

"I was 19 at the time," he recalled, "writing my way through college grinding out pseudo-scientific stuff at a half cent a word for *Amazing Stories,* Hugo Gernsback's old *Wonder Stories* and *Secret Agent X.*" After joining the American Fiction Guild, Weisinger launched Solar Sales Service, a science fiction literary agency, with Julius Schwartz.

"It was while hustling for my clients in and out

The "fingers" of DC Comics' Hand (from left: Red Dragon, Big Caesar, the Needle, the Dummy and Professor Merlin) as visualized by artist Mort Meskin (right)

of editorial offices that I met Leo Margulies, chief at Standard Magazines. A short while later one of Leo's associate editors left, leaving him in a hole. He hired me to plug the dike.

"I edited *Thrilling Wonder Stories, Startling Stories, Captain Future, G-Men, Thrilling Detective, Phantom Detective, Black Book Detective, Popular Detective, Thrilling Adventures* and *Thrilling Mystery.*"

After Margulies was inspired to announce a new pulp during the 1939 World Science Fiction Convention, Weisinger created Captain Future, a character envisioned as "Doc Savage in outer space." Mort and fellow Standard editor Jack Schiff soon sold a Doc Savage plot to Lester Dent that became *Birds of Death.* "I had the feeling that a personality character and a team—a science fiction parallel to Doc Savage—would go," Mort explained. "And we gave him some unique props, a robot, an android, and a living brain."

On the recommendation of Superman-creator Jerry Siegel, DC Comics editorial director Whit Ellsworth hired Weisinger as a story editor in 1940. Mort later claimed he created three successful characters on his first day at DC: Aquaman, Green Arrow and Johnny Quick. During his thirty-year tenure at DC, Weisinger incorporated many established conventions of science fiction and hero pulps into the Superman mythos, eventually bequeathing the Man of Bronze's Fortress of Solitude to the Man of Steel.

Weisinger introduced his own villainous Hand organization in the premier Seven Soldiers of Victory adventure in DC's *Leading Comics* #1.

Photo by Forrest J Ackerman

Mort Weisinger circa 1932

The 56-page tale, scripted by Mort with a single chapter by Jerry Siegel, chronicled how a "Napoleon of Crime" organized prison breaks to assemble his criminal band (just as Zanigrew did in *Shadow Over Alcatraz),* and sent each "finger" to launch a crime wave in a different region of the country.

Since few of The Shadow's foes survived their initial confrontations with the Knight of Darkness, Gibson's Hand was made up of newly created mobsters. Weisinger improved upon Gibson's concept by assembling a criminal team composed of the Seven Soldiers' previously defeated arch-foes. This Hand's "fingers" included Green Arrow's enemy Professor Merlin, the Needle (from Jerry Siegel's Star-Spangled Kid), the Red Dragon, Big Caesar and the Vigilante's foe, the Dummy.

Weisinger's Hand set the pattern for such future super-villain teams as Wonder Woman's Villainy, Inc., the JSA's Injustice Gang of the World, the Frightful Four, The Avengers' Masters of Evil and the Secret Society of Super-Villains.

The opening chapter of Weisinger's Hand epic was illustrated by Mort Meskin, one of the finest artists from the Golden Age of Comics and a devoted fan of *Shadow*-illustrator Edd Cartier.

"Mort Meskin was a huge fan of Edd Cartier's work," Jack Kirby recalled, "and so was I." One need only compare Meskin's and Kirby's spotting of blacks with Cartier's, and the villainous clutching hands from Kirby's Golden Age stories with Cartier's inset panels in this volume, to recognize the influence Cartier and *The Shadow Magazine* had on the pioneer comic artists. —Anthony Tollin •

THE ARTISTIC EVOLUTION OF EDD CARTIER *by Maggie Thompson*

In a 1950s home in which science-fiction pulps were shelved alongside Dante, P. G. Wodehouse, and collections of *Pogo* comic strips, what was it that especially caught my eye as an 11-year-old? It was the confident, clean sweeping lines and

Edward Daniel Cartier circa 1939

remarkable characterizations of the pictures that accompanied many classic stories of some of the finest science-fiction writers of the time. The stories were memorable, but I only read many of them in the first place because of the illustrations that accompanied them: illustrations by Edd Cartier.

I'd seen a lot of imagery of the future: rocket ships and aliens, spacemen and distant planets. And it was competent art that captured the essence of many tales of imagination. But Cartier's art was more than competent, more than simply skilled. He conveyed the strength of men, the voluptuousness of women, the menace (and sometimes the comedy) of monsters.

I wanted to draw the way Cartier drew. As time went on, I traced several of his illustrations to try to unlock his secrets of composition and line. I realized that his tools and the way he used them must differ from my pencil and my ballpoint pen. A brush? Yes, a brush for those clear lines—but more than that, because there were other textures in the art.

But try to copy him or not, I was attracted to every story he illustrated. As far as I knew, Edd Cartier had always been the commander of the dark hero and his luscious love interest, the master of fantastic sprites of extraordinary loveliness—or ungainly comedy. The stories he illustrated, I felt at 11, were always worth reading. Because he'd already made them fascinating.

Readers of Sanctum Books' *The Shadow* #16 (and also this volume) are treated to the rare opportunity of seeing in the same publication some of Edd Cartier's earliest Shadow illustrations and those in the style he developed when freed from the need to imitate his predecessor's style.

Until I read that edition, I had never seen Cartier's early work in pulp illustration, never appreciated how far he had come in such a short time. Moreover, that volume provided a foreword by Cartier, in which he discussed his early artistic development and the influence of his skilled instructors. He noted that, as his professor Harold Winfield Scott was an important Western pulp artist, Cartier, too, had wanted to draw for the Western pulps. Though he had sold some Western pulp illustrations while majoring in pictorial illustration at the Pratt Institute's School of Fine and Applied Arts, he was also turning out professional work in a variety of genres. And, upon graduation, he found himself with the assignment of illustrating the adventures of The Shadow.

And so it was that he was locking in a place for himself in magazine illustration, starting six years

Edd Cartier illustration for *The Sledge-Hammer Crimes*, his premier outing on *The Shadow*

before I was born in a process that led me to know him only as a master.

The work of fiction-magazine illustrators is, these days, largely forgotten. Unless a collector accumulates the original publications in which stories appeared and actually reads them there, the impact of the original presentations, complete with artists' interpretations, is gone. And that means the artists' works are, too.

There are a few exceptions. I have five books on the work of Virgil Finlay, for example; in his case, it is the art that has often outlasted the stories with which it appeared. Sherlock Holmes' delineator Sidney Paget is considered important enough that he merits an online census of the location of his surviving original art.

But many histories of fantasy and science fiction treat the field's art as of only passing interest — or as examples of cornball, albeit amusing, cheesecake. Despite his receiving the 1992 World Fantasy Life Achievement Award, among other tributes, illustrator Edd Cartier's work is remembered today by few readers who are not also pulp fans. (Shadow buffs, obviously, have been able to enjoy his art in conjunction with Sanctum Books' reprints. But, conversely, those who are admirers of his fantasy and SF work may be as unaware as I had been of his major role in defining The Shadow.)

Mind you, Cartier's work has garnered a few brief tributes in histories of fantasy and science fiction, especially in those focusing on such pulps

as Street & Smith's *Unknown* (aka *Unknown Worlds*) and *Astounding Science Fiction* (both edited by John W. Campbell, Jr.).

The Brian Ash-edited 1977 volume *The Visual Encyclopedia of Science Fiction,* for example, included samples of Cartier's work from Jack Williamson's *Darker Than You Think,* Eric Frank Russell's *Sinister Barrier,* and Isaac Asimov's *Foundation and Empire.* Following the comment that *Fantastic Adventures* artist Rod Ruth is almost unknown today appeared, "Edd Cartier is perhaps more fortunate, and is remembered for his illustrations to such stories as [L. Sprague] de Camp and [Fletcher] Pratt's *Castle of Iron* and [Jack] Williamson's *Darker Than You Think* in 1940. He ended the decade by illustrating de Camp's "The Hand of Zei" in *Astounding."*

And Randy Broecker's 2001 *Fantasy of the 20th Century: An Illustrated History* ran three samples of his work and calls him "talented" and *"Unknown*'s resident da Vinci" and provides this evaluation: "Cartier produced some impressive covers for *Unknown,* but his black and white illustrations are a delight to the eye, perfect for the type of fantasy material that *Unknown* was publishing. His gremlins, dwarves, gnomes, and other fanciful creatures were all executed with a certain sense of personality, and he created a wonderful mood and atmosphere with his compositions."

Given that the award-winning Cartier is unfailingly praised whenever he's mentioned—however

Edd Cartier art for
Crime Over Boston (1938)

fleetingly—how did he evolve from the student who imitated the style of other pulp artists? Cartier outlined it himself in 2008 in *The Shadow* #16, beginning with his work as a student, pulling down $8 per illustration for Street & Smith's pulps. Upon his 1936 graduation from Pratt, he was offered the job of illustrating alternate issues of *The Shadow* with longtime Shadow artist Tom Lovell. "Initially, [Editor William] James wanted me to work in Tom's darkly shaded style. I was given a batch of his originals to use as a guide … At first, I felt quite inhibited imitating his style. However, no one complained when I later subtly started changing things and began illustrating in my own way."

And his "own way" continued to develop. "My illustrations evolved with each new issue. I abandoned pen-and-ink, preferring to use a combination of brush, ink, tempera and lithographic pencil. I worked almost exclusively on the lightly textured surface of illustration board, usually Bainbridge #8, roughing in my Shadow drawings on the board with a pencil, then outlining the illustration with brush and ink. Next came brush and tempera, combined with ink for the darker areas. Finally, I would erase my original penciling and finish up by adding shading with a lithographic pencil. Some-

times I added a bit of red ink to my originals, usually in the eyes or as dripping blood, the red ink reproducing as black on the printed page. A typical drawing was usually one by one-and-a-half feet in size, or one-and-a-half by two feet, or sometimes larger, even though it might be reduced in the pulps to as small as a quarter of a page—or smaller still, as a spot illustration."

Aha! Had I but known that when I was 11, I, too, might have become a major illustrator! If only it weren't also a matter of talent …

A look at the two stories in this volume clearly displays his development, given his changing use of tools and styles. The cross-hatching evident in *The Strange Disappearance of Joe Cardona* is gone in *The Hand;* the litho pencil has confidently taken its place. The outlines are sharper, the action even more dynamic. He's working with the same storyteller and the same types of character—but his work is more exciting, the layouts more captivating. And the reader, already, was even more drawn into what was already a world of compelling stories about a classic character.

Galaxy Press published William J. Widder's *Master Storyteller: An Illustrated Tour of the Fiction*

"Edd Cartier was my favorite pulp illustrator. I used to read *The Shadow Magazine* and I marveled at Cartier's work. I liked the way his figures moved and how he lit a room. No one drew darkness better than Edd Cartier."
—Jack Kirby

Edd Cartier illustrations for:
"Crossroads" by L. Ron Hubbard (1941),
L. Sprague de Camp's "The Animal-Cracker Plot" (1949),
Jabberwocky Thrust **by Maxwell Grant/Bruce Elliott (1947),**
and "The Cold Trail of Death" by John D. MacDonald (1948)

Edd Cartier 1947 *Super Magician Comics* interior page and *Red Dragon* cover, 1948 cover painting for *From Unknown Worlds,* 1953 illustration for Poul Anderson and Gordon R. Dickson's "In Hoka Signo Vinces"

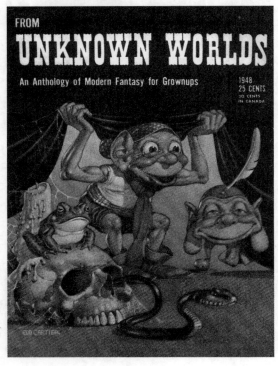

of L. Ron Hubbard in 2003 and provided fascinating behind-the-scenes communications involving Hubbard's work as a storyteller. One of his finest illustrators was Cartier, and samples of Cartier's illustrations of Hubbard fiction appear in the volume. The book also includes an essay by Cartier himself, who provided other insights into his work methods: "I illustrated more stories by Hubbard than for any other author during my years of work for both *Unknown* and *Astounding Science Fiction*. Illustrating Ron's tales was a welcome assignment because they always contained scenes or incidents I found easy to picture. With some writers' work I sometimes had to contact Campbell for an idea. That never happened with a Hubbard story. His plots allowed my imagination to run wild and the ideas for my illustrations would quickly come to mind."

Cartier's evaluation of his own work continued in the essay, regarding Hubbard's tales for Campbell's Street & Smith magazines: "They offered fantastic opportunities to draw blustering, swaggering heroes and wickedly depraved villains. In the novels *Slaves of Sleep* and *Typewriter in the Sky* Ron gave free rein to the swashbuckling, historically costumed characters I loved to sketch. I was able to fill my illustrations with humorously grotesque faces and to add atmosphere with old guns, burning candles, rope and swords. Ron's other novels in *Unknown* allowed me to depict my visions of his ghouls, devils, demons and old hags. Those type of ghastly characters in 'Death's Deputy,' 'Fear' and 'The Case of the Friendly Corpse' were among my specialties. I relished the chance to draw them and often enjoyed adding a smile or hint of humor to their gruesomeness."

That confirms what I'd thought as an 11-year-old: Cartier's own likes and dislikes led to illustrating some of the stories I liked best. Because he liked them, too. Because the characters he loved to sketch were precisely the ones I liked to read about. And because he loved to draw them,

he added an expression of their already fascinating characterization.

Cartier produced a small amount of comic-book material, most notably for three issues of Street & Smith's second try at a *Red Dragon* series. He provided covers for #1 (November 1947), #2 (February 1948), and #4 (August 1948), where he also illustrated "Through the Looking Glass." As opposed to an assortment of other illustrators' versions of the character over the years, his *Red Dragon* covers interpreted the character as merely bored by an assortment of surprising, menacing fantasy characters. (Interestingly, the other artist who specialized in Red Dragon's comic-book existence in the late 1940s was Bob Powell, whose style most closely matched Cartier's at the time but whose career from that point took place mostly in comic books, whereas Cartier focused on illustration of textual material.) What other illustrator would have dreamed up boredom as a reaction to menace? It subtly conveyed the strength of the character while it compelled the reader to find out what happened next.

Cartier's work today is seldom seen. His Red Dragon stories have yet to be reprinted in book form. His newspaper work for King Features Syndicate from 1948 and 1949 has never been collected and was lost to fans for decades, though random panels (roughly 7x7-inch originals) turn up at auction now and then. (The panels illustrated a series of detective fiction, and stories included "Murder in the Shower Bath" by Carl G. Hodges (1948), "The Case of the Death Idol" by Robert Carlton (1948), "Case of the Red Headed Girls" by "King of the Pulps" mystery writer Harry Whittington (March 1949) and "The Blonde in the Bay" by Whittington (June 1949). The panels are Cartier at his polished best: controlled lines conveying wild hard-boiled action.)

For the most elaborate look at Cartier's assorted artistry, readers will have to hunt for the 1977 book compiled by Gerry de la Ree: The 128-page

"Unknown Worlds had some excellent illustrators... but the greatest of all was Edd Cartier, the perfect illustrator for a fantasy magazine. His gods were more divine, his devils more diabolical, his feckless heroes even more feckless, and his villains nastier, than those of anybody else. He combined exquisite draftsmanship with an ebullient humor and sense of the fantastic—a combination not often found."

—L. Sprague de Camp

1951 illustration for Clifford D. Simak's "Courtesy"

Edd Cartier: The Known and the Unknown was limited to 2,000 hardcover copies, but a few can still be found here and there on the Internet. The Internet Speculative Fiction Database (http://208.100.59.10/cgi-bin/index.cgi) provides 27 cover identifications by Cartier from 1939 to 2000 (though some may be reprints) and 113 interior identifications. However, by its very nature, that listing covers only a portion of his work. And such projects as images for calendars from Gnome Press, his design of the Gnome Press logo, and even the contents of *From Unknown Worlds* don't seem to have a home on the list. Nor do his 800 illustrations from *The Shadow Magazine*.

Despite the glories of that concentrated focus, perhaps the best showcase of the work of Edd Cartier as an illustrator appeared long ago in an oversized 25-cent Street & Smith 1948 "bedsheet" pulp (reprinted in England as a dustjacketed hardcover by Atlas Publishing and Distributing Co. Ltd. in 1952). *From Unknown Worlds: An Anthology of Modern Fantasy for Grownups* contained 13 stories and four poems, several of the entries featuring more than one Cartier embellishment. And that has been the strength on display in Sanctum Books releases, as well: the artist's consummate skill in drawing the reader into the narrative by capturing the action with verve and tantalizing detail.

Cartier was a master of a craft that is only slowly experiencing a resurgence: adventure illustration. And even in that resurgence, his art from the 1950s stands out as distinctively his. Whether as an 11-year-old science fiction fan or as a 67-year-old comic-book commentator, I've always judged Edd Cartier as one of the very best.

Edward Daniel Cartier died on Christmas Day, 2008. This volume is dedicated to his memory. •

"By me, Cartier is *the* greatest and always will be.... Whereas Finlay, with infinite love and meticulous craftmanship, made the utterly impossible photographically real, Cartier with a flick of the brush could pinpoint the fantastic, the whimsical, the 'otherness' in the most prosaic details.... absodamlutely nobody else could put a tyrannosaurus into a freshman's beanie and sweater and have it come off! No— there are no successors to Edd Cartier."   —Frank Kelly Freas